The Ember Stone

Book 1 of The Ember Files

Revised Edition

Shari Marshall

Writing Sparkle Books
sharimarshall.ca
Alberta, Canada

First Edition Paperback/eBook released by Twin Horseshoes Publishing 2022

Marshall, Shari
The Ember Stone: Book 1 of The Ember Files Revised Edition 2023

eBook ISBN 978-1-7782531-2-6
Paperback ISBN 978-1-7782531-3-3

Fiction | Fantasy | Urban
Fiction | Humorous | General
Fiction | Women

Praise for *The Ember Stone*

" . . . Marshall's law enforcement background brings a gritty, true crime quality to the book's many action scenes . . . The Ember Stone is a promising debut and should provide a fun romp for fans of the genre." – *BlueInk Review*

"In the fantasy novel *The Ember Stone*, a gifted woman struggles to establish her place in a supernatural war . . . While her heritage and shunned gifts drag her into the supernatural conflict, she also has to do the inward work of self-discovery." – *Foreward* Clarion Review

"The story moves at a blistering and exciting pace, and the premise and plot are endlessly creative, resulting in an engrossing and boundary-crossing series debut."
– *Self-Publishing Review*

Dedication

For absent family & friends – forever in my heart.

In memory of my mother, who taught me about humour and always encouraged me to believe in magic.

To my husband and my boys, thank you for your support while I indulged in this writing & editing frenzy.

The Ember Stone

Chapter 1

I'm unsure if I'll ever come to terms with my life. I live a life governed by the motto "when crazy calls, Kori answers." That's me, Kori Ember. I'm five foot three with an athletic build. I love wearing studio pants and a sporty tank top.

It's been a dry spring so, today, I slip my sandals off and walk barefoot through the well-manicured grass of the cemetery. If I can do it barefoot, I do, and if not, sandals are my next favourite choice. The cool tickle from individual blades of grass has a calming effect as I walk the familiar path toward the headstones for Dad's side of the family. It's where we buried my older brother Jaxton after . . .

I shake my head, not wanting to let in the memories of the dark magic that took his life. I move lazily, enjoying the heat from the sun and the pleasant floral scent in the air.

"Kori, we were just talking about you," Grama Pearle points to the urn of ashes on the bench beside her. Grama Pearle keeps her parents' and beloved husband's ashes, my Grandpa Ian, like companions. She has regular-sized and jewelry urns with their ashes encased for times when having them with her on a small scale is more manageable.

Grandpa Ian's remains rest in a blown-glass spherical urn. Today's urn is not his. The urn beside Grama Pearle is a companion-sized, silky white cremation-lidded vase with silver branches and leaves adornments. The inside is customized to hold the remains of two people on each side of a divider. My eyes survey Grama Pearle and the urn. I sigh; her expectation isn't a surprise, but the act itself is unorthodox. I fix the urn with a pointed stare. "Hello, Great-Grandmother Effie. Hello, Great-Grandfather Luther." I let my stare linger for a few seconds.

The sun reflecting on Grama Pearle's blue-silver hair gives it an eerie glow. She smiles and cocks her head to the side, and I see the secrets flicker in her eyes. "It's finally time, is it?"

I scrunch my face at her. "How do you—"

"Kori, that's why you're here, isn't it? You're here to tell me you're going away?" She pauses while her hazel eyes continue studying my face. "Tell me what happened."

I close my eyes, swallow, and nod in agreement. When I open my eyes, I glimpse movement by the far tree line. "Others visit the cemetery," Grama Pearle says.

"Yes, I know, but this looked like the short man with bulky muscles that thinks he's a bird." I continue to watch the tree line. "Every time I arrest him for causing a disturbance, he tells me he needs someone like me on his 'task force.'" I swipe my hand through my hair. The stress must be catching up with me. "Anyway, Grama Pearle, what happened is straightforward. I surprised them in the living room—"

"Wait, who is them?" Grama Pearle interrupts. Her eyes track from the tree line to me.

"My husband, Carter, and his police partner, Kinsley Reun." I pause, blinking rapidly to clear the image from my mind. "This is going to spread like wildfire through their detachment and mine." I sigh. "Anyway, I don't know who was more surprised, them or me. They were standing up, lip-locked, as they shed the last of their clothing. Kinsley saw me over Carter's shoulder, and her eyes grew as big as saucers. That's when Carter panicked and turned. I threw my right fist into his washboard abdomen, hoping I could reach in and pull an internal organ out.

"Sadly, I had to satisfy myself with his forceful gust of air and gasping sounds. Of course, when he doubled over, I performed 'nose to toes' and laid his naked ass out! Then I ejected Kinsley from my house in her birthday suit."

Grama Pearle's laughter has her bent forward, holding her stomach. I roll my eyes and wait. When she comes up for air, she locks eyes with me. "I never liked that asshole!"

"Smoke and ashes, Grama Pearle!" I say with mock admonishment. "Do you know what people will say?" I ask in a serious tone. "They'll say Little Kori, or Smouldering Ember, as they like to call me, snapped."

"Who cares!" Grama Pearle exclaims. "I plan to embellish this story to include sacrificial offerings of

Carter's manhood and a cursing of Kinsley's ovaries."

"You can't!"

"Kori, I know you and I are both incapable of hexing people, but why not have a bit of fun with it?"

I try to keep my eyes from bulging out of my head. "Because people will believe that!"

Grama Pearle shrugs. I take in a big gulp of air and almost choke on it when she starts in on magic genetics. The last thing I want is for people to be encouraged to think of me as abnormal, whether in jest or in reality. I also don't want to be reminded about the less-than-normal things that are part of my heritage.

"Magic runs in the family, Kori. You spent your adolescent years, after Jaxton's death, denying your abilities, but eventually, you'll have to understand them. Because you were a headstrong teenager, you're behind in learning to use your magic or knowing what your magical strengths are. We never forced you. We respect your choice to not learn, to not see, and to pretend you're a normie. You're exceptional at deceiving yourself and at ignoring the magical world."

"I'm not doing this!" I cross my arms, cutting off the conversation. My nostrils flare. "Magic killed him, Grama Pearle. I was there. I—" The hair on the nape of my neck rises in response to my recall of cloaked faceless forms. "Aberrant Spellbinders . . . unearthly creatures in their movements, breached our home! There was a complete absence of sound, not a peaceful tranquillity." A sneer pulls the flesh of my face tight. "The silence was threatening, suffocating." Just the recollection has my hand clutching my chest, my pulse racing. "It was the silence that pressed down on me, my access to oxygen growing smaller, and my field of vision narrowing with it.

"Magic wasn't saving me, it was killing me. To this day I've no idea why. Just a senseless act of murder by magic, that's all they wanted. It should've been me, but they didn't care, any Spellbinder would do. Then Jaxton was there. He attacked with magic so bright it was blinding, but it wasn't enough."

I palm the warm tears off my cheeks ignoring the saline stickiness. "The noiselessness became a wail; whose? I don't know. The shadows in the corner of the room deepened to impossible darkness and the intruders vanished into them. But not before . . ." The pain in my throat constricts my voice box. When I speak again bitterness drips from my words. "I held his head as he died."

Grama Pearle's voice is soft but firm. "His death was investigated within the Spellbinder community; experienced adults couldn't stand against that attack. You were ten, Kori. Ten years old. You aren't responsible for what happened that day and Jaxton isn't either."

Something in the shade of the trees stirs. Thankful for the distraction, I strain to see what's there. A tiny hawk with a lengthy square tail lifts from the branches. When I look at Grama Pearle, she's smiling in the direction of the retreating bird.

I set my jaw and steady my voice so it comes out low. "I'm sure you and the rest of the family will think that I joined the ranks of the certifiable after this. Divorcing Carter aside, I quit the police force, and now I'm leaving the entire country. The family can draw all the conclusions that they want." I give a half-hearted shrug and let my gaze wander.

"Money?" is all that Grama Pearle asks after my big revelation.

I puff my cheeks up with air and nod. "Lottery winnings," I'm unable to stop myself from scrunching up my nose and pulling back my lips. "Substantial winnings and also my well-kept secret, until now."

A yellow cab parks a few feet away and honks. I hug Grama Pearle. Her slight frame is strong in my arms. She returns the squeeze. "I'm here if you need me, Kori."

"Fin will know how to contact me," I call over my shoulder as I enter the cab.

I haven't been visiting Mexico for long. I'm planning for it to be a short stopover on my way to wherever my lottery winnings take me next. The last six months have been filled with Caribbean travel and an ever-increasing surge of magical powers that scare and confuse me. Why is the magic I've rejected imposing on me, and why now? They used to tell me rejecting magical abilities couldn't be done because the laws of our nature forbid it, but there's no evidence to support that, at least until now. Grama Pearle's warning about eventually having to understand my magic takes on new meaning.

My surges centre around the air with phenomena like unexplained gusts of wind, swirling air vortexes, and interruptions to the natural movement of air in varying stages of potency. Out of desperation, I started making attempts to control it. Taking time to manipulate the currents every day has lessened the surges.

Tonight, as I enter a busier section of the market, I allow the seven tiny chakra stones to settle into my hand. Even though the human race is conditioned not to see magic, it wouldn't be subtle to walk through a crowd of people with my hand outstretched and seven stones floating in circles over my palm. Practicing manipulation of the air currents with palm stones has become akin to meditating for me and, lately, I do it often without being aware.

As I stuff the stones into my pocket, my curiosity is drawn to a shop displaying racks of vibrant beach wraps, cheap hammocks, and handmade purses. A variety of local birds flock to this striking store, but the one with long legs and a square-tipped tail is my focal point. This hawk is familiar. Before I give it much thought, a second bird starts to sing.

A blue bird perched on the beach wrap rack at the front of the store is whistling a song. Its strange eyes follow me, and its head flicks back and forth with curiosity. The shopkeeper's voice rises and falls musically, drawing my awareness away from the birds. "*Bienvenida a mi tienda.* Welcome to my store."

The blue bird takes flight into the night sky, and the hawk is gone too. I dismiss them and stay where I am, watching the mingling tourists. They're drawn into the store by the silver necklaces with light blue-green gemstones and pink-peppered stones with red veins. Both kinds dangle from the front wall. The necklaces hang overtop a table full of charcoal onyx sea turtles, colourful sugar skulls, and simple leather sandals. I smile at the shopkeeper and continue walking.

The air that stuck to my skin all day has a breeze to it now, and it licks away the moisture from the day's heat. My senses are alive with the tang of brine and the distant sounds of the ocean set against the hum of vendors at the market.

Walking the market is one of my favourite activities because of the bright, cheerful atmosphere. The hum of conversation punctuated with laughter is relaxing and uplifting. Then there are the market buildings which provide a breathtaking combination of colours, from yellows, oranges, and reds to fuchsias, greens, and blues. Even as I walk out of the market zone, the buildings remain impressive, with straight lines and sharp angles.

Since my self-imposed retirement, I've no desire to return to the gun and badge, but cop instincts never leave you. Now that sixth sense that burns deep within my psyche tingles. An unknown threat is present behind me, closing in.

I pick up my pace, but the faint pat of my heels contacting my flip-flops lets anyone close enough know I'm moving faster. The corner of a building looms. I scoot around it and plaster myself into the shadows. I force my breathing and heart rate to regulate by reminding myself that I'm trained for these situations.

Silent, a shadowy figure continues past my hiding spot. It's shaped like a man, but it glides in its movement, unnatural, and there's a chill in its wake that smells of damp leaves. It presents as an unearthly mix of human and something bestial. I tense, bracing for an attack, but the shadow doesn't slow, tilting its head up to taste the air, snake-like. I respond with a slight pull at the air currents, bringing them toward me so that the creature doesn't scent me, and my hiding spot remains just that, a hiding spot. Sure enough, my follower moves on.

Before I can leave the cover of the wall, a second shadow breaches the alleyway. This one is human. He has a powerful frame that pauses in the exact spot as my first stalker. I know by instinct that he's tracking me. I watch him now as he strains to hear. He's searching for any sign to show him which way to go next. Before he looks my way, I slam my eyes shut, cursing their unique colouring. The amber in them glows. Cat-like, they would give me away for sure. Silent and sightless, I wait.

A banshee-like scream slices through the night. My eyes fly open by reflex in time to see the shadowy character crash into the large man. The man is looking right at me! He mouths the word "run" before grunting as the blow knocks him backwards and out of my line of sight. Gliding, the shadow keeps its momentum aimed at the big man, and I don't wait to see the outcome. I've no interest in a face-to-face with either unknown follower, and I'm thankful for the distraction their confrontation creates. I flee.

My breath is loud in my ears, and all other sounds fall away until an angry voice breaks through my trance, "*Ve más despacio!* Go slower! *Ve más despacio!*"

My ability to translate is equivalent to trying to find a path out of a maze. The Spanish words flow along that complicated network of neurons trying to find an English translation and eventually land on the realization that I'm being told by multiple displeased pedestrians to decelerate.

"I'm sorry. *Lo siento.*" I call out to everyone who's demanding I relax my pace. I grind to a regular stride, casting my eyes from side to side. Satisfied I haven't been followed, I turn into the hotel where I'm staying. The beautiful open-air lobby is full of tropical vegetation and Mayan works of art. The marble floors shine under the dramatic lighting and pockets of people occupy the oversized wicker furniture, each lost in their own world of conversation, social media, and rum-filled glasses.

"*Senorita?* Miss?"

"*Buena Noches*, good evening, José."

José, the front counter clerk, is like everyone's favourite grade-school teacher. I enjoy practicing my limited Spanish vocabulary with him. He has a big smile and shadowed, brown eyes that display the soul of a serious young man. He's currently waving an envelope in the air and yelling, "*Para ti*, for you. *Un mensaje para ti*, a message for you."

"*Gracias*, thank you, José. Excuse me, *perdóneme.*" I'm about to hurry away with the unopened envelope when I realize that there isn't anyone in Mexico that would leave me messages. "*Espera un minuto*, wait a minute," I say out loud to myself. José thinks I'm talking to him, and he pauses with his head tilted to the side. "José, did you see who left this message for me?"

"No, *senorita*."

"Did anyone else at the front counter see who left it?"

"No, *senorita*. I am sorry."

I blow out a heavy sigh and think wistfully about Canadian hotels and my police ability to check security cameras. A non-existent capability now since I have no authority to view surveillance footage in any country and no relationships in Mexico to leverage for a sneak of it. "Okay. Thanks, José."

I exit the lobby with the envelope crushed in my hand. My mind is racing, and I barely notice the people giving me strange looks and a wide berth as I pass them, talking to myself. "Nobody knows I'm in Mexico and, if someone does, they wouldn't know where in Mexico I am. So, who is leaving me a message?"

I pass through my room to the balcony so I can read the message without turning the lights on. The balcony offers a soft glow of light supplied from the world beyond its boundaries. The message inside is to the point. It's typed and unsigned.

They've taken your sister. You might be in danger. Come home.

My younger sister, Alivia, is a paper-thin mother of two. Her response to Jaxton's death was the opposite of mine. She embraced the crazy, plus some, that I fled from and she spiralled from there. Her rebellion involved sex and drinking. Now, she's a recovering alcoholic who works as a night nurse at the hospital.

I admire the way she turned her life around. Just the thought of her has me pulling my chin up, my shoulders back, and thrusting my chest out. The way she exchanged parties and liquor bottles for textbooks and study time like there was no question is awe-inspiring. I've no words to describe the power of seeing the tiredness clinging to her, but the beaming smile on her face when she was with her boys.

Being a mother to Jayce and Holden is Alivia's life. After the boy's father, Jett Anders, just up and disappeared, she refashioned her entire world for them. It's sad to say that Jett's leaving was one of the best things that could've ever happened. She would've kicked him to the curb anyway, but it was one hard thing that she didn't have to do.

"What could you possibly have gotten mixed up in, Alivia? Hmm? Something doesn't fit with this scenario. You worked too hard to relapse into a life of addiction. I hope you are okay, little sister." I take a small bit of comfort from talking out loud like she's present to hear me.

Jett's involvement in Alivia's disappearance is a fleeting thought. He doesn't have what it takes to orchestrate something so complex. There's speculation that he made the wrong people mad, the kind of people who are thorough and don't take unnecessary risks, so Jett disappeared. The word "disappeared" more likely means murdered. The possibility of their connection to Alivia's abduction is nil. They would've known she isn't a threat, which means eliminating her is an unnecessary risk, plus their thoroughness wouldn't have left the children alive.

Considering the note, my mind flashes with new meaning to the strange shadow figure and the big man. I don't know who they are or what they want, but it's reasonable to assume it has to do with this message. Many questions layer this note, but the most important one is whether it's genuine.

I paw through my travel bag, unable to remember the last time that I connected to the world of social media. "Come on. Where are you? Why in the blazing hell are phones so small and easy to lose?"

When it bumps my fingers, I snatch it out with hastiness and I almost fling it across the room. I clench my teeth as I power it up. My feeling of giddiness from the lack of notifications on my phone doesn't last, and I feel as if my stomach has dropped into my feet when the silence is shattered with texts, emails, and voice message alerts. The bulk of the messages are from my best friend, Finley Salinger. *Why are you calling, Fin, when we agreed you'd wait to hear from me?*

Fin is dramatic if nothing else and she's trustworthy. Her messages start out urgent and get increasingly intense. "Kori, I was told not to go to the police. Noah said Alivia's abduction is beyond the scope of their training, whatever that means, but I trust his judgement so I haven't gone. Kori?"

As I listen, I'm reminded of Jaxton's death. The Spellbinder community kept his murder within locale. *Jaxton, I won't fail Alivia the way I failed you.* The air currents gust through the room in response to my pledge, and my throat tightens at the unspoken implication.

Fin's final voicemail is strangled. "I'm so sorry, Kori. I gave your number to Noah. He said he'd be able to find you. We need to find you! Kori, where are you?"

I blink back memories. Growing up, Fin and Noah were my people. It's hard to say if I was Noah's shadow or if he was mine. The friendship between the three of us is so solid we're like family.

Before I left Canada, my sensible side identified the possibility that someone should be able to reach out to me in the event of a family emergency. So, Fin is the sole person who is privy to communication with me. She knows that I don't want to be found and that I don't want to interface with anybody from home. I trust her to not violate that. If she broke confidence, then something is wrong. I swallow hard and close my eyes to steady myself.

There's one message left. I punch the number one into the keypad and the voice of my closest childhood friend fills my ears. For just a brief second, I can feel him behind me, close enough that I'm aware of the energy that he radiates, both strength and warmth. Then that husky, matter-of-fact voice says one thing, "You're coming home."

"Yes, yes, I am," I say to the air.

Chapter 2

Six months away and I come home in the fall. The aroma of fresh-cut grass clings to the crisp morning air. It's chilly enough that a shiver travels over me and I decide to wait inside the café. The vibration of my cell phone distracts me, and I glance at the screen to see a text from Fin. *Almost there. Starving. Going in.*

Fin is a friend I can count on without exception. She's always game, doesn't ask unnecessary questions, and can adapt to any situation. I can tell her anything— I imagine anyone could—and she wouldn't cast judgement. I might go as far as to call her jaunty and airy. These are reasons she was my first call when I returned to Canada.

I stare at the café name, "Just Flavours." After blowing out a sigh, I wander in. I need a strong black coffee. Just Flavours is quaint and cozy, with the counter situated at the rear. There are eight tables set up with four on each side of the room and a space running down the middle to line up and order.

As I'm staring out the window, I see the cutest soot-coloured truck with a thin lime green line on the side drive into the parking lot. It's a compact pickup. It has vintage rectangular chrome side-view mirrors, and old-school exterior door handles. I smile in memory of the old roll-down windows; this truck has them. I'm so caught up in the shape of this truck that the bronze face framed by an ebony-layered bob almost goes unrecognized. Fin sashays toward the café, smiling from ear to ear at every person coming out the door.

"You have a beautiful sweater," Fin compliments a woman who's exiting. I order my coffee, so I don't hear their brief conversation. I eyeball the coffee cake and close my eyes wagging my head no. Then Fin's arms encircle me in an embrace that's crushing. "My Smouldering Ember."

I pass my credit card to the cashier. "I'll get her order too, please."

"Um, can I get your glazed-donut breakfast sandwich and a Turkish coffee, please," Fin says with her arms still encircling me. "Girl, you should try their loaded Mexican egg and cheese melt. Did you order food?"

"No, just a coffee."

Fin releases me and calls the barista, who has moved away to start our order. "Excuse me, we'd also like a Mediterranean egg white breakfast sandwich with roasted tomatoes. Thanks."

"Good grief, Fin. How hungry are you?"

"That's for you, silly. You look like you're in a healthy mood. For lunch, we can come back and order avocado, strawberry, and goat cheese sandwiches!" She kisses the tips of her fingers and pushes the kiss out into the air in an elaborate gesture that sends her wallet flying. We watch in stunned silence as it arcs through the air and lands with a plop in an open container of egg salad.

After an exaggerated round of apologies, we move to a corner table with our order, Fin's wallet, and napkins to clean it with. I position myself with the wall behind me, giving me an almost complete view of the room, the exception being the extended hallway that leads to the bathrooms and second entrance.

"Old habits die hard, I see." Fin smirks, settling into her chair and stretching out her long legs.

"Fin?"

Her facial features rearrange, taking on a grave expression and her voice is devoid of humour. "Okay, your sister went missing. I don't know much beyond the fact that she's gone and Noah needs you. Jayce and Holden are safe. Noah has them holed up somewhere. I wish I could tell you more, but he said it was better if I didn't know. I'm sorry, Kori."

"My family, do they know?"

Fin has a mouth full of food, so she's bobbing her head, which I understand to mean "yes." Through her chewing, she spits out words. "I thought I would take you there first. Chances are Noah will show up."

With returning to my childhood home about to become a reality, my coffee turns to ice in my stomach, and I close my eyes, drawing a deep breath.

"I can come in, if you need me." Fin's voice is low and soft.

I crack my eyes open and peek at her from the side of my vision. "Thank you, Fin, but this initial family meeting is an act I should do alone."

I inspect my food while Fin rattles on about her life,

the main topics revolving around food, men, books, and changing careers. I sink my teeth into my sandwich. My first few bites are crunchy, creamy, and cheesy. Under other circumstances I would find it delicious, but today it sits like a lump in my gut. I set it down and focus on finishing my coffee.

"You ready, Fin? We can catch up more later."

Fin crams her last bite of breakfast sandwich into her mouth. She finishes chewing and points at my half-eaten meal. "Are you going to eat that?" Her face disappears behind her coffee cup while she drains the remaining liquid.

"You can finish it in the car." I wrap the rest of my sandwich in a napkin. "Come on."

The air outside is brisk. The chill of the pavement penetrates the thin sole of my flip-flops. I stand next to the truck, waiting for Fin to get in and manually pull up the lock mechanism on the passenger side door.

"What's up with this truck?" I ask, the bucket seat enveloping my bottom.

Fin scrunches up her nose in a knowing smile. "It's a '68 Ford Bronco half cab. As a mini pickup, it wasn't a popular body style, so they stopped producing them in 1972. I, however, love it!"

"Wow, how did you—"

Fin cuts me off. "Nope. All you need to know is that I know a guy who knows a guy, who knows a guy. Don't ask beyond that."

The conversation ends there with me nodding in silent acknowledgement and wondering what goes on at the body shop Fin took over. Two years ago, Fin quit her job at the bank because she was dying of boredom. That job was her greatest frustration. She constantly told me that no amount of feather pens, quote mugs, or coloured highlighters could give a workday zest. It's surprising she didn't get fired because she'd slide notes to clients at her wicket with comments like "stick 'em up."

Given that she always wanted to ride a sparkling unicorn to work, I wasn't surprised when she found herself a job that involved vehicles. Buying the body shop to be the owner was shocking because Fin isn't a mechanic or a business expert, but in typical Fin fashion, she adapted and excelled.

The closer we get to the house, the stronger my reluctance and discomfort. Do Mom and Dad think Alivia's old life has resurfaced? Will they blame me for her going missing? *If the cop in the family was home . . .*

I've no idea how Mom and Dad are going to respond to me just disappearing and popping up again. I'm restless and my thoughts are dancing with *what-ifs*. "Damn, Alivia, I'm coming," I keep whispering to myself like a mantra with an additional silent thanks to Fin because she just keeps driving.

It's a short drive and all too quickly I find I'm waving goodbye to Fin over my shoulder. I feel like if I wait outside the house for a prolonged time, I'll catch a glimpse of everyone who lived here when I was growing up, from Grama Pearle and Grandpa Ian, to Mom, Dad, Jaxton, Alivia, myself, and Noah. Given that the house doesn't show any signs of the passing of time, Noah's parents might be alive and stroll outside, too. A gush of warmth accompanies my thought of Noah's parents; they were like family.

Eyes closed, I take deep breaths. The air smells musky and sweet like the leaf piles Alivia and I used to play in as kids. *Time to stop procrastinating.* I put one foot in front of the other and I push through the front doors into the foyer. I'm not sure what I'm expecting, but it damn sure isn't what I get.

This never-empty house is vacant. The silence feels like it's reaching out and embracing me. I shake and wipe at my arms to brush away the silent, invisible fingers enclosing me. It isn't just the silence though. The house is in disarray, leaving no doubt that it's been ransacked. *Could this be in connection to Alivia? Where is my family? Fin couldn't have known about this.*

There's so much to take in between tipped furniture, strewn books and knick-knacks, and broken glass. However, my mind notes that there's no blood. Before I can register more, the back door in the kitchen bursts open and a familiar voice calls my name. Noah comes down the extensive hall at a flat run, straight from the door. His lean body is a blur as he rams into me.

"Quick," he whispers breathlessly as I become aware of a commotion in the front yard.

Noah's hand grasps mine, and he's pulling me down the hallway toward the kitchen. I keep my footing as we thunder through the debris. Loud footfalls move outside the kitchen door. Noah's stop is abrupt and I ram into his solid frame. He doesn't notice. His head is swivelling in the direction of the front entrance and sideways to the stairwell leading up to the second floor. No doors separate the hallway from any adjoining rooms, so we can see the main entrance. No time.

The front door flies open, banging into the wall, and cold air streams in filling the space with a damp scent. It's powerfully familiar, and it mentally transports me to the alley and the strange shadow figure.

Noah pulls me to the left, leading us into the library off the kitchen. I stumble over a heap of books and drop to my knees. He has me under the armpits without missing a beat. He opens the secret room and stuffs me in and he follows, sealing us in.

The hidey-hole is a twenty-eight by fifty-three-inch space designed to resemble a solid wall between the library and the front living room. Both rooms have an access door. The other two walls making up this hidden space include an exterior wall and the back wall of the powder room. Noise is kept in and out with soundproof insulation. It's also lightless. The room is so well concealed that nobody outside the family knows about it, and I had forgotten it.

"Wow, I missed those amber eyes and the way they smoulder in all settings. A mystery amber that glows without light reflecting in them." Noah's voice is gravelly as he squeezes my hand in reassurance.

I'm aware of the proximity of our bodies and his spicy fragrance punctuated with sweet, bitter notes of fruit. I'm also aware that after all this time and amid all this chaos, there's still that energy there, an undercurrent questioning whether we could be more than just best friends. A part of me still grieves how close Noah and I came to being a couple in our youth, but a larger part of me is thankful for the strength of our friendship and the depth of our love. Like Fin, Noah is one of those friends who neither time nor distance affects, but it's not the time to get lost on memory lane, so I refocus on the wall that's pressed tight against my shoulders.

The silence is heavy and I'm grateful for the strong, calloused hand that's gripping mine. Seconds slip by. Noah's voice cuts through the quiet. "Ready? One, two." He shoves the door open, and we emerge into the library.

A noticeable chill hangs in the air with a weak undertone of dampness. We move cautiously toward the doorway to the kitchen and creep out. Voices in the front living room dictate we escape through the kitchen door, but as we get closer, the shadows move and two men we hadn't noticed, draped in cloaks as dark as night, block our way. They don't hesitate. Their voices fill the surrounding space with cries for help.

Noah turns and heads up the stairs. I follow, taking two steps at a time to keep up with his long legs and swift pace, all the while thinking that the damp stench and cloaked men in the hallway don't match my memory of the shadow figures from the alley in Mexico. I have to refocus my thoughts when Noah continues past the second floor. He bolts down the hallway to the back stairwell that leads to the attic.

Our getaway through the second floor is so fleeting that I can't take much in besides the area being dishevelled. Noah is yelling instructions at me as we pound up the stairs, and it takes an effort to focus on his words. He must have realized because he stops and grabs me by the shoulders, locking his eyes on mine.

"I know you grew up in this house, but you never allowed yourself to see." His voice is soft, and I think I see a hint of sadness before it's lost to stern seriousness. He fears whoever is pursuing us through the house. "Kori, when you hit the top hallway, head diagonally across the hall to that bedroom, and when you breach the doorway, drop and slide. Aim for the built-in shelves with your feet."

My head is swinging searching for alternatives. "Slamming into things with my feet doesn't constitute a plan—"

"GO!" Noah pushes me in front of him.

I'm running. Dropping into a slide, I give thanks that hardwood replaced the old carpet. I brace for what I'm sure will be a jarring thud when I hit the wall, but when the bottoms of my feet make contact, a rectangular section of the cabinet's base gives way. There's no floor and I'm falling down a tapering chute. I pull my arms and legs tight and pray Noah doesn't crush me when we hit the ground.

The perfume of lavender is rich and I gulp the calming scent. I drop out into Grama Pearle's basement store behind the checkout counter. Noah slides in behind me. We both realize at the same time that we aren't alone.

An enormous shadow detaches from the corner and shock runs through me as I recognize the man from the alley fight a few nights before. *Here? How?* Thoughtless, I find my belt knife in my hand and I'm crouching low in a fighting stance.

The large man freezes. His eyes lock on mine, smoky gray eyes with the softest hints of blue.

Noah's hand clasps my wrist. In my peripheral vision, I see his head give a slight wag from side to side. I risk a look at him, and he mouths the word "friend."

Voices at the top of the basement stairs drift down. They're searching the house for us. It's just a matter of moments before they'll be coming our way. I leave my questions about this so-called friend unspoken and transfer my focus to survival. There's no exit besides the stairs. The chute that discharged us is unnoticeable, but even if it wasn't, climbing up is unfeasible based on the design.

Littered with several kinds of shelves, the store has nothing large enough to conceal us. The thought of hand-to-hand combat doesn't bother me, but I don't relish confronting unknown hostiles. I don't know what or who we're running from. I do know that if Noah is running, then there are too many for us to challenge alone.

I can hear feet descending the stairs. I draw my vigilance from the store entrance and see the big man disappear, soundless, into the shadows leading to the storage area. Noah tugs me to the floor as a loud crash indicates that someone's inside the store. One of our pursuers has knocked over the shelf with a basin full of various stones.

In my mind's eye, I see the obsidian, limestone, sandstone, marble, and quartz covering the floor.

Focus, a hushed voice whispers in my mind.

From my crouch behind the counter, I close my eyes

and inhale a calming breath, locking on an image of the air stones. The stones become foremost in my thoughts, and I imagine them swirling and flying on the increasingly aggressive air currents.

"She's down here somewhere," a deep voice hollers.

I imagine the air currents turning violent. I hear a soft rustle turn into a raging wind and the stones begin pelting things. Voices cry out in pain as the stones batter them with progressive frequency.

Noah pulls me toward the shadows. I push up from the floor and stretch my head higher, trying to see over the counter to get a glimpse of who's after us, but it's a string of LED lights illuminating the dark space. With a quiet sigh, I drop down and crawl into the shadows. Noah and his friend are whispering but come to a conclusion. With brief nods, they're leading the way deeper into Grama Pearle's storage room. She keeps it like a strange labyrinth of weird, witchy supplies. It's well organized so there won't be anywhere to hide.

The big man rises to his feet, and I can just make out that his muscled body is straining to complete a task. A clicking sound rings out like a gunshot in the storage space, and a grating noise follows. He's opened a concealed door and positioned himself to the side gesturing us forward. Noah sees my hesitation and leads the way. *Noah trusts him, and I trust Noah.* The big man just stands there, like we have all the time in the world. I'm sure that he can see me shake my head, but in the darkness, my raised eyebrows and eye roll are for my own satisfaction.

I enter. The doorway and the tunnel it leads into are

narrow and have to be navigated sideways. I'm relieved by the high ceiling because it helps to ease the feeling that I've just walked into a tomb. The man wedges into the space alongside me, and I hear him grunt with the effort it takes to pull the door closed using one arm. The grating sound echoes in the confined space and the darkness is complete.

"Kori, we have to move. It's unlikely with all the ruckus they're making that they'll hear us in the walls, but I'd rather not risk it." Noah's disembodied voice floats into my left ear.

"Okay," is the best response I can muster. The muffled crashes from shelves being overturned fade out as we move into the tunnel.

This is far from the homecoming I expected. My hands grope the wall. It's cold and rough. The air is damp, stale, and earthy. We move in silence for what feels like hours. The only sound is our soft breathing and the occasional shuffle of a misplaced foot. I have the distinct impression that we're going down, but in the dark, cramped space, I'm not sure if it's just a trick on my senses. Regardless, the tunnel never gets wider, and I'm overjoyed that it doesn't get any more constricted.

Once my eyes adjust, I can discern shadows but those are limited to the side profile of Noah to my left, who I'm following, and the man behind me. There are walls sandwiching us. Although the walls are rugged, there aren't any large obstacles protruding from them.

The big man's voice carries over me. "There should be stairs soon, Noah." He speaks over my head as if I'm not trapped, walking like a crab between them. I clench my jaw and stop walking, overtaken by a childish urge to trip him, but my frustration grows when he senses I have stopped and he doesn't stumble into me. Instead, he speaks over my head. "She stopped!"

"Kori, are you okay?" Noah asks.

"Fine," I huff and start shuffling to the left. I imagine the big man smiling to himself and I huff again, this time at myself. I revisit Noah's use of the word *friend*; this man has shown up twice when I'm under attack. Setting aside the fact that being attacked is abnormal, it can't be a coincidence that he keeps showing up, but that doesn't brand him a friend. Or a foe, I add as an afterthought.

We travel sideways up fifty-three steps and stop at what I think is a dead end. The thought of retracing our steps is almost too much for me.

"There should be a release latch, Noah," the big man says.

Noah's hands scrape over the rough surface, trying to find the supposed latch. I wait. There's a swishing sound from the big man's direction that blends into a low hiss and a crackle. The surrounding tunnel is now bathed in a mellow glow.

"Thanks," Noah offers without turning, like this is what he expected to happen. I, on the other hand, whip my head so fast that I almost graze my nose on the wall.

Behind me, the big man has raised his far arm high in the air. In the palm of his elevated hand, he holds a florescent orb that coils with burnt orange, lemon yellow, and hints of umber. It flickers like a live flame.

There's a clear blur of heat haze above the orb that distorts images on the opposite side of it in a shaky, disillusioned way. But there's no smoke and no smell of fire.

It takes a great effort for me to pull my eyes from the hand holding the orb to the face of the big man. He's looking past me as if I'm not there, which isn't a shocker. He's focused on what Noah is doing on the other side of me, which affords me a minute to check him out. I'm surprised by the rough handsomeness in his chiselled features. My eyes slide lower, curious about what I might find.

When a clicking noise indicates Noah has found the latch the orb makes a sound like roaring fire. I pull my eyes up to see it grow, the colours washing over each other, giving a rich, grey smoke off the top before it winks out. The door behind me gives way, allowing light to flood in.

As I blink stupidly, Noah grabs me and yanks me from the tunnel. He guides me to a sitting position to keep me stable as I try to blink the sight back into my eyes. Meanwhile, I hear the big man step into the room and close the tunnel door.

Chapter 3

What I thought was natural light I now see is a series of well-placed candles. As my eyes adjust, I note the proximity of walls and the crypt-like feeling. The ceiling is lower than in the tunnel; I can graze it with my fingers if I jump.

We're in a space that's about six feet by six feet, lacking windows and doors. Because of the lack of light, I can't see the hatch we entered through. The air is stuffy like a damp basement with poor venting and there's a fine dust in it that tickles my nose when I breathe. My rational mind acknowledges that there's some sort of ventilation system, but the non-logical part of my mind focuses on the intense sensation of being buried alive.

"Are we underground?" I ask nobody in particular.

Noah flashes a smile that makes his mouth, cheeks, and eyes light up. "We are. We're under the old Lindsay Street Cemetery."

"You're enjoying this, aren't you, you big ass?" I cast my eyes from side to side. "Is there another unnoticeable door?"

Noah pats a cramped spiral staircase in the centre of

the room. It leads up into complete darkness, and I can't determine how much of its top half travels through the ground. "At the right time, we'll go up and out."

"The right time?"

"You sound skeptical, Kori. Doesn't she sound doubtful, Alaric?"

I eye the big man whose name I've just learned is Alaric. He remains silent and observant. His thick arms fold over and he leans against the cold wall, expressionless. I raise my eyebrows, clear my throat, and turn to Noah. "I'm not skeptical. We just walked," I pause, considering what I know about where my family house is in relation to the cemetery, "three and a half kilometres in a secret underground tunnel from the basement of my childhood home to the local cemetery while being pursued by humans, something not human, and—"

"They were human once," Noah interrupts.

"What?"

"You said, 'while being pursued by humans and something not human.' Well, the 'not human' is a magical person, a Spellbinder, who let their greed for the magics, particularly dark magic, subvert them into the Warped," Noah explains. He reads the blank look on my face to mean I want him to explain more. "They're Spellbinders who are chronically drawn to dark magic and display abnormal and often violent behaviour. Oh, did I mention that they're members of The Society of the Blood Wind?"

I stare at him, blink a few times, and continue as if he hasn't spoken. "We're in a crypt. An underground tomb lit with candles, but there's not a soul in sight. That big man over there was in Mexico stalking me, and now he's here. My family is missing, but I'm assuming you know where they are because you weren't surprised by anything at the house and the message I received in Mexico didn't refer to them at all. Someone took my sister. So, if I sound skeptical, I would say I'm doing well because I feel like I took a direct flight from reality into the depths of absurdity."

Noah places his hand on my shoulder. "Pearle," he says without hesitation.

"What? Grama Pearle, what?"

"She lit the candles for us, of course, then she went to get us an inconspicuous ride out of here." Noah waves his hand in a circle as if he's answered everything.

I can feel a twitch behind my eye, accompanied by a slight throbbing. Eyes closed, I move my neck from side to side and finger my temples. "Okay, is that a bad joke about Grama Pearle's love of cemeteries? No. You know what, Noah, I know it isn't a bad joke, but I don't know what you're trying to say. So, let's try a different question. Who in the blazing hell is he?" I jerk my head in Alaric's direction.

Noah and I are both looking expectantly at Alaric, but he's close-mouthed, with no verbal or physical response. I spread my hands apart in a questioning gesture and glance at Noah, whose head is bobbing up and down. "Let's just say that he has a vested interest in stopping the group that's hunting us."

"Right," I mumble. "Who's hunting us then, and

why? Any why would anybody kidnap Alivia?"

"Alivia's magic is limited, but her talents in the healing magics are too advanced for the most powerful of Spellbinders to detect. Alivia placed an awareness charm on Nekane, son of Dolion Adelgrief the head of The Society of the Blood Wind, to alert her to subtle variances in his knowledge. He didn't detect the charm, but it tipped her off that he had become aware of the Emb—"

Noah cups his left ear and tips it up toward the ceiling. "Shh, I think our ride is here."

Nothing he said strikes me as sane or realistic; the degree of my confusion is astronomical. Noah moves to the spiral stairs and starts up as Alaric peels himself off the wall. When I can't see Noah anymore, there's the distinct sound above me of one rough surface scraping another, followed by a mumble of voices.

Alaric catches my eye and lifts his chin at the stairs. I don't hide my frown before beginning the awkward climb. I spiral up through at least six feet of the stairs that are encircled by ground. Blindly moving in the absence of light is clumsy and disorienting, and the effect on me is suffocating. My breaths are quick and shallow. *Climb, climb.*

At the top, I find an enclosed crawl space. I'm not sure what kind of structure I'm under but there's pale light filtering from an opening in one wall. I have to drag myself across the ground on my stomach to get off the stairwell and over the dirt to the exit point. I reach my hands out into the daylight and Noah locks onto my wrists and drags me the rest of the way. An interment niche! I exited the underground tomb via an interment niche. I stare as Alaric squeezes through the opening.

"Let's go guys, now!" a familiar voice orders.

"Fin?" I note a hearse idling by the columbarium we just crawled from.

"Did Pearle call you, Fin?" Noah has opened the hind door of the hearse, and while I've been immobile, trying to wrap my mind around everything that just happened, he and Alaric are already inside. Noah pops his head out to speak to Fin again, "Is she with you?"

"In a manner of speaking," Fin yells, her head hanging out the driver's window, as I scramble forward, too dumbfounded to ask whom they're talking about. Noah's remark about an inconspicuous ride takes on a whole new meaning.

The rear windows of the hearse are almost opaque, offering privacy from outside eyes. The interior of the hearse is the cleanest I've ever seen, new vehicles aside. A chemical smell fills the air. Rails for moving caskets with ease line the floor, making the space itself uncomfortable for live passengers. An untinted glass window separates us from the driver and passenger area of the vehicle. There's nothing to do but wait as Fin takes us wherever she plans to go. The hearse bumps over the curb onto the main street and we blend into the flow of traffic.

"It's The Society of the Blood Wind, that's hunting us. It's a detailed story that spans back generations." Noah points at me, "The part you need to know is that we're in the middle of The War of Magic."

"The War of Magic?"

"It's a conflict of power between two opposing groups of thought among the 'Spellbinders.' The Embers, that's your family, are the strongest magic bloodline and the strongest resistance for The Society of the Blood Wind. The Society of the Blood Wind was formed after a Spellbinders' vote in favour of living peacefully amongst humans, also known as 'normies.'" Noah stretches his legs out, trying to get comfortable before he continues.

"The Society of the Blood Wind wants to destroy humans instead of living among them, mostly for power, domination, and from a belief that Spellbinders are superior. Those who side with your family have always been a larger group. So, The Society of the Blood Wind bides its time recruiting in an attempt to tip the balance in their favour and by committing crimes that can't be directly linked to them."

I cross my arms and cock my head; there's no keeping the exasperation out of my voice. "So, you expect me to believe that we're being hunted because we live with humans? What's your magic, Noah?"

Noah's eyes stray to Alaric. Alaric's shoulders rise and fall non-committal, and Noah nods in response. "First, I don't expect you to believe that we're being hunted because we live among humans. This is way more complicated than that, but it's what I'm able to share with you right now. It's what's at the core, along with power and domination.

"Second, there are some magics almost all Spellbinders can do but are specific to family lines and other magics are individual Spellbinders. I have limited magic, Kori. I'm skilled with shields. It's more of a protective magic, which complements my fighting skills. And this works for me because I have a different responsibility. For hundreds of years, my family has worked with yours as protectors of your bloodline, warriors."

The hearse stops suddenly and I'm thrown forward by the momentum. "Did I hit my head, Noah?" I ask. "What you're saying makes no sense."

Fin flings the hind door of the hearse open. "You guys look dead hungry." She laughs and slams the door. Fifteen minutes later the door pops open, and Fin passes in food bags from Just Flavours. The shadow of a person darkens the area behind her and we all tense. I can't see who it is, but Fin visibly relaxes. Her smile slips before she forces her lips to curl up again.

"I know I'm an asshole, Fin, but I had to stop and see what you'd be feeding in a vehicle designed to carry dead people." The familiar voice rises in pitch, making the statement an unofficial question.

I barely have time to register Carter's coin phrase of "I know I'm an asshole," before his brown eyes peek into the hearse. There's a sharp intake of air as Carter registers my presence. Then Fin shoves Carter backward, two-handed. I watch as he stumbles far enough that Fin can shut the door.

Fin is in the driver's seat and reversing. I'm sure she's going to run Carter over as his hands bang down the full length of the passenger side of the vehicle, unable to keep up, but trying to get Fin to stop. His voice sounds strangled as he calls my name. Flabbergasted, my eyes pop in their sockets.

I turn to Noah and Alaric but drop my head in defeat because they're both oblivious and munching on the grilled chicken burgers. It's clear that I'm not going to get answers from them, so I bite into my sandwich. I chew mechanically and taste nothing as my thoughts race from one wild idea to another.

Carter looked rough, like he hadn't washed or cut his hair in a while. Even his normally pristine clothing was stained and crumpled. It's abnormal behaviour for him. His voice calling my name as he beat at the hearse is haunting. I'll have to ask Fin about this.

We've reached our destination. The door to the hearse pops open and fresh air flows in. Before I close the door, the hearse pulls away with one of Fin's employees behind the wheel. She must've pre-arranged for him to collect the vehicle here.

"Take it to the funeral home, Pete. The work on it is complete," Fin yells at the disappearing hearse. "Errr, that guy. I'll find it at the shop when I go in tomorrow like we didn't already do the brakes. Come on. Let's go in."

I turn and see that Fin has taken us to her place. The two-storey, red brick house feels like home to me and I'm eager to get inside.

"Grama Pearle brought some clothes for you, Kori. They're in the smallest bedroom. You can shower first."

I pad up the carpeted stairs, grateful that things in this house feel like they always have. The solitary bathroom is off the main bedroom at the end of a short hallway. After the stress of the last few days, I need a few minutes to myself. So, I don't waste any time taking up the offer to shower first. My questions can wait. A shower will help me refresh so I can assemble my thoughts, formulate relevant questions, and be primed for the answers.

I close the bathroom door, turn the radio on, and strip. I spare a quick second to make sure it's me in the mirror after these unwonted activities of secret tunnels, unnatural pursuers, and prattle about magic before I step over the tub edge and disappear behind the shower curtain. The spray of the shower hitting my skin feels refreshing, but it isn't enough to inhibit thoughts of the last few bizarre hours. Thankful that I turned the music on, I focus on the beat until it takes over and I'm caught up in its rhythm.

Without warning, the shower curtain pulls back and out of my reach, and Alaric is there. Attempting to jump free of what I think is an attack, I slip. Arms flailing, I plunge out of the shower into him. He catches me and places me on my feet in a single fluid motion. "We have to go now."

"I'm naked, you asshole!" I'm not sure if I'm madder that Alaric is seeing me naked or that he seems unphased by my nudity.

Alaric pauses, and looks down and up. He locks eyes with me which I construe as appreciation and an electric current jolts through me. I'm sure that the water beads on my skin are sizzling. *It's been too long since I've been naked with a man.*

Much to my horror, Alaric drags me from the bathroom. I grab a towel and hold it against the front of my body before I'm yanked into the hallway.

Goosebumps pimple my skin and I stop struggling, casting a glance toward the stairs all thoughts of my clothing abandoned as I realize our pursuers have found us.

Alaric lets go of me as we enter the main bedroom. In one fluid motion, he rips my towel away and yanks an oversized t-shirt from Fin's bed down over my head. I'm happy that I don't have an opportunity to think about why this shirt reeks of both men's cologne and Fin's perfume. Instead, I ram my arms through the shirt sleeves, thankful that the shirt hangs down past my lady bits.

My head is on a swivel for something to pull over my lower body as Alaric herds me and Fin toward the window on the far side of the room. It's the first time I notice that she and Noah are upstairs. "We gotta go," Noah announces with a smile as he disappears out the open window onto the lip of roof that overhangs Fin's front deck.

Fin has the uncanny ability to read my thoughts regarding my lack of wardrobe. "No can do, Kori. Besides, if you've seen one cookie, honey, then you've seen them all, and yours isn't dusted in gold. So, haul your naked ass out that window before this well-built man throws us both out."

I take a deep breath and follow her out the window. I've been home for less than twenty-four hours on a quest to help my family and I'm going almost butt-ass naked out a window while being pursued by a bunch of crazy lunatics; nothing about this is normal.

"How'd they find us?" I scramble over the rough

shingles aiming for a group of trees that hug the side of the house.

"Carter!" Noah yells. I think that he's talking to me, but as I steal a glance groundward, I see Noah yelling at him. Carter is yelling for me in a voice full of desperation and he won't stop. Noah cocks his arm and lands a solid blow into Carter's midsection. He doubles over, gasping for air and grunting, but he stops yelling.

Fin is backing her truck up. Alaric is dragging me from the tree. We grab the tailgate, jump onto the bumper, and tumble into the mini truck box. I note human shadows in the upstairs windows and wonder how many others there are in the house. Noah miraculously got into the front passenger seat before we hit full speed. I fix my eyes on Carter trying to straighten into a standing position. Two cloaked figures are converging on him.

I'm moving as if I can leap over the tailgate and save him. Alaric's hand clamps on my upper arm. I whip my head in his direction to see him blowing grainy particles out of his other hand toward Carter. His lips are moving, but his words are too quiet for me to hear, and he isn't paying heed to anything other than the three figures on Fin's front lawn.

Alaric's focus is so intense that I peek to see what's happening, just as Carter gives a shriek that turns into a loud squeak. Carter has changed into a brown rat. *Is this a glimpse of Alaric's humour?* The sudden transformation takes the shrouded assailants by surprise, giving Carter enough time to scurry into the foliage and disappear. The cloaked figures turn their heads in our direction and stare until we are out of sight.

I feel Alaric's eyes on me, so I turn. He releases his hold on my arm, reaches down while holding my eyes with his and tugs the shirt lower over my exposed bottom half. All I can manage is a blink of acknowledgement.

"Carter will change into the human rat he normally is in a few hours," Alaric tells me as if my questions are visible on my face while his remains deadpan.

I nod before I pop my head in the open back window of the truck. "They found us fast, how?"

"Carter," Noah replies.

"Why would Carter tell them where we are?"

"I got this one. I've been dying to tell her." Fin winks at Noah. "He's obsessed with you, Kori, and has been since his erectile dysfunction." Fin and I are staring at each other in the rear-view mirror; I'm dumbfounded and speechless. "You know impotence, limp dick, softie, wang fail, mopey dick—"

"Ahhh, stop it!" Noah glances at his own crotch.

"Floppy jalopy," Fin smirks.

"He believes that you're responsible for Kinsley's ovary trouble and his sexual difficulties," Noah explains. Grama Pearle's threat to spread rumours to that effect pops into my mind, but Grama Pearle isn't malicious. She wouldn't, nor could she, be responsible in any way for Carter and Kinsley's misfortunes. *Coincidence?*

Noah's narrative continues. "Carter has convinced himself that his infidelity and impotence connect, and you're at the core. Not so much a curse as a negative action earning negative consequences.

"Either way, he's been trying to find out where you are for months. He's obsessed with fixing things with you to try and fix, well, everything else." I glance at Fin. She shrugs like it isn't something she felt I needed to know right away. "It was bad luck that he was at Just Flavours when we pulled up in the hearse and even worse that he found us at Fin's place," Noah says to me before speaking to Fin. "Who would've thought he'd figure it out so fast." Fin nods in response.

"What?" I ask.

"You and Alaric need to lie down in the box," Noah says.

"No."

Noah turns to me, his eyes softening as he takes in my current dishevelled state. "Bet you wish you went second for a shower." When I say nothing, he nods. "Okay, I see that you need a bit more information before you duck down. Lots happened since you've been gone. Carter was involved in an unpleasant scene at work. We know that he stumbled into some kind of magical crime that was set up to suggest The Society of the Blood Wind was involved, but we aren't sure if they were." Noah scans the scenery before he continues.

"We aren't sure about much of it including why whomever it was let Carter live. But he hasn't been the same since; it was after that that his erectile dysfunction became public and his preoccupation with you started. His memory of what happened is obscured by normie conditioning that magic doesn't exist outside of stories and movies so we can't get any answers.

He isn't a cop anymore. His parents disowned him. Kinsley left after Carter's work incident, she'd been vocal about her ovary issues before she left. Who knows where she went? She was bad news. Anyway, Carter just fell through the cracks. Mixed into all that, he became convinced that you were the key to solving all his difficulties."

"Well, that explains why he hasn't signed the divorce papers," I mumble low enough that the wind carries my voice away. *Alivia first. Finalizing the divorce second.*

"Floppy jalopy? I've never heard that one," says the faint voice of Grama Pearle.

"Who called Grama Pearle?" I push my head as far into the cab of the truck as I can, craning my neck to find the cell phone that's on speaker. "Where's the phone? I'd like to talk to Grama Pearle privately."

"No cell phone, sweetheart. I'm right here," says the voice of Grama Pearle.

"Grama Pearle, there are two people and my head inside the truck cab," I say. Without skipping a beat, I address Noah. "Give me the cell, Noah!"

"She's here, Kori," Fin says dipping her head and thrusting her chin at her chest.

"Pearle brought you into the fold, eh, Fin?" Noah says.

"I've waited years for Fin to choose to see the magic in the world, most normies never do. Now she's really part of the family," Grama Pearle says.

"Give me the cell phone guys and stop teasing."

"Forever unbelieving, eh, Kori? I'm right here in Fin's pocket," Grama Pearle insists. "Been here since the cemetery. I'm being stealthy and having a bit of fun."

I glance down and sure enough, a four-inch-tall Grama Pearle is smiling up at me from Fin's breast pocket. Her blue-silver hair is a sharp contrast to Fin's pink shirt. There's no mistaking that it's her. Even at this miniature size, I can see the strange green-gray glow of Grandpa Ian's ashes in the onyx and glass cremation necklace Grama Pearle wears. Not for the first time in the last few hours, my eyes grow round as saucers. I look from mini Grama Pearle to Fin. Fin is all business with her eyes on the road and Noah is observing this exchange.

"Kori, honey." Grama Pearle says. "I'd love to give you a hug, but right now I'd pinch your nose, so it will have to wait. Noah and I need to figure out what to do next, and I feel like I'm going to get sucked out that window. It needs closing. We'll talk soon. If I were you, I would snuggle that hunk of man and catch a fast nap." Grama Pearle winks and gives me a dismissive gesture with her hand. I swallow and slide down into the box of the truck.

Alaric is keeping vigil of the road behind us. "This is what it is to be home," I mumble. *Alivia I'm home for you.* Alaric says nothing, but his big arm enfolds me. I don't resist. Instead, I lean in for his heat and I shut my eyes, hoping that wherever we're going, I can find some pants.

Chapter 4

Somewhere in my sleep-filled brain, I realize the speed of the truck is changing. It's now marked by the crunch of gravel under the tires as we ease to a stop.

Way more tired than I care to admit, I'm surprised that I fell asleep, half-naked in the box of a truck, with a man I don't know. Said man, Alaric, sits patiently, while I compose my thoughts enough to untangle myself from him. As the drowsy part of my brain registers this, my body jerks aside bumping into the box wall.

The truck doors open and close. There's a flurry of conversation from Fin, Noah, and Grama Pearle, none of which I'm able to comprehend.

Thankfully, nobody is observing me as I climb over the tailgate because there's no way to maneuver myself without flashing my lady bits. Once my feet hit the gravel, I tug my shirt down and follow everybody up the extensive driveway. The rocks are cold and pointy, and although I prefer bare feet, it's a reminder that certain situations require sandals.

Tall trees, just starting to show the colours of fall, obscure the road. To the left, there's a large, gray, three-car garage, and across the driveway sits a ranch-style house. The house is built into the terrain. Viewing it from the front corner, I imagine the front door enters on a split landing to go up to the main floor or down to the basement.

The front door is in the middle of the house under an overhung roof. Two lion gargoyles sit guarding the door with their gaze directed toward the intersection where the driveway meets the road. They have sleek bodies. Their fangs are visible even with closed mouths, but it's their oversized paws with claws layered like rows of shark teeth that capture my fancy. Before I can register more, we're marching past the walkway.

A wooden deck comes into view with a woman posed on it. Feet spread, hands on hips, she's watching our approach. She's almost five feet tall, but she radiates an air of authority and no-nonsense. The voice that booms out of her is shockingly deep and loud. "Who goes there?"

Before anyone can respond, the woman's stance changes. She must feel we're a threat because she's postured to fight with her feet staggered, her chin down, and her hands up. Without warning, her arm arches in a throwing motion. A bubble-like ball rolls through the air, growing bigger as it gets closer to us.

"You blind fool! Where are your glasses?" Grama Pearle, regular-sized, brings her hands in front of her. I can see she's braced against the faint outline of a materializing clear wall.

Alaric moves behind her and braces. When the bubble hits the wall, it's grown to a size that would envelop us all if it didn't crash into Grama Pearle's barrier. Its strength is stunning. I hate to think what its purpose is, but given Grama Pearle's response it can't be good. Hers and Alaric's feet are grinding backwards in the gravel. Fin and Noah move to brace behind Alaric and I follow suit.

"Birdie!" Grama Pearle yells. "BIRDIE, shut it down!"

The woman, best described as birdlike with her small quick movements, is alert and perched on the stairs. Her body leans forward and she squints as if she's straining to see. Her countenance changes at the sound of Grama Pearle's voice.

The woman's thin arms flutter and wave at her sides. She twitches once and there's an audible pop as the bubble becomes a dissipating misty vapour. Fin and I fall into a dusty heap, unable to adjust to the sudden lack of pressure, and I feel a slight wave of irritation that nobody else is in the dirt with us. My vexation switches to self-consciousness as the chilly air blows over the skin of my exposed lower body. I crank the shirt down and scramble to stand, rubbing dirt off myself.

The woman descends the stairs and is hopping raptor-like across the driveway at full speed. Grama Pearle is moving, matching her pace. They both come to an abrupt halt, laughing, and lock each other in a hug. "Where are your glasses, you blind old bat?"

There's a short, high tweet. "Left them in the house, Pearle. I raced out the door thinking I was going to war, but it's just you and some younglings. Besides, it's my opinion that I see fine without them." Her voice changes to one of suggestion, as she peers at Grama Pearle. "It must be significant if you didn't send a message ahead." The little woman cranes her head with snappy movements. Her voice is musical. "Shhh, first, let's get inside."

We enter a screened-in sunroom, an addition to the original house. It's littered with various plants, some I can identify and others that appear very exotic. Among the plants are numerous Buddha statues, ranging from plain but cute to ornate and complex. In the centre of the rectangular room is an old dining table.

The room is warm and tropical and I'm aware that there are birds amid the plants and Buddhas. I ignore the bird droppings and instead I survey the room, trying to determine how many species of birds are present, when my eyes drift past a hawk the size of a dove. It's perched on a branch close to the ceiling. I whip my eyes to the hawk, thinking that I've seen it before, perhaps in Mexico or maybe at the cemetery, but it disappears into the foliage in a flurry of feathers.

Birdie leads us by a set of closed sliding doors that lead to a family room. As we move through the room, Birdie chirps and tweets to the birds, sounding like a real bird and not a person making bird noises. The birds chirp and tweet replies. Fin casts a questioning glance at me, but I muster a shrug. I regret the action as I feel the shirt slip up to expose the lower half of my buttocks.

Noah's body is close behind me. His hands are tugging playfully at the bottom corners of my shirt. "Birdie is the lone name we know her by. She's a great old bird," he whispers as we pass through a doorway into a well-sized kitchen, to find Birdie's eyes on Noah and me. Noah clears his throat and bobs his head at her before moving.

Birdie says nothing. Instead, she crooks a claw-like finger at me and gives a snap of her head toward the exit on the far side of the kitchen. When I remain unmoving, Birdie peeps at Grama Pearle, who cracks a smile and a bark of laughter. Birdie gawks at my naked legs and barely covered private area. She hops forward, making a clucking sound and staring; her examination of me makes me feel like a worm caught by a bird.

When Birdie is in front of me, she lifts her claw-like finger and flicks it in the exit's direction. "First bedroom on the right has clothes in the dresser that will fit those beautiful legs like a charm." She cocks her head to one side, her tone leaving no room for discussion. "Off you go." She slaps her hand on my behind, not quite missing the shirt, but causing me to hop and give a short shriek. I leave everyone snorting or full-out laughing at my expense. I don't give it a second thought because I'm thankful for the promise of pants.

Not wanting to miss much of the conversation, I open the first drawer to find a pair of olive-coloured studio pants in my size. The next drawer has undergarments, again in my size, and the third drawer has tank tops. I scoop out a beige tank, dress with a smile, and hurry out to find everyone. I follow the sound of voices down the hallway, past the kitchen, bathroom, and stairs that lead down to a landing, confirming my original assumption about the front door being a split level.

The group is in the family room, all seated and talking. Fin fills me in that we're in a safe house warded by magic alarms, our temporary home. I can't help rolling my eyes, *magic*, even though my brain struggles to believe.

"Kori Ember," Birdie sings. She has found her glasses, which are big, round, and thick. They magnify her owl-like eyes as she addresses me. "Your Grama Pearle and I have decided that you'll all stay here while you learn a few fundamental things and gather resources. Now, I'm going to send messenger birds to some helpful Spellbinders. Then tonight, Kori, I will teach you to fly," she hoots as she disappears through the sliding glass door.

I have an intense urge to back peddle down the hall. "Um, say what?" I mumble through the sour taste in my mouth and the ache in my throat.

"Yes, yes, she said learn to fly." Grama Pearle shakes her head. "There's so much to tell you, but . . ." her voice trails off.

"Grama Pearle?"

"It'll be easier if I show you." I feel Grama Pearle's hazel eyes probe into my amber ones as she assesses me. "Kori, whether or not you want to, it's time you discover the secrets of the family. Close your eyes and trust."

Grama Pearle doesn't wait for an answer. Her dainty, wrinkled hands move toward my eyes, and I close them in reflex. I feel two warm fingers slide gently over my eyelids and pause. The warmth from her fingers grows and I swallow fear as a white light burns through my eyelids and penetrates my internal eye. Grama Pearle's commentary is in my head. It sounds like she's speaking from miles away. "Trust me Kori, trust. Trust and let go."

On some level of consciousness, I feel my body shudder and give over, allowing the white light to take on colours and shapes.

There's no mistaking the family resemblance. This teenage girl has glowing golden eyes like my own and her height and build could be any one of the Ember women I know. It isn't Alivia, but the family likeness makes me think of her. Her hair is butterscotch brown, and she exudes a strong spiritual energy of honour and strength. Her clothing looks like a costume. Is it Halloween? I can see her magic.

Because Grama Pearle knows who these people are, I know too. I know that I'm seeing my ancestor, Evelyn Ember. I cringe and fight a wave of anger as I watch helplessly. Her boyfriend, Bert Becker, moves with anger. His face is red and spit flies from his mouth as he yells, "It isn't normal! Just be normal! Can't you just be normal?" Evelyn's mouth is moving with words that can't be heard over Bert's yelling.

The voice of Grama Pearle is with me as she answers questions that I haven't spoken out loud. "Evelyn was an extremist with her beliefs in how magic should or shouldn't be used. As for Bert, we don't know if he knew she was a Spellbinder. We assume that he didn't know because normies are conditioned not to see, and some choose to not see even if their conditioning fails. Bert had a temper, and he used to yell the same thing as he beat his previous girlfriend, and she wasn't a Spellbinder."

This can't be modern times; the snippets of the house show straw insulation and a dirt floor. Evelyn raises her arms to shield her face. The first blow is to her stomach, doubling her over. Without pause, Bert's knee smashes up into Evelyn's face, sending her flying. As she falls, the back of her head, where the neck and head meet, cracks violently off the corner of the table. Blood spills from the wound and her life with it.

The vision jumps.

A medieval table is awash in the flickering light of candles. Bodies sitting in chairs line the table and more people stand in the shadows. I see people with Ember family features, but I don't recognize any of their faces. Questions, accusations, and vows of revenge come from raised voices. Ember family or not, the question foremost is why Evelyn didn't use her magic against this monstrous human to defend her life.

"She could've destroyed Bert and his whole human family," Sephtis Adelgrief's voice sounds like thunder clashing in the small room. The proposition pitched by the Adelgrief family is to rid the world of humans keeping a few for servitude. Sephtis slams his hand down as he stands. He angles his body to lean across the expanse of the table as far as he can while keeping his feet on the floor. "Evelyn's death is an insult to Spellbinders and an embarrassment! Allowing a normie to kill her . . ." He turns and stalks from the room. His last words, "Magic will rule!"

Images continue moving through my mind while Grama Pearle talks. "That day, Kori, a distinct line was drawn between the Adelgrief and the Ember families.

It's the day that The Society of the Blood Wind was born." The tone of Grama Pearle's discourse, in my head, is sad and tired. "It wasn't long after that the Ember, Pickingill, and Greensmith families went into hiding from the Spellbinder community. Many of those families, including ours, needed protectors. That need developed the honoured Guard Families to protect the bloodlines. Spellbinder families who had an affinity to protect created the honoured Guard. Noah's family is of the honoured Guard."

So many memories of families and wars rush through my mind that they blur. "Breathe, Kori, just breathe." Grama Pearle's voice is a soft overlay on the destructive images. "This is the last thing I'll show you, and it's paramount. Approximately every one thousand years, a Spellbinder child is born into a strong family bloodline, our family. This Spellbinder is very powerful in the magics. This child's job is to purify and lead our people."

Without delay, the images continue, and my throat tightens.

A man becomes clear; the likeness to my deceased brother Jaxton is unnerving. This man could've been Jaxton, grown older. This man is The Cleanser, which makes this image roughly a thousand years old! He's standing with his eyes closed. His feet angle about a foot apart, his head tips skyward, and his arms are reaching high. Smoke is coming off his body with a soft red glow that's growing stronger. The Cleanser is the sole person I see, but it's clear other people are present by the way The Cleanser's eyes travel the room, like he's acknowledging and greeting others.

Fearless, like my brother. Flames are lighting in patches on his person. His face is serene even as a loud cracking sound fills the air, marking the appearance of a long, glacial-blue lightning bolt a few feet in the air from The Cleanser. Torpedo like, it's moving toward him. It penetrates the smoke and fire to drive through The Cleanser's heart with a sickening sizzle. The smoke and fire die out as he crumples, dead. The lightning bolt evaporates in the dissipating heat. Voices rise and confusion reigns.

The vision ends, but my eyes remain unfocused while my brain races to catch up. It's a lengthy piece of Spellbinder history dated a thousand years or more and not presented in chronological order. Instead, the images start with a human killing a Spellbinder. A Spellbinder who could've defended herself with magic, but chose not to even at her own expense.

This choice creates the division in Spellbinders that results in The War of Magic. However, the war started on its projected path with the murder of The Cleanser, the one person whose job it was to purify the Spellbinders of evil and hate. Realizing the truth, I can feel it all rippling through me like nanoscopic sparks growing stronger and brighter by the second.

"Is she okay?" There's concern in Fin's voice.

A large, warm hand squeezes my shoulder. I can't reply. My eyes are unfocused, and my body isn't responding. The squeezing hurts. The pain pulls me from my unresponsive stupor. A wave of anger and an urge to protect myself starts to simmer. The squeezing continues. My eyes fly open, and my body launches off the sofa, twisting to escape the grasp on my shoulder. As I turn, I pull my fist back but a strong hold pins my arms to my sides.

"Easy, Kori." Alaric's voice whispers soothingly. "Breathe. You were catatonic. Breathe. I used pain to trigger a combat response. Breathe." I know it isn't just his voice that he's soothing me with, a soft tickle of magic is being fed into my system to counteract my fight or flight reaction. I can feel my mind and body unwind. Unhurried, Alaric releases my arms.

Every face in the room is watching. I ignore them and turn to Grama Pearle, my police brain dominating my thinking. I'm not sure whether to ask about The Cleanser first or Bert and Evelyn. I go for the murder where I didn't see the killer. "Who killed The Cleanser?"

I watch Grama Pearle's face as she ponders her answer. She gives me a dissatisfied look. "We don't know."

"What?" The word is a roar. My fists clench and unclench.

She sighs. "The type of magic required to make that weapon, the lightning bolt, is rare. The family line with that magic has kept it sequestered so nobody outside of themselves knows about it."

"Wait," Fin cuts in. "You don't all have the same magic?" I admire Fin's adaptability. She doesn't question that magic exists; she questions that it isn't the same for all Spellbinders.

Grama Pearle speaks with patience. "No, Fin. We're all born with different magical skills and our magical strengths differ as well." She holds her hand up to Fin to halt further questions. Fin's mouth keeps moving, but her words aren't audible.

Subconsciously, I know Spellbinders have magical variance, but I hope it doesn't show on my face that I've no idea how many varieties of magic are available in the Spellbinder community. Almost everything magical that I've experienced since that last night in Mexico has been shocking to me on some level. It's possible that Fin knows more than me with the way she has embraced the Spellbinder world. I dismiss the thought.

My line of questioning about The Cleanser and his murder isn't getting me anywhere, so I switch gears. "What happened to Bert? I know laws were different hundreds of years ago, but what happened to him?"

"That's the part she focuses on?" Birdie chirps. I wasn't aware she had returned from the sunroom.

Grama Pearle breathes deep. "They killed him: death by magic. Normies would see a body without a cause of death, but the killer marked the body with a magic message that said 'Magic is Superior.' To this day, it's unknown who was responsible for his death." She pauses, and I wait because I know she isn't finished talking. When she speaks, her voice is stronger and edged with anger. "It's believed the Adelgrief family was responsible for several deaths, normie and Spellbinder, after Evelyn's. They killed whole family bloodlines off." This time the tone of her voice leaves no question that she's done talking about this subject.

"Grama Pearle, all those things you showed me," I pause, thinking about how to ask my question, "those things happened before you were born. How do you know the details?"

"Some happened in the 1500s." A smile pulls at the corners of Grama Pearle's mouth. "I'm a Memory Keeper, Kori. People can pass their memories to me. I accept them as I see fit—so, typically, salient pieces of history—and I store them in my mind. I can share them with others if I choose. However, Memory Keepers can perfectly retain them like their own memories, without limit. Anybody else might keep bits and pieces, as if I told them a story."

I can feel her watching me as my mind sifts through my personal memory bank.

"I can't take things from your head or see things you aren't willing to show me, Kori. Your secrets are safe." She pauses for a conspiratorial wink. "But do you see them, Kori, those memories I shared with you? They're yours now and they're retained, aren't they?" She sounds certain, but I note that she's asking me.

Grama Pearle says no more, and I take a few minutes to let the implication sink in that I'm a Memory Keeper.

"Grama Pearle, if memories must be shared, then how can we have Evelyn's memories? She died before she could share them."

A snort of disgust escapes her and her jaw tightens before she flaps her hand in dismissal. She closes the distance between us and speaks so only I can hear with her eyes downcast. "Bert lost consciousness after his fit of rage. Eyes store representations of external life. For up to ten minutes after a person dies, those portrayals can be accessed and they become a memory for the person accessing them. But," her tone is strained, "it's an act that was once punishable by death. We still have laws around it, but we no longer kill people for doing it." She studies my face with her eyebrows raised.

"So, you're saying someone found Evelyn within ten minutes of her death and took the memory from her eyes? Why? Who?"

"I took this memory because it's an important piece of history regarding the divide in our people. I only know who shared the memory with me. I do not know the chain of Memory Keepers that had it before. I assume that whoever originally took it did so because they feared what it could mean for Spellbinders and normies. It seems probable that whoever it was that took the memory is also who reported the crime." Grama Pearle rolls her shoulders to release the tension she's holding. "I don't want to speak of this anymore now."

The rest of the afternoon passes in a blur of conversation; I don't involve myself. Fin and Noah have a good handle on hypothesizing my bird form. If they came to a conclusion, I wasn't made privy to it. They've discussed eagles, falcons, hawks, the phoenix, and so many others it becomes exhausting. As a result, I'm thankful for bed when Grama Pearle leads Fin, Alaric, Noah, and me down to the basement.

She marches us all into a large room set up with four single beds piled with hand-knit blankets. There are a couple of antique pieces of furniture in the room and nothing else. The floor is unfinished, and the cold cement sets the atmosphere. The chilly air will make for a beautiful sleep once I'm nestled under my mound of blankets.

After spending a good chunk of the day parading three-quarters naked, I shamelessly shuck my pants and bra to climb into bed in my tank top and undies. I don't know who is kind enough to turn out the light and navigate to their bed in the blinding darkness because my whispered "Thank you" receives a grunt in return. I fall asleep thinking about Alivia.

Chapter 5

The room is a dark hole when Birdie shakes me awake. "Dress, girl, it's time to fly."

Without argument, I follow Birdie through the dark house. She leads me out the sunroom door and we trample through the damp grass to the edge of a farmer's field that stretches for miles. The blades of grass tickle the exposed sides of my flip-flopped feet. The night is bright with no clouds and an almost full moon.

Abruptly, Birdie turns. "Watch," she commands. With that, she hops into the air and becomes a grayish-mottled owl with beautiful white tufted ears, a great horned owl. I'm relieved not to find a pile of her clothing on the ground; they must alter with the magic. The owl takes a flight run and she must be travelling at forty miles per hour. Her flight is silent as she comes in with her deadly talons posed to attack. I'm in awe of this predatory bird. She completes her demonstration and shifts into a tiny woman—clothed—who holds me with her intimidating, yellow-eyed stare.

"Now you," she says as if everything is clear. She stares at me.

I hop as she did and try to exude a bit of hope. I land

on my two human feet. Birdie doesn't even blink. She just stares. Seconds tick by. I hop. Birdie bursts out laughing and hops in a circle. She looks so ridiculous that I laugh.

"Good, good. Now we shall try for real. It comes from here." Birdie crooks her finger at my heart. "Your bird is already decided. It's a part of you. Because we are shapeshifters, the traits of our birds are modified from the original species. Sometimes it's as simplistic as a colour change, but it can be strength, speed, or wingspan. You get the idea, but it's another of the ways that makes our bird unique to the Spellbinder. Now don't think about it. Just fly."

She hops and morphs into her owl and then into her human self. "Watch." She repeats the transformation a few times and as I observe, I see misty wisps of energy that I read like an instruction manual.

Seeing the threads is so exciting that I jump and shift without thought. There's a strange pressure all over my body. It isn't uncomfortable, it's just there. I can't see myself as a bird, but I know that my wingspan doesn't compare to an owl, which is over forty inches. I can sense my bird body like I would my human one. I know in my mind's eye that I'm a hummingbird. The shock of it causes me to shift back, dumbfounded. Birdie swallows in a motion that makes me think of a bird swallowing a worm before she starts laughing.

Arms crossed, I curl my toes in the sole of my sandal. "Serious? A hummingbird?"

"Amazing," Birdie chirps through her laughter. "Swift, with maneuverability to hover and fly sideways, backward, and dive at up to sixty miles per hour! Those hummingbirds can be aggressive, and they've fended off larger birds like hawks."

"Birdie, you said that my bird is a predestined part of me, right?" I'm curious about who transforms into what bird, so I try to remember family members and birds I saw growing up. I don't recall seeing hummingbirds, and I can't connect any family members to birds. But if I'm being honest with myself, I made a point of my magical ignorance. I glance at Birdie. She's staring at me with her magnified eyes, expecting more questions. I sigh. "Are all the members of my family hummingbirds? Is Alivia?"

Birdie smiles. "I don't know what Alivia's bird is and I don't believe there are any other hummingbirds in your family, at least your immediate family, anyway. Your ancestors don't dictate your bird. There's a unique quality about you that determines it; we don't know what.

"Spellbinders can't shift at birth. It's a talent that develops as we age, quicker for some than others. Most of us grow up knowing it'll happen at some point," she pauses to study me. "For those who don't have that knowledge, they may never shift." She cocks her head to the side and I'm hopeful there's going to be more explanation, but there isn't. "No more questions, girl. I'm done with answering. Now fly."

I spend the next few hours shifting and learning to fly and steer with my fast-moving wings. As the sun makes its lazy ascent into the sky, Birdie yells, "Race you!" She hops, shifts, and soars away.

With much less grace, I follow suit and make my flight across the yard. Birdie gets there first. My sluggish speed at transforming and my inability to flawlessly control my bird-shaped body gives her the advantage, but I was successful in shifting and manipulating my bird form. When I open the door to the sunroom, Birdie is feeding the birds and laughing with Grama Pearle.

"Are you laughing because I'm a hummingbird, Grama Pearle?"

Birdie pinches her nose. "It could be worse. Some birds stink, right Pearle?"

Grama Pearle sticks her tongue out at Birdie, and I can't help feeling like I'm missing the punchline. Before I can think too much about it, Grama Pearle fixes me with a stare.

"Hummingbirds are incredible flyers, they . . ." Grama Pearle stops mid-sentence. Her strange expression coincides with Birdie rushing toward the door with a wave of her hand that calls the birds in the room forward in a hurricane of wings. I get the impression that she's using the flurry of birds to hide something because their flocked movement obscures visibility.

I hear it, the unexpected feet moving up the steps. As the door wrenches open Grama Pearle grabs my arm, and my stomach feels as if I've just gone speeding over a hill in a car. Although Grama Pearle is intent on the scene unfolding at the doorway, I feel as if I'm going to pass out. The world isn't in proportion to my five-foot-three height. Grama Pearle shrunk us!

My eye twitches. The plants feel like thousand-foot-tall trees and the table we're now standing on is over half a football field in length. As I'm contemplating diving into the drooping ruffled leaves of a Boston fern, an intense agoraphobia grips me, and I close my eyes. I feel like I'm bird food and I feel helpless to change that because I've no idea how to return to regular size. Thankfully, Grama Pearle is still gripping my arm.

"Just the delivery boy, Pearle. That's why he got past the wards without setting them off. He's a normie and harbours no ill intent. He's gone," Birdie explains.

So, Birdie called the birds forward to obscure us from whoever was approaching and give Grama Pearle time to react. *They were hiding me.*

Grama Pearle makes no move to unshrink us. I creak one eye open and peek at her. She's staring at the door. However, while she waits, the birds are searching for food. From this size, they're prehistoric dinosaurs. I clear my throat loud enough to gain Grama Pearle's scrutiny, but hopefully none of the birds. She turns and I can see on her face that she's wondering why I'm slant-eyeing her from my open eye. "Can we please change from the size of bird food into our regular non-edible size?"

"Ha!" she exclaims, and I can see the misty threads of magic modify to make us our regular size. I can't help the urge to brush at myself with my hands like the action will wipe off the feeling of being scaled down and vulnerable.

Birdie assesses my reaction. "Rarely feels that way, right, Pearle?"

"Nope. Sorry, Kori. When you expect it, the shrink

feels natural and fun. The best way to experience it the first few times is to try it yourself in a controlled environment, assuming you possess the ability. Birdie told me you can see magic molecules, so you should try shrinking now and then practice when you can. It's a handy tool that requires little effort to master and you don't expend any extra energy as a four-inch-tall Spellbinder."

I pause, trying to think of a response, but nothing comes to mind. "I need a drink of water and a cold cloth for my eyes."

"Your eye is twitching, girl. Are you sure you're okay?" Birdie asks.

"Nope." I stalk from the room, longing for magic reprieve.

I've no idea where anybody else is and in my present mood, I don't care. I flop down on the sofa and pull my chakra stones out of my pocket. The sight of them makes me feel thankful that the surge of magical powers I experienced when I was travelling involved air currents. I don't want to think about what would happen if those magical surges made me randomly transform into a bird or shrink on the spot. With the air surges, I was able to refashion my meditation techniques to control them. I slap the cool, wet cloth over my eyes. "At least I'm wearing pants," I tell myself over and over, like a mantra, while I float my chakra stones.

"They're nice pants, too," Noah whispers having sneaked into the room.

"Was I talking out loud?" I tuck my stones away.

"Yeap. Personally, I think it was more fun when you weren't wearing any pants because . . ." He doesn't finish the sentence as I hurl the cloth at him. He ducks and laughs. "I see you got the twitch under control; your feelings of exasperation must have calmed."

"You know about my twitch?"

"Kori! I know about your everything." He raises his eyebrows with a smug grin.

"Noah, I don't like what you're implying!"

Laughing at my discomfort, he reaches out and pulls me to my feet. "Maybe you're misreading my implications. Perhaps you're allowing a subconscious message to slip through."

"Put your eyebrows back in place, Noah Ward, and stop teasing me!"

"You're beautiful when you smoulder, you know? But come on, Pearle wants to show you how to make orbs."

"Orbs? Do you mean like what Alaric did in the tunnel?"

"You bet. She said you're a quick learner, so we're all going to watch. After, maybe you can show me your hummingbird?" He's struggling to keep a straight face. I slit my eyes at him in warning, and he throws his hands up in the air and retreats a step. "I wasn't talking about the feathered vertebrate." He turns and bolts out of the house.

I grit my teeth and follow.

Grama Pearle is in the yard with her hands on her hips, as if I've made her wait an eternity. "No instruction here, Kori. I want you to watch the threads. Ready?"

I nod.

In a quick spinning of air and light that wouldn't be visible to the human eye, Grama Pearle forms a tiny orb in her hand. She's controlling the colours of the orb so that they shuffle through the rainbow. The colours sweep across each other like fun-sized balls of flame no matter what colour she holds. Then she lets it blink out.

"That's your homework tonight. Birdie and I must go take care of some business," she tells me. "No questions." Before she walks away, she hugs me. "I'm proud of you."

"Let's see you do this, Kori," Fin says.

I face them and raise my hand to show them I'm already holding a fire orb. It's someone else's turn to put their eyeballs back into their heads.

Alaric stands up, arcs his arm, and releases forward. A brilliant fire orb sails out of his hand and crashes against the wood pile stacked by the garage, catching the wood on fire. A second orb that's a mix of vibrant blues follows crashing over the fire as water. The fire goes out and Alaric looks at me out of the corner of his eye, with his eyebrow raised in challenge because he threw two orbs in rapid succession with the second designed to control the first.

Fin, quick to find her voice and read the challenge, says, "You should make it a game. I'll set up our water bottles as targets and the loser makes dinner."

About an hour later, I trudge into the kitchen, exhausted from my dauntless efforts, and start pulling out the dinner supplies. I was a worthy opponent for Alaric, but I'm bummed I have to make dinner.

Chapter 6

It's the thought of hot coffee that gives me the drive to get out of bed. As I climb the stairs, I hear Fin's voice and nobody else's. Curious, I detour from my pursuit of coffee to follow the sound of her monologue down the hallway to the bedroom with the dresser that I've been getting my clothing from. Fin is facing the dresser. She's standing alone, talking, wearing a soft blue bra and panties.

"Fin?"

"Oh, Kori, I've got to get myself one of these dressers! Is this where you find your clothing?"

I move beside her so I can have a full view of the dresser. This antique piece is as high as my hips. "The whitewashed distressed wood with gold drawer pulls isn't your style, Fin." I reach to put my hand jokingly on her forehead to check for fever.

She smacks my hand away. "Don't be ridiculous. That's not what I mean!"

"Okay?"

"The clothes, Kori! It's like the dresser self-generates what the person opening the drawer needs. Did you know that Alaric and Noah are getting clothes out of here too?"

I prolong my blink to keep from rolling my eyes. "What are you talking about?"

Fin says nothing. Instead, she opens the top drawer and pulls out a very Fin-like pair of pants. "You need to be curious, Kori. Be hungry for knowledge like me. I'm learning so much about the Spellbinder world. Have you read any of the books from the bookshelf?" She slides the pants on and adjusts the next drawer, plucking a blue and white striped V-neck T-shirt out. She tugs the shirt over her head. "Now you."

"You and I know the drawers are empty," I respond with a note of displeasure in my voice.

"Try. I'm telling you, it's like there's a hallway behind each drawer leading into the store of my choice, or in this case, yours!" She smiles at me while fingering the layers of her hair into place.

I slant my eyes but tug the top drawer open. Goosebumps ripple over my flesh. I'm awed as I lift out a light gray pair of studio pants. "I've been so distracted with everything else that I didn't give the clothing situation any thought." Fin nods at drawer two, raises her eyebrows, and smiles. The next drawer I open isn't empty anymore either. It displays a seafoam-green tank top.

"See? We need to get one! It doesn't even require a credit card." Fin laughs.

"Enchanted," Noah says from the doorway. We turn to find him leaning against the doorframe wearing a towel. His chiselled chest is damp from the shower. I swallow and blink.

"A pleasure, as always, Noah." Fin's voice comes out sultry and she follows it with a light, sexy laugh.

"Can we help you, Noah?" I snap, misdirecting my impatience with Fin's flirting.

"Time for me to use the enchanted chest of drawers, ladies." Noah moves past. Fin and I are moving to exit the room. "If you want to stay and help," he continues, and there's a soft thud as his towel hits the floor.

Fin slows and turns her head in Noah's direction.

"Fin!" I propel her down the hall.

"What?" She's all innocent and pretends to pout.

"Give it a break," I say, but I can't help the smile that steals over my face, just because I don't have romantic feelings for Noah doesn't mean I don't appreciate his attractiveness.

"Ladies." Noah sticks his head into the hall with a mischievous grin. "Alaric is by the field waiting for you, Kori. Fin, if you're free, I have a task for you. I'll meet you in the kitchen." He ducks into the bedroom.

I stifle a sigh and go in search of coffee. "Alaric will have to wait," I whisper to the coffee as I watch the rich brown liquid fill my mug. I lean on the counter and draw in an ample whiff as Noah prances into the kitchen. He stops dramatically and rolls his eyes at me still being in the house, drinking coffee.

"Are you mocking me, Noah Ward?" I demand as I try to keep the smile out of my voice.

Fin's laugh is explosive, spraying her immediate area with coffee. Noah casts a wicked grin at her. He tosses her the paper towel before grabbing my coffee cup and upending it into a travel mug. He thrusts it back into my hands and ushers me through the kitchen.

I cross into the sunroom with my face lost behind my coffee as I drink deep. Over the rim I see Birdie; I feel surprised that Grama Pearle and her—my assumption is they came back together—have returned from their classified errand so soon. I also see a person shift and fly out the open sunroom door, but because my view is obstructed by my mug, the person is blurry.

"Another messenger bird?" I ask Birdie as I continue through the room.

Birdie makes a sharp, uncommitted sound.

"There are so many lately," I mumble as I head outside. "Yet no word on Alivia's whereabouts . . ."

I trudge through the grass toward the field. This has become the magical training ground. Fin was so kind as to set up lawn chairs and a folding table. It's a nice place to sit, but Fin, hungry to know about the Spellbinder world, has taken extra interest in my training. As if trying to learn this stuff isn't difficult enough, why not have an audience to critique me? With a quick look skyward, I give thanks that the chairs are empty.

Alaric is staring into the field. He doesn't show that he's heard my approach even when I plunk myself down in a chair to finish my coffee. I drain the last of my cup and set it down on the table before I kick off my sandals and stretch out my legs. I close my eyes, content to let him stare. Without warning, my chair tips sideways and I'm deposited into the grass like a sack of potatoes.

I see Alaric standing by the field, but before I figure out who dumped my chair, he disappears before my eyes. A large hand reaches down and pulls me to my feet. I make a marked effort to keep my eyes in my head when I see that it's Alaric who offloaded me from my chair and is now helping me up. *How can he be in two places at once?* My brain is spinning, trying to figure out this new impossibility. I can't get the words out. I just point to the place where disappearing Alaric had been.

Unspeaking, Alaric lifts his hand and points. Squinting into the sun, I see a likeness of Alaric staring at me from the deck. I can't help myself. I reach out and pinch the man close to me. He's real. I keep one hand on his muscled arm as I look in the new direction he's pointing. Sure enough, there's another Alaric, throwing orbs at a target.

"Okay, Alaric. What's this lesson?"

The corners of his mouth turn up, and he points to the chair. I see myself in the chair and jerk my head down to see if my body is where I expect it to be. Satisfied that my physical self is intact, I raise my eyebrows at Alaric. I catch a fast glimpse of the strands of magic that make up the version of me sitting in the chair before it disappears.

"Projection," he says in his typical fashion, with brief and controlled responses.

I swat at the air, brushing away imaginary microscopic bugs. "You're a man of so few words, Alaric," I huff. "Projection? As in astral projection?"

"Did you leave your body?"

"No!"

He raises his eyebrows at me but doesn't speak.

"Okay, not astral projection then. So, projection as in the presentation of an image. Okay," I say, having realized since arriving at the safe house that my skepticism is futile.

Alaric just watches me. I watch him, waiting. So much time passes, I feel uncomfortable, but I'm too stubborn to do or say anything. As my patience wears thin, he points to himself sitting in a chair. I realize that this has been my lesson. The tendrils of magic, which are well concealed for someone that either isn't attuned or can't detect them, cling to the projection in the chair. Eyes closed, I draw a breath. When I open them, I move and plunk myself down on the Alaric sitting in the chair. I drop right through him because his physical person is standing in front of me and not sitting.

"So, projections aren't physical, but they look like a solid form?"

His answer is a nod. "You should always be aware of the filaments of magic. There aren't many Spellbinders who can see them. It's a powerful advantage." There's no reprimand in his voice. For him, it's just a point that I can take or leave at my own choosing.

"Okay, now what?" I ask, hoping that there's more of this lesson.

"Practice. You saw the threads." Alaric stands up. "If you can see them, then you can copy the magic."

"Wait, is that it?"

He looks at me, assessing. "No, not for you. The stronger you get at projecting, the more you'll be able to do with it, actions and multiple projections. In time, you'll get your projections to talk and control physical objects." With that, he walks off.

I smile and plant a projection of myself in his path.

He marches right through it and calls over his shoulder, "Your lesson is scheduled 'til lunch."

I practise alone. As the morning passes, my patience seeps away with it. The steady stream of birds swooping in to investigate what I'm doing before flying to the house isn't doing much to help my ever-souring mood.

When a green, yellow, and black parakeet circles my head chanting, "Practice, practice, practice," I imagine the thin, tapered wings of a falcon. I watch as my life-like bird of prey soars toward the parakeet. The budgie isn't ready to risk what's reality, and it flies off. I let my projection reduce its speed and come to rest perched on my outstretched arm. I hold it there as I march across the field to the deck.

You must learn to do these things in the same manner as you draw breath! Go and practice. Return when it flows. The words echo in my head. Over and over, I have heard these words spoken by Grama Pearle and Birdie since arriving at the safe house.

I practice hoping that this time we accomplish something that'll lead us closer to Alivia. Shifting and shrinking quickly became second nature and yet we still sit and wait. Birds are the only things coming and going from the property, which fuels my frustration. I'm not naïve. I know the birds are assisting with our search for Alivia by carrying messages and information, but I feel like *I* need to be actively doing more than learning and practicing magic.

Storming into the sunroom in a self-inflicted rage, I interrupt a whispered conversation between Grama Pearle and Birdie. "What are we waiting for?" I ask with more aggression than appropriate. Both women level their stares, but I refuse to be cowed. "Alivia's out there somewhere and we're doing nothing!"

Grama Pearle's face becomes pained and Birdie makes a clicking noise with her tongue. I shut her down before she can break into a speech about me practicing. "At least tell me what we're waiting for?"

Birdie's look conveys the message that I need to calm down and get a grip. Her large eyes are magnified behind her thick round glasses. She gives me a drawn-out blink and returns to feeding the birds as if I'm not there.

"Are you going to stomp your foot now, Kori, like you used to do as an angry teenager?" Grama Pearle's features soften. "We wait, Kori. Understand?"

I adopt a hard smile, blowing air forcefully out of my nose. "Alivia! Grama Pearle, we're talking about Alivia—"

"We wait." Her voice is steady and low-pitched.

I'm fuming. "I'm tired of being told that's all I need to know. Blazing hell, it's obvious there's way more I need to know."

"You spent the bulk of your life denying the Spellbinder world and now you think we can explain everything to you in the blink of an eye."

I flinch. Her words affect me like a slap in the face. She continues like she didn't notice. "Kori, we'll tell you things at a time and pace that we feel won't overwhelm you and send you running from your true self again! We're working to find Alivia in the safest way we can. It's happening even if you aren't aware of it."

I see a faint glow and I throw up a shield by instinct just in time for it to be hit with one of Grama Pearle's air orbs. The force pushes my shield enough to let me know it's there.

"Good, Kori. Fast. What do you call it, you police people? Muscle memory?"

I shut my eyes, stomp my foot like a defiant teenager, spin, and storm out the screen door, narrowly avoiding getting hit by a pretty blue bird that's swooping in. I turn to the side and watch as it glides around the room once before shifting.

The bird reminds me of the one that was watching me in Mexico, but I'm unsure from my cursory glance what kind of bird it is. I can't tell if this visitor is a man or a woman. This person has short spikey hair the colour of gray ash and a long black cloak. Before I observe more, Birdie uses a puff of magic to push the door closed in my face. I contemplate pushing the door open with my puff of magic, but satisfy myself with a huff before marching off the deck to find Fin.

I find her in the front yard alone, sitting on the ground and leaning on a gargoyle. Fin's eyes are closed with a book nestled on her lap. She's comfortable, reclined with a blanket made of the warm sun. I hesitate, thinking maybe I should let her rest, but before I decide, she pops one eye open. I smile and take up a piece of grass, not beside a gargoyle, and I stretch full out to let the sun cover me as well.

Neither of us says anything, just enjoying the kiss of the sun and the quiet. I might have dozed off because the crunch of gravel jars my eyes open. I blink against the blazing sun. Fin's Bronco is making its way up the driveway and I see the outlines of Noah and Alaric inside. With a sigh, I push into a sitting position. I flick my head at Fin's lap, "What are you reading?"

"It's a book on rock trolls, you know, like we learned about in folklore? They're real. Spellbinders have designated rock trolls for eons as guards for valuable magical items that are too dangerous to leave in the hands of any one person." Fin is turning the book over in her hands like it might spit out facts. "I found it on the bookshelf, along with some other strange and interesting titles. I'll tell you more about it over lunch. Come on, I'm starving." She gets up and stretches.

At the top of the driveway, the Bronco pulls into the big garage across from the house and the door lowers down. The soundproof garage is bunker-like, if they're closing the doors, they'll be in there for a while. I nod and follow Fin to the deck entrance.

"Kori," Fin hisses at me from the doorway to the sunroom. She's paused there, unmoving, and she isn't saying anything.

I hurry up the stairs, across the deck, and peek past Fin to see what's captivated her. Hunched on the far side of the table is the fattest cat I've ever seen. It's a calico cat of grays, tans, and whites, with a unique black shape over its nose. Its eyes are pale hazel, but the left eye has an intense green patch that makes me think of a wedge of cake. Its strange eyes are fixed on us, and its tail is twitching in jerky motions. I have a clear view of the cat's sharp front claws. I'm wary, but my gut suggests there's more to this cat.

"Is that blood-red nail polish on its toenails?" Fin whispers from the corner of her mouth.

"Let's hope." The birds are motionless and quiet, but they aren't acting threatened. I swallow and whisper to Fin out the side of my mouth. "What in the world are we supposed to do?"

"It was watching the doorway, waiting. It doesn't seem interested in the birds." She keeps her voice soft.

"It's a cat! It's a cat in a room full of Birdie's precious birds, Fin," I hiss.

"Exactly, and where are Birdie and Grama Pearle?" Fin's meaning isn't lost on me. Clearly, they're gone because the cat is encroaching on the bird room and neither woman is anywhere to be seen. I can feel the layers of an extra ward, which makes it stranger that this cat is inside. Neither the cat, Fin, nor I have moved. Then, without warning, Fin is lunging toward the cat. "We can't stay deadlocked all day. This pussycat must go!"

Fin pulls up short as the cat releases a deep-toned snarl and transforms into a short, round man. The man and the cat have similar features and his eyes haven't changed at all. He has short, shaggy hair framing his face. Once I get over the fact that there are cat eyes staring at me from a human head, I'm able to note that he has a flat, wide nose that's almost drowned out by the puffiness of his mouth. He even has random white whiskers protruding from his cat-like cheeks.

His lips withdraw to reveal normal human teeth as a low guttural sound appears to come straight from his throat. "I'm assuming that Pearle isn't here, ladies, and what I have to say cannot wait." His mouth moves a small degree when he talks, so subtle that the movements are difficult to see, making everything about this moment more surreal.

Fin has straightened and taken the shifting cat in stride. "Okay, cat, speak!" She lets her cautious distrust come out in her tone.

The cat is unphased by Fin's abruptness. I move into the room, shocked that birds aren't the unique alternate form of Spellbinders. As if reading my thoughts, the cat man looks at me. "I'm the last of my kind. I'm the last cat shifter, Kori Ember."

He lets the astonished impression fall over my face before pressing on. His eyes rove constantly, searching for an unseen threat. "I'm the last of the Frone family line. After the Adelgriefs stripped my ancestors of their respect and influence, they used them mercilessly. I couldn't subject myself to it and I fled.

"Pearle found me and brought me to Birdie. They treated me not just as a Spellbinder, but as a Spellbinder of value. They gave me their trust and their kindness. I can never repay them for that." He pauses and I half expect him to purr, but he shakes himself. "Anyway, I used to care for the birds when Birdie was away, but some time ago my duties changed and as a result, I need Pearle to know the danger that's coming. Do you understand? She also needs to know that we have a confidential ally."

Fin and I exchange a brief glance. We've advanced so the kitchen door is behind us and if we move properly, we can herd the cat man out the deck door. I'm wondering if his visit has anything to do with Alivia when Fin speaks. "Yes, cat," she says.

"My name is Mouz. It's a pleasure to meet you, Finley Salinger," He purrs.

"A cat named 'Mouse' that watches birds!" Eyes skyward, I make a silent plea for patience.

"Not mouse, Kori Ember, Mouz. Like Maui, but replace the i with z, Mau-zzz. It means 'to hunt and catch,' which are my duties. There's no time for further explanation. Pearle needs to know—"

Before he reveals his message or I question how Mouz knows our names, an unfamiliar hawk drops from the high foliage. Mouz sees it and stops talking. He sends a blast of magic at the bird, which transforms into a man and counterblasts in one fluid motion.

The shock wave of the two magics colliding knocks me into the plants and Fin goes sailing through the kitchen doorway. I hear her hit the table hard, expelling a rush of air. I waste no time refocusing on Mouz. He's struggling furiously behind a shield of his magic. He's braced against the wall, but he can't do anything other than hold. The attack coming at him is so aggressive that I can't pull the strands of magic apart to see what's being thrown to counter-attack with it; my brain is scrambling for a safe but effective plan.

The attacker is an unattractive, short, thin man with a bald head and scars covering his face. The scars add to his menacing air. His eyebrows pull down and his eyes tighten, glaring with hatred at Mouz. It's impossible to estimate his age. With his full onslaught locked on Mouz, his tight, turned-down mouth is moving, like a chant, but I can't hear what he's saying. His nostrils are flaring, and I'm reminded of a bull getting ready to charge.

Mouz is making a very high-pitched sound in an effort to hold off the assault. I step from the plants, preparing my orbs, when the pretty blue bird from earlier swoops in the open deck door. I recognize it as the mysterious visitor with the spikey ash-gray hair and black cloak.

Before I can act, the blue bird transforms mid-air and hits me with a rope of magic. The rope entangles me and whips me through the kitchen door, but not before I witness the scar-faced man leap over the table and charge with a terrifying magical assault on Mouz.

Spinning like a top, I bang into Fin who has just managed to untangle herself from the clutter of being tossed into the room the first time. We tumble over the already toppled kitchen chairs. The air fills with a high-pitched scream that's distinctively cat-like and it's followed by yowls of pain punctuated with blasts of magic.

"It sounds like a war zone, and we're trapped in the trenches," Fin whispers.

I give no verbal response. I'm up and running toward the kitchen door, but the mysterious spikey-haired visitor backs through the doorway and drops her magic defences. The stink of rusty iron sticks to her. She raises her arm to me in a stop gesture without glancing my way and I spy blood smeared on her hand, although I don't see an injury. "The doorway is warded against enemies. He can't get through."

"Mouz?" I choke his name out.

The woman's head movement is slow and pained. "Mortally wounded."

I start, despite myself, as the scar-faced enemy steps into view. He flicks his finger at the doorway, testing it with a bolt of magic. It sizzles and dies out. His face, marked with a snarl, is locked on the woman. He never takes his eyes off her as he raises one hand, slow and deliberate, and points at me. Then he withdraws from the doorway.

Mouz's yowls fade into silence.

"Oh, Mouz," the woman whispers. When she turns to face us, her cheeks are wet with tears. She bows her head. I can see her energy depleting in thin wisps as she works her own magic to heal the through-and-through gash in her side. I reach out to grab her, anticipating correctly that she'll fall. "Don't leave the house, and avoid the sunroom for now," she breathes before losing consciousness.

Fin and I carry her into the bedroom and make her as comfortable as we can on the bed. I peek at her wound. She's mended it better than anything we would've been able to manage conventionally. Out of precaution, we apply a medical ointment and a clean bandage. The woman is sleeping with a steady breath and regular pulse.

I return to the kitchen with Fin. I busy myself with the coffeemaker. "Fin, I admire your ability to adapt, but even for you, this must be beyond the scope of going with the tide. Don't you have questions or doubts?"

"My question is, how did I not notice this stuff

sooner? But then I said to myself, 'Self, Kori grew up in this world and she chose not to see,' so . . ." Fin lets the statement hang and we sit without speaking because there isn't anything else for us to do.

I've no desire to risk going to the sunroom or outside with a Spellbinder killer on the loose. I've no idea how to contact Grama Pearle or Birdie. Fin's cell phone is dead and her charger is in the sunroom with my cell phone. So, we drink coffee in silence.

It's dark before Noah and Alaric come in. By the way someone thunders through the sunroom, it's clear there's destruction, but no body. Noah launches himself into the kitchen in full fight mode. I'm sure that my face is a mirror of Fin's annoyance. "Thanks, hero, but you missed this one." She purses her lips.

Alaric strolls in like he could take or leave a fight with no difference.

Noah ignores Fin's comment but drops his fighting stance. "What happened?"

Fin and I relay the events of the afternoon and watch as Alaric breaks off and heads toward the bedroom and Noah turns on his heels to inspect the sunroom.

"Mouz isn't out there, alive or dead," Noah says.

"It's Astrid in the bedroom. She'll live." Alaric advises.

"That's good about Astrid. Mouz isn't in the sunroom. Can you read the room?" Noah asks.

"Who is Astrid?" I ask.

"Astrid is a close friend to Birdie and Pearle. My best guess is that she's been around Birdie and the safe house most of our lives. Since Pearle and Birdie have been friends much longer than that, I assume Pearle met Astrid here. And keep in mind I've never asked about Astrid, but from conversations over the years, and since we've been staying here, I hear that she's something of a fighter. She and Mouz were like family."

Alaric ambles through the kitchen and glances into the sunroom. Everything goes quiet for a few seconds. "Dead."

"Body disintegration magic?" Noah asks.

Alaric nods.

"That means whatever message he was trying to get to Pearle was a doozy if he set that kind of spell on himself." Noah scratches his head. Grama Pearle's disclosure about reading a dead person's eyes fits with Mouz disintegrating himself.

I'm taking drawn-out blinks and darting my eyes between Noah and Alaric. They seem to share unspoken thoughts.

Noah spins on us, eager to identify the man. "Okay, you described the man. Can you describe the bird?"

"I didn't see either, since I was blown from the room like a grain of sand in a windstorm." Fin tips her chair back on two legs, folding her arms.

I shut my eyes. "Why describe it? Do you think Mouz knew something about Alivia?"

"It's a possibility that he had information about her, but it died with him. Why describe the bird is simple. The Society of the Blood Wind, particularly Nekane, employs two very special henchmen who are trusted with major tasks. Entering this refuge would be a task for one of them. Each of them has their own," he struggles for a word, "area of expertise. They're identical twins, but they can be distinguished by their birds. I want to know which evil specialist he sent." Noah makes this sound like everyday news.

I roll my eyes. "Of course, they're twins! Hmm, the bird was a hawk, but it was bigger than most, if not all, of the other birds in the room. It was brown with a pale streaked belly." I pause, trying to recall what I saw. "It might have had a red tail, but it shifted into the man as it dropped. I didn't get a good look."

"Okay, did you see its beak?" Noah asks.

"Typical, I think. Short, curved, and blackish."

"Sounds like a red-tailed hawk. That means it was Kyson that was here," Noah says, more to himself than anybody else.

"Okay, so what?" Fin asks.

I cast a glance at Fin because I hadn't been aware she was following along. "I agree with Fin. So what? How does this help us find Alivia?" I can feel my already thin patience disappearing.

Noah's pursed lips suggest I'm missing a relevant point. Alaric is leaning on the counter and peering out the window. His head is angled to listen, and he's going to let Noah lead the conversation. I gaze at Fin; she shrugs, as lost as I am. "Noah!" I snap.

"If they sent Kyson, then he was here to kill, which he did. He killed Mouz to stop him from telling Pearle something crucial. Kyson wasn't concerned with you in the sunroom, Kori, or you'd be dead too," Noah continues. "Furthermore, he didn't make any overt attempts to get you once you were in the kitchen, but he let you know he knew who you were."

"So?" I huff.

"So, that means Kieran will be sent on his brother's heels to get you!"

Fin stands. "How did they, Kyson and Mouz, get past the wards?"

Noah narrows his eyes. "Mouz isn't an enemy, so he would know how to get in. Kyson is a powerful Spellbinder with a very different set of skills. I'm not sure how the current safe house wards are set, I'll speak to Birdie when she gets here. Obviously, the wards need to be changed. In the meantime, we'll need to be on guard."

"Like changing the locks?" Fin asks with big eyes.

I ignore her. "Great, Noah! And this helps us find Alivia how? Do you know where Kyson came from or returned to?" I feel hopeful, but it doesn't last.

"Nope, he wouldn't be so sloppy as to take a direct path to wherever he was dispatched from. The Adelgriefs are a lot of things, Kori, but sloppy and stupid aren't among them. The Adelgrief mansion is often where everybody is found, but nobody has ever been able to link any crimes to their house or the people there. They're good at covering their tracks. Regardless, we're watching it and monitoring its lesser-known entrances and exits." Noah leans against the counter, satisfied with his analysis of the situation.

I try to draw a few deep steadying breaths, but it isn't helping, and I blow like a top. The chair flips over in a clatter as I stand. I advance on Noah with my voice getting louder by the syllable. "So, they know where we are and they're moving in on us, but we have nothing? NOTHING!"

Noah's voice matches mine. For the first time I sense his frustration, but I'm too emotional at this point to yield. We're toe to toe, yelling over each other. My body is quivering with anger, frustration, and restraint because I want to throw and smash things. Every muscle in my body is primed to fight, but all I do is yell. Slowly, my yelling allows the pent-up stress-related hormones to release.

By the time we've exhausted our words, my throat feels raw from yelling and we're alone in the kitchen with the moon lighting the room. A warm dampness snakes down my cheeks and I realize I'm crying, then Noah's arms enfold me and I return the embrace, grateful for the comfort.

"I'm scared for her," I whisper.

"I'm scared too," Noah breathes into my hair. "But we'll find her."

Chapter 7

I wake late to discover that Grama Pearle and Birdie haven't returned. I stomp through the house, but I can't find anybody. Even Astrid is gone. After mine and Noah's blowout last night, it would seem Fin and Alaric are trying to give me a cool-down period. My throat feels scratchy from yelling at Noah about why we aren't doing anything to help Alivia and why he won't tell me where he has hidden my family.

I continue outside. By the time I've marched my way to the front, I'm somewhat depleted of my angry energy. As I turn the corner, I come to a complete halt and my mouth drops open. Fin is seated on top of one of the lion gargoyles like she's going to ride it off the yard and down the road, except that the gargoyle is resting with its front paws crossed over one another.

Fin clearly hears my noisy approach, but she doesn't turn my way when she speaks. "I need a break from this property, Kori. Are you still feeling murderous or just smouldering?"

I clear my throat and scan myself before answering; I feel less sour. "No, Fin. How can I be angry when I see you trying to ride a cement gargoyle off a property warded by magical charms? No, what I'm feeling is something else!" I say with a smile and a snort of amusement.

Fin cracks a smile and motions to the empty gargoyle. "Try it. It makes you feel like a kid again."

"I don't know what kind of strange-ass childhood you had, but riding cement creatures wasn't a part of mine."

Fin scrunches up her face and shrugs.

"I could've sworn these gargoyles were sitting when we arrived the other day."

Fin tilts her head, considering my statement. "Nah," she says without conviction.

I move to inspect the face of the gargoyle Fin mounted. The haunting stare of its vertical pupils keeps its bulging eyes from being comical. Its face is recognizable as a lion, but it has huge fangs protruding from the top and bottom of its mouth. I decide it must be female because instead of a mane it has a series of tiny spikes that line the base of its jaw.

I believe the other gargoyle is male because he has a full dagger-shaped mane. I hoist myself up, careful to avoid the edged blades. "Where are Alaric and Noah?"

"Alaric is out in the field dealing with messages and birds. He didn't say why, but I assume it has to do with Mouz's death and the threat of Kieran and Kyson. Don't know where Noah is."

I'm sure there's nobody to hear us, but I lower my voice anyway. "Let's go. We can't keep hanging out here waiting for nothing. I came home to help Alivia, and I need to be in town to do that."

A smile plays at the corners of Fin's mouth. "I'm

listening."

Before I can go on with my plan, a soft growl fills the air and the gargoyle I'm resting on stiffens under me. "Did your gargoyle just . . ." I pause, trying to find a word that doesn't sound stupid when describing a cement, inanimate object, but I can't. "Stiffen?"

Fin nods her head. Her eyes are downcast at the gargoyle.

"And growl?"

I can see Fin swallow and shake her head no. "That was yours," she whispers.

I cast my eyes down to my gargoyle with a prickle of fear blossoming. Cement objects aren't supposed to move or make noise, but this gargoyle's shoulder blades are hunching up, like it's trying to sit. My eyes go wide to match Fin's.

"I'm starting to think they aren't cement. Did your plan include riding these gargoyles to town?" she asks quietly.

"Nope and nope!" I fling my leg off and slide down. The drop's farther than I expect because the creature has started to get up.

Fin hits the ground. "Shouldn't things on the safe grounds be safe?"

I snatch up my sandals. "Something stirred them up and there's no part of me that wants to wait and learn we're wrong about that safety assumption."

"Do you think they're reacting to us talking about leaving the property?" Fin asks, as we bolt.

At the corner of the house, Fin turns to run toward the back door, but I grab onto her and tug her after me.

Thoughts of fleeing the property are still on my mind, but if anybody has returned to the house, then going in will shut that option down. We need concealment, so we run until we're behind the garage. We skid to a stop and Fin looks at me, but I don't have a next step.

Eyes closed, I give my head a mini shake, and breathe deep through my nose. When I open my eyes, Fin is beaming. I turn and I smile too. Parked to the side is an army-green, World War II Jeep. It's clear this vehicle hasn't just been parked here rotting; someone has been restoring it.

Beside me, Fin sucks air through her teeth and lets out a low whistle. "Do you know what this is, Kori? This is a 1947 Willys MB!"

I say nothing as I take in the small-scale circular side-view mirror mounted on the body. The front windshield angles out to allow air flow up under it, more like a front window than a front windshield. Before I assess further, I see Fin behind the wheel, fiddling with something. The Jeep sputters to life.

"Come on, Kori. We just found our ride."

"We can't steal a vehicle, Fin!"

Fin laughs. "We aren't stealing it, Kori. We're borrowing it. I'm sure Birdie told us, at least once, to make ourselves at home." She emphasizes her point with a glance in the direction of the gargoyles. "Borrow the vehicle or risk what the gargoyles had in mind for us? I don't think they'll eat us, but the last I checked growling isn't a friendly action."

The sizeable crunching of gravel helps me with my decision and I climb in to sit on the folding front seat.

It's an uncomfortable experience. Engrossed by the large dark metal circle with three spokes holding it to the lengthy steering column, I stop my struggle with my lap belt. I observe the world's puniest key. I'm blinking at the diminutive key that was left in the ignition, assuming that the owner was scared to lose it in the depth of a pocket, when Fin mumbles about original gauges.

"Um, Fin. Do you know how to drive this?" I gesture at the three strange gear sticks on the floor between us. "I don't know how far those gargoyles can move, but something is prowling across the gravel. Let's go."

With a laugh, Fin drives us off the property and we don't look back, which for me is mostly because there's no rear-view or passenger-side mirror. Fin takes us straight to her shop and drives the Jeep into an empty single-car garage. We jump into a dull, four-door sedan, a less conspicuous vehicle, and power off the lot in less than five minutes.

"Okay, now where?" Fin asks.

"Alivia's place. I'd like to comb for clues."

"You don't think someone is watching the house?"

"Probably, but I'm hoping that we'll have enough time to scavenge before Noah and Alaric find us. Noah will expect us to go to Alivia's place."

The drive to Alivia's is short. I note her house feels as empty as Mom and Dad's. However, Alivia's house hasn't been messed up; there are no signs of a struggle. They took her from somewhere else or she didn't put up a fight, but why wouldn't she resist? We're departing, disappointed with our lack of results, but when I open the front door, Carter is there.

"I figured you'd visit Alivia," he says. "I came by yesterday but nobody was home."

"Now isn't a good time, Carter." He steps back as I continue out the door with Fin behind me. Carter is unsatisfied with my response and refuses to move farther.

"Kori, can you just hear me out?" He doesn't wait for an answer, and I can't get by him to go down the stairs, so I stop. Fin slips in the door to wait, watch, and listen. I'm sure I can feel her amused smile working to keep the laughter off her lips.

"Kori, my life doesn't work anymore. My BODY doesn't work anymore," Carter continues with a brief wave of his hand over his genital area. "I realize now that it all goes back to you, me, and Kinsley. It's karma, and I need to correct it." Again, he waves at his nether region.

Fin stifles a giggle before Carter speaks. "I've been thinking of ways to fix it all, to make us whole." The crotch hand wave is more pronounced this time, and it's clear which *we* he's referring to. Fin gives a full out bark of laughter and I hear her shuffle away.

Eyes closed, I suck in some air, and reopen them, focusing on Carter. "I don't have time for this, Carter. Sorry that you aren't in the best place in your life, but you aren't the only one with problems, so if you'll excuse—"

Carter cuts me off with a full out wail. "Kori, if you'll just give us another chance." He pauses and I'm so surprised that I miss my opportunity to escape from this embarrassment. "Maybe if you'd look at it?"

"At what?" My voice rises an octave.

Carter's head is down. His uncut, greasy hair has fallen forward into his eyes, causing him to fumble with the zipper on his jeans while mumbling about breaking the curse and being made whole. For a second, I think I see a faint thin twine of magic over his crotch, but my glimpse is so fleeting that I can't be sure if I saw it at all. The last thing I want to do is look in the direction of Carter's groin, so I'm going with the assumption that my nerves are making me see things that aren't there. Why would there be magic on his penis?

I'm in a state of shock about the current situation when the door behind me bangs open and Fin moves past. She two-hand shoves Carter into the bush, fumbling with the front of his pants.

"Sorry, Carter. They're looking for us, not you," Fin yells as she grabs my hand and yanks me down the stairs. "I hope," she says quietly. "The back door burst open and I didn't think we should wait to see if it was friend or foe," Fin hollers, sliding across the hood of the car as I jump in the passenger side.

We pull away from the curb as a bear of a man charges out the front door with another, more handsome, male specimen behind him. My glimpse of them suggests to me that the big man is the muscle, but it also has me spin in my seat. I strain to get a better view of the second man as the distance between us and the house increases.

"We just dodged a magic bullet! That handsome guy had magic clinging to his body. I didn't notice if the muscle guy did," I announce as I turn forward. Based on Fin's face, it's clear her thoughts are on Carter and his problem. "Don't bother! DON'T!"

I have to give her credit for not saying a word before she's snorting with laughter. She's laughing so hard there are tears on her cheeks, and I wonder how she can see where she's driving. I establish that there's nobody following us, then I look straight ahead at the road to make sure Fin isn't going to run into anything while I wait for her to stop laughing.

I glance sideways at her and she snorts but manages not to laugh. We travel a respectful distance in silence before she finds her voice. "So, that was fun. Did you notice that Carter's wearing clean clothing, Kori?" Fin changes the tone of her voice so it comes out sexy. "He must've been hopeful to see you!"

"You mean happy?"

"Nope, I mean hopeful." She makes mock bedroom eyes at me and gives a dramatic imitation of Carter's groin wave. She waits to see my eyes goggle at her before moving on. "Now what?"

I try to relax my eye muscles and steer the conversation from Carter and his penis. "Well, I don't think they took Alivia from her home, and the hospital she works at would be too public. We know she wasn't at Mom and Dad's house or Grama Pearle's store. So, that leaves the cemetery."

"Where I picked you guys up the other day?" Fin asks.

"No, not there. We have a family section farther in. Alivia likes to visit Jaxton's grave." As always, the thought of Jaxton's murder is painful. It's a hurt we never talked about as a family; bringing him up caused Mom and Dad intense grief. This unspoken thing— Jaxton, his murder, how he was killed—is a defining event in our lives, one that I'm realizing shaped me more then I care to admit.

I close my eyes against his homicide, but it pervades in a flash of blinding light: the light that came from Jaxton's hands before the dark figures literally disappeared into the shadows. Fin puts upbeat music on the radio. I keep my eyes closed for the rest of the drive.

Fin parks and we go in on foot. Thanks to Alivia and Grama Pearle, Jaxton's grave is well kept. I plod toward it. It's been so long since I visited, and my emotions are doing somersaults. Fin recognizes my need for privacy, so she engages in a deliberate search for any of Alivia's items in the grass by the bench.

It doesn't go unnoticed to me that the grass is soft under my knees as I kneel and place my hands on his stone. I dip my head, trying to create solitude. *Ah, Jaxton. It's been twenty years.*

I remain leaning forward, locked in a silent battle with my emotions, fear is foremost. I'm gripping the stone so tight my knuckles are aching. To bring my feelings under control, I slide my hand over the top of his stone. It's quite unexpected when I hear a soft click and grinding sound like a lock disengaging.

I open my eyes. A camouflaged drawer in the tombstone has popped open. I've no idea what I did to open it or why it's there.

"We have company, Kori." Fin's voice has an edge to it that I know means we're in trouble.

I drop my hand into the drawer, blindly grab the two small solid objects, and stuff them into the pocket of my studio pants while closing the hidden drawer and standing up. In the meantime, Fin has moved closer to me, and she continues backing up as I assess our situation.

There's a high fence behind us, rimmed with trees and other foliage. Not a great escape route. The expanse of the cemetery leads away to our right, but I question how successful our escape would be, running willy-nilly deeper into the cemetery. The bear-man from Alivia's house is coming straight at us. To our left, the handsome man stalks us like a predatory cat, and he now has a second beast-like man with him.

I'm playing through options when Noah comes out of nowhere and plows into both the handsome man and the bear. To a normie's eye, Noah would look like he always does, but I can see multiple shades of red magical threads coating his body like armour. The handsome man disappears on impact in a puff of thick smoke; he's just gone. Then Noah and the bear hit the ground in a tangle of flailing limbs. My mind tells me there's no time to worry about Noah. I refocus on the other big beast moving toward Fin and me.

"Where the hell do you find guys built like this?" Fin has retreated almost to the fence. "He must be six foot five and two hundred and fifty pounds, if not more. And those shoulders." I risk a glance behind me when I hear the dreamy note enter her voice. She clears her throat and hitches her chin in his direction.

Blocking all thoughts of Fin out, I put the bear in my crosshairs. I can't see any sign of a magical attack; either his magic is too limited, or he likes old-school fighting.

I bend my legs slightly and reposition my weight forward onto my toes so I can move quickly. Knowing I'll need to maintain my body posture when I get hit with what I'm sure is going to be a violent assault—physical or magical—I square my hips. I'd prefer a physical altercation; at least I'm trained for that. I hunch my shoulders to protect my neck as I bring my bent arms up to block my face with balled fists.

Feeling as ready as I can be, I watch as he stalks toward us. He's confident in his size and self-assured in his abilities. Even with the two of us facing him, he doesn't feel threatened. I reassess him for signs of magic, but don't see any. I hear Noah grunting with the force of the struggle he's locked in. There are sharp intakes of air and the sound of one body hitting another. I wonder where Alaric is. However, my consideration returns to the oversized thug moving in.

Without warning, an object zooms past my head and with a loud thwack hits the thug square in the face. His hands fly up as he stumbles, loses his balance on the uneven ground, and falls, making a sickening thud as his head bounces off a tombstone, knocking him unconscious.

"Did you just throw your shoe?" I ask Fin without moving a muscle.

"Yeap, seemed like a good idea." Her tone is flat as

she balances on her left foot. Her eyes are flicking from the unconscious man to her black and white zipped platform sneaker on the ground not far from him.

"Good throw, Fin!" Noah says as he emerges from a group of bushes with Alaric behind him.

"Thanks, Noah. I gave up competitive darts and took up throwing axes. Nice tackle."

Noah nods at her. "Great shoe, too. Here, catch." He tosses Fin her shoe and turns to Alaric. "What do you think? Should we give her knives?"

"You can't be serious?" I ask.

"Everyone has a sorcery, and I think we just discovered that Fin's brand of magic is throwing," Noah replies.

"I threw the shit out of that shoe, didn't I?" Fin laughs. "Sign me up. I'll take some knives."

"Smoke and ashes," I say, as my mouth falls open.

Noah gives me a sharp glare. "You and I will talk about ALL of this later, Kori. Right now we need to go before Mister Vanish returns with allies or the guy I knocked out in the bushes and Fin's shoe man wake up."

Fin pulls her cell from her pocket and barks into the phone to someone about attending the cemetery to collect the car.

"Time to hustle. We have company." Noah jumps into the driver's seat of Fin's Bronco. He and Alaric borrowed it to come find Fin and me.

"Kori, in the box," Alaric says. "Time for target practice."

The truck is moving as I launch myself into the box.

We're picking up speed, but I can smell the dampness in the air, and I know the hooded figures called the warped are after us. A flash of light shows Alaric has armed himself with two fire orbs. He wastes no time sending them flying behind us. Crouched low against the cab, I form up a fire orb and let it fly.

Our orbs hit their marks, and in a brilliant flash, two of the four cars catch fire. The first fiery car veers to the left crashing into a tree. Alaric is fast, throwing a water orb big enough to fill a couple of family-sized swimming pools. It pounds onto the crashed car and the flames go out.

The occupants of the second fiery car are bailing out, leaving the car to steer itself. I fling a water orb at it, but I don't see if it hits its mark because there's a gigantic explosion in front of car three, which flips it end over end, filling the air with dirt and chunks of grass.

"What in the blazing hell was that orb you threw?" I finger my ears to try and stop the ringing.

Alaric doesn't take his eyes off the road behind us. "Explosive orb."

"Um, happy learner over here, big man! Teach me that one, please?"

"Later. Right now . . ." A silver-gray orb appears in his hand. He pauses with his arm cocked. His muscles are taut and his stare is unwavering.

I see why he paused. The fourth vehicle has stopped and the handsome man, also known as Mister Vanish, is standing alongside it with his arms crossed, leering at us like he has plans to even the score later. No threat to follow us or continue this battle. We bounce over the curb and exit the cemetery, continuing to gain speed.

"Somehow, I don't think that we've seen the last of that Tall Drink of Water!" Fin yells from the open cab window.

Exhausted from the adrenaline dump, I sink down and stare at the cemetery as it disappears. Alaric settles in, taciturn.

"I'm not sure that accomplished much." I say. Alaric casts his eyes sideways at me but remains quiet. "I just want to find Alivia. I want to feel like I'm actively trying to find her." Alaric gives me another sideways glance to acknowledge he heard me without encouraging further conversation. I give him a scowl before I reposition to talk to Noah. "How'd you find us?"

Fin laughs. I cut my eyes to her with a glare. "What?"

"Well," Noah says. "After we fished Carter out of the bushes at Alivia's with his penis in his hand, we got him to tell us that you had run from two scary guys. I knew there weren't many options left for places you would go, so—"

"Holding his penis." Fin laughs. "He was trying to show it to Kori on the front steps before those two thugs showed up."

Now it's Noah's turn to cut his eyes at me. I shrug my shoulders and give a head shake before I slide down into the truck box. Alaric has a smirk tugging at his mouth and his sideways glance includes a slight eyebrow raise.

"What? It isn't like I haven't seen it before," I snap at him.

A full grin cracks across his face, and he directs his musings to the road behind us.

Chapter 8

"What were you thinking, Kori?" Noah thunders as we walk toward the deck.

"You know what, Noah, save it! I'm tired of this bullshit. I came home to help Alivia and nobody else seems to be trying to do that. So, I will not keep sitting here. Tomorrow I'm going to Alivia's and—"

"Like hell you are. The Spellbinder world is a part of your life that you didn't take the time to learn about. There are things at play that can and will kill you!" Noah rages. "It's not a typical cop investigation, Kori. You can't make it conventional. And you know zero about any of the things that govern the Spellbinder world. Plus, none of us know if or when you might choose to stop seeing."

"I'm going!"

"Like hell!"

We've reached the deck, but Noah and I are blocking the stairs. Alaric and Fin are stuck waiting for us to finish arguing, but we aren't done. We're toe to toe, trying to stare each other down.

"It's like they're kids," Fin says to Alaric, who just grunts in response. "This is how I used to deal with them then."

Noah and I are so focused on each other, neither of us understands the meaning of Fin's words as she marches between us. In a throwback to our childhood, she grabs one ear on each of us and keeps walking, yanking us behind her painfully. The result is a refocusing of our anger. She parades us right up to the screen door wearing a satisfied smirk while she waits, holding our ears.

Noah and I stare at each other. He speaks first. "Okay, WE will go together tomorrow."

"Deal." I sigh.

Fin lets go of our ears and pushes us together, encouraging us to hug, and then she pulls the door open. I ignore Alaric as he comes up the stairs, my experience with him hitherto dictates that he'll be impassive.

The birds in the sunroom are chirping and singing loudly when we walk in, but our entrance casts a shroud of silence over the room. It feels like we have interrupted a conversation about us. Not one bird makes a single chirp and they each take up perches where they can see us. Fin, Alaric, Noah, and I stop like we're one person.

"Does anybody else feel like a teenager that got caught sneaking into the house after a night out partying?" I ask.

"You should," says Birdie. "Ha! We do. The Fermented Grape was a brilliant place to call a meeting and—"

Grama Pearle attempts to squash her hand over

Birdie's mouth, but pokes her in the eye. It accomplishes what I'm sure was her desired effect, stopping Birdie from telling more, which begs the question, what have they been up to?

I can't speak for any of the others, but I hadn't seen Grama Pearle or Birdie in the room until Birdie spoke. They're both standing with their arms crossed and stern parental facial expressions fixed in place. I manage a dramatic blink and narrow my eyes before Grama Pearle and Birdie both burst out laughing.

Grama Pearle's explosive laughter sends her ass over teakettle into the jungle of foliage behind her. Birds fly off the branches with angry shrieks and cries. Birdie wobbles, hiccups, and follows Grama Pearle into the greenery, arms and legs flailing. Birdie must have tried to shift into owl form because there's a puff of feathers, a hiss, and the clacking of a beak.

The room falls silent and then there's hysterical laughter inside the jungle from Grama Pearle and Birdie as a human. We freeze in stunned silence, not sure what's going on. The laughing stops. There's more hiccups, followed by the soft drone of snoring.

"They're drunk," Fin barks. "What the hell is The Fermented Grape and when can we go?"

"The old birds are drunk." Grama Pearle giggles from in the plants. "Wake up, you old bird," the disembodied voice of Grama Pearle continues. There's a thump, a forceful exhale of air, and then the hiccupping starts.

I'm trying to process the appropriateness, or inappropriateness, of the situation so I don't remove my eyes from the plants. "It's a fancy wine bar. Membership only," I say with no inflection.

"Spellbinders only." Noah adds. "They say, 'membership,' but when they grant membership, they make sure no normies are successful with their applications. Normies, of course, have no idea that they're denied for being human. Their rejection letters say that The Fermented Grape is at their maximum capacity."

Fin snorts. "Kori, you're goggling." I turn my wide eyes to her and blink. She laughs, "I love Grama Pearle!"

I stifle a heavy sigh and make my way to the plants, where Noah is already fishing to find Grama Pearle and Birdie. Fingers crossed they haven't shrunk themselves. He latches onto Grama Pearle first. He yanks her from the coverage of the plants, not shrunken, and passes her to me. "Let's get you to bed, Grama Pearle."

"Nope, not doing it. I'm waiting for my bestie. Yeap, my bestie Birdie!" She whoops. I scramble to get my arms around her waist as she pitches to the side, narrowly avoiding another plant dive.

It's Birdie's turn to whoop next. Her voice comes out in a shriek. "I'll thank you to watch where you're putting your hands, young Noah."

The rest of what Birdie says is drowned out because Fin is laughing so hard that she's choking. I ignore her but catch sight of Alaric, watching the fiasco from the sidelines, straight-faced except for a low-key twitch of his lips. Wondering what it takes to make that man laugh, I muscle a surprisingly strong Grama Pearle away.

Thirty minutes later, I stalk into the living room like

an irritated parent with a first-time drunk teenager. "Did someone get Birdie to bed? Grama Pearle was a handful! She performed a magic light show, sang a few songs, and somehow had three different brimming cocktail glasses magically appear in her hand, three different times! What a mess to clean. Anyway, I'd no sooner get one sock and shoe off her to find that she had got the other sock and shoe back on. I'm exhausted!"

"Birdie wanted to hide and let us seek her!" Noah replies. "Do you know how hard it is to play manhunt with a drunk Spellbinder who can shapeshift, alter her size, and do several other disappearing tricks?"

I swallow and blink, waiting. When nobody answers, I shrug and lift my hands.

"Well, it took three of us to find her because first she shrunk herself and hid. When we found her, she changed into an owl, and sped from the room, just missing the wall. Once she was out of our sight, she transformed into a human and shrunk herself again. We had to follow the sound of the hiccupping, which is quiet when you are four inches tall," Fin answers.

I've a hard time imagining Alaric participating in the debacle Fin described and feel sorry I missed it. When nobody offers anything else, my impatience escapes in a snort. "Dare I ask where you found her?"

"Nope, don't bother. All you need to know is that she's in the kitchen, sleeping in a box of cookies with a marshmallow pillow," Noah says.

I purse my lips and nod. "Do we know why they're intoxicated? It's out of character, especially under the circumstances."

Noah's brow crunches up. "Birdie chirped something about finding answers over drinks."

"She said, 'Old school truce, sharing bread and wine with enemies,'" Fin corrects. "I think they were drinking with someone to try and get information. I'm just not sure if the drinks were meant to loosen lips and tongues, or if drinking together works as a truce to do each other no harm." She smiles. "Maybe both."

I take a melodramatic blink. "Enemies?"

Alaric, reclined in an armchair, crosses his ankles but remains impassive.

"She wasn't making complete sense, Kori. She was chirping names. Weir, Hoar, and Grogan." Noah watches my face for recognition and, thanks to the memories Grama Pearle gave me, I do recognize the names.

I grin feeling pleased with my ability to access my Memory Keeper impressions. "The Weirs are a supporting family for the Adelgriefs. The Grogan and Hoar families realigned their support in favour of the Adelgriefs. Did she mention the Rist family?"

Noah rubs his chin. "No mention of the Rists, which is good because that family is unpredictably violent with their support. Given the state Grama Pearle and Birdie were in, I doubt they could have kept themselves safe."

My eye starts to twitch, and my brain begins to hurt. "I'm going to bed."

"The words I wait to hear." Noah scoops me up and heads toward the stairs.

"Not with you!" Horrified, I try to wiggle out of his

arms. With a smirk, he sets me down at the top of the stairs and the four of us march down single file to our shared accommodations.

Morning dawns, and it's filled with the aroma of maple bacon and coffee. Grama Pearle is busy in the kitchen, making a breakfast of champions that includes not only the lovely foods I smell but orange juice, scrambled eggs, French toast, and fresh strawberries as well. She's finishing setting the table by putting breakfast out as we all slide into place.

"Morning, Grama Pearle." Fin greets her with a soft voice and a tiny smile.

"Don't you start, young lady." Grama Pearle has a smile of her own. "Do you know where Birdie is?"

There's a commotion on the counter by the fridge, accompanied by the sounds of tearing paper, crinkling plastic, some crunching, and a tired voice. "Here."

Everyone turns to see a full-sized Birdie sitting on the countertop. The left side of her mouth arches up in an attempt at a smile before she tips her weight to the right. She plucks a destroyed box of crushed cookies out from under herself, having disfigured it as she expanded into regular size. She lifts her head and stares at Grama Pearle with such a look of complete surprise that we all bust out laughing. Birdie gives us each an individual glower of disgust, slides off the counter, marches to the table, and sits down.

Everyone's quiet. The sounds come from the clinking of cutlery and the movement of food. After everyone has eaten, Grama Pearle breaks the silence. "There's much to talk about."

"Yeah, like where have you been?" I ask.

"We'll be asking you the same, Kori." Grama Pearle challenges with pursed lips and raised eyebrows.

"First, let's take our coffees to the living room. I need comfort. Sleeping on a bed of cookies and marshmallows isn't as agreeable as I remember it to be," Birdie says. Without waiting for a response, she heads for the living room.

Grama Pearle continues talking as we move. "We're trying to find where Dolion Adelgrief is and what he's up to. Even if Nekane has taken over as head of The Society of the Blood Wind, Dolion won't be sitting by idle. He'll be a driving force till the day he dies. He'll have a hand in Alivia's disappearance."

"Dolion Adelgrief? Is he related to Sephtis?" I interrupt.

Grama Pearle looks at me strangely. "Sephtis is dead. He lived in the middle of the 1500s, Kori." She pauses, waiting for my reaction. I blink. Grama Pearle continues. "So, Sephtis is a distant ancestor of the living Adelgriefs. Anyway," she hurries on, "what we learned is that Dolion, who is my age, has handed power of The Society of the Blood Wind over to his son, Nekane Adelgrief. Nekane is mid fifties, with a son a few years older than you."

"And Nekane is in the wind, searching for something that in itself is questionable because we don't know what he's looking for," Birdie chirps.

"Pause," Fin interrupts. "I have questions. First, who were the thugs at Alivia's place? Maybe Mr. 'Tall Drink of Water' was Nekane. Second, why did Mr. 'Tall Drink of Water' not take a more active role?"

"Where is it?" a low, rough voice demands.

The only person who doesn't seem startled by the interruption is Birdie. "It's okay, Roger. Come out of the corner."

It isn't until Roger rises from a crouch that I become aware that he's in the room. He was statue-like until he stood up. At a shocking seven feet tall, he's a very solid young man. His skin has a gray tint to it that reminds me of rock.

He moves with a heavy, purposeful step and stops when he's in a position to be included in the conversation. His eyes are the same curious colour as his skin, and I blink twice as I register what I'm seeing. This young man has no visible hair. No eyebrows, a bald head, no facial hair, and he's close enough to me that I can see there's no hair on his chiselled arms.

"Roger, this is a safe zone, and these are my friends," Birdie says sternly.

Roger says nothing. Instead, he looks at each of us, evaluating.

"Grama Pearle?" I say, not bothering to hide my tone of cautious distrust.

"Roger is a hybrid. He's half human and half rock troll."

I blink at Grama Pearle a few times and then turn my head to Roger.

Roger is done with pleasantries. "Where is it?"

"Roger?" Birdie says, her tone both concerned and questioning.

Roger scowls and eyes each of us. "My Willys MB, Birdie. Someone took my Willys."

Birdie shakes like she's ruffling her feathers. She implicates Noah first but glances past him and Alaric to fix her stare on Fin and me. When neither of us speaks, she taps her fingers on the arm of the chair.

"Yeap, it was us," Fin offers matter-of-factly.

I shut my eyes and tip my head. "Blazing hell . . . the lion gargoyles at the front of the house started to move and their intent wasn't clear. That, coupled with the fact that I'm ready to come unglued about doing nothing to find Alivia, sparked the decision for us to bolt. The Willys MB was ripe for the picking." I glare at Fin. "We just borrowed it."

Roger's features become furious.

"It's safe, Roger. We parked it inside one of the parking sheds at my shop," Fin assures him.

"Let's get it now." All of Roger's passion is fixed on Fin. He must have noticed her discomfort because he adds, "Please."

Fin looks at Grama Pearle, but she's staring at Birdie, who nods reassurance.

"Yes, Roger, Fin will take you to your Willys MB." Birdie says. "Fin, Roger is the best kind of friend you could ever ask for. He'll protect you outside of the safe house. The Willys is his project and he needs it. Keeps him busy, gives him focus, and makes him feel productive. So, if you could please take him to his Willys?"

Roger scoops Fin up like he's a child picking up his most delicate toy and he's out the door with her faster than I thought possible.

Birdie turns to Grama Pearle. "Roger is living with me while his tribe decides if a half-breed is welcome within their ranks. We're hopeful, but he always has a place with me either way."

Grama Pearle bobs her head, satisfied with that scant explanation. Roger will get his fair share of questioning from Fin, and she'll tell me all about it, I'm sure.

"How long has he been here?" Noah asks.

"Let's see," Birdie squints into space, "almost twenty years." She smiles. "You should have seen how cute he was as a boy! His birth name is Rakash, which I feel is a bit too Trollish for everyday in the human world, so I've called him Roger since he came to live with me. It worked out well when we went to get him his driver's license because his identification now reads Roger Rakash. A very nice-sounding name."

"You bet. It's a great name. His tribe must be close to a decision." Noah scratches his head. "They've lived a long time and they're a cautious species, so twenty years is a normal decision-making timeframe for rock trolls."

I jiggle my head, trying to empty it of the last few minutes of strangeness. I clear my throat and re-direct the conversation. "So, the guys at Alivia's place, could one of them have been Nekane?"

"Not if it was the same men from the cemetery," Alaric says. He's been so quiet that I forgot about him.

"Why?" I ask. Alaric's mention of the cemetery sparks me to remember the object from the hidden drawer in Jaxton's tombstone. But as I watch Alaric, I see hostility pass across his facial features as he formulates his response and I pause with my hand halfway into my pants pocket.

"I would know Nekane anywhere and when I see him again, he'll die." Alaric responds in such a low, quiet tone that chills creep up my spine.

"Nekane would be your father's age, Kori." Noah clamps a hand down on Alaric's shoulder.

I resume my search into my pocket. "Who were the guys at Alivia's?"

"Belamey Adelgrief," Grama Pearle answers. "Has to be Nekane's son, Belamey. We heard Nekane is trying to toughen him up, give him some responsibility."

With a question paused on the tip of my tongue, I yank my hand out of my pocket unable to wait any longer to see what I took from the gravestone drawer. I'm holding two very fascinating stones. Both are cut into the shape of two-inch long flames, an inch wide, and they curve slightly.

A closer inspection shows a person blended into each of the flames. Their faces draw me in with their closed eyes and a guise of complete serenity etched into their features. Each flame person has one prominent hand holding an object, but this is where the stones differ.

The first stone is agate and it's composed of rich

coloured bands that radiate out from the centre to the edges of the flame-shaped figurine. This figurine is clasping a piece of amber. The amber ranges in colour from a deep reddish-orange to a bright medium-orange, depending on the angle of the light. The play and movement of colour in this stone screams of fire.

Stone two is translucent, with black inside, corkscrewing in a design like mossy fern. This stone's flame-shaped figurine clutches a piece of coal-like amber that's dark as deep night. They're not like any kind of stones I've ever seen.

The room has grown silent. I was so engrossed by the stones that I'm surprised to find that Grama Pearle and me are alone in the room with Birdie peeking at us from the sunroom doors. I look at Grama Pearle questioningly.

Before either of us speaks, Alaric enters the room and I watch the construct of magic he throws over us to create a dome. The temperature, which I realize minutes before felt infernal, cools to the point that I shiver. He's thrown an ice dome over us, one so thick that I can't see out. Grama Pearle and I are alone.

"Kori, do you know what you're holding? Can you feel what you're holding?"

I examine the two tiny flame-shaped figurines in my hands and notice waves of heat both in and on my body. Without explanation, I know what I'm holding. The image of The Cleanser with flames coating him pops into my head, unbidden, but giving the ice dome a hint of context. "The Ember stones."

"Not stones Kori, just *stone*."

"I don't understand." A drop of water lands on my forehead and draws my wariness to the roof of the ice. The increasing heat is causing the ice to melt. Grama Pearle, is watching me.

"I know you don't understand," she says in a quiet voice. "But first you need to fit the stones together, making them one stone. Then you need to put them in your pocket to make them safe." Her words are slow but firm. "We don't know if you can activate them, so they aren't safe like that. We aren't safe."

I look at them. "You take them." I shove my hands forward simultaneously.

The action of my hand thrust stimulates the stone figurines. I can feel the reaction as a red-hot flame shoots out from the stone figure holding the orange amber. Grama Pearle is fast, throwing a defensive shield in front of her.

The flame streaks toward Grama Pearle, but before it hits her shield, it disappears. An unseen substance dispelled from the figure clutching the dark amber hit the flame. The substance acts like an antidote that counteracts the flame. *I could've killed her!*

I yank my hands back and mash the stones together before ramming both figurines into the depth of my pocket to avoid accidental activation. Grama Pearle drops her shield. We're both stunned. The dome disappears, and we're left standing as if we've come inside dripping wet after being caught in a rainstorm.

Swallowing, I close my eyes and I draw a deep breath before I open them. Grama Pearle is watching me. Moving, my arms encircle her while both of us tremble.

"I'm so sorry, Grama Pearle," I whisper into her blue-silver hair terrified that I could've killed her.

"Shh, Kori. It's okay, you didn't know, and we'd never have expected the Ember stone, separate or together, to just appear in your possession. We didn't know what Alivia did with it before she was . . . And, with all your rejection of magic, who would've guessed that you'd be the next Cleanser? We initially thought they were Jaxton's responsibility to carry. Now we know they're yours, there's no point to pass them off to me."

My trembling stops and my body feels rigid. "Jaxton," I breathe. "This is why they killed him, isn't it?"

Grama Pearle's hold on me tightens. "Yes, Kori. They, like us, believed that Jaxton was the next Cleanser, the Spellbinder that would wield the Ember stone. Our assumption was calculated based on the estimated return of The Cleanser; theirs likely was too."

She releases me and continues. "It was time to start testing members of the Ember family to see if there was a Cleanser among us, so the rock trolls, as custodians of Spellbinder artifacts, were bringing it to me." Grama Pearle weighs the value of explaining the larger history to me, but settles on limited details. "Rock trolls have guarded valuable magical items for Spellbinders for a time that predates me. Anyway, Jaxton was a perfect age, fourteen, to start training with the Ember stone, so it was a natural assumption given the estimated expectancy of a Cleanser. Before I brought the Ember stone home for him to try, he was killed. I was here getting the stone from Roger the night Jaxton was killed."

I slam my eyes closed, trying not to see the blinding flash of light that preceded his death. Magic thrown from his own hands to protect us both. Magic I was helpless to wield effectively. Magic failed us that night and magic killed Jaxton. That night changed my entire life and set me on a path without magic on a quest for a conventional life.

"Kori, you were a child, ten years old. He was fourteen. There wasn't anything either of you could have done to prevent what happened. You're not responsible for Jaxton's death."

I choke on arguments to the contrary because I know she's right.

"I know your parents don't speak about it because they find it too painful, but I'm here for you for support, to listen, and to answer questions the best I can. Kori, nobody blames you."

I can't look at Grama Pearle, but again I know she's correct. It's easier to avoid the omission that the only person who blames me is me. Each member of my family got lost in their own grief and blame after we lost Jaxton; whether it was right or wrong, we strayed from one another and from our responsibilities, with me holding out the longest. I pushed the belief that if we weren't Spellbinders, Jaxton's death never would have happened and from there, I chose to not be a Spellbinder. Run from the pain, to run from the fear. Until now, it just seemed easier than accepting it.

"Is it safe?" Birdie calls from the other room.

Grama Pearle breaks our hug. "Yes, come in. Kori was about to tell us where she found the Ember stone."

Once everyone has re-entered the room, I explain about the secret drawer in Jaxton's tombstone and how I forgot about the Ember stone in the aftermath of everything that happened.

"Was there anything else in the drawer?" Grama Pearle's hope crumples when I give her a thumbs down.

"Should there be?" I ask.

She nods. "There's a holder that Alivia had mounted on a necklace. The holder makes the stones into a cohesive amulet by keeping them secured as one. When they're one, their power is in balance. One stone can't be activated without the other being in proximity. The closer they are the more balanced," Grama Pearle explains.

"I don't understand. First, why didn't Roger just reclaim control of it? Second, why did Alivia have it?" I ask. Fin, Alaric, and Birdie are watching and listening to the exchange.

"There was no point in placing it back under guard until the Cleanser was identified and had successfully used it. Based on the timeline and if Jaxton wasn't The Cleanser, keeping in mind we didn't get to test him, someone else in our family was. We tested all the adults first. Remember we dismissed you because we thought a grasp and acceptance of magic was required to wield the Ember stone." Noah scrunches his face at me and my gaping mouth and continues.

"Alivia was testing Jayce and Holden, but they're so young we wanted to test them over a few years. The easiest way for her to test the boys periodically was to wear the stone on a necklace. It was stable that way, she always knew where it was, and nobody outside our family was aware it was with an Ember. I haven't seen her take it off since we tasked her with the responsibility," Grama Pearle answers.

Noah chimes in. "If it wasn't one of the boys, we planned to send it back to the rock trolls under the presumption that Jaxton was the Cleanser. At this point, Kori, you were the only Ember who hadn't tested with the Ember stone. But now—"

"You knew about this?" I say, enraged.

He shrugs. "Of course, I did. Kori, it's part of my job description."

"That doesn't matter right now, kids," Grama Pearle interrupts. "We need to find that necklace and holder. Alivia separated the Ember stone from the holder and hid them in different locations. She knows that without a proper holder for balance, the Ember stone is unpredictable, but the risk of it falling into Nekane's hands was too great. There wasn't time for her to do anything else once he became aware the Ember Stone was with her."

I continue to glare at Noah. "We're going to Alivia's tomorrow and we can scour for it."

"Good, good." Grama Pearle glances at Birdie. "We'll go to the Ember family house then. Right, Birdie?" Grama Pearle nods, not waiting for Birdie's response. "Knowing Alivia like I do, the holder will either be at her place or ours, unless someone from The Society of the Blood Wind found it already."

"Grama Pearle, I don't think it's a good idea for you two to go to the house. What if Nekane or someone who works for him shows up?"

Birdie and Grama Pearle share a look, and then they laugh at me. "It's decided then. We'll go tomorrow. Fin, Noah, and Alaric can go with you. And Roger will come with us," Grama Pearle says.

"Roger should go with Kori, Pearle," Birdie interrupts. Birdie flicks her eyes to me and away again like she's creating a morse code for Grama Pearle to decipher. My assumption is that the stakes have changed, with Alivia's kidnapping and my unexpected connection to the stone. Roger being with me means that if I fall or fail in some way, best case scenario, he can take the Ember stone to his people; the worst case isn't something I want to give thought to.

Grama Pearle clears her throat. "Right. Fin, Roger, and Alaric will go with you Kori. Noah will accompany us. Now you need to go practice some of the magic you've learned. But, Kori, leave the Ember stone in your pocket. You're doing well with the basics we're teaching you, but to use the Ember stone safely requires an advanced understanding and command of one's magic."

Chapter 9

Later that night, Fin sashays into the bedroom as I'm about to turn out the light. She's glowing with excitement and her hair is dishevelled. The energy radiating off her person stops Noah, Alaric, and me in our tracks.

I wonder if she's having sex with Roger, but that seems quick even for Fin. I decide not to ask because I know with Fin, if I don't want to know the answer, especially a response so detailed I'm left blushing and trying to cleanse my ears and purge my memory, I shouldn't ask.

"Fin?" I brace for her response. "Are you okay?"

"You won't believe this." Without drawing a breath, she continues. "We were at the shop getting the Willys when that damp stench filled the air. I tried to get Roger's attention so we could hide, but he wasn't interested in hiding."

"Fin, where's Roger? Is he okay?" I slide into my blankets to avoid freezing to death while Fin talks. Noah is perched on the edge of his bed listening frozen in the act of taking his shirt off.

"He's fine. He's in his own apartment in the big

garage. Guys, Roger is an amazing person. Did you know that he's 105 in rock troll years?" she asks. "Anyway, turns out Roger is familiar with that malodour! There were three guys and they had me surrounded. The first guy never saw it coming. Roger grabbed him from behind and squeezed. The guy went poof."

"Poof?" Noah's look is one of concern, but I don't know why.

"Poof," she repeats. "It was like squeezing and popping a balloon filled with dirt and dust! He just exploded. Nothing left but a pile of powdery particles. The second guy went at Roger and the same thing happened. The third guy bolted. We jumped in the Willys and made our way back."

"Shit," Noah groans.

Alaric is in the same spot he was in when Fin entered the room. He listened to the exchange, unspeaking. Based on Noah's swearing, Fin's story means something different to him and Alaric than it does to me. In addition, Alaric nods at some unspoken communication between them and leaves the room.

I scootch further into my blankets. "Where's he going and what does this 'dust death' mean?"

Fin yawns and stretches. "I need to do what you're doing, Kori. You're cozy in your blankets. I'm so tired. Sorry, Noah. What were you going to say?"

"Hollow people," Noah says, lost in his own thoughts.

"Noah?" I say louder to draw him from wherever his thoughts have taken him. "What are hollow people?"

Fin has paused, watching Noah. The wind outside

has picked up, and it sounds fierce as it batters the house. I've one thought as I listen to the gale, waiting with trepidation for Noah's retort. *A storm is coming and I don't mean a weather front.*

Noah weighs what we need to know. He nods to himself before supplying a remark. "They're normies who've had the essence of their beings removed. There was a group of Spellbinders who believed sucking the essence out of one person and into themselves strengthened them and increased their life span, but it's an obsolete practice for hundreds of years. They performed it on humans, but . . ." Noah pauses as if gathering strength. "Occasionally, there were rumours that Spellbinders were having their essence collected. If that's happening now—"

"Their essence?" Fin has paused listening to Noah's explanation. I had the same question, so I stay quiet to wait.

"Yes, essence in the sense of a person's mental abilities of reason, feeling, consciousness, character, memories, perceptions, and thinking. Taking a Spellbinder's essence offers the same increase in life span as taking a normie's, but the essence itself has no magical history with a normie. They take it, leaving behind a hollow shell that does their bidding for a time before the body becomes dust. The shell doesn't crumble easily. Roger must've been exerting a fair amount of force. He's part rock troll, so . . ."

I manage a perceptible nod as I try to digest what Noah is telling us.

"This isn't a great bedtime story, Noah. So, shut up."

Fin drops her clothes and climbs between her blankets in her bra and underwear. She rolls to face the wall and I can hear the soft sound of her breathing change to that of someone asleep.

I cock my head, wondering how she can do that. I sigh and turn to see Noah retreating. Where he's going is one of my many questions. "Noah?"

He stops with his hand on the light.

"I'm just thinking about something Fin said. She said that she smelled the hollow people before she saw them and . . ." I scratch my head wondering if I'm going to make a fool of myself with my question. The words race out of my mouth before I decide not to ask them. "Do the warped smell bad? Because I've been associating that stink to them, but now I'm wondering if it's been hollow people all along. Maybe the warped are with them sometimes but . . ."

Noah's face goes through a series of emotions in rapid succession. "The warped don't reek." His words are tight and clipped, but I know Noah's tone reflects dissatisfaction with himself. "How did I miss that?" he asks under his breath.

I know he isn't asking me, but I answer anyway in a whisper. "You said it's a hundred years' obsolete practice, so why would it even have been on anybody's radar to be watching for. Plus, we've no firsthand experience with them. I imagine your knowledge of them comes from books."

He gives me a sad attempt at a smile. "We'll talk more tomorrow. You need to sleep because we have a big day, and you'll need to be on your toes." He flicks the light off.

"And you?" I ask the darkness, assuming he's already gone.

I'm startled that he's crossed the darkness to my bedside. He slides his hand tenderly over my hair and whispers, "Sleep now, Kori. I'll return before you know it." With that, he disappears into the darkness, leaving me to lay there pondering the things this day has revealed, things that challenge the core of my reality. My reality, the one I worked so hard to create for myself, the one removed from magic, is becoming harder to trust. It exhausts and terrifies me.

Thunder cracks and lightning illuminates the room. I'm determined to stay awake until Noah and Alaric return, but I'm also too tired to drag myself from my warm blankets to see where they went. The rain beating a rhythmic pattern outside is soothing and I succumb to a wave of sleep.

I don't hear Noah during the night, but as the morning light creeps in, I'm not surprised to see him stretched out on his bed, sleeping. Alaric's bed is empty and it's impossible to determine by looking if he slept in it. Fin is up and gone, which doesn't surprise me either. I stretch and yawn before I slither out of bed, get dressed, and climb the stairs to the main level of the house.

I find Fin working on the Willys with Roger and I convince them to leave right away for Alivia's. I don't want to wait for anybody. Alaric isn't here, and Noah is going with Grama Pearle and Birdie to the Ember family house. Two teams of three make sense.

After a stop at Just Flavours, we pull up to Alivia's with hot coffee and breakfast sandwiches. Fin's plan, of course, is to eat and then forage for the holder. We're armed with a brief description of the holder and a hope that it won't be hard to find.

Grama Pearle's pride in Alivia is strong. I can hear Grama Pearle telling me, "Alivia's knowledge of the healing properties of various metals led her to silver because of its medicinal properties. Silver, a moon metal, is cooling, calming, and soothing and it brings balance. On top of that, silver improves intuition, love, and emotional wellbeing, and repels evil and negativity."

"Grama Pearle said that the holder is on a silver necklace," I remind Fin and Roger as we enter the house. "It's too bad there aren't pictures, but it makes sense since the family was keeping the fact the Ember stone wasn't with the rock trolls a secret. Anyway, she said the holder holds both stones back to back, with one set somewhat above the other."

Fin licks her lips. "Yes, we'll look, but first breakfast."

"Yes, first breakfast," Roger repeats.

Fin and Roger sit down at the table. I've no knowledge of rock trolls but Roger's face while he watches Fin unpack the food bags reminds me of a smitten teenager. I turn away from them to sift through the vintage apothecary box.

The smell of egg and sausage fills the room and overpowers the familiar scent of old wood and herbal medicines. Regardless, I smile as I swing open the two front doors of the apothecary box to reveal three drawers and shelves of unique glass bottles lining the inside. Alivia filled the bottles with herbs, powders, and tinctures.

It's the lowest drawer that I'm interested in because Alivia told me that there's a false bottom in it. Before I open the drawer, I hear movement from the hallway leading to the bedrooms. I turn, arming myself with two sound vibration orbs strong enough to temporarily counteract the effects of gravity for whoever, or whatever, I blast with them.

When Carter comes into view, my eyes go wide, and I let the orbs dissipate. I scan him up and down, looking for an explanation for his presence. As my eyes pass over his groin area, I think I see a hint of magic, but it's so short-lived I again dismiss it, reasoning that with my desperation to find Alivia being tied to my acceptance of magic, it must be making me see magic in places where it isn't. I don't let my eyes linger, the last thing I want is for him to think I'm checking out his junk. "What in the blazing ashes?"

Carter flashes a winning smile at everyone. "You didn't lock up, so I crashed here to wait for you." He lowers his voice to a whisper as he hides one hand behind the other angled away from Fin and Roger, but not from me, and points the hidden hand at his genitals. "I need your help with my problem."

I don't look at his crotch. I focus on his face and just blink.

Fin taps the space beside her and slides an unopened breakfast sandwich into it. "Dude, nice haircut. Sit down and have a breakfast sandwich and let's talk about your penis." Carter views the sandwich,

Roger, and then me. "Carter," Fin says, trying to draw his perception to her. "Carter, you need strength for your body to work. ALL your body." She nudges the breakfast sandwich. "This is Roger, a new friend. Guess what, Carter?"

"You can go ahead and tease me all you want. Laughter solves problems." Carter eyes the breakfast sandwich.

"One of the things I like about you, Carter, is that you're a good sport. Anyway, Roger has a penis too, so maybe he can help shed some light on your . . ." she pauses dramatically, pretending to think of a socially appropriate word. She clears her throat. "Flaccid penis." She casts her eyes sideways at Roger and lifts her eyebrow.

Roger says nothing, choosing to take a big bite of his breakfast sandwich and ignore the rest.

"Carter, strength," Fin repeats and pokes the sandwich before pulling the chair out.

"Okay, you're right. I need strength and I'm hungry." Carter slides into the chair.

I roll my eyes and turn to the apothecary box.

The hidden drawer is easy to find when you know it's there, so it doesn't take any time for me to open it. Inside is a leather-bound book that Alivia keeps notes and drawings of herbs in. There's also a small glass bottle, stoppered, with a curled note in it. I unstopper it and shake the bottle 'til the paper tumbles out in my hand.

It's brown recycled kraft paper. As I unroll it, whiffs of lavender waft off the paper. There's a drawing of bloodweed on it. Alivia's use of colour, reddish-orange and yellow, creates a flame-like feeling to the flowers. "Thank you, Alivia," I whisper. I turn to tell them Alivia left me a cryptic message, but I stop with my mouth open and my eyes bugging out. Carter is standing close to the table, unzipping his jeans, an active participant in Fin's charade.

"Lay it out here on the table, Carter, and let's have a look." Fin unfolds a napkin and slides it in front of him. "I've been learning about alternative healing with diet, nutrition, herbs, and that kind of thing, and I think, no . . . I know, this is going to work."

"Fin!" I say, horrified by what's unfolding and knowing she isn't studying any forms of alternative medicine.

"Hang on, Kori," Fin says. "Carter is ready to try this remedy for his penial deficiency." A smirk plays at the corner of her mouth.

Carter's penis is on the table and he's preoccupied with it.

"Okay, you take this." Fin produces a tiny cloth bag from her pocket with who knows what inside and slides it toward Carter's exposed manhood with a piece of red string. "Just tie it to your little friend there and—"

"Little?" Carter's head snaps up. "Did you say little?" His voice is high and squeaky with distress.

I flick imaginary lint off my shirt. Fin enjoys pushing Carter's buttons and he's never minded her teasing. It's the hallmark of their relationship, but sometimes I think they take it too far. This is one of those times.

Fin clears her throat to hide a giggle. "No, I said tie this bag onto your friend there. In three nights, dance naked under a starry sky, calling out Kori's name."

"FIN!" I shout.

Neither Carter nor Fin acknowledges that I'm in the room. Before I can say anything more, that fetid odour of damp, rotten earth hits me. Fin recognizes it too because she whips her head up, looking for the source. We both note the movement going past the windows, which are cracked open.

"Outside," I whisper. "Let's go now. Where's Roger? We can't leave him here."

"He went out to the garden shed, and he hasn't come back," Fin whispers. I suspect Roger went outside to avoid being part of the penis fiasco, but I don't point that out. I don't know much about Roger, but I do know most people don't possess Fin's flair for theatrics, teasing, or the same skewed filter for thoughts, feeling, emotions, actions, and words.

Carter, who doesn't know what's going on, is in the same position, with his penis out, trying to ask Fin questions about her instructions. "Shut up, Carter," she hisses.

Suddenly, a powerful orb crashes into the table and it upends. Fin flips over with her chair and hits the floor hard. Carter flies across the room, slams into the wall, and slumps to the ground. Both are unconscious.

I whip my head in the blast's direction, unsure who or what I'll find. Belamey Adelgrief is standing there, having entered through the front door, tall with his shoulders back.

I assess him, noting his black outfit of untied boots, which are loose on his feet with tucked laces, but lead up to a nice fitting pair of cargo pants, topped with a perfectly fit T-shirt. His body faces me with a wide stance, his head and chin are up, and his eyes lock on mine with such an intense yearning that I feel it travel through my full body, creating a tingling desire that confuses me. Belamey is the enemy and therefore equals vile.

"Kori Ember, at last." His husky voice draws me in. "I assume you know who I am?"

The tendrils of magic that cling to him are visible to me as thin whisps. I try to lash out with my magic but find that it's wrapped tight, and I can't access it. There's nobody to help me; both Fin and Carter are unconscious and Roger is outside somewhere, locked in his own battle, for all I know. I keep my fear from my face as I continue struggling against the invisible magic bonds.

He tuts at me in disapproval. His deep brown eyes probe mine while he talks. "You should have studied with single-mindedness. You're so powerful, I can feel it. Forgive me for bonding your magic but, as I just said, you are powerful and inadequately trained. With that fiery personality, this is for both our protection." He gives a sad sigh. "I understand now why my father wants to turn you."

A wave of nausea washes over me at Belamey's comment about his father wanting to flip me; it would be my death before I'd become part of The Society of the Blood Wind. I barely keep my stomach contents down when I think about Alivia being held prisoner by them.

A different training takes hold. My magic is bound by

Belamey's, but he hasn't physically bound me. I launch myself at him. With my head down, I go for his legs. Because of the element of surprise coupled with his habit of fighting using magic, he doesn't anticipate my physical attack. We hit the floor hard, but he recovers quickly, and I don't have a chance to scramble out of his arm's reach.

He grabs me by the ankle and drags me toward him. I flip as he drops his body weight overtop of me. He's so close I sniff cardamom, cedar, and lavender with undertones of cinnamon, vanilla, and earthiness. It's a heady bouquet that I find exhilarating. I shake it off as Belamey pins my arms on either side of me and lowers his face close to mine. But I'm not done yet.

I toss my head to the side and thrust my hips up forcefully. It has the desired effect of knocking him off balance by throwing him forward. I grab his legs and roll us so now I'm on top of him. He stops struggling, folds his arms behind his head, and just lies there.

"Well, that was fun." His low, husky voice makes butterflies take flight in my stomach.

I stop fighting, intending to climb off him. He's looking over my shoulder. That musty offensive odour replaces Belamey's intoxicating fragrance, and I know hollow men have entered the house. I try in vain to access my magic, but Belamey still has it wrapped so I fail. I decide that it's better to accept defeat and wait for another opportunity to strike.

Clambering off Belamey, I put my hands in the air, rising to my knees. Before I get any farther, Roger appears behind the two hollow men. He grabs the first and squeezes 'til dust fills the air. The second man tries, but isn't fast enough to get distance from Roger's crushing arms. He gives a slight howl that's cut short when he's reduced to teensy particles.

It occurs to me that Roger's familiarity with hollow men is curious, but I don't have time to ask. Belamey's eyes are wide with shock, the hollow men aren't with him. I use this moment to my advantage. I turn and coldcock him hard enough to knock him out. Shaking off the pain in my fist, I jump to my feet. "Roger, we need to get to the Ember family house. Grama Pearle and Birdie are in danger if they're there. If The Society of the Blood Wind is looking here, they'll be looking there, too!"

Fin is waking up, but not fast enough. I gesture at her so Roger will pick her up, but he's already moving to lift her to her feet. I glance at Carter.

He's unconscious, with the cloth bag that Fin gave him tied to his exposed penis. I'm startled to find that I feel no anger; instead, I feel sympathy for his struggles and an appreciation for his ability to perceive humour and accept a joke at his own expense. I also feel a sense of sadness that this was the man I thought would give me normalcy, yet I hope that maybe one day we can be friends. To say it was a love of necessity isn't fair. I did love him, but so much of our relationship was about my fear of who I am.

Carter's chest is rising and falling. Satisfied that he isn't dead, I tell myself that he has no value as a target and I dash out the door with Roger on my heels.

From the outside, my old brick family home is silent and empty, but as we make a circumspect approach that musty fetor is in the air. It isn't overpowering, but strong enough to let us know there are hollow men on the property. I motion to Fin and Roger that we need to circle the house in separate directions. I'm hoping we can find Grama Pearle, Birdie, and Noah quickly, which seems easier if we split. With luck and stealth, maybe we can get in and out without a fight.

An icy shiver tugs at the base of my spine and my nose clogs with stink. Fin's arm arches up and she releases it forward. Something sleek whizzes by my head so close that I can feel a breeze. I turn to see a knife lodge in the chest of a hollow man, who scatters into ashes. I'm left staring at the knife lying on the ground as the ash drifts down like dirty snowflakes tickling my skin.

Fin pushes past me to collect it. "No problem, Kori. I got your back."

"Fin," I hiss. "What the blazing hell was that?"

"Ordered these online." She flashes three more well-concealed knives at me. "Don't look at me like that Kori, I practice with Noah and Alaric when you do your magic homework. They say I'm fantastic. These are just my practice knives, steel-fixed blades, but Alaric says he has some special ones that he'll give me. You won't believe how many of them I can hide on my body. I'll have to show you to make you a believer."

My eyes have been growing wider with each word out of Fin's mouth. Our conversation is cut off when Roger grunts behind us and we turn to see him grasp another hollow man and squeeze.

"Let's get inside and check if Grama Pearle, Birdie, and Noah are here. Then we all leave fast," I say. "Split up. Roger, you go in the rear and clear the main level. Fin, go with Roger, but once in, you go upstairs. I'll enter through the front and head downstairs to the store."

We don't make it anywhere. The front door blasts open and Noah tumbles down the stairs, locked in combat with someone I assume is a normie because they're in physical combat and not a magical one. Noah isn't using his protective magic either. Fists are flying, but they seem evenly matched. Grama Pearle evacuates the house, but stays on the stairs, as all hell breaks loose.

We're surrounded unless we escape into the house, but given Noah came out fighting and Grama Pearle exited fast it suggests that there are enemies in there and I've no idea how many. Better to fight our way clear of the property.

The musty stink in the air is so thick that it's hard to breathe, which suggests to me that most of our assailants are hollow men. They must've exited from the rear of the house. Roger is stalking across the yard, grabbing and squishing whoever is foolish enough to get close to him. His stone-like skin offers him a measure of protection the rest of us don't have.

Fin is partially concealed, she takes a knee behind some bushes to aim and throw her knives, taking out her first three targets. She misses the fourth, who is hunting her with clear intent; her knife now in his hand. Without hesitation, I fling an orb at him, and he explodes into dust on impact.

Fin scrambles from the bush and stays low as she collects her fallen knives. I turn to the front of the house, pelting orbs as I move. I feel panic when I can't see Grama Pearle. Hearing her voice calling for Birdie, edged with fright, does nothing to calm me. Grama Pearle has moved up the few stairs she descended to position at the front door and shielded herself. She's screaming for Birdie with a note of fear in her voice as she continues to sling her own orbs at approaching hollow men.

I'm moving like I'm in quicksand, unable to reach them fast enough to help. The man Noah is fighting has produced a knife. Noah is bleeding and tiring. Hairs on my arms and the nape of my neck rise; Noah's magic is protective, a complement to his fighting, but I don't see any magic shielding. *Does it even defend against non-magical assaults?* Growing up, Noah enjoyed a fair fight whether it was fists, a board game, a bike race, or whatever. I feel like screaming at him to not let his honour get him killed, but that might be a deadly distraction.

I scan the yard. My analysis lands on Grama Pearle. She makes a fatal mistake in looking too long into the house. She's unaware two hollow men are approaching from behind. There's no way I can lob an orb to help either Noah or Grama Pearle without hurting them.

Tunnel blind, trying to get to them, I'm side-tackled by someone. Instinctively, I lash out and my attacker explodes leaving a cloud of ash enveloping me. I crawl, still trying to reach Noah and then Grama Pearle. My vision clears to see Alaric materialize out of nowhere and hurl himself at the two hollow men moving in on Grama Pearle. A cloud of ashes engulfs Alaric.

At the same instant, Grama Pearle opens the cremation urn on her necklace containing Grandpa Ian's remains. She tosses some of his ashes into the air. They don't scatter like I expect. Instead, his ashes pull together in the air and form a ghostly snowy owl. Its yellow eyes assess its surroundings.

This massive bird starts hunting, targeting hollow men. I watch as it swoops down on the hollow men, their remains scattering in the wind. Between Grandpa Ian's owl and Roger, the hollow men's numbers deplete, leaving a few normies fighting us.

I don't see what happens to Grandpa Ian's owl because I'm distracted by a shriek ringing out from the interior of the house. The shriek, a high-pitched owl noise, has come from Birdie. Her large owl form barrels out of the house, swooping down and attacking the man with a knife pressed to Noah's throat. The man is lifted off the ground in a spray of blood as the owl, strengthened as a unique shifter quality, carries him a few scant feet away before releasing his body to fall into a wooded area neighbouring the house. The sickening thunk that follows is a sure sign that he hasn't survived. Our last remaining enemies run from the fight.

Birdie, as an owl, makes a low pass around the house and I see blood and other things clinging to her feathers. When she returns, she shifts into her human form. I swallow hard as I take in her appearance. She's covered in blood, dust, and what appear to be chunks of flesh.

"There are more of them inside. Let's go," Birdie says. Her eyes are wide, her hair is dishevelled, and she's so tired I'm amazed she's standing. Roger is at her side in seconds. He lifts her from the ground and strides toward the Willys MB that we left parked half a block down the street.

Grama Pearle doesn't bother pulling the door closed as she hastens off the steps. Alaric is already helping Noah up. When we reach the edge of the property, I grab Fin so that she stays with me for a second, I don't want anyone else to hear me. Things have been so outside the scope of my normal that I only want Fin to know about this until I figure out what *this* is.

I lean in close to her and whisper. "Did you see a dove-sized hawk with square tail feathers sitting up in the trees just watching everything happening?" I eyeball the trees. "I think it's following me."

Fin scrunches her nose at me and shakes her head, but she looks at the treetops.

I sigh and roll my eyes. "I must be losing it. A bird following me? Yeah, right," I mutter.

Fin glances at me and then at the treetops. Before she can say anything, I grab her arm and pull her toward the Willys.

It isn't until later that night, as we're all finishing dinner, that I bring out the note I found in Alivia's apothecary box. "At Alivia's place. I found a clue." I pass the note for everyone to see.

"I don't get it?" Fin hands it to me. "Lavender scented paper with a drawing of a plant?"

"It's a drawing of bloodweed," I explain. "It was used to induce vomiting, but it's toxic when ingested. Grama Pearle used it topically on customers to remove warts when they came into the store." I can see Grama Pearle's head bobbing up and down in agreement.

"Okay?" Fin questions.

"I know where the holder is and I'm hoping she left another clue with it that might help us find her. The problem is we need to go back to Grama Pearle's store to get it!"

Chapter 10

As a group last night, we established that The Society of the Blood Wind won't leave the Ember house unmonitored. Fin and I plan to sneak out in the morning for a drive-by of it. It's unlikely that we'll escape the safe house unnoticed, but I hope to break free from the bedroom. However, as Fin and I tiptoe, Noah's voice is an unwelcome taunt, "Don't go into the Ember house without us!"

I march up the stairs, ignoring the rest of what he says.

"Roger is in the driveway, waiting for you girls," Birdie chirps the moment we enter the sunroom.

I give Fin a look of sheer frustration. "It seems everybody knows our plans. Fin?"

Shoulders raised, she says, "Wasn't me. I didn't tell a soul."

With pressed lips and narrow eyes, I march through the sunroom. I slide into the back seat of the Willys MB with a scowl. Roger shoots me a good-morning grin and beams at Fin as she gets in the passenger seat. "Breakfast?"

"Need you ask?" She laughs.

I rub my eyelids and shake my head.

"Oh, come on Kori! You know you need a coffee!" Fin and I lock eyes in the rear-view mirror. I'm happy to stare her down but my shoulders and head hit the back seat in surprise as Roger, overzealous, rockets down the driveway, gravel flying.

Recognizing that coffee will benefit my ever-souring mood, I sigh. "We should switch vehicles first. The Willys won't go unnoticed." Arms crossed, I close my eyes, content to leave that plan up to them.

I must have dozed off because the next thing I hear are keys jingling. I crack my eyes open. We're parked by the rear exit to Fin's favourite food joint, Just Flavours. "Fin?"

"I love the perks of owning my own car lot, Roger is going to grab us a drab Jeep Cherokee from there while we order food. It's a vehicle that'll blend with local traffic."

I bob my head up and down, thinking a new vehicle only benefits us if we aren't being watched before we retrieve it. At the same time, the Willys and the Bronco draw attention regardless of what we're doing, so we couldn't lose a tail if we had one, or be confused with another vehicle. So, there are benefits, whether we're seen getting a new vehicle or not.

"Your employees?" I hear Roger ask.

"Too early! Meet you back here." With that, Fin hooks arms with me and drags me toward the door.

"Fin, are there any other restaurants in town?" I ask.

"Yeap, but I don't like them." She pulls the door open and the rich smell of coffee and breakfast food hits me like a wall, and my tummy rumbles in response. Fin tightens her hold on my arm, pulling me closer. I can see a smile spreading on her face. To her credit, she says nothing, but I note that her usual sashaying walk has a bit more of a swagger.

I switch my steps to match hers and dramatically move my hips from side to side. Fin's laughter competes with the noise of the restaurant. Through it all, I hear a well-known voice. The voice is like a familiar hum against the sounds of food being prepared and cooked, so it doesn't register in my brain. It isn't until Fin's laugh causes his voice to fall silent that I realize it's Carter's voice among the restaurant's chatter. I stop dead, jarring Fin.

"Carter," I hiss, disgruntled that he keeps showing up.

"Fin, is that you? Is Kori with you?" Carter calls.

I can't see him because the expanse of the restaurant isn't visible. Fin's face is flipping between amused and deer in the headlights.

"Shit, we don't have time. You need to start eating at a less popular food joint," I mumble as I cast my eyes down the hallway. We won't make it out of Just Flavours before Carter rounds the corner, he doesn't go away when told, and he's overall a big pain in the ass that we don't need to deal with right now.

The washroom sign catches my eye and I yank Fin through the door. I can hear Carter calling for us. Given his current single-minded obsession, the symbol of a stick figure wearing a dress won't provide a blockade if he thinks we're in here. There are two stalls. Stall one is occupied and stall two is marked as out of order. I kick stall two open and stuff Fin inside, motioning for her to climb on the toilet seat and crouch down.

Carter's voice gets closer. "I know by the laugh it's you, Fin!"

Fin and I balance on a single toilet seat, knees to knees, our backs braced against the walls. All the restaurant noises die away as I strain to hear Carter. Instead, my ears fill with the soft sound of a vibrating rectum releasing gas in the next stall along with the low, continuous droning of the same occupant as she hums and poops. The unpleasant smell of fecal matter wafts from her stall, and my nose scrunches in response.

"She's so happy," Fin whispers.

I see the wheels turning in Fin's mind. I give her my I'm-going-to-kill-you face, but it's too late. She stands up and I recognize the white and pink packaging of a tampon in her hand. She launches it at the door to the hallway. It makes a soft thump. Fin ducks. The pooper keeps on pooping as if nothing else is happening.

"Carter won't appreciate this experience." Fin winks.

The bathroom door bangs open. "I know you're in here, and . . ." Carter doesn't finish his sentence because the pooper stops humming, lets out an explosive fart, and resumes humming. Carter finds his voice, but it's high-pitched when he calls out. "Uh, wrong room."

The door swings shut. Fin and I wait a few minutes before we dismount the toilet.

"Think he's gone?" Fin asks.

I pinch my nose. "You bet. He won't even be in the

restaurant after that!"

"Happy pooping," Fin calls. A stream of farts is the only response.

Ten minutes later, we're armed with a tray of hot coffees and a bag of glazed-donut breakfast sandwiches. Roger is waiting in a Jeep Cherokee. The tinted windows and shiny custom rims give the vehicle a gangster feel, and I wonder how it's inconspicuous. It is drab.

We drive by the Ember house, staying with the regular flow of traffic. The house sits quiet, with no immediate signs of movement. I'm looking so hard to find life forms that I almost miss the thin wisps of magic hanging over the doors and windows. Houses typically aren't warded unless they're designated a safe house, so that suggests to me this is more of a trap than a ward and not one that's friendly.

"The windows and doors are framed with magic. A trap of some kind is my guess," I whisper.

"What?" Fin asks.

Blowing out a sigh, I take my seven chakra stones out of my pocket to calm my nerves and thoughts. "I can see foggy threads of lime-green and coal-tinted magic twining over the windows and doors. Remember, the Ember house isn't warded. Plus, these colours just feel evil and it isn't like anything I see at Birdie's haven." I pull the air currents enough to float and spin the stones over my palm while I try to figure out how to get past the traps without tripping them.

Roger drives us a full city block, but the twines of magic are all I see when we make a second pass. "I won't lie. I was hoping we would learn a bit more than this today. We need to know more so we can plan how to get in." I say.

Silence fills the Jeep.

"I have an idea," Fin yells. "Roger, can you head toward the restaurant where we got breakfast, please?"

"Fin?" I ask, but she smiles and lounges in her seat.

Just Flavours comes into view minutes later and Fin points to something I can't see but Roger can. He speeds up.

"Can you stop with him on my side of the vehicle, please?" Fin asks Roger. He nods and pulls a U-turn. She jumps out. The back passenger door flies open, and Fin unceremoniously shoves Carter in. The "he" she was referring to is Carter. He plops onto the floor between the seats. The chakra stones I'm floating over my palm speed up and clatter out of my hand.

"Geesh! Fin, you usually fight fair, but—" Before he can finish speaking, Fin reaches down, grabs his legs, and flings them up in the air inside the vehicle. She slams the door. We're driving before Carter can unwedge himself from the floor. I try to absorb myself in the act of finding my scattered chakra stones.

"Sorry, Carter. There's no excuse for my behaviour," Fin says with an apologetic smile. Then in her best business-as-usual voice, she says, "How's it hanging?"

If he heard Fin's apology, he doesn't acknowledge it, as he hurries to comment on his penis. "That's all it does, Fin. It just hangs!" Carter groans with his head down. Roger glances in the rear-view. "It just hangs," Carter mumbles.

Roger turns briefly in his seat, assessing Carter,

before putting his eyes on the road. At this point, I'm trying to stay stationary and quiet, hoping that Carter will continue contemplating his lap.

"We have a deal for you, Carter," Fin says with a big smile. "You interested?"

I hear the word *we* and cringe. Carter's head pops up and he sees me. Just as quickly, his head drops down, and he makes a move to expose himself, absorbed by his belief that I'm the solution to his impotency.

"CARTER!" I holler.

He pauses and lifts his eyes to me. I suck in a calming breath of air before I look from Carter's face to his crotch and back. This time I'm sure I see magical threads, but I'm not sure what it means. It's clear from Carter's behaviour that he doesn't know there's magic attached to his penis; in his mind, the world is magic-free, which is one of the reasons I married him.

I'm guessing that it's the magic that encourages him to expose himself in my presence. Fin said that he hadn't tried to show his penis to her before my return to Canada and she hadn't heard of him exposing himself to anyone else. I swallow and try to infuse my voice with sweetness. "Carter, the back seat is not big enough for me, you, and your penis." For emphasis, I raise my eyebrows.

He drops his eyes down, glances up quickly, and then down. "Kori, you just need—"

I'm not sure who is more shocked when Roger's hand clamps down on Carter's knee and tugs him forward. Whether Roger was tired of Carter's foolishness, or just couldn't handle it in the confined space, I don't know.

Fin takes advantage of it and turns, pushing her nose against Carter's. "This vehicle has a 'no dick exposure' rule, Carter. No dicks! Got it?"

It's Carter's turn to swallow and choke out a response. He gives a perceptible nod. Fin smiles and turns to face the road. Roger releases Carter's knee, gives it a pat, and puts his hand on the steering wheel. Silence fills the vehicle until Roger eases it to a stop a block and a half from the Ember house.

Fin twists in her seat and gives me one of her winning smiles before focusing on Carter. "Okay Carter, here's the deal. We need you to go to the Ember house. Ring the doorbell like you're there to visit Kori. Feel free to yell about her and your erectile dysfunction. Shouldn't be too hard, right?" She clears her throat. "Oops, I mean, it shouldn't be too difficult. Then leave by walking straight that way." Her slender finger flicks in the opposite direction from us. "We'll pick you up at the corner, up the street from the Ember house. You can tell us everything you see, hear, and smell. Got it?"

"What are you going to do for us?" Carter asks with a slight head bob toward his penis.

If I hadn't been watching so closely, I wouldn't have believed it was possible for Fin's smile to get brighter. "We'll take you with us to the place we've been staying and get you some special help for you and Mr. Dangles Down." Fin pauses. She bats her eyelashes at him and cocks her head. "Deal?"

Carter opens the door and hops out, mumbling as he walks away. "Seems like an easy deal for the fee of curing our erectile dysfunction doesn't it, Jack?" I'm happy Fin doesn't hear Carter talking to his penis because my eye is already twitching and I'm not sure how much more I can take.

"You can stop the incessant blinking, Kori," Fin says.

I give her a poke in the shoulder. "What in the fiery blazes, Fin? He can't come with us! He's making me crazy just being in the same town. What's going to happen when he's in the same house?"

Fin dismisses this with a hand wave. "You could float him on air currents, and that man would never see magic."

I sigh, shake my head, and slump into my seat. "I need to talk to Grama Pearle about him anyway. It'll be easier if he's around when I do."

"Why do you need to talk to Grama Pearle?" she asks, with her hand on the radio's volume knob.

"I think I see magic clinging to him, and I can't help wondering if it's related to his peculiar behaviour."

"Hang on, I love this song," she says, blaring the music.

I'm glad that she was distracted enough by the radio to not hear what I said because I don't want to explain what part of Carter's body the magic is associated with. The less I have to think, speak, or otherwise engage with Carter's penis, the better.

After twenty-five minutes, we pull onto the almost empty street. There's no change at my childhood home and no sign of Carter.

"Um, where is he? We should've seen him by now," I say to nobody in particular.

"There," Roger says, jerking the Jeep to a stop. He

jumps out and sprints away.

Carter is running into an alley three blocks from the Ember house with two men chasing him. Roger's long legs are closing the gap.

Fin springs into the driver's seat as I scramble up into the front passenger side. How she makes the turn into the alley I'll never know. Roger is already thirty feet in and his hands are on the first guy, who disappears in a puff of dust. Carter continues running. He hasn't noticed us.

I lean out the window and pitch a water orb at the man behind Carter. The arch of my throw is perfect. The orb lands on the guy's head. I can't see his face, but I imagine the force of the water is blinding. His left foot catches his right, and he goes down in a wave of water and mud, giving Roger time to close the distance. As the man lifts his head, Roger cold cocks him and rolls him into the grass, out of the way of traffic that might travel the alley. Not a hollow man because he didn't poof out, and no magic, so just a normie.

We pull to a stop and Roger jumps in the back seat. "That Carter guy can run! Where's he going?"

"Good thing he can run," Fin says as she hammers on the gas. We shoot out of the alley in a cloud of dust. Carter is nowhere to be seen.

"That can't be good, can it?" Roger asks.

Fin and I exchange a glance but neither one of us says anything. Carter is a lot of things, but we don't want to see anything bad happen to him. We drive in silence. He doesn't turn up. We drive by his apartment, but the lights are out and there's no noticeable sign of movement.

"We have to get to the safe house," Roger points out. "The Society of the Blood Wind will start to wonder why their people haven't checked in and they'll come out in full force to investigate. We don't want to be here then."

Fin directs her voice at me, not the front windshield. "Sorry, Kori. I didn't mean for Carter to get caught."

I pull my gaze from the side window to respond to Fin and catch sight of a form moving quickly out of an alley into the street ahead of us. "FIN!" I shriek.

Her foot jams down hard on the brake, and the tires scream in response. The vehicle fishtails before grinding to a halt with the front bumper kissing Carter's body. He doesn't move, he just stands there with his eyes wide, staring at us.

"Where's he running to?" I wonder aloud.

"Who knows," Fin says, reversing the vehicle. Carter doesn't move, and now we can see he has both hands, overtop his pants, cupped protectively on his penis. Roger has the presence of mind to jump out and steer Carter into the vehicle.

Carter's hands appear to be permanently in protection mode, but he's able to let go of his penis with one hand to fasten his own seatbelt. When he lets go, a fibril of magic trails from his hand to the seatbelt but snaps toward his groin area. I'm reminded of a magnetic attraction. Checking to see if anyone else notices, I remember that I'm the Spellbinder in the vehicle and the only one we know that can see threads of magic.

Glancing at Carter I see that he doesn't have any visible injuries. He's sweating and winded, but otherwise seems unharmed from this escapade. I gaze at Roger, who is watching Carter hold his penis. Roger looks at me. Confusion marks his chiselled features. "I don't get it either, Roger." *Although, I might have a better idea now.* I face the side window.

"We have no choice now, Kori." Fin eases the vehicle onto the highway. "I feel like we put him in danger, not to mention he won't stay anywhere we try to leave him anyway." She flicks her eyes at the rear-view mirror to indicate that she means we have to bring Carter with us.

"Yeap, but first we need to know where he was because we can't have him leading anybody to our refuge," I mumble. "Carter!" He doesn't respond. "Carter," I repeat, louder.

His head darts my way. It's like a faint light is glowing behind his dark brown eyes, which gives them a heated, reddish-orange tinge shrouded by a haze. I swallow hard, trying to remember what I was going to say, but it's Roger's voice that brings me to my senses. "Dude, where'd you go?"

Carter blinks but doesn't take his eyes off me as he answers still winded. "Running."

"You were running the whole time?" I say, exasperated.

"Yeap."

I know Fin has eased the vehicle onto a tree-lined road. "Did you not see us in the alley behind you?" I ask.

"Yeap."

"Why did you keep running?" I huff.

He shrugs and I get the impression by his vacant

expression that he has no idea why he kept running.

"Listen Carter, before we go any farther you need to let go of your penis because you're creeping me out," Fin says.

Surprised, Carter notices his hands cupping his penis. He releases it. He struggles for a few seconds, trying to figure out where to put his empty hands, and settles with clasping them over his knees.

"What happened, Carter?" I ask.

He pinches his nose. "I went to the house—"

"Was it a rotten yet sweet stench?" Roger interrupts.

"Yeap, kind of like a decaying leaf pile. I can't explain why I ran. It just didn't feel right. It felt empty and unfriendly. I felt like something unfavourable was waiting. That was enough for me. The shadows moved and I saw two men, and they chased me."

I scrunch my face. "Did they say anything?"

"Nope."

"But you ran?"

"Yeap, my self-preservation is strong. My penis already doesn't work. I couldn't risk losing the use of another body part or losing Jack completely," he says with complete sincerity and no comprehension of the full situation.

I stifle an eye roll. "But they didn't threaten you?"

"Nope."

"Carter, that makes zero sense." I huff. "What happened to you?" I ask with frustration not meaning at the Ember house, but since our marital separation.

Fin leans over and whispers, "Kori, he isn't who he used to be!"

"Think about Jack, Kori," Carter says as if that's all the explanation in the world. His hands are drifting up his thighs toward his penis, where threads of magic are flashing in and out of sight.

I'd like to have a closer perusal but given the location and the delicate nature of the whole situation, that isn't going to happen. Plus, I know nothing about spells and charms. Wait and talk to Grama Pearle. I reason out that this has been going on for a while, and although he's suffering from it, it isn't going to kill him. Carter, not to mention his penis, seems like a very unlikely place to put a tracker.

Fin flips the radio on and turns it up to muffle our conversation. "Who's Jack?" She's quiet for a second as she works through it. "He calls his penis Jack?"

"Yeap," I mutter. "It's short for Jackhammer." I can't say it without my eyes rotating skyward.

"Yikes, that doesn't sound very pleasant!" Fin gives me a fast assessment.

I pinch my eyes shut and move my head side to side with measured movements. I can feel Fin's eyes on me, so I look at her and push my left eyebrow to my hairline.

"It's just, well, why Jackhammer?" She asks.

I let out a deep breath, "Because I refused to sleep with him if he kept calling it Womb Raider."

Fin gags. I nod in agreement before staring out the window at the darkening sky while Fin transports us to our temporary home.

Chapter 11

When we return, Roger doesn't come in with us. Given how late it is, he retires into the garage for the night. The house is in darkness, but I can't imagine that everyone has gone to bed. The birds barely stir when we enter the sunroom. Carter says nothing, but I can see his eyes drifting, taking in the plants, the birds, and everything else in plain sight.

"Kitchen is this way, Carter," I say, as Fin and I retreat through the doorway.

"Where is the bathroom?" Carter asks.

"I'll show you," Fin says. "I'm going that way anyhow."

Before moving to the dresser for clean clothes, I wait for them to disappear. When I hear a commotion in the kitchen, I'm staring vacantly at the dresser, wondering how having Carter here is going to play out. I race toward the sounds of the ruckus.

The first thing I see is Fin standing with her mouth hanging open. She's rubbing her eyes, looking at something, and repeating the action like she can't believe what she's seeing. Her voice is shaky with disbelief, "I told Carter I was going to bed because I wanted to see what he would do! This isn't what I expected."

The second thing I see is Carter's tight white ass. His body is facing the sunroom, but he's looking at Fin over his shoulder, so he doesn't see Birdie come into the kitchen. His eyes are strange, not lifeless but dazed. I remember his hazed eyes in the vehicle earlier. It has to be connected to the magic loitering on his penis.

"Holy peacock!" Birdie hoots. Her already magnified eyes bulge as she stops with her mouth open to stare at Carter's exposed manhood. Carter whips his head forward. I wish for a second that I could see his face.

Grama Pearle pokes her head over Birdie's shoulder. "Next time you should yell 'small cock' and not 'peacock.' I thought there was something good to see." Grama Pearle's laughter is hearty.

"Ladies," Carter says in greeting, cupping his hands over his genitals.

"What's wrong with it?" Birdie asks Grama Pearle like none of us, including Carter, can hear.

"You know normies and their strange beliefs, in this case, karma and curses? It's how their conditioning works; anything that can't be explained by science or medicine is coincidence, karma . . . He thinks Kori cursed it with karma. The sum of his actions, the affair and hurting Kori, decided the fate of his penis." Grama Pearle explains.

Both of them go silent and tip their heads to the side, judging Carter's penis. "Did she curse it?" Birdie asks.

Grama Pearle wrinkles her nose. "Nope, she wouldn't know how. He must have a medical condition because

Kori couldn't curse it and what other Spellbinder would benefit from this?" She flicks her finger at Carter's genitals. I ignore her and Birdie's continued discussion.

Fin is struggling with a bout of nervous laughter. I drive my elbow into her side. "There's something wrong," I hiss at her. "Magic filaments are visible, real faint on his . . ." I take a drawn-out blink and sigh, "penis."

Fin stops laughing and the grin falls off her face. "I'll speak to Grama Pearle when Carter isn't in the room."

"Thanks, I need to get away from this," I say, flailing my arms at the scene. "I don't think Grama Pearle or Birdie is versed in healing or reversing this kind of magic, but I'm sure they'll know someone who is."

Aware that Alaric has wandered down the hall to this kitchen entrance, I wheel on him, grab his arm, and start walking. My feet keep going, but the top half of my body bends backwards because Alaric isn't moving. I let go, straighten myself, blow out a heavy sigh, and turn to Alaric, who I'm surprised to see is looking at me and not the scene in the kitchen. I draw a steadying breath. "Come on, it's lesson time. Teach me. Anything is better than this." I grab his arm, happy to feel his body move with me.

Noah's voice carries from the kitchen. "Shit, man. Have you no dignity?"

Fin's voice breaks in with her explanation about what she calls, "his magical penis."

I hear Carter grunt, then some shuffling and feet moving. "I'll take him to Roger's tonight," Noah says, and I can picture his face.

Alaric stays wordless as we tromp through the darkness of the backyard. I appreciate the silence and note that this is one of his strengths, composure. There's a power to it that provides calmness. The air smells crisp and clean, refreshing, but I wish that I had a sweater to guard against the fall chill.

When we reach the chairs, he fashions a light orb and hovers it over the table so that a soft glow washes over the immediate area. He gives a nod and disappears. I look for a projection, but I don't see anything. In this lighting, I missed the telltale wisps of magic that have become a helpful learning tool for me.

He blinks into his hulking self in the same place that he disappeared from. I narrow my eyes and hope he understands that I'm not impressed with this game. Just like that, he's gone. Nothing is different, but I drive my hand forward in the air in frustration. Pain lances through my wrist with the unexpected impact and Alaric reappears, holding his side where I made contact. I blink at him and shake my wrists. He's not moving, just vanishing from sight.

"You'll master using this magic before we go to Pearle's store." He moves toward the house, letting the light orb fade out.

"Hey! There's more to this lesson, right?" I hurry to catch up to his stride. "I didn't see the threads?"

He grunts and keeps going. "Think about what you heard, saw, and smelled." I fall behind, shaking my head and feeling an overwhelming tiredness with this day's events, being frustrated regularly is exhausting. Stupid magic. I'm moseying up the deck stairs, thinking about my soft bed buried under mounds of blankets, when Noah crests the stairs behind me.

"Don't start. Don't say a word." I glare as I hold the door open for him.

The corner of Noah's mouth twitches, and mischief burns in his eyes. He's mumbling as the door bangs shut. It sounds like, ". . . of a size that is less than normal."

"Pardon, Noah?"

He clears his throat with a word, "Small."

I shove past him with a shake of my head.

"Did you shrink it, too? I mean, I've been told you cursed it, but you must have hit it with a bit of shrinking potion too, right?" He teases. "I have to make a penis joke when someone just has it hanging out there." He's laughing as I stomp down the stairs, flop into bed with a thump, and I stare into the darkness.

When my eyes ease open, the glow of early morning light bathes the room. I stretch and freeze mid-yawn. A mildly spicy odour with woody yet sweet notes hang in the air. My eyes snap wide as my mind recalls mixed images from what I thought was a dream, but the scent is real. *Belamey?*

Alaric's disappearance last night, could Belamey be using a version of that here? His scent is in the air and not a smell born from lingering dream memories. There's an abundant intake of breath close to my head. I launch myself sideways off the bed, tossing a sound wave orb at the spot where somebody just enjoyed an ample sniff of my hair.

From my defensive crouch, I search the room, to

discover that I'm alone. It's my turn to take a sniff. The air is absent of scent. Rising warily, I survey a second time.

I'm certain that someone was present, and even though it makes no sense, I'm certain that it was Belamey, but I've no idea how he could've been in the safe house or why. I feel like I'm fighting a losing battle when it comes to magic. There's just so much I don't know and trying to play catchup is vexing.

I keep telling myself this is all for Alivia, but my magic was flaring up before she disappeared so I would've had to come back for help with it at some point. Alivia's kidnapping got me here faster. She's helping me even if she didn't know she was doing it.

Noah hollering my name from the top of the stairs gets my attention. I snatch at the studio pants on the end of my bed. The last thing I need is any comments from Noah about me being in the middle of the room wearing my panties and a tank top. I ram one leg into my pants while on the move toward the door, hopping on one foot, trying to get my other leg in.

Noah is nowhere in sight when I enter the kitchen, but Fin is waiting. She rams a travel coffee mug into my hand, and she physically escorts me right through the house. Something has her out of sorts.

"Fin," I grumble.

"We need to get this show on the road before Carter and his penis take over," she says without stopping.

I'm surprised to see birds and no people in the sunroom this morning. "Where's Birdie and Grama Pearle?"

Fin, who is pulling me now instead of pushing me, gives a puff of air out her nose and cups her ear dramatically. "They're teaching Carter to relieve stress. Their explanation is a lifestyle change to help his body. They told me they wanted to create a plausible normie solution for solving the magical problem with his penis. I think Birdie's getting a little sexual excitement out of this." Fin stops talking to allow me to hear voices speaking in soothing tones before I see people.

It's Grama Pearle that I see first. Her fluorescent-orange toenail polish matches her yoga mat. Even Fin stops dead at the scene unfolding. Grama Pearle balances in a one-leg chair pose with her opposite leg crossed over the other at the thigh. She's bent forward at the waist with her arms up and twisted together like a tree branch. Carter is across from her, mirroring her pose and he's red faced with concentration but supple and balanced.

"Good, young man. This pose will increase the blood flow to your pelvis," Birdie instructs from her mat beside Grama Pearle. "Now unwrap and follow what Pearle does."

My eyes wander to Grama Pearle's yellow leggings and brown sports bra. The skin in between her pants and bra is weathered and slightly saggy, but overall, Grama Pearle has a surprisingly fit appearance. Regardless, I feel my eyes pop and my eyebrows travel skyward. I can't imagine wearing that outfit at my age, and here's my grandmother rocking it. Fin takes no notice of me, but I don't miss the twinkle of mischief dancing in her eyes.

"I think we should get him to do head-to-knee pose and bow pose because they both help with blood flow to the groin," Grama Pearle explains to Birdie.

Birdie comes into my line of sight wearing a similar outfit to Grama Pearle's except that hers is green and gives the impression of a withered pickle. "He should hold a pose like camel or bridge," Birdie says, eyeing Carter's boxer shorts.

Grama Pearle casts a disapproving glance at Birdie, who snubs her. Grama Pearle clears her throat and continues. "We're going to flow through two more poses and then end in Shavasana. Birdie and I don't like to call it corpse pose for obvious reasons."

Grama Pearle explains to Carter the importance of finding hobbies to help alleviate stress. I can feel my eye twitching when she explains the various ways stress could affect his body, particularly his penis. I pound back a deep mouthful of my coffee, ignoring the burn as it slides down my throat.

"Have fun." I shove my mug at Fin, and I shift into my hummingbird to avoid notice from Carter when I flee this yoga display. I hover in front of Fin, sweeping my wings in figure eights, backwards and forwards, pushing the air downwards. She raises her eyebrows and smirks before I accelerate away.

I'm not surprised to see Alaric stretched out in a lawn chair, eyes closed. There's no doubt in my mind that he's heard or somehow sensed my approach. I transform and flop my human self into an empty chair. Alaric slits his eyes open and glances at me out of the corners before closing them again and resuming his rhythmic breathing.

After a few breaths, I interrupt. "I know there's more to last night's lesson. When you vanished, I couldn't see, smell, or hear you. A useful tool for covertness. So, how is it done?" I take my turn sitting still and just breathing, I try not to think about the possibility of Belamey being in the bedroom earlier. I choose not to mention it to Alaric or anybody else because I have no evidence it was real, and if it was there was no direct threat to it.

Just like before, Alaric gives a low-key head bob and disappears. I examine the area where he was because I'm sure there's a clue there. I see the thinnest wisps of magic, but they're so delicate that I'm uncertain if it's magic or just the sunlight catching scattered air particles.

This time I use tiny feelers of magic to study the wisps, a magical exploration that I wouldn't be able to do if I couldn't see the strands of magic. Alaric is in the same spot that he disappeared from. He reappears and on his face is what passes for satisfaction.

"What is this?" I ignore the look, knowing it'll fade once I ask questions and attempt to copy his crisscross of magic.

Alaric is watching me. "Masking Yourself, Magic 101."

I snort like a bull, but otherwise, let the challenge go. In silence, I acknowledge the role I played in my lack of magic mastery. "Masking? Like hiding?"

He gives one distinct head bob. "Watch."

I reposition in my seat and lean in close, focusing. He

vanishes at a pace that allows me to view the path his magic takes. It's a complex meshwork that hides his physical body, his sound, smell, and, to some extent, his magic.

"There's a sparkle to it that suggests the magic is exploiting the light and air to shield you from view," I whisper in awe. I can tell from the wisps that you can choose to mask everything or just certain aspects, but given that it's for a furtive purpose, why would you not hide it all? This makes me question even more if I'm going crazy or if Belamey was in the bedroom.

I hear the chair creak and although I can't see Alaric, I'm aware he's resumed his stretched-out position in the chair. "Now you."

This design is a bit more complex than the others I've tried. I'm surprised by how easily it comes to me, and I'm also surprised that Alaric hasn't left. "You feeling okay, big man?" I smirk. He reappears in the chair and just stares at me. Eyes closed, I suck a deep breath. "I mean, 'are you feeling okay?' because you never loiter when I practice."

He stands. "Let's play a game."

"A game!" My voice squeaks out, high with surprise. "You play games?"

Alaric grunts his amusement and walks away, expecting me to follow. With clenched hands and a shrug, I stomp through the grass after him. He marches straight into the big garage and closes all the doors. He locks eyes with me. "Find me," he challenges as he flicks the lights off.

The garage is blanketed in a darkness so thick that

it doesn't matter if I try to complete this activity with my eyes open or closed. I can't see a physical person or the wisps of magic he's using to hide himself.

Before we plunge into darkness, I see Alaric vanish. I grope the darkness with my hands, but he's moved from the spot where I saw him last. I rub my eyes as if that will restore light to my retina. Then I reach out with magic to probe the area. Without warning, he sinks a fist into my stomach, expelling the air out of me.

"I can see you," says Alaric's disembodied voice, challenging me to mask myself.

"Oh, so that's the game we're playing?" I've caught my breath, changed my position, taken a defensive stance, and masked myself.

"No game. It's combat." He's too close to me. I don't have time to brace before he bowls me over.

I don't know how long we score points for tactical attacks against each other in the dark, but I'm enjoying this learning experience too much to discern anything else. The garage door gives a groan. The mechanic grind of it lifting off the ground acts as a buzzer, ending our wartime. I dash out past Noah and Fin, holding onto my invisibility.

"Where's Kori?" Fin asks.

I've gained the deck stairs when I let my physical self reappear. Alaric flicks his finger in my direction, and both Noah and Fin turn. I wave and pop the screen door open.

"New trick?" Noah asks. I envision Alaric's silent nod. "Nice," Noah says.

"That a girl," Fin chimes in.

I waste no time hitting the shower. The telltale aftereffects of fighting are already manifesting in my body. Tomorrow I'm going to be stiff. After my hot shower, I slide into studio pants and a sweater and seat myself at the dinner table with my legs bent up and my feet resting on the adjacent seat.

I'm relieved to not see Carter anywhere. Birdie, flitting between the sunroom and kitchen, could've spared telling me that Carter was resting his body after all the groin blood flow exercises today. It didn't help to dispel the magic attached to him, but Birdie is attempting to contact a friend of hers who might be able to help.

We're on the move with barely a shred of morning light. My head feels too heavy for my neck and the one thing that keeps it from thumping down onto my chest is a whiff of coffee. Somebody stuffs a coffee into my hand and I'm half aware of the fact that I've been shoved into the hearse again. If anybody is bothering to watch me, I resemble a human bobblehead because my head continues to dip and snap.

"What did you do to her yesterday, Alaric?" Fin asks from the rear door of the hearse. "I'm alarmed."

Alaric, of course, says nothing, but he has an Alaric version of satisfaction pasted on his face. Fin closes

Alaric, Noah, and I in the back and she's driving within seconds.

I yawn and don't cover it, which is a big mistake on my part because Noah seizes the opportunity, snatches my travel mug and pours warm coffee into my gaping jaws. I sputter, cough, and choke it down.

"Come on, Kori. You got a lot ahead of you here," Noah says.

I slit my eyes. "Yes, I know, and I'm mentally preparing." I purse my lips at him before slamming my eyes shut while sucking back the rest of my coffee. I make a half-assed attempt to get comfortable and ignore everyone for the rest of the drive.

For me, the drive is going quick. It's with a deep sigh that I maneuver out of the hearse when we arrive. Roger has opened the interment niche and I'm staring at it in disbelief because Alaric has already wedged his hulk-like self through the hole and disappeared. An amazing feat of speed to cram himself through so fast; the hole is about twenty-two inches wide and eight inches high.

I've no desire to army crawl through the niche to the stairs that lead farther underground. Eyes closed, I tip my head to the sun, which is now cresting the skyline.

"I recommend you hit the opening for the stairs feet first," Noah breathes in my ear.

I glare at him in response, and I'm satisfied when he pulls his shoulders toward his ears and steps away. "Just a suggestion, that's all. Up to you, you're going. I'm not."

With a sigh of resignation, I drop to the ground, facing the open niche, and stifle a moan. My body feels like a train hit it. I'm so sore that just the awareness of having a body is painful. I disregard Noah's advise to go in reverse. I set my mind on Alivia and start dragging my reluctant parts forward with my arms. Alaric is out of sight, already down the spiral stairs. The ground under me is unforgiving and my arm muscles are screaming with the effort of pulling my body like dead weight. I hear the niche being sealed up behind me. Alone, I try not to panic in the darkness of the burial chamber.

There's a faint glow in the ground that shows where the hole to the stairs is located, and I wiggle and squirm until I'm at the edge. I grip the sides of the opening to carry my body over the hole into the space on the other side of the stairs so that I'm able to aim my feet at the entry point. It's uncomfortable and in hindsight Noah's advice would've been worth taking.

The air changes as I start down the stairs, taking on a damp basement staleness that I tell myself isn't the stink of death. Alaric is standing in the room below, watching my descent. I brush the dirt off my body, straighten myself, and blink at him, unimpressed. His lips twitch. I squint at him. "What?"

His hand snaps out and flings something from my shoulder that makes a soft crunch with its impact against the wall. I shudder. "Joys of crawling through a tomb, I guess. Can we get on with this, please?" I mumble.

Alaric's strong fingers work themselves into finger groves in the wall and he gives a forceful pull. A sharp sound echoes and fades. Then the door grinds open to allow us entry. There's no reason to think the tunnel has been compromised by foes. I roll my neck to crack it, spark a light orb in my hand, and slide sideways into the tunnel in front of Alaric. I brace for the silent, shuffling gait that awaits me.

Everything is as I remember it, but this time I can see the uneven surface of the wall illuminated by my orb. The cold, rough surface of the wall is made up of rock and dirt. It's a dug out tunnel and not a man-made bricked structure. Certain sections are grainy and crumbling, suggesting this might not be the safest passage into the Ember house. There's a dampness that works its way into my bones with each tedious movement, and I'm shocked to arrive at the end of the tunnel in what feels like no time. I see the latch to release the concealed door and I pull it.

I mask myself and slip into the storage room of Grama Pearle's store. The familiar lavender perfume is welcoming, but the house is eerily silent. My cop instinct activates, and I sense we aren't alone. I send out soft feelers of magic to test the immediate area and then push them out farther into the depths of the store while Alaric pushes the door so that it's almost closed. "Nothing," I whisper as I allow myself to appear.

I feel the weight of his hand on my shoulder, and I blink out of sight. With caution, we move forward, joined hand to shoulder. The store is empty. I'm relieved to see minimal damage from my stone storm the last time we were here.

Alaric releases my shoulder to double check we're alone in the store and I glide off in search of the stone holder. Without question, it'll be on the wooden bookshelf on the other side of the store because that shelf was Alivia's and my favourite to play on as children.

I reach the bookshelf and consider the options. I disregard the four cupboards and the two drawers. Alivia's message is meant specifically for me, so I disregard the bottom three shelves because they're to easy to access. I head to the attached ladder, remembering the hours we spent playing on it as kids. The fifth shelf is where Grama Pearle kept all the cool stuff.

The ladder slides over with ease until I spy the glass jar that holds the bloodweed. I pop the jar open and drop my hand in. The jar is a smoky glass and can't be seen through. I move my hand with my eyes closed. My fingers knock a hard object inside the jar, creating a clinking noise as I accidentally bounce it off the glass. It booms through the quiet space. If anybody has amplified their hearing, I've just made enough noise that someone will want to check on it.

I grab the necklace, pull it out, and ram it into my pocket. I lock the jar, slide down the ladder, and I'm almost to the storage room when a voice resonates upstairs. "They're in the basement!"

Alaric blinks into sight at the store exit and hollers with a rage that freezes me in place. "Prepare to die, Nekane!"

Alaric has the presence of mind to fix me with a glare. He gives me a commanding gesture to leave now and then he re-masks himself to go after Nekane.

There's a thunder of footsteps on the stairs and a taint of damp decay overpowers the lavender. Sounds of battle erupt on the floor somewhere above me. Alaric has found Nekane. The footsteps change directions and start up the stairs to protect Nekane. I run to the stairs myself, dropping my masking so Alaric will be aware of me when I get up there, but I barely take a couple of steps before powerful arms and a net of magic grab me. I mask myself, but it's too late.

"I knew you were here, Kori Ember. You can't hide from me." The intoxicating smell of Belamey fills my nostrils. He takes a deep inhale of the top of my head even though my masking is blocking my scent. He sighs. "Forgive me for physically restraining you, Kori. You attacked me last time, so this is for my safety."

His body presses against my back. I can feel his arms, but when I look down, it appears as if he's hugging air. He isn't trying to hide himself like I am. I can see his arms holding my invisible body. Body heat radiates off him in waves that make me dizzy. I know I should feel threatened, but I don't. My body responds to his without my permission. He laughs seductively in my ear and bites my earlobe. "You're so beautiful when you're sleeping."

My blood runs cold with his admission that he was in my bedroom when I woke yesterday. Anger surges through me. "That's not okay, and neither is restraining me," I say, assessing my options. Unless he lowers his head, head-butting him will be ineffective. My head would just bounce off his chest. I stomp my foot down on his toes.

Belamey grunts and releases his hold on me. Wide-eyed, I see Alaric, having deserted his attack on Nekane, moving like a charging bull from the stairs toward us. I drop my mask, since it isn't doing anything.

Because I can already see magic attacking Belamey, I satisfy myself by shooting a death stare at him. Alaric has wrapped him in webs of magic. As I'm making note of Alaric's weave, he uses those webs to fling Belamey hard against the wall. Another grunt leaves Belamey's body as he slumps slightly, but he flashes a wicked grin at me before Alaric grabs me and yanks me into the storage room.

"Kori, she's alive. Your sister is alive. Pretty thing, not like you, of course, but pretty none the less," Belamey taunts.

"Is that a threat?" I spin and head back, intending to beat Alivia's location out of him, but Alaric fastens my arm in an iron grip, drags me to the doorway, and stuffs me through.

"There's too many of them upstairs, Kori. We wouldn't have time to forcefully extract Alivia's location from him. He could be baiting us so we get captured too." Alaric pushes his body in after me, thwarting any hope I had of reaching Belamey. He strains to pull the door closed. This time, he does something from our side. It sounds like he dropped a series of stone latches into place.

I don't move. Alaric presses into my side, ready to go, but I can't yet. "He knew I was there. Belamey, I mean. He knew! How?" Faint sounds of a search penetrate the wall. There are shouts and the crashing of shelves, but

I stand firm, staring at Alaric even when there's a hammer smashing off the brick.

"He must have an intimate connection with you. Now move!" he says, pushing sideways into me.

I don't ask anything else, too dumbfounded and put off by the intimate connection comment. Besides the smell of Belamey, I also smelt the offensive scent of the other things pursuing us. I call up a soft glow orb and start moving toward the crypt that leads to the outside world.

We move in silence, each of us lost in our own thoughts. When we reach the end, I swivel my head toward Alaric. "What happened upstairs?" I search his face for a sign. He gives me an empty stare. "With Nekane?" I ask.

"I wounded him, nothing more . . . this time." He's so quiet that I almost don't hear.

I'm unresponsive but continue staring at him.

Alaric thrusts his chin at the door. "You're the mission this time; keep you safe and prepare you for the Cleansing. Nekane will be my final business."

Not for the first time, I find myself wondering about this man and all the unknowns he embodies. Releasing the latch, I move to the stairs and start my climb. I lie on the ground in the darkness, hoping that I don't have to wait for someone to open the niche. I'm aware of Alaric's breathing behind me, but there isn't enough room for us both to be stretched out. We pause in silence. Before long, I hear tires on the pavement.

I slide through the niche into the deepening twilight and come face to face with Roger. He's lying in the grass on his stomach a few feet from the open hole, waiting for us. "Roger? Where is everyone else?"

Roger's features tighten with displeasure.

Not a good sign, so I interrupt before he can say anything. "Let's pretend I didn't ask." I stuff myself into the back of the hearse while Roger and Alaric close the niche. I'm relieved when Alaric climbs into the front with Roger because I need time alone with my thoughts.

Chapter 12

It's late evening when we get to the house. Sullen, Roger stomps off to his apartment without a goodnight. I glance at Alaric, hoping for an explanation, but he just shrugs and marches into the night. With a slight head shake, I trudge toward the house.

The first thing I notice when I enter is the overwhelming smell of coffee. Sounds of hiccups and stifled giggles drift out from the kitchen, followed by a sigh of resignation.

Noah is leaning on the counter, stone-faced, and he doesn't acknowledge that I've entered the room. I follow his gaze. Fin is squinting at her empty hand, which is positioned out to the side like it's holding a glass. Her other hand has a mug in it, with steam clouds billowing out. She's hiccupping wildly, and brown liquid is sloshing out of her mug.

I cross the room in four strides and take the mug from her. Fin just goes on hiccupping and staring at her other empty hand. I make the mistake of tipping the mug to my lips. The taste is so bitter that I choke and spit it into the mug.

I side-eye Noah as I dump it into the sink. "Did you

triple brew this coffee?"

Before he can answer, Fin realizes that I'm present. She pretends to set a glass on the counter before launching herself at me and locking me in a crushing hug.

"Fin? Honey, are you okay?" I ask, as I wiggle free.

"Watch this, Kori." Fin thrusts one hand out in front of her and waves her other hand over it yelling "abracadabra" and she finishes with a wild flourish of her fingers. She's smiling at her hand, which remains void of objects. She tips a pretend cup up to her mouth and takes a big swallow.

I keep my eyes fastened on her and paste a smile on my face. With limited movement of my lips, I mumble, "Um, Noah, how much has she drunk that she's convinced herself she's doing magic? And why was she drinking?"

Noah removes himself from his leaning perch on the counter. He yawns. "Before we left for the cemetery, Fin convinced Pearle to meet her at The Fermented Grape after dropping you and Alaric off. Roger brought Pearle in the Willys, which he left for me to bring them home and he took the hearse. I don't know what he did after that."

Noah yawns again. "They're a handful when they're sober, but put a little liquor in the pair of them . . . They shouldn't be alone together. They fuel one another's mischievousness. Their 'plan'," he says, making air quotes, "was to try and gather more information. Fin's argument was basically that they needed to contribute to today's efforts to find Alivia. And since Pearle and

Birdie got particulars the first time—"

"Did they?"

Noah's eyes go wide and he pulls his lips tight. "They drank like fish."

"But I thought The Fermented Grape was Spellbinders only." I wheel on him.

He cuts me off with a hand to my face. "Pearle can bring in anyone she wants and I babysat her and Fin! By babysat, I mean I kept them from getting into too much mischief while they were drinking."

I can't ask my next question with my eyes open. "Is Grama Pearle in the plants with Birdie?"

This gets a chuckle from Noah. "Nope. Birdie took Carter to some special Spellbinder doctor friend to have his penis magically inspected."

Shocked, I'm gaping at Noah, but he's blatantly ignoring me. The corners of his mouth are twitching, but he keeps talking. "Because of your ability to see threads of magic, we know all of Carter's strange behaviours connect to the charm," Noah screws his face up, ". . . hex? Hex is a more fitting word, but whatever it is that's on his genitals. Why his genitals? Anyway, none of us know anything about this kind of magic, so we can't help him. There isn't a set anti-hexing fix all. However, we speculate the hex happened the night of the incident that cost Carter his job."

I blow out a sigh. "Why?"

Noah shrugs. "The timing all fits."

"Abracadabra!" Fin yells. She's staring at her hand, still containing nothing.

"Noah?" I ask without taking my wide eyes off Fin.

"Pearle is in bed, asleep. Fin is all yours. I'm going to bed. Keep an eye on her. She has plans to hitchhike to The Society of the Blood Wind house to do who knows what. I made the mistake of taking my eyes off her for a second and she was out the door at lightning speed. I had to chase her down the driveway and carry her back. It was like carrying a flailing orangutan with coordination problems."

He looks at Fin. "Lunatic," he says to her and I hear the humour in his voice. His face disappears behind an enormous yawn. "I recommend you keep her practicing her fake magic so she doesn't run on you." He stuffs a hot cup of triple brew into my hand and takes his leave.

"Abracadabra!" Fin yells.

"Fin?"

"Hang on, Kori." Fin slurs. "You need to try one of these drinks that Grama Pearle taught me to make." With her right hand moving over her left, she just keeps saying "abracadabra." I understand what Noah was doing when I came into the kitchen. I sigh and take a seat at the table.

"Abracadabra," Fin enunciates. Her hand, of course, remains empty. With her drunken eyes on me, her bottom lip pushes out and curves. "There isn't anything in my hand, Kori."

"Ah, honey, here." I push the coffee mug into her grasp. She grips it but she doesn't move, so I hold my hand over hers. I grab her other hand and I guide it in a series of wild movements over the coffee mug. "Say it with me, Fin."

While moving her hand together, we whisper

"abracadabra," and I direct her into a chair at the table. "Taste that now," I tell her gently.

She looks at me with big doe eyes, then at her mug, and then at me.

"Go ahead," I encourage.

Heedful, she raises it to her lips and takes a generous sip. She pauses and downs the contents of the mug. Her mouth puckers and she flicks her tongue out and in. "It doesn't taste the same, but let's do it again."

"Okay, honey." I slip the mug from her hand and cross the kitchen to refill it with Noah's triple brew. When I return, Fin has folded her arms on the table and laid her head on them. She's snoring.

"That's going to hurt tomorrow," I whisper unwilling to risk waking her and not being able to get her to settle again. I turn off the light and sneak from the room.

I peek my eyes open. Noah's sleep breathing fills the space with a ragged echo that's almost a snore. The unmoving lump in Fin's bed signals she must have crept downstairs at some point. Alaric's bed is empty, but rumpled like he slept sometime during the night. With a dramatic stretch that reminds me my body still aches, I oust myself from bed to go find him.

Armed with a hot coffee, I stride barefoot through the chilly morning grass. Alaric sits in a chair, looking off into the field. I lower myself into the seat, and cross my legs so that my feet tuck under me, hidden from the crisp morning air. I sip my coffee in silence. When I can see the bottom of the inside of my mug, I set it on the grass and readjust my position.

"I'm sorry, Alaric," I say, with my eyes on the side of his face.

He turns his head, saying nothing, assessing my sincerity. This is the first he's moved since I sat down. With no words, he nods acceptance and resumes staring at the fields.

I breathe deep through my nose, and release the air from my lungs. "Alaric, I don't know what happened, but I can read the pain that was re-awakened after your encounter with Nekane yesterday. I want to help you. Is there a way I can do that? Maybe you need to talk about it . . ." I let the sentence fade on my tongue, knowing Alaric is a man of few words.

The silence stretches on, but I hold my place, hoping that my company is enough. I'm startled when he breaks the silence. "It's better if you see." He closes his eyes and dips his head. "It's easier for me that way."

I stutter as the meaning of his words sink in. "Alaric, I . . . I . . ."

He lifts his head fixing me in a steady stare. "I have remained isolated too long." He bows his head.

I know enough about this man to know what this act of trust means and what it'll do to our friendship if I decline. My mouth has gone dry, and my palms are sweaty. I haven't tried using any of my Memory Keeper skills yet, but I recall Grama Pearle telling me it's a skill like breathing. Unfortunately, where magic is concerned, I feel like I'm learning to breathe water; it's scary and unnatural.

A skill like breathing, I repeat in my head as I wipe my hands on the fabric of my pants and slide into the grass on my knees. I glide my fingers over Alaric's closed eyes, like I remember Grama Pearle doing to me. "Breathe," I whisper, without being sure if the command is for me or Alaric.

Warmth grows between my hands and Alaric's head. As the hotness radiates up my arms into my body, I wonder how the relay of heat feels for him. There isn't a white light burning into my vision like when Grama Pearle transferred her memories to me. There's a lack of colour; it's ashen.

I feel a barrier that isn't sure it wants to allow me to see the other side of its shadow. Then I'm falling through it and images tumble past my mind's eye. They're just rapidly moving blurs and I feel scared until I realize the blur of images are conveying a feeling of happiness.

This is what Alaric desires, I see: happiness. It's his happiness and it's associated with the three most-valued people in his life: his parents, and his partner Soraya. The Alaric I've come to know is serious, reserved, and recluse—a lone wolf. But this suggests he was a man who was genial, open, and not alone.

Without being aware of what I've done, the images come into focus, but the noises grow clear first. It's sounds of battle, not a typical one, but magical attacks with a mix of hand-to-hand combat. The environment becomes clear and sharp.

The house is familiar from the memories that Grama Pearle shared with me, but I don't know whose house it is; a horrible fight rages. The Society of the Blood Wind has launched a surprise attack. I don't have time to give it a second thought because the yelling is louder. I have a front-row seat to an intense clash.

An aged version of Alaric, clearly his father, is fighting three men. They strike in rapid succession, coming in and out from multiple sides in varying patterns, but Alaric's father is physically conditioned to outlast his opponents; he's composed, fluid in his movements, observant, and self-assured.

Soon the three attackers become two and they revamp tactics to pounce as one unit. Alaric's father holds his ground. It's like a scene from an action movie and I'm so enthralled that an ear-piercing scream scares me to the core.

Alaric's memory tells me it's his mother. I watch as her screech distracts Alaric's father for one fatal second and he falls too, with his hand stretched out toward the corpse of his beloved wife.

Alaric is trying to fight his way to them across a large room. He's back-to-back with a stunning woman and they're fighting for their lives. Her black braid swings with the movements of her body. Her skin glistens with a sheen of perspiration and their bodies move as one. Without warning, the foot soldiers for The Society of the Blood Wind withdraw. Alaric and Soraya move in a circle, keeping their backs together as they survey their surroundings.

There's movement to the side of Alaric's vision, but his eyes lock on the bodies of his dead parents. He doesn't see Nekane or the death orb in his hand. Alaric doesn't see Nekane's hand prepare to throw the orb marked to end his life.

But Soraya sees it.

With a scream professing her love, Soraya dives in front of the orb. Her body explodes into millions of misty, sparkling particles just as Alaric turns to respond to her call. Nekane disappears in a puff of smoke, like an evil magician, his haunting laugh echoing in the room. It's clear that Nekane has assumed in his arrogance that he couldn't miss his intended mark.

It's now just the darkness of my closed eyes I'm aware of and the feel of Alaric's head resting in my out-stretched hands. We're locked in what my whole body is acknowledging as an intimate moment, and my knees feel stiff and chilly in the ground where they're nestled.

The sun pelts down on us. Opening my eyes, I nod my head in acceptance of this enlightenment about Alaric. I'm conscious of his memories, which are prominent in my mind. I drop my hands from his head. "Store them," he says, as if he can see my thoughts.

I screw my face into one of confusion. I'm not orientated enough to formulate a response to Alaric's statement. I feel like my internal compass is spiralling and can't lock onto any specified position.

"My memories, Kori. You have to store them."

"Grama Pearle said she stores other people's memories like her own. This doesn't feel like my own. It feels planted in my head. It isn't mine and doesn't belong." I shake my head like it'll somehow dislodge the discomfort.

Alaric's big hands close on the sides of my head and he waits until I focus on his face before he talks. "She stores them similarly, but the process is different. Soraya," his voice cracks. He tries speaking again. "Soraya had Memory Keeper skills and she explained things about it. Try imagining a container. Place the memories in and put it somewhere in your head for later."

Alaric says nothing else, but he continues to hold my head. I swallow and close my eyes. I imagine a solid container and I'm surprised when a tempered glass box appears. The glass pattern is reminiscent of rolling flames and it's obscure, not quite opaque, but it'll keep the contents mysterious. I imagine etching a warrior's arrow into the side and I transfer Alaric's memories into the box before sliding the tempered glass lid over it.

The process has created a sense of relief, but I can feel that it isn't quite complete. I take the box and move it through my mind to a shelf and I dismiss it. The result is instant; his memories aren't infringing on me, but I'm left with a memory of a special moment shared between us.

I open my eyes. "How does it feel to you?" I ask, out of curiosity. Alaric releases my head and reclines into his seat without answering. Deep horror rises in me. "They aren't gone from you, are they?"

Alaric closes his eyes. "No, they're not gone," he says quietly. "They're alive in a way that suggests I have honoured them by sharing their story with you. They're close in a way I haven't felt for a while."

I wait, but Alaric says no more. A desire to be alone emanates from him. I stand, pausing to view him with a new understanding. He's the last of the Alden family line, a family line believed to have been wiped out years ago.

Mouz was also the last of his family line. How many Spellbinder families have been obliterated? Are there families that remain in hiding? There's so much I don't know about Spellbinders' history. I pick up my empty coffee mug and turn toward the safe house. I position my hand on Alaric's burly shoulder to convey comfort before I set off through the grass.

The birds chirp their greeting to me when I stroll through the door. Their welcoming song makes me smile and lightens the emotional load from Alaric's memories. I set my coffee mug down and shift into my hummingbird form to chirp a greeting in response. I zoom through the room and complete a flying transformation to my human self, aiming for the kitchen door. My shift leaves my feet moving pell-mell and I'm trying to catch my balance before I ram the table. My abrupt entry causes Fin to scrunch up her face and cover her ears while Noah braces the table for impact.

Thankfully, I don't bang into anything. I'm able to turn myself and aim for the far counter where the coffee pot is. I grab it up and move to sit down. Noah is smirking at Fin and Fin is holding her head with her eyes closed. Her hangover must be a painful one. She makes no move to acknowledge me. I fill myself a new coffee cup and I top theirs up.

"Advil, Fin?"

"I gave her some a few minutes ago." Noah gestures at the pill bottle beside Fin's elbow.

"Grama Pearle still sleeping?" I ask.

"She went out." Noah's smile is still smug and aimed at Fin.

The timer on the oven goes off and Fin's eyes crinkle tighter. Noah laughs at her and moves to the oven. I watch as he places a big pizza on the table. "Best hangover food. It's hot, cheesy, and saucy, just like Fin was last night."

Fin grabs the pill bottle and launches it at Noah, who was expecting the throw. He dodges it with ease.

In between bites, Noah bombards me with questions about mine and Alaric's visit to Grama Pearle's store. Fin listens, chews, and by the time we start talking about the holder, the meds, caffeine, and pizza are kicking in; she's regained some regular Fin energy.

"Wait," she rasps at us. "What do you mean, a connection between you and Belamey? This sounds erotic," she says with a bit too much excitement. She cringes and rubs her temples.

Noah swipes his hand over his face and closes his eyes.

"What?" I ask him. "Does this mean anything to you? I mean, can you explain what Alaric means by connection?"

He glares at me. "Nope, but Belamey Adelgrief is the last person anyone should have a connection with."

I feel my eyes go big in my head and my blinking

momentarily stops as I return his glare. "Leave it to you to suggest that this is my fault!"

"I think I'm going to be sick." Fin runs from the room, leaving me and Noah stunned.

Before we revisit what I'm sure is going to be an all-out argument, the birds in the sunroom sing a welcoming greeting, meaning either Grama Pearle or Birdie has returned. I use it as an opportunity to leave Noah sitting there with the words stuck in his mouth.

I'm happy to see Grama Pearle when I enter the sunroom. "You're better off than Fin," I chuckle.

Grama Pearle smiles and laughs. "Learned my lesson the night Birdie and I went to The Fermented Grape. How did things go, Kori?"

Noah slides into the room, interrupting Grama Pearle. Snail-like, Fin follows.

"Wait, Kori," Grama Pearle moves toward Fin. I can't see what she pulls out of her pocket, but I see Fin has no problem chewing it up and swallowing it. Within seconds, colour blooms on Fin's skin and all the signs of hangover that were clinging to her fall away. "Better," Grama Pearle says to Fin as a statement of fact and not a question. Then Grama Pearle turns to me. "Did you find it?"

I reach into my pocket and pull out the holder. "Alivia didn't leave another clue, though." My voice is so soft that I don't know why I say the words aloud, "I'm desperate to know you're okay, Alivia."

I'm aware of the weightlessness of the chain. Each silver link has a unique oval shape that's wavy and crinkly. I dangle the necklace on two fingers. A link lock secures the holder to the necklace. Customized, the holder itself is like a spiral gemstone cage. The top and bottom of each stone fit into the bowl-shaped wire wrap to nestle back to back, with one stone marginally above the other.

"You haven't put the stones in it yet, Kori?" Fin whispers.

"Well, things were a bit wild at the Ember house, then you were drunk as a skunk last night, and if I'm being honest, I feel intimidated enough to not want to fit the stones into the holder without—"

"Your support team," Fin finishes for me, with a slight wince as the hangover cure still works its magic. I was thinking of Grama Pearle, but Fin looks so happy with her assertion that I don't correct her.

I'm not sure what to say as we stare at the necklace. Fin breaks the spell with a dramatic throat clear that moments before would have made her own head pound. "Can we secure the super dangerous Ember stone in the amulet holder, please?"

I scan the sunroom. Everyone is eyeing me with a constrained caution, and I wish that Alaric had come in from the field to toss his ice dome over us. I rather not cause an accidental disaster just trying to fit the stones into the holder. I attempt a smile, but there's no strength behind it. So, before the quivering at the corners of my mouth becomes apparent, I let it slip off my face. I set the necklace down and reach for the zipper of my studio pants pocket. I nod at Fin. "The enchanted dresser gave me a zipper. That dresser is forever answering our needs."

"Stop stalling, Kori." Fin says.

Remembering what happened last time I moved the stones quickly, I drag my hand out of my pocket, conscious that I've no idea how to work them. I move to set them on the table when a jarring whistle fills the air. Simultaneously, I note that Fin drops into a crouch with her eyes squeezed shut and her hands clasped over her ears. A deep-red liquid is visible between the cracks of her fingers.

Noah is struggling with invisible ropes and his howls of pain overpower the chaos as the ropes sear his skin. He can't get his protective shield to form under them. I'm not sure if he can access his magic at all. Marks on his skin suggest rope abrasion and heat blisters.

A medium-sized bird with a curved dark bill is swooping toward me. I'm grateful that Noah drilled Kieran and Kyson's bird details into my head. There's no doubt an angry thrasher bird is in our midst.

Without thought, I mask myself and dive to the side in time for the wiry, bald man to plow through the spot where I was standing. I see the tangled ends of a magical net sprawl uselessly on the plants. I can feel Grama Pearle is in the room, but she's nowhere to be seen, which makes me happy because the twins are ruthless and magically strong.

The Ember stone is in my pocket, but in my haste to avoid Kieran, I left the necklace on the table. He'll have heard our whole conversation; he's after the necklace and the stones.

Kieran lunges for the necklace. An air orb blasts him off course. I realize that Grama Pearle isn't able to attack with anything stronger because she has no idea where I am, but by throwing her orb, she has given away her position. She explodes up into her full five-foot-one height and flings another air orb that shoves the necklace hard to the side, causing it to zoom off the table and out of sight.

I drop my masking so Grama Pearle can see me, and I throw a bubble orb at Kieran. Bubble isn't a representative word for it because although it looks like a thin sphere of liquid, the inside is impossible to escape. This weave of magic is designed to allow things from the outside to move in. So, I know once I catch Kieran, I can keep him inside, but I can reach in and access him for the purposes of stimulating pressure points to get him to talk.

My blood is racing. If I capture this minion of The Society of the Blood Wind, maybe he can be forced to share Alivia's location, or maybe Nekane's hero could be traded for her.

Kieran is waiting for me and uses a braiding of magic to take over my bubble and imprison me with it. I bang futilely against the inside with my human and magical strength, but it's no use. Not even sound penetrates out. I watch in horror as he throws an orb at Grama Pearle that launches her hard into the plants.

Kieran turns to me. The smirk on his face doesn't reach his lifeless eyes, but his intent is clear. I catch a flash of silver as a filleting knife appears in his hand. With his other hand, he tosses a frayed magic rope toward my bubble prison and they connect like magnets. There's nothing I can do as he pulls me closer.

He presses his body against the bubble, narrows his eyes, and cracks his neck left and then right. His eyes find mine and we stare at each other with mutual hatred. My hatred stems from revulsion about the pure evil he represents. His hatred is ingrained in him, it constitutes who he is.

His voice comes out low and rough. "We're going to have fun before I hand you over, just you and me." He pauses and closes his eyes. "I'm going to take you to the point that your fire is about to go out," he whispers with a sound like a sigh.

There's a sharp pain in my side and my eyes go wide with the realization that with nimble proficiency he has run his filleting knife through the side of my abdomen. His eyes open and he watches my face as he withdraws the knife from my flesh and out through the bubble. I clutch at the wound and double over, fighting the pain. My blood feels warms and slippery.

"That's a good girl," he hisses. "Don't worry, I know what I'm doing. No liver damage. No rupture to the lungs. I'm knowledgeable about how deep to insert my knife and all the fun places to slide it." His body shudders as if his own words have brought him to climax. "Let's go somewhere private to finish our game."

There's an explosion of red. My fading thoughts think a can of red paint has been thrown at me. Then the bubble is gone. I hit the floor with a jolt that increases my pain. I curl into a ball. My stomach churns, and I retch violently, the sour smell warring with the coppery scent of blood.

Through blurred vision, I see pieces of Kieran. His

body exploded, which explains what I thought was red paint, but how? Telling myself I'm wrong, I blink several times, trying to put him back together, but it's Alaric that comes into focus.

He's moving toward the chunks of Kieran. I can hear Noah. His voice sounds distant, even though I can see him in front of me. His face crinkles with concern. "Alaric, don't do it!"

I blink, trying to make sense of Kieran's head without a body. Alaric positions his hands over it. His thumbs move toward the eyes. Noah and Alaric exchange a glance, suggesting Alaric isn't planning to return from this journey as the man he was when it started. Then I lose consciousness.

Chapter 13

I come awake to the sounds of hushed whispers. I lie with my eyes closed and run a mental scan of my body. My side has a dull ache and an unfamiliar tingling that tickles like hundreds of insect feet are moving over my skin and inside my flesh.

Bolting into a sitting position, I rip my shirt up and swipe at my mid-section, but my hand doesn't encounter anything other than my skin. I adjust my focus and instead of insects, I see faint stitches of green magic working to heal my stab wound. *Mojo, a magic spell for healing.* As I accept my heritage, small things I've blocked out return and will continue to return. As is the case with the mojo, I recall that the green stitches incorporate into tissue and organs to repair damage.

I blow out a loud breath. They've moved me to the living room. The sunroom sliding door is closed and a clear, sparkling barrier of magic covers it. The whispers have stopped, and I take stock of everyone; they're all present.

Noah has bandages wrapped around his arms. I can see red angry skin where the gauze isn't covering: his collarbone, neck, biceps, and the backs of his hands.

He gives me a grimace before I evaluate Grama Pearle's injuries. Shoulder-length hair is sticking out in strange directions, but beyond the bits and pieces of flowers and plants stuck in it, she emerged unscathed.

Fin perches on the sofa by my feet. She has a pale glow of green magic at work over her ears. My eyes almost miss Roger, standing statue-like off to the side with his arms crossed. He's uninjured. So, he came inside after the attack.

If it wasn't for Fin sitting near me, the impression would be that Roger was staring at my legs. I stifle an eye roll and continue scanning the room. I see Birdie has arrived home, which must mean that Carter is here somewhere too.

"Where's Carter?" I say without trying to hide my concern. He hadn't been in the sunroom, but I feel the need to confirm everyone's wellbeing.

Fin's head bobs toward the corner of the room behind me. I rearrange myself, careful to avoid pulling open the wound that's being healed. Carter is curled up on the floor, sleeping with his hand between his legs. I relax. Birdie is about to say something about Carter.

"Don't bother." I flap my hand in Carter's direction. I clench my teeth. "I want to know how Kieran got into the sunroom, a warded room!"

All heads turn to Birdie, who gives a hop and adjusts her oversized glasses. "We changed the wards after Kyson's visit. The sunroom is now warded differently," she begins. "The wards allow birds entry. All birds," she adds when she sees our confusion.

"How is that safe?" Fin is flourishing her hands in my

direction.

"It should be safe because although all birds can enter, only those that are Spellbinder friends can shift, so—" but before she can go on, there's a stirring in the corner.

"Look," Carter's voice cuts in.

Startled, we all turn. Carter's head is down, blocking his expression as he ogles his penis, which is out there for all of us to see. It's coated with a shimmering shamrock-green magic mist. The mist is working to combat the other magic, to fight it off and leave him healed; a battle raging on his groin. I almost miss the third layer of magic, a subtle pastel-blue sleep interlace.

I whip my eyes to Birdie and then Grama Pearle. They both duck their heads to hide their smiles. "You're tricking him," I hiss. I know that Fin teases Carter mercilessly, and I don't get upset or involved, but she's up front about it and their relationship is built on it; they understand each other that way. Grama Pearle and Birdie are deceiving him and it feels wrong.

"It's . . ." Carter yawns and falls asleep. There's a collective sigh of relief from the room as he curls into the fetal position, hiding his manhood from view.

"It's a sleep charm! You coated his penis in a sleep charm!" I say with accusation.

"If he doesn't know what's going on, he's safest. And to be honest, his penis was the easiest place to put a charm without him becoming suspicious. Plus, we don't know how long it'll take for one magic to defeat the other," Grama Pearle offers.

"He trusts you!" I throw at her. I know that I'm

reacting to this more than I should. I'm trying to avoid the harder things that I need to deal with. So, I stop.

Birdie makes a chirping sound. "Now where was I? Oh, yeah. Kieran, when he was here, would've been in continuous pain in his human form, a pain that would cripple anyone else who tries to shift with negative intentions. And no, you can't hide your intentions!" Birdie's gigantic eyes fix on me. She's quiet for a minute. "Kieran and Kyson were different as children and that difference was fostered and fed. They were raised to feed off pain."

I blink and try to fight off a yawn, but it wins the battle. Fin has sunk onto the sofa. She's struggling to keep her eyes open.

"Healing will make you tired, especially mojo healing," Grama Pearle explains. "Before you sleep, though, you need to address that." She jerks her head at my legs.

The necklace and holder are nestled in the blanket on my legs. I nod and yawn. Through blurred vision, I pluck the stones out of my pocket and fit them into the holder, too tired to care if I set us on fire or freeze us to death. Each stone gives a soft click as it snaps into place and I can hear a faint hum of energy.

"Is it talking to you, Kori? Memories and books suggest things, but this is the first I've known anybody experiencing it firsthand," Grama Pearle says with an unprecedented note of awe. I muster a nod, and she returns it. "In time, you'll learn to listen only when you need to."

I fumble with the clasp, trying to get it on. Nobody

makes any move to help me, but after a few tries, I get it. The necklace is warm on my skin, but the amulet gives off alternating waves of cool and heat. "I need to know about Alaric. Where is he?" My focus is on the amulet nestled between my breasts. "I need to know . . ." but I'm too tired. I stop fighting it and let the sleep wash over me.

When I wake, the sensation of insect feet crawling on my skin is gone and my body feels whole. I'm aware of the amulet in a way that suggests that it's there, but it isn't intrusive. My body must have acclimated to it as I slept. The constant hum is gone and now I can hear it if I listen. The hot and cold waves have harmonized into a consistent temperature, like that of my body.

I rise from the sofa. Sleeping Carter and I are alone. Voices and the smell of coffee drift from the kitchen. I fight the urge to touch the new magic ward on the sliding door as I walk by. I've learned enough to know that as pretty as that barrier seems, it isn't meant for admirers to touch.

The first thing I see in the kitchen is the other door to the sunroom has the same sparkling barricade. After what happened in the sunroom, it seems appropriate to take extra precautions in relation to that room.

Grama Pearle, Birdie, Roger, Noah, Alaric, and Fin sit

at the table chatting. They are expecting me because there's a fresh mug of black coffee in front of the chair that Fin is patting. I lift my chin at Noah as I sit down. He's wearing bandages over his injuries. Fin snorts.

"Fin? What?"

"Well, Noah wants to heal on his own, no magic. He thinks it's beneficial to his role as a guard, his ability to fight through pain in case there isn't someone to heal him or no time to be healed, blah, blah . . . I think it's macho bullshit. Either way, it's your turn to change his bandages and add burn cream." She gives a dismissive flick of her hand in his direction.

Noah ignores her and turns to me. "Glad you're awake. We were just discussing if we should send a message to Nekane about the untimely death of one of his two top henchmen."

I sit back. I raise my mug to my lips, blowing thoughtfully onto the hot liquid and enjoying the pillows of hot steam that drift at me. After a few seconds, I allow a sip of the bitter liquid to flow over my lips before responding. "What have we come up with?"

"No message," Birdie says with an individual head jerk and a stare directed at each person at the table except Grama Pearle.

I tip my head sideways at Birdie. "Okay . . ."

"Birdie is right. If we can keep this from Nekane, we should. Let him think Kieran has gone rogue with Kori." Grama Pearle eyes me. "Which means you, Kori, need to stay inside for a bit. Just a couple of days, Nekane won't buy Kieran taking longer than that to satisfy his twisted craving to torture. He'll assume, correctly, that

Kieran is dead. Dead and not ensnared because Kieran and Kyson would maim their own bodies to avoid being captured."

"Okay, and to what end is this?" I ask.

"You might be catching on to basic magic, but Jayce and Holden can do the magic you're learning. The Ember stone usually takes years of advanced magic to wield. This will give you time to get at least acquainted with the stone." Grama Pearle falls silent as her eyes land on Alaric. I'm startled by his sunken eyes; he's haggard. My wide eyes question Grama Pearle.

"Second, we need time to figure out what Alaric learned from Kieran." She makes an unsuccessful attempt at a smile.

"And what to do with it?" Noah adds quietly.

I have a fleeting image of Alaric's hands and Kieran's eyes. The vision is direct and clear, it's the last thing I saw before I lost consciousness; I'm nauseous. "What happened?" The table falls silent, and everyone has their eyes downcast. Even Fin is conscientiously studying the tabletop. "Guys?"

Noah's eyes rise from the table to meet mine. "He looked through a dying man's eyes, Kori." His words are quiet and clipped.

Not to mention he blew a man's body to pieces; I think to myself. I hadn't thought of Alaric as a man I should be scared of, but maybe I misjudged him. My mouth is dry, my brow scrunched down. His actions saved me from Kieran. If I hadn't tried to catch Kieran, if I chose to defend and protect . . . My throat constricts, but I force my question out. "Is he alright?"

Noah nods.

I gulp my coffee. "Is he having trouble coming to terms with what he found?"

"No, with what he did. What he did is marked in Spellbinder laws as unforgiveable." Noah is watching Alaric. "There are sometimes exceptions made . . ." Noah considers Alaric. "Nekane won't report Kieran as missing to the normie police or to the Board of Magic because it opens the door to questions he won't want to answer. As for The Recruiter, if I was a gambling man, I would say he knows because he has a way of knowing. If he plans to pass judgement, that's between him and Alaric." Noah says nothing else, but he claps a hand on Alaric's shoulder and gives a squeeze.

My nose and forehead scrunch. "Grama Pearle?"

She lays a wrinkled hand over Alaric's calloused one. "Lifetimes ago, killing a normie or a Spellbinder from The Society of the Blood Wind's elimination list was initiation into The Society. Looking through a murdered person's eyes earned an initiate special privilege. The eyes hold images like the brain holds memories. You can get a view of the images stored in the eyes up to ten minutes after death. You can control what images you view all the way to the beginning of a person's life." Grama Pearle must hear the monotone of her voice because she pauses and coughs to clear her throat.

Her mouth has a grim twist. "The belief is that most, if not all, Spellbinders can do it but because it's a violent disrespect to the deceased, there's no way to test the theory. It's very intrusive and there are Spellbinder laws against it. Our laws are like the normie laws about improper or indecent interference with or offering any indignity to a dead human body or human remain."

Alaric looks at me for the first time, but I don't know what to say. We stare silently at each other. I hope my eyes convey my gratitude, but the longer our gazes remain locked, the more I realize that this isn't a sacrifice that he made. This was a calculated risk done to achieve our end goal and, after that, his own. I nod and break the stare. "So, what did we learn?"

"They don't know who has Alivia!" Fin blurts.

"What?" My eyes have gone so large it almost hurts. "Nekane doesn't have her?"

"It would appear not, but they're searching because they want the amulet, all of it—the stones, the holder, and the necklace. And they don't want us to know that they don't have Alivia," Grama Pearle says.

"I don't understand. Belamey said she was alive. How would he know that if Nekane isn't holding her prisoner?"

Noah glares at me. "Belamey is not to be trusted, Kori. It was obviously a lie."

"None of us understand, Kori," Grama Pearle whispers. I can see she's thinking. "Nekane was there. He was right in front of Alivia and then she was gone. There were no clues about who or what helped Alivia escape him. At least that's what he told Kieran in confidence." Grama Pearle reads the confusion on my face. "No, not on her own. Alivia doesn't have that kind of magic; she's a healer. Plus, we would've heard from her by now. Nope, someone else has her."

"Who?" I wonder out loud. "It would have to be

someone with knowledge of Nekane's plans."

"How long do we have?" Fin asks.

"What?" I ask her.

"When will Nekane figure out that something happened to Kieran? And will Kyson feel anything? I mean is the twin bond a real thing? How much time do we have to make our next move?"

"It'll be short-lived, Fin." Noah says.

"I'll be returning the warding on one door to the sunroom to what was there previous to the attack. I'm just waiting on extra help to arrive," Birdie chirps.

As if on cue, there's a strange noise coming from outside. Some trick of magic amplifies the sound. It's the signal she was waiting for because Birdie is hooting and hopping full speed. She hops right through the shimmering ward without stopping, indicating it was a ward set by her. The sparkling barrier shatters and crumbles to the ground like shards of broken glass.

I stare wide eyed at the broken ward. "Grama Pearle?"

Grama Pearle makes a flicking motion with her hand. The glass sweeps aside, and she marches through.

I don't know what I expect to find when I enter the sunroom. I'm not prepared for two tall birds with shaggy black backs and bright blue heads pushing each other as they each try to get through the door first. Like a cartoon spoof, they both pop through the door frame, frazzled and angry.

Each bird is over five feet tall and they remind me of emus, but before I can register anything more, Birdie's hand shoots up at us in warning. We all grind to a silent halt. The tension emanating from her body is palpable, as if this help she's called for us is dangerous.

Fin, crammed behind me, brings her hand into my line of sight, and points. My mouth goes dry, and my eyes go wide. The legs on these birds are muscular, with feet that are terrifyingly prehistoric, but it's the dagger-like claw on its inner toes that brings the terror home. The claws are five inches long. I rate these birds as dangerous, and I would have taken a few steps backward if Noah and Roger weren't crowded in behind me and Fin. Alaric must still be sitting at the kitchen table because he isn't in the doorway with us.

"Amazing," Grama Pearle whispers.

"What's that, the murderous feet on these oversized birds?" Fin hisses.

Grama Pearle doesn't register that Fin spoke. "It's the cassowary siblings."

"Did she say cassowary, as in the bird?" Noah asks.

I nod, staring at the weapon-like feet, waiting for one toe to tap like a velociraptor toe in the movies. Birdie makes a bird sound and each bird's neck tips to the side, highlighting the intimidating black casques on the tops of their heads.

"Cassowaries are known for their ability to jump attack their victims and kill them with puncture wounds and lacerations, so we better hope Birdie knows what she's doing," Noah pauses for dramatic emphasis. "These are not birds to mess with."

"Why are they here?" Fin hisses to nobody.

Birdie makes the noise again, causing one bird to make a low hiss. She eases back until she bumps into us huddled in the doorway. Slowly, she reaches over and pulls a bit of foliage in front of us. My eyebrows draw toward my hairline.

Without warning, both cassowaries shift into humans. The birds were scary, but the man and woman put the birds to shame, with unkempt hair and untrimmed fingernails. They're both dressed in brown, baggy clothing and besides the length of their hair and the fact that one of them has obvious, saggy breasts, they look the same. The woman gives a startling laugh and everyone flinches, except Birdie and the man.

"Meet the twins, Dugal and Hellzel Grogda, also known as the Grogda siblings or the cassowary siblings." Birdie performs a sweeping bow and arm flourish. "Dugal and Hellzel, meet everyone."

Hellzel's laughter cuts off my musings about why Birdie introduced us as a group and not individually. Dugal jumps and grasps Grama Pearle in an embrace. His muttering about it being an honour to meet Pearle Ember is what keeps him safe because it takes the threat out of his jerky movements. Dugal jumps from one of us to the other, mumbling a greeting of some sort. It takes a marked effort not to scrunch my face up as I breathe in the smell of fruit and vinegar that lingers on his person.

Hellzel only seems capable of random outbursts of laughter, but as Dugal springs to Birdie, she forms her first sentence. Her tone is biting, her jaw is tight, and her squint is harsh. "Enough fool! Birdie wants protection, not affection."

When Dugal doesn't respond, she stretches her neck

up and he tips his head to the ground and recoils until he's behind her. "Instructions please, Birdie." Hellzel turns to face our group, which is spreading out into the space of the sunroom. She gives off another creepy crow of laughter.

"Hellzel, we need you and Dugal to guard the entrance to the sunroom," Birdie begins, but Hellzel's laughter cuts her off. Birdie is assessing Hellzel. Although Hellzel dwarfs her, Birdie makes it appear like she's peering down her nose in disapproval of the frenzied laughter.

Hellzel is unfazed. "Let's keep it simple," she says. "Kill anything that isn't on the approved entry list that you sent me when you requested our help."

Dugal has heard all he wants to, and he transforms into a cassowary as he walks out onto the deck. I'm expecting to hear Birdie correct Hellzel. When the silence stretches on, I whip my head in her direction.

Birdie's head is bobbing up and down in agreement and the only indication that this troubles her is the way her eyes are squeezed shut. I incline my head as my eyes grow wider.

Amid her laughter, Hellzel says, "Kori Ember." Her abrupt shift into a cassowary cuts off any further laughing. Her bird form cocks its head at me before strutting out of the sunroom to take up guard on the deck with her brother. I'm left blinking idiotically in her wake.

"Birdie?" Grama Pearle's eyes lock on the screen door. "Are they safe, Birdie?"

Birdie's eyes lock on the screen door as well. She

opens and closes her mouth, soundless.

"I heard that the Grogda siblings were a dangerous duo because their grip on reality is marginally slipping. And, Birdie, from what I saw, marginal is a minimalization." Grama Pearle pulls her eyes from the door to Birdie.

Birdie opens and closes her mouth again without making a sound.

"Birdie!" Grama Pearle yells.

She turns to meet Grama Pearle's stare full on. "You shouldn't believe everything you hear, Pearle. Dugal and Hellzel never had a grip on reality!" Birdie looks at the screen door. "With them out there, there will be no breaches in this sunroom! They're capable guards."

I study the screen door, wondering if the reason there won't be breaches is because the Grogda siblings will kill anything that moves.

Chapter 14

It's hard not to be fascinated with the Grogda siblings, both as humans and cassowaries. I'm not one to stare, but my coffee-sipping activity this morning involves watching them move on the deck as large birds.

They plant their feet, toes first, and take deliberate steps, going in opposite directions from one another across the deck. I'm so busy enjoying the way their heads move, forward and back on their necks with each step, that I've missed most of the conversation happening between Birdie, Grama Pearle, and Fin while Birdie tends to the birds.

Fin's elbow in my ribs breaks the spell and I follow her, Grama Pearle, and Birdie into the kitchen. Noah, Alaric, and Roger sit at the table with a fresh brew of hot coffee. I slide into a chair and refill my mug.

"Well, someone has to ask." Fin grins mischievously. "What's a magic penis doctor?"

I close my eyes to block out the room and take several deep breaths. Carter, his crotch, and the magic penis doctor aren't the first questions on my mind. It isn't a question in my mind at all.

"What?" Fin directs the question at me. "A magic

penis doctor? How aren't you curious?"

I open my eyes and fix them on Fin, who shrugs and smiles. I fold my hands. "Well?" I ask sharply.

"Wait," Fin interrupts. She casts her head from side to side before she starts exploring the corners and under chairs. "Where is Carter?" She stops with her hands on her hips. "I hope he isn't masturbating somewhere!"

Noah chokes on his coffee. He wasn't expecting a typical Fin comment. Birdie's hand flies to her mouth in mock shock and Grama Pearle bursts out laughing. Alaric sits stone-faced, stretches out his legs, and leans back, at ease and in control. It's Roger that starts filling in the blanks.

His tone reminds me of a know-it-all teenager. He's not condescending, but boastful and smug. "She's not a magic *penis* doctor. She's a magic doctor. Right, Birdie?"

"She?" I blurt out.

"Yes. *She*, Kori. And no, she doesn't specialize in penises. Her specialty is memory and mind control," Birdie says.

"You took him to see the Child of the Shadows?" Grama Pearle asks with astonishment.

"I did, Pearle, and don't make her sound so ominous! Where do you think I got that sleeping charm? And we can't have him running willy-nilly with his willie hanging out. He's a liability and one whose safety is our responsibility since the botched attempt to use him as a spy at the Ember house."

Birdie and Grama Pearle have gone silent, staring at

one another. After an uncomfortable few minutes, Grama Pearle nods. "Good thinking, Birdie."

"So, she isn't a magic penis doctor?" Fin's disappointment is dramatic. "Is there a good part to the story? Hold up, did you say the Child of the Shadows?"

"No wait," I cut in. "Where is he?"

Birdie eyeballs me like she's reassessing my intelligence.

Grama Pearle's eyes lock on Birdie. "Sleeping."

"The sleeping charm?" I ask.

"The one on his penis?" Fin perks up. "I knew there was a story here, but can someone please clarify this scary-ass name?"

"A penis sleeping charm." Noah chuckles.

"Made the most sense," Birdie says. "The man will whip it out and lay it down anywhere if he thinks one of us will look, listen, and help." Birdie flaps her hand like it's a wing, "A symptom of the magic—"

I clear my throat and tap my foot, feeling like I know enough about the troubles with Carter's penis. "But you said she specializes in memory and mind control?" I say to Birdie with confusion. "And why, Grama Pearle, did you sound so scandalized about doctor shadow child?"

"Not doctor shadow child, Kori," Roger corrects. "Her nickname is Child of the Shadows, but her real name is Dr. Ague Draven. And Ague is pronounced Ah-g like the hard 'g' sound in good, and not Egg-you. She's particular about that. Anyway, because of her specialty, her charms last in ways that other Spellbinder charms don't, and her charms have a different effect on people's consciousness."

I just stare at Roger and blink.

"We need to make a plan for him, Kori," Grama Pearle's voice is soft as she tries to avoid my questions. "He can't continue staying here. Like all normies, he's defenseless in this battle, and his common sense and self-preservation failed with his penis. So, we need to figure out where he can go and still be safe. Until then, he sleeps."

"Someone has a destructive sense of humour. You don't mess with a man's penis," Noah says.

Fin acknowledges Noah's discomfort with a nod. She searches "Dr. Ague Draven" online and passes me her cell phone. A middle-aged woman with dark eyes and a pale face is shown in an article. She's smiling and her bright red lipstick is melting off her lips. The article title is, "Escaped Patient." A quick scan clarifies that Dr. Ague Draven escaped from one of the psychiatric wards in the greater Toronto area years ago and vanished. With intentional movements, I push two fingers into the corner of my left eye to hold the rapid twitch in check. The muscle jumps under my fingers.

"Oh, it isn't like it sounds, Kori." Grama Pearle is staring at my fingers rammed into the side of my eye.

"It never is," I mumble, closing my eyes tight.

"We view memory and mind control, not to mention a person claiming to be a doctor in that area, differently in the Spellbinder community. She shouldn't have tried to breach that line. It made her appear to normies as if her mental stability prevented her normal perception, behaviour, and social interaction and she was perceived as a danger to herself and others. So, they locked her away," Birdie says.

I slit my eyes to peek at her. Her head is bobbing up and down as fast as my eye is twitching. I sigh and close my eyes.

Birdie chirps. "Anyway, all that's behind her. She set herself up in the Blue Mountain area in southwestern Ontario, hidden literally in the mountains. It's about a fifteen and a half hour flight from here by—"

"And Carter?" I ask through clenched teeth, choosing to ignore the comment about this supposed doctor being within flying distance. I don't want to know how Carter got to the mountains.

"Hold the fort," Fin interjects before Birdie can answer me. She's leaning toward Birdie. "How did Carter fly? Did you shrink him and tie him to your tail feathers? Or maybe you put him in a wee basket and pulled him under your feet like a hot-air balloon, I mean hot-owl balloon."

My eye is twitching so much at this point that my vision is blurry.

"Helicopter," Birdie hoots, crushing Fin with this very human answer. "It would take my owl self over sixty hours to fly that distance. And Kori, Carter will sleep until we figure out what to do with him. He's in a waking dream state that allows him to eat, drink, and use the washroom when needed. Roger will check on him in scheduled intervals and help when necessary."

"So, his penis is still deflated, then?" Fin asks. "What? I'm just clarifying, getting all the story?"

"You know what? I don't want to talk about this anymore." Abruptly, I march from the room with no exact idea of what I'm doing.

I surprise myself when I find I'm watching Carter sleep. He's peaceful. The tenseness, desperation, and sadness that mark his waking self aren't evident, and I feel a bit of my worry about him slip away. *It may be for the best.* "Sorry to drag you into this mess. I can't imagine how scary it must be to not be in full control of your actions." After watching him for a few minutes, I realize that I feel heavy with sleep.

I tiptoe to the chair and flop into it. My last waking thought is about why I chose to tiptoe; Carter wouldn't wake if I jumped up and down on the bed.

No more sleeping for me. The storm outside picked up, and it's hard to imagine how everybody, except for Carter, is sleeping through it. The last thunder crack shakes the foundation of the house, causing me to spring from bed and pad to the kitchen. The mug of coffee nestled in my hands is a comfort as I laze in a chair at the table and watch the storm through the window. The lightning is brisk, illuminating the world outside.

It's a gray day, absent of life forms. With horror, I realize that the Grogda siblings never came inside when the storm started. I creep to the sunroom door, timing a peek with the flash of lightning. The sunroom is empty and quiet, even the birds are nestled away, sleeping. There's no sign of the Grogda siblings.

I can't imagine them on the deck in this weather, but I also can't imagine them abandoning their post. Intrigued, I creep into the sunroom and I'm halfway across when the hairs on the nape of my neck prickle. The lightning illuminates the room and I spin. The shadows are alive as I cast about. Memories of Kieran's breach are fresh.

I cast aside my curiosity about the Grogda siblings and turn to make my way to the kitchen. The lightning strikes and from the corner of my eye, I see a shadow move with distinct human movements. It's too tall and athletic to be one of the Grogda siblings. Could someone have sneaked passed them using the storm as cover?

As I blink into the darkness, I note a familiarity to the predatory-like movement of the shape. My mouth goes dry. I shut my eyes and inhale deeply. That rousing smell of Belamey fills my nostrils. He hasn't bound my magic, which my cop brain interprets as a truce, but I'm alert to the risks he poses.

He locks eyes with me, "I'm not going to hurt you." His voice is low and I can see in his eyes that he means what he says. I don't resist when his warm hands grip the flesh of my upper arms to turn me so I'm facing the door to the deck. His arms snake around me and he presses himself tight. I swallow as I try to ignore the electric warmth radiating off his muscled body.

Lightning flares and I see the outline of two cassowaries pacing on the deck. Not once do they look my way. The sound of the storm muffles the limited noise that Belamey and I are making. If I yell, they might hear me, but for now, I feel more enthralled than threatened.

"I bring a message, Kori Ember." His husky voice is in my ear. "Let's find your pocket."

Belamey's left hand slides over my body, taking extra liberties as he searches. My skin tingles in response and confusion makes my brain fuzzy. He moves his hand like he has all the time in the world and like the pain of shifting in this sunroom isn't crippling him. *He couldn't be on the approved entry list, could he? His presence makes no sense!* He makes a soft noise into my ear. His hand slides up over my right breast to the neckline of my tank top.

"No pockets," he whispers. He pauses and I can feel him smiling.

I've no desire to struggle, which confuses and angers me. His hand resumes movement and his fingers feel electric as they find my skin and slip into the edge of my bra. I know that he has placed an item there, but before I can register anything else, he vanishes. On cue, the lightning flares and I'm alone.

I move to the kitchen table in a haze. Fishing the object out of my bra, I set it down. I wrinkle my nose at it before heading for the coffee pot. The storm is being replaced by pre-morning light and I'm not surprised to hear sounds of people waking.

Finding me sitting at the table staring at strange-shaped foil ball is odd. From that, it takes a few moments for everyone to realize something offbeat occurred in the house.

"I don't understand how Belamey could've been in the sunroom," I say.

"Perhaps it had to do with the storm," Fin offers. She responds to my raised eyebrows with a shoulder shrug. "Now, answer the prime question. Was it hot?"

"You know what? Perhaps Fin is onto something," Noah interjects. "Maybe the electrical discharge and imbalances caused by the storm gave Belamey a brief window of time to enter. You said it all happened fast, right? He was here. He was gone."

Grama Pearle is quiet. She and Birdie peep at each other like they have a different theory before returning to the message that Belamey passed me. "Open it, Kori," Grama Pearle says so quietly that I can hardly hear her. I scrunch my face up. "Birdie and I have suspicions about Belamey and his loyalties. Open it."

I huff but move my fingers to the foil. I peel it off. There's a collective gasp from everybody for what I'm sure are different reasons. On the table is a miniature replica of an unkempt, wartime house. There's nothing about the replica house that's familiar or striking, but before I can comment, the replica makes a low hiss and disintegrates.

"The safe house!" Grama Pearle mumbles as she suddenly shrinks.

The replica is another haven? I don't get a chance to put my thoughts into words. My eyes nearly pop out of my head when Birdie swoops her hand down and grabs a shrunken Grama Pearle and tosses her into the air. Birdie shifts and Grama Pearle lands on Birdie's owl back, clinging to her feathers as they rocket away.

I'm blinking at the empty spot they left behind, wondering why Grama Pearle never transforms to bird form. I jump when Fin's voice breaks the shocked silence. "Do you remember Mouz?"

Noah and I turn toward her.

"Well, remember he used the words 'secret ally' the day Kyson murdered him?" Fin asks. "And remember Mouz said 'he,' as in Mouz himself, switched his loyalty?"

I nod and blink as I see where Fin is going.

"My point is, if Mouz turned sides, is it possible that someone else within the ranks of The Society of the Blood Wind did, too?" Fin has a self-satisfied grin painted on her face. "What if it's Belamey? Grama Pearle said she and Birdie question his loyalties, he shifted in the sunroom without being crushed by it, and he doesn't seem interested in hurting you."

Noah's hand claps down on my shoulder, causing me to jump. "I think I better get Alaric to send some messenger birds," he says, wagging his finger at Fin like she might have figured it out with the idea of a covert ally. "It's not Belamey," he growls at her.

"Wait. Why can't it be Belamey? And what do you know about Mouz Frone?" I ask him.

It surprises me when Noah gives out a sizeable sigh. "It's not Belamey," he says through clenched teeth. He takes a deep breath. "Mouz was good at hunting and catching. The Society of the Blood Wind was brutal in their expectation and treatment of his skills." Noah turns to leave, as if that's explanation enough, his irritation controlling him.

"How was he trustworthy?" I ask his backside.

Noah whirls and locks me with misty eyes. "Do you know the fierce loyalty that a wounded stray animal shows its rescuer, especially a rescuer that asks nothing of it but its friendship?" There's a pause while Noah wipes a solitary tear from the corner of his eye. "Mouz used his skills to help. He wasn't asked. There was no expectation of him. From what I know of Mouz, if he was willing to die sharing information, there's NO question about its value!" With that, Noah storms away.

Fin and I lock eyes, nodding in recognition. "Thank you, Mouz," Fin whispers into the air. I nod with heartfelt agreement.

After a moment of silence, my mind slips to the replica wartime house, a safe house, and Birdie and Grama Pearle's breakneck exit. *Why? What do they know?* Fin distracts my thoughts. She has a look on her face that I haven't seen before. "So, Noah is having some jealousy issues about Belamey's interest in you, eh?"

My mouth falls open and my body stiffens. My voice is shaky and soft. "Excuse me?"

Fin's eye contact is unwavering and she speaks like she's citing facts. "Noah is responding to Belamey like he's a rival. He gets all bitter every time Belamey's name comes up. Noah has feelings for you still."

"Don't be ridiculous, Fin," I hiss, the pitch of my voice rising. I've an intense urge to hide.

Fin shrugs. "I'm just saying. I know you have a little brother vibe for him most of the time. You got over your and his almost-couple thing all those years ago, but he hasn't yet. He's trying," she says, like she's privy to direct information."

I turn away suddenly feeling exposed. I'm grateful when Fin switches her train of thought.

"So, what was Mouz trying to hunt and catch that got him killed?" I ask.

"Intel," Alaric says as he enters the kitchen from the hall and continues straight through, disappearing into the sunroom.

"Makes sense that his mission would be intelligence gathering," Fin says, as if she had come to this conclusion on her own and Alaric hadn't just one-word bombed us as he passed through. "But where did Grama Pearle and Birdie race off to, I wonder?"

"To get Kori's family and bring them here. We had them stashed at the wartime haven," Noah says as he enters the kitchen and marches through it to the sunroom. We hear the sunroom door bang shut.

"I bet they went to get your family and bring them here," Fin says, edging her voice up on the word here. "They must be at the life-sized version of that replica." She tips her chair legs like she's a top detective solving a case. "Why, though?" she asks, eyeing the spot where the miniature replica sat.

"Compromised location," Roger says as he enters the kitchen from the sunroom and walks toward the hall for his timed check on Carter. His voice carries to us as he heads down the hallway. "The replica was a warning that the wartime safe house and its occupants were in peril. Astrid is stationed there, so I'm sure she's already working to get them out."

Before Fin can parrot Roger's words, I stand up.

"Why the hell is everyone marching through with purpose and throwing out limited answers as they go? Errr!" *Birdie gives Roger a lot of responsibility and he seems to know a lot about what goes on at this refuge*, I think.

"Kori?" Fin whispers.

I direct my glare at her. Her hands fly up in the air in a gesture of surrender. "Easy!"

"Sorry." My shoulders sag.

"Did you process that? Your family is coming," Fin says as she moves over and squeezes me tight.

"My family," I whisper as I drop my head to her shoulder and draw some stability from the comfort of her embrace. *Maybe they'll have some information about Alivia that'll help us.* Roger returns to the kitchen, moving as if he has another task. I call to him, my assumption, based off his knowledge of the replica being a safe house, is that he will be able to answer my next question. He stops and turns, waiting. "How long 'til they get here?" I ask.

"If all goes well, expect them for dinner," he replies before continuing on. He leaves before I can ask him how they'll get here.

I watch the entrance to the sunroom to see if Roger is going to reappear. "Fin, do you find the whole thing about Roger living here for twenty years while he waits on a decision about his status in the tribe to be strange?" Fin doesn't respond. Her is head tipped to the side and her nose is scrunched up in thought, working to come up with an answer. "I mean, do you not think Birdie left stuff out of her explanation?"

Fin shrugs. "Would it make a difference? He's one of us?" She widens her eyes at me and smiles.

I sigh. "Okay, let's prep for my family. We need to set up beds. There are rollaway cots stored in the basement and three or four will fit into the room we're sharing. Someone can sleep on the sofa and the boys can sleep in sleeping bags on the living room carpet. And we should make dinner."

"One, two, three, go!" Fin runs from the room.

"Where are you going, nutball?" I call.

"Dresser, I need a fun cleaning outfit!"

I snort. I'm staring into the fridge when Fin comes in. She's wearing a navy silk blouse unbuttoned just enough to clarify that she has nothing under it but a push-up bra. The lower half of her body is clad in tight navy shorts with white stockings held up by garter belts and, of course, she didn't forget the apron. A thick white ribbon cinches her waist, and it flows down into a short lacey edge.

"Well, you're playing the part, aren't you?" I smirk.

Fin pirouettes. "Let's get this done because I have a snazzy outfit picked out for dinner!" She thrusts a pile of clothing at me. "Your cleaning clothes, Mademoiselle Ember."

I judge my current outfit. "What's wrong with what I'm wearing?"

"No fun. Fun reduces stress."

I shrug and let her steer me to the bathroom and usher me in. I change, muttering about the off-beat things I'm exposing myself to. Fin's ideas can be eccentric, but she means well and I love her, plus she has a way of making things fun and uplifting.

Fin has picked a pair of form-fitting gray slacks for me topped with a short-sleeved, low-cut, V-neck silk blouse that has gray cuffs and a gray collar. The apron she picked for me is a match to her own but in denim. When I come out, she plops a pleated cloth on my head that she ties on with a ribbon. She steps aside to assess.

"Beautiful!" she drawls.

Alaric picks this moment to enter the hall. He takes one look at us. Expressionless, he turns and walks away, unspeaking. Fin pauses, like the lull after a funny joke, then she howls with laughter. The corners of my mouth pull into a smile, and I laugh too.

Chapter 15

The sky is deepening into night when Astrid swoops into sight. She shifts out of bird form mid-air and lands in a cat-like pose on the deck banister. Her thin lips smile at the cassowaries. A surge of panic forms in me as I wonder if the Grogda siblings are going to tear her apart.

Even through the cloak, I can see Astrid's muscles are tight. Her smile lines intensify as she jumps down and moves between the cassowaries to enter the sunroom. My alarm fades until I realize that she's alone. None of my family is with her.

Her eyes lock on me. She shakes her head and covers her ears. Her slight frame marches past me into the kitchen. I glance at the deck door. The cassowaries have resumed their pacing, and the sky remains empty.

"I see you made dinner." Her tone is soft with understanding. Without waiting for a response, Astrid continues. "Unfortunately, you'll have to make breakfast instead."

"Astrid?"

"A few slight complications, but everyone is safe. The haven was being watched. So, we had to be sneaky getting everyone out and then, of course, nobody can come straight here." She pauses. "I played decoy in bird form, and I was chased by five Society of the Blood Wind birds. It took a lot of fancy flying to lose them. I don't have any other details, but people should start arriving in groups by the morning."

"You're well, Astrid?" Noah tips his head toward her midsection.

"I am. Thank you for asking, Noah. But I need to rest now."

Astrid disappears into the house to a spot that's known only to her. The rest of us eat in silence. The food has no flavour in my mouth, as I wonder about my family and their safety, but I continue through the motions of eating for lack of anything productive to do. We tag team the clean up before each of us retreats be alone.

The kitchen has a hum of activity when I wake. I stop just before the entranceway. I haven't seen my family since I skipped town all those months ago. My mouth is dry with anticipation. Eyes shut, I pull a drawn-out breath before stepping into the room.

I'm smiling before I realize it. Two little bodies are dancing and talking animatedly on kitchen chairs pulled over to the counter by the stove. Jayce and

Holden are flanking Noah while he flips pancakes. Holden's plump legs bend at the knees but never fully straighten, bouncing, his three-year-old version of a happy dance. Jayce has a more sophisticated rhythm that involves a bum wiggle.

I peek at the table to count the place settings. Only my nephews have arrived. I rub my neck and roll my shoulders, trying to shrug off the feelings of unease about the rest of my family. I push the syrup and juice away from the edge of the table and clear my throat. Two chubby faces turn my way. Their eyes go big and there are shrieks and squealed words that I can't decipher.

Jayce jumps from the chair. I drop to my knees to catch his tiny frame as he collides into me. He holds on tight with his face buried in my shoulder. Holden is clumsily climbing off the chair, chanting, "Auntie, Auntie."

Jayce releases me and peers into my face. "You look like Mommy."

"Oh, sweetie," I whisper as I pull him into a hug. My vision blurs with unshed tears and my chest tightens. I draw comfort from the warm little body cuddling me and I put on a gentle smile to avoid upsetting him with my own emotions.

He lets me hold him for a second before he squirms. "Uncle Noah needs me to help him cook the pancakes."

He races away as Holden wobbles into my open arms. I scoop him up and take a deep breath of the baby smell that clings to him. "Noah," I say. "My nephews did not travel from one safe house to another on their own.

Who brought them?"

Noah flicks his eyes to me and back to the pancake he's flipping. "Astrid had a friend named Cian, or something like that. He collected the boys from your parents early this morning. Did you know both boys can shift into birds already?" Noah flips a pancake. "Jayce is a potoo and Holden is a morning dove. Cian flew into the sunroom with Jayce and Holden, but he didn't stay. He didn't even transform. Some tiny hawk that I think I've seen in the sunroom before." Noah doesn't see my eyes widen because he's busy with the pancakes. "These need to go on the table now, bud." Noah ruffles Jayce's hair.

"Me do! Me do!" Holden yells, wiggling in my arms. I set him down on wobbly legs as Noah places a plate with a few pancakes into his chubby hands. Before I can ask Noah about the hawk, he hands me a second plate and shoos me in the direction Jayce and Holden are going. I start when I see Alaric and Astrid are now seated at the table. I hadn't heard anybody enter the room, but they're sitting in silence, observing the pancake cooking.

"Go find Great-Grama Pearle," Noah says.

I put the plate down. Noah comes up close behind me. Slipping his hand around my waist, he leans in to put the coffee pot on the table. "I'm hungry for sweetness this morning. How about you?" I'm not sure if he means the pancakes or me. Regardless, I twist and shove him away. He smiles devilishly.

"I'll take that as an after-breakfast invitation." He makes his eyebrows wiggle up and down. While I look for something to throw at him, he dances away. Alaric is four years older than me, but his manner mimics Astrid, an impassive but watchful parent.

"Auntie! Auntie!" Holden is yelling. I turn to see him and Jayce pushing and hurrying toward me.

"I want to sit with Auntie," Jayce says.

"No, me. No, me." Tears well up in Holden's light brown eyes. "No, me!"

"Boys, Auntie has a chair on each side of her." Noah scoops Holden up and plops him down alongside me. "Uncle Noah will sit here." He sits on Holden's other side.

I decide that I'll wait until after breakfast to ask Astrid about Cian the hawk. Jayce and Holden are so excited to be with us they haven't stopped giggling and telling stories. We've finished our breakfast when a commotion alerts us to someone's arrival.

I discover Aunt Rune standing in the sunroom with her shoulders back, her chest stuck out, and her pointed nose high in the air. Always a stark contrast to Dad, who has a quiet quirkiness where she's eccentric. She's dressed in a classic black witch's dress. Fin pokes her head around me. "Where's the hat and broom, Mrs. Greyson?"

Aunt Rune fixes Fin in an intense stare, then cackles so loud we all flinch. "Miss Finley, you know you address me as Rune."

"My mother's broom is at home." Brynlee scowls as she enters the sunroom. "The old witch," Brynlee says so quietly that I'm not sure I heard correctly until Aunt Rune's hand flies up in a blur to flick Brynlee on the nose. All the while, Aunt Rune is mumbling unintelligible words.

When Aunt Rune stops mumbling, she looks at us pointedly before saying, in a commanding voice, "Grow!"

An ugly wart pushes out on the side of Brynlee's nose where Aunt Rune just flicked her. "MOM!" Brynlee screeches, her hands fly up to her face, as she yells various combinations of words to not only stop, but reverse Aunt Rune's spell. For Brynlee's twenty-year-old self, getting a pimple is upsetting; having her mother curse her with a facial wart is devastating.

Brynlee dashes at us with her head down. There are five of us stuffed in the doorway so tight that we can't move. It's like a charging bull is running at us. I brace for impact, but Brynlee shrinks herself, tight-lipped, and dodges between the openings in our legs. The sight of her over my shoulder is a blur as she returns to normal size and continues her flight through the kitchen to the sound of Aunt Rune cackling.

"With her over-the-top representation of your magical heritage, I can't believe Rune is your father's sister. Your dad does odd stuff like sweeping bows to say hello, but he looks like an average dad. I grew up thinking Rune was crazy and obsessed with Halloween. And I've always wanted to know if that's her real laugh or if she practises," Fin's amused whisper tickles my ear.

"We better move before she turns us all into frogs," Noah jokes.

Aunt Rune stops cackling. "Brynlee should know better than to tease her mother, especially when her mother is me." She smiles at us. "Are there apples in the kitchen?"

"Auntie Rue-Rue," Holden screeches as he totters at full speed. She scoops him up and kisses his cheek.

"Do you want an apple, sweet boy?" she whispers. We move out of the doorway to allow Aunt Rune and Holden to walk through.

Alaric and Astrid have disappeared, but they've cleaned the kitchen in the few minutes we were gone. I have a brief thought of anthropomorphic brooms from the movies. We spend the next forty-five minutes listening to Aunt Rune chronicle the events since her family, the Greysons, left the wartime safe house. All the while, she's inspecting the bag of apples from the fridge. Each apple turns a deep red and increases a bit in size as her hands move over the skin.

Aunt Rune takes her leave, and as she slides from the room, she says to nobody in particular, "Is the potion room locked? I'd like to prepare." Then she cackles, "As if a lock could stop me."

Aunt Rune has filled a wooden bowl in the centre of the table with beautiful red apples. Our brief distraction is all Mom and Dad need. True to form, they entered the house silent as mice. They enter the kitchen undetected. Dad makes a flourishing bow as his way of saying hello when we turn his way. Mom twirls and curtsies.

Mom's soft clearing of her throat with her eyes locked on me is a sign that she has questions for me. She grew up under the fierce quizzing of her own mother, Grama Opal. So, Mom's line of questioning takes on the air of an inquisition, needing to be one level more intense than the examinations she experienced.

I sigh and start mentally preparing to be interrogated. There was a time when I would've resisted Mom's probing questions, but with Jaxton's death, the hell Alivia and I put her and Dad through as teenagers, and everything that's currently going on, I kind of get the fierceness of her love.

"You're okay. I've been worried," Mom is mumbling over and over. During my eye roll, both Mom and Dad cross the room and surround me in a group hug. Mom sobs and rubs my shoulder blades.

"Do you have all of your fingers and all of your toes?" Dad asks, and I can't tell if he's serious or joking.

With a gasp, Mom steps back. "You still have all your lady bits, right? I expect grandchildren from you one day!" She punctuates her statement with a foot stomp. "You and Carter weren't compatible, but your next husband . . ." her voice fades out, and her eyes go wide. She snatches my left hand. "Are you remarried?"

Fin is laughing so hard behind me that she's snorting like a wild pig.

"Mom!" I yell stamping my foot.

Noah takes this opportunity to hug Mom. I see her visibly relax. "Hello, Noah, my boy," she says, stepping aside to scan him. "Are you well?"

"I'm well," he grins.

Satisfied, she gives him a gentle slap on the cheek. Mom's eyes fasten on me, but before she can say a word, I turn to Dad. His face leaves no doubt that he's done all the peopling he can handle, he's never been big on socializing. "Dad?"

He narrows his eyes on me. "We'll talk later." His gaze softens for Mom. "Cora?"

"Wade?"

"I'll be excusing myself until dinner."

"I excuse you, Wade, my darling."

He kisses Mom on her forehead and strides from the room. Mom smiles after him for a few seconds. "I love that man. Kori, find a man like your father."

I'm happy that she misses my eye roll.

"Hello, Mother Pearle," Mom says formally to Grama Pearle without skipping a beat.

Grama Pearle sticks her tongue out at Mom.

"Unacceptable, Mother Pearle," Mom reprimands.

I'm smirking with enjoyment about Grama Pearle's long-standing game of getting Mom worked up. Plus, it takes the focus off me. Meanwhile, Mom considers the people in the room.

I'm thinking I'll come out of this unscathed. I register her voice talking to Fin, and I zone out. It isn't until she clears her throat that I realize she's talking to me. There's a notable change in the tone of her voice, firm, leaving no question of obedience. "Kori, you and I will prepare dinner and discuss your life choices."

Mom turns to face me. I nearly hyperventilate when Roger marches past the doorway to the kitchen with Carter in tow. I risk a glance at Fin. She's grinning and enjoying my discomfort more than she needs to be.

"Kori," Mom stomps her foot. "Dinner!"

Everybody else decamps before she can put them to work. I hear the rest of the family arrive over the next few hours, but I don't get to greet them. The house, outside the kitchen, is a hive of conversation, but I spend my afternoon under intense questioning. The result is that I'm exhausted by the time Mom catches her voice in magic bubbles and sends them floating on paths to call everyone for dinner.

I'm thankful that I know her as well as I do because even in my exhaustion, I've sense enough to watch her weaves. It was her manner of teaching Jaxton, Alivia, and me. No matter what it was—dishes, making a bed, or tying a shoe—she expected us to watch and then replicate.

"Now, you call your father," she says to me with a tone of voice that suggests she expects not to be let down.

I copy her framework and cast my voice into the bubble. I do it with no extra lectures. Mom says nothing but nods, her classic expression of approval. She returns to setting the table.

Jayce enters the kitchen first in search of food. "Where's my Holden?" His honeyed voice draws attention to the fact that they aren't together, which is strange for them.

"Shhh." Mom cups her ear. I see the magic intertwist and amplify her hearing. "Outside," she chokes. "And someone is coming, not a familiar Spellbinder."

I shift without thinking and speed from the room. A bird with an amazing wingspan is soaring toward Holden from the opposite direction and it's closer to him than I am. It's creepy the way it seems to ride the air currents its wings not flapping and I'm struck by the way its wing feathers resemble outstretched fingers.

Holden is unaware of the danger. He's bent over poking at a tube-like object in the grass. I can hear him humming and I can see his bottom swaying.

I push my wings, willing them to go faster, but it doesn't matter. The bird dives. I transform and scream. Holden's plump face pops up with terror-filled eyes, which change to shock as he swipes at his T-shirt, which is pulling back like it's being blown in a breeze I don't feel.

My brain registers the currents of air forming behind him. The currents have an increasing suction that forces Holden to bend in half. He's sucked backwards and disappears. I freeze and scan the area, but he's gone.

I look at the diving bird, and blink at its feet because one foot has changed into a human hand. The bird grunts as it hits the now-empty spot where Holden was moments before. Its human hand scoops the cylinder off the grass and as it pulls up to fly away, it grabs at my face with the blunt claws of its empty bird foot.

I'm conscious of a growing fire trying to force its way out of me as all my pent-up anger and frustration starts to crest. Holden is gone but the bird isn't and I've no plans to let it escape. My hands flail, trying to get hold of any part of it. The Ember stone on my chest is pulsating with waves of hot and cold.

Some part of my brain hears the bird hissing and me screaming. Its sharp curved beak tears at my face. With its attack on me complete, it wants to get away.

I'm unaware of the dome that I instinctively threw

over us to keep the bird from escaping. Mom's voice bubble transmits her voice into my ear telling me to release the dome and let Alaric in. I drop to a crouch and watch the bird soar up toward the highest point of the dome on the wind currents that I haven't blocked. It's just out of reach. The burning in me is fading. I drop my eyes from the bird and see Alaric at the dome's edge, waiting for me to let him in, patient and neutral.

Mom's voice has gone silent, but I know that this bird won't escape. I release my dome. The bird doesn't get any higher in the air. There aren't any moving air currents in Alaric's new dome. The heavy body of the bird can't fly without the help of the thermal currents.

Blood from the gashes in my face obscures my vision, but I see a blur of coiled magic hit the bird, causing it to shift forms. A woman hits the grass with a thump that knocks the wind from her lungs. Alaric slowed her fall enough to keep her from injury. Her magic and physical person are bound by Alaric before she hit the ground. She can't run, shift to fly, or fight.

My energy sapped by my adrenaline dump and face injury, I watch Alaric remove the tube from her hand to tap out a piece of paper. His expression never changes.

"What does it say?" I croak.

"It says they're coming," he says with a look at the skies.

Chapter 16

Alaric floats our prisoner to the house, still bound by his magic. He looks to me to see if I need help, but I wave him away weakly. "I can make it." He doesn't push it, understanding that my wounded pride for losing Holden needs to feel like I can accomplish something. My feet are clumsy as my weak body and dizzy brain try to work together to get across the field.

Noah meets us halfway to help me walk. He's shrewd enough to recognize that same internal demand in me that Alaric did. He offers his arm to me for support and ignores my uncoordinated footsteps. Alaric passes him the paper.

"There's something in the sky to the north," Fin yells from the deck.

"Inside now!" Noah swings me up into his arms and breaks into a jog. "There was a warning sent saying that people are coming. Everyone inside now!"

"Holden," my voice comes out hoarse. "Holden." I try to wriggle free from Noah.

"Shhh, Kori. We'll find him," Noah says.

I tussle harder, my voice growing louder until I'm screaming.

"Someone knock her out! She needs sleep," Noah hollers over my yelling.

A hand comes into view, but I can't see who it is. The hand forms a sparkle of magic that breaks into tiny falling particles over my head. My yell turns into yawns and my eyes grow too heavy to hold open.

I struggle consciously against the sleep forcing itself on me. *Can't sleep. Must find Holden.* I refocus on the pain from the missing chunks of flesh on my face and the sleepy feeling recedes. My eyes open, I push free of a surprised Noah, and I drop to the ground, barely staying on my feet.

I turn toward the screech of the screen door opening. Aunt Rune is in front of me. "Sweet Kori . . ." Her hand opens inches from my face, and she blows a powder at me.

It stings my wounds. I swipe at it and turn away, but not before breathing in the potent smell of lavender and chamomile. The powder coats the inside of my nasal passage.

"This way is more effective because it guarantees ingestion into eyes, nose, and sometimes mouth. The sleep sparkle is a sleep aid. My spell powder can be compared to a general anesthesia," Aunt Rune barks with a cackle. "Sleep," she commands, and I feel my body and mind complying. Strong hands hook under my armpits as my legs give out.

"It's temporary, Kori," Noah whispers.

I wake to the feel of tingling on my face and know that my wounds are being healed. The ground underneath me is cool and hard. I ease my eyes open. The kitchen lights are above me and I realize that someone has unceremoniously dumped me on the floor. My assumption is that they wanted to keep eyes on me, and since the kitchen tends to be the gathering point, the floor became my bed.

My body isn't ready to move yet, groggy from the sleep powder, but I can hear people talking close by. I hear snippets about rudimentary magic starting to come without conscious effort. I'm not too befuddled to realize they're talking about me.

I remember Noah rushing us to the house after Fin saw something in the ether. "Th-the sky?" I call out.

"It was just Ague," Aunt Rune answers.

"Mad at y-you for . . ." I close my eyes.

Aunt Rune cackles. "Fair enough, I guess, but I plan to teach you control over some of the more potent elements in my potions."

I open my eyes to yell at her, but choke on my words. An unfamiliar face is so close to mine that our noses are touching. Dark eyes set deep into a pale face are burrowing into my own. I fight the urge to pull away and create personal space. I'm not in a mood to be intimidated, and being laid out on the floor limits my options, anyway.

After what seems like an impossible amount of time, the face moves enough for me to see a smile dressed with melting lipstick. I wonder if this is her trade-mark look of insanity or if she's clueless about how crazed it makes her look. The lips move. "I like this one. She has a powerful fire in her." The face returns to nose-bumping proximity. "I think you and I will be great friends, Kori Ember. With your smoulder and my mind control—"

"You're th-the Child of the Sh-Shadows?" I interrupt with frustration as my groggy tongue trips over my words.

The face recoils as if slapped. The label isn't a favourable one. The Child of the Shadows stands, and her mouth flattens into a line, transforming her into an intimidating figure now leering down at me. I can hear Aunt Rune cackling from somewhere close by, but I don't take my eyes off the woman standing over me. My cop instinct tells me that this woman has a dangerous side, and these initial moments of our introduction are setting up the hierarchy for our relationship. Eerily, her haunting smile slides into place.

"I love your fire but please, call me Ague." She reverses from my line of sight.

Fin bends over me. I see the mischief in her smile. "We have no time for games or naps, Kori."

I scrape a hand through my hair and lever myself off the floor. My world is dizzy but comes into focus when Jayce charges at me from across the room, trying to wrap his arms around me. His chubby face is red and tear stained.

When it becomes clear he has no intention of letting go of me, I stand up slowly with him in my arms and ease us into a chair. I settle him on my lap. He rests his head on my shoulder, closes his eyes, and I can feel some of the tension drain out of him. Besides the Grogda siblings, everybody is here. "Um, so what's the deal with the ugly bird?"

"It's an Andean condor," Ague advises me.

I scrunch my nose up at her. "Yeap, I don't care! What's its deal?"

Before Ague can form words, Noah jumps in. "She, the Spellbinder who was the condor, isn't talking. At least, not yet." He cuts his eyes toward Ague.

"She?" I ask. "*She* isn't talking? Let's do better here, folks!"

"We saw a pretty bird in the grass!" Jayce announces. He's nestled in my lap, smiling at me. "It was pretty, and Holden wanted to touch it."

His tone unsettles me. "Jayce, when did you see the pretty bird?"

"Before," he says, fidgeting on my lap.

"Before when?"

"Before I wanted a snack," he answers, looking at the food still spread out on the table.

"Did Holden touch it?" I ask passing him a dinner roll.

"No," he answers, pursing his lips out like his mother does when she's thinking. He squishes the bun in his hand.

"What, Jayce? What happened?" I continue softly.

"Holden touched a thing."

"A thing?" I ask. "What thing?"

Jayce's lips purse out and tears form at the corners of his eyes. I squeeze him and kiss the top of his head. "It's okay, Jayce. You aren't in trouble. Auntie just wants to know what happened so she can help."

His voice is shaky, and I can hardly hear him. "In the grass." His body shakes and he starts crying. He buries his head into me and clings on. I rock him until he lolls and then sleeps.

I roll my neck, the ligaments voicing their displeasure with a series of pops and crackles. "Okay, so what do we know?"

"We know that a pretty bird left a message in the grass. We can surmise that the bird hadn't planned to be seen, but when it was, it left the message in the grass for Holden to bring to us and therefore avoid further detection. And we know that an ugly bird was trying to get that message before we could," Fin says. "Pretty basic."

I look at her and blink, but I direct my next question to everybody else, "Where is the ugly she-bird? I think it's my turn to try to get her to talk," I say sharply.

"Oh, that fire," Ague says.

I turn what I hope is my fieriest stare at her. Her lipstick-melting mouth twitches and she laughs.

"Love it, love it!" She gasps. Jayce sleeping on my lap keeps me from wringing her neck. When she has herself composed, her eyes lock on me as if I'm the only person in the room, "The condor is a woman named Aza Tier."

"That means nothing to me, Ague."

"She works for The Society of the Blood Wind and soon she'll work for us as a double agent," Fin cuts in.

I cut my eyes to Fin and see that she's almost vibrating with excitement. "Okay," I say, turning to Ague, "where is this Aza Tier now?"

Ague's eyes flash to the corner of the room and she licks her red lips. I swallow, feeling uneasy with the idea of creating a double agent and the methods for doing it. The slender female strapped to the chair is a feral-looking adolescent with unfocused, darting eyes. Her dark hair is greasy and matted. I'm horror struck that we've captured a child, but when she lunges against her restraints, I can see the signs of age that cling to her waxy skin. This tiny woman must be mid-forties.

Ague has no emotion when she says, "I've extracted all the useful intel from her already."

"It was so cool," Fin says with wide eyes.

"How long was I asleep? You know what? Never mind," I say. Moving my fingers to my temples, I make firm circular motions and turn to face Ague. "And?"

Ague says nothing, her smile never falters, and her empty eyes just watch me.

I breathe deep and hold my stare on this crazy lady. "Anybody?"

"Kori, The Society of the Blood Wind doesn't know who has Alivia, but they believe it's an inside job. Someone from their own ranks. They suspected the message today, perhaps even orchestrated it by letting people in their ranks know an attack was coming. Aza was supposed to watch the safe house. Her mission was to see who was handing the message off to us and to stop us from receiving it. She was unsuccessful on both tasks," Fin says.

I'm sucking in large gulps of air to keep myself calm. I shrug in a how-does-this-helps-us gesture.

"The plan is to alter and control her loyalty in our favour for a while, override her free will." I can hear a note of disapproval in Aunt Rune's tone.

The disapproval is lost on Fin. "Like a programmed spy," she explains with a huge grin.

I flash Fin a look of disgust. "I can't be a part of this." But I'm not one hundred percent sure of my commitment to the statement; Alivia, and now Holden, are missing. I turn to the ever-smiling Ague. "I know the reason for this 'programmed spy' is to see if we can learn anything about who has Alivia and Holden and what The Society of the Blood Wind is planning. But how can we gain control of her quickly enough to make her useful?"

Ague cocks her head to the side and stares at me.

I sigh and drop my hands from my temples. "That kind of control requires isolation and psychological, not to mention physical punishments, and—" I stop myself because Ague's head has cocked the other way and her mouth is moving without sound. Her eyes lock on Aza, but Aza has her eyes shut and is moaning and fighting against her restraints. Ague is subjecting Aza to her magic and Aza is resisting.

I can't see the weaves, but I know they're there. The air is electrified as the seconds tick by, creating bolts of flashing fluorescent lighting. The flashes increase in intensity and frequency like an indoor lightning storm.

I wrap Jayce protectively in my arms. Aza has stopped moaning, and she isn't fighting as hard. A few seconds pass and then Aza stops moving and slumps in the chair. The lightshow ends, leaving an inorganic, burnt smell of wire and plastic.

"Is she dead?" Fin whispers, less impressed with the situation than she was a few minutes ago.

"Release her restraints," Ague says flatly.

Fin glances at her but doesn't move. Ague straightens her head and flicks her chin in Aza's direction. Fin manifests complete surprise as her limbs move forward like they're attached to a puppet's strings. Ague's head is moving slightly, like she's controlling Fin's body with slight movements of her own head.

Fin releases Aza's restraints and we watch as Aza's body slides into a heap on the floor, unmoving. It's unclear to me if Aza has zero control of her body or if she's so exhausted from Ague's attack on her that she can only lie there. I've no desire to draw Ague's attention, so I accept my ignorance.

Unsure of herself, Fin lifts her arms up and down, then her legs. She jumps on the spot and wiggles. When she seems satisfied that she has control of her body, unmoving, she looks at Ague. "How?" she squeals with delight instead of anger.

My eyes go round in response and my scalp prickles. My heart is beating a heavy, sluggish rhythm of dread. *Where do we draw the line of ethics?* Aunt Rune turns on her heels and retreats. Her escape from the room appeals to me.

There's a soft rustling in the plants closest to the

sunroom doorway. I glimpse a bird with round wings and a square tail flying deeper into the foliage. I jump in my seat when Brynlee speaks from the hallway entrance to the kitchen. "There are a few glorious minutes right after the charging, that's what we call what Ague did to Aza, when anyone present can be susceptible to manipulation. It wears off fast for everyone except the person the charge focused on."

"Can you do it?" Fin asks her, wonderstruck.

"I'm learning," Brynlee comes completely into the room. The wart is gone from her nose and she's smug and satisfied with herself.

I blow out a sigh, making a mental note that I'm doing it a lot today. "What happens to Aza now?"

"Aza is loyal to us," Ague answers as she moves over to Aza's motionless body and bends over her. I hear Ague whispering, but her voice is too low for me to make out the words.

Brynlee is watching Ague with awe. "Brynlee," I hiss. I wait until she looks at me and then I flick my chin at Ague and Aza.

Brynlee surprises me with a cackle, very much like her mother's. "Ague is planting suggestions, and then Aza will be on her way."

"Just like that?" I ask.

Brynlee turns to Ague's bent form and nods her head. "So simple," she breathes.

Either everyone is so caught up in Ague's control of Aza that they aren't noticing Brynlee's concerning response or they're so used to it they take it in stride. For me, it feels like another aspect of Spellbinder life that I cut myself off from and I'm realizing this is a dangerous game I am playing on so many levels: an in ability to understand the world around me and the people in it, a disadvantage protecting myself and the people I love . . .

Ague rises and steps back. Her lips pull up at the corners as she watches Aza stretch like a cat on the floor before getting to her feet. Aza studies the room. Her haunting eyes land on me and there's a distinct rousal, like I've startled her out of a deep sleep. She takes a menacing step in my direction, shudders, and runs from the room. The deck door bangs.

Outside the kitchen window, I see a condor flying off. I turn to speak to Ague, but she's disappeared. Swallowing, I stare out the window until the sky is empty. I'm staring at the ether when I see a pigeon speeding toward the house with an erratic flight pattern.

I scoop Jayce up and move to the window to see better. As I pull the glass open, I hear a faint raptor-like scream. The pigeon dives and a hawk comes into view, diving after it. The pigeon spins and pulls up, but the hawk mimics and is closing in.

"Help the pigeon, Auntie," Jayce says, having come awake in my arms. I set him on the counter and he opens the screen and starts yelling for the bird to come to us.

The pigeon changes course for the open window. I ready an orb, but I can't get an angle that won't hit the pigeon. The hawk pulls up and arches its talons. Everything is in slow motion.

"Bounce it," Brynlee says. "Some orbs can be bounced."

When my response is a questioning look, she forms her own orb and lobs it out the window. It hits the ground at an angle and rebounds up behind the pigeon and clips the hawk with just enough wind to blow it off its attack path. It screams and flaps its wings wildly, but the pigeon sails through the open window, causing us all to duck as it loops toward the sunroom.

The hawk stays its course. Brynlee closes the window. At the last second, the hawk shrieks and curves up before it hits the glass. The flash of red on the tail is all I need to see to know the pigeon escaped a brush of death from Kyson Adelgrief's talons. I scoop Jayce off the counter and follow Brynlee to the sunroom.

The plump bird is on the table, watching Birdie with its orange eyes as she prepares a fresh dish of grains, seeds, and berries for a job well done. It feeds happily while Birdie removes the message from the carrier tube on its leg. She gives the bird a few strokes and its bluish-gray feathers almost glow in response.

"No shifting?" I ask curiously.

"Hmm, no. No shifting," Birdie chirps absently as she unfurls the paper. "This is one of my messenger birds." Her hand waves around the room, she says nothing more, and her owl-like eyes stay focused on the message.

I take a fresh look at the room and the birds. "Wait, not all messenger birds are Spellbinders?"

Birdie flicks her hand at me, head shaking, and her

eyes move over the words as she speaks. "Spellbinders can shift into bird form, but we don't do it to courier communiqué. Obviously, we could, but why? Messenger birds are just that, birds."

She's distracted by the paper and her words are flowing out without thought. "I love birds, and this is my bird sanctuary. I thought someone told you that. Spellbinders come and go from here in bird form just as often as they drive up in vehicles under regular circumstances, but with everything going on there have been more Spellbinders flying in then usual. That isn't to say I haven't provided safe house services to Spellbinders who shelter here in bird form."

I should've thought that one through, I think. *Why would we put a tube around our leg when we can shift and speak for ourselves? Although it could be an interesting disguise.* "Birdie?" I ask.

"I need to speak to Alaric." She passes the note to me and hustles from the room to find him. The paper rolls into a tight scroll the minute it's released from her fingers and it topples into my hand.

The clicking of Brynlee's fingers is a tip-off that she's lost interest. She's sitting on the far corner of the table, swinging her legs. I watch for a second as she clicks her middle finger and thumb together and produces a reduced flame of fire on her fingertip, letting it wink out, and then she snaps to create a different condensed element. I raise my eyebrows at her, but she doesn't notice.

The paper in my hand rocks. A flash of heat scorches my palm, and the note burns to ash. "Awesome, self-destructing messages," I mumble hanging my head and brushing the ash onto the floor. Jayce is content feeding the birds seeds and stroking their feathers, so I leave him and Brynlee in the sunroom to go find out the details of the message from Birdie.

Birdie and Alaric are alone in the kitchen. She's talking lively at him, and he's listening, poker-faced. They turn toward me when I come in. "Bad news?" I ask.

Birdie makes a growling sound as she turns. "Our enemies have set upon our reinforcements, causing their delayed arrival here." She blinks her enormous eyes at me and hops away.

Alaric is deadpan. He shrugs and heads toward the sunroom, leaving me alone in the kitchen. I stand there for a second, considering the information and my options. I scratch my head and reach for the coffee pot. It feels like this is going to be an exhausting day.

Chapter 17

The morning passes in a blur, with just about everyone pulling me off to the side to teach me new useful magic, intent on cramming me full of it. I'm happy to find that each skill comes to me with ease, but I'm happier to discover that I've grown stronger and faster with the tricks I originally learned. Regardless, the distraction from my mounting frustration is nice, but time is moving. We've no leads on who took Holden or why, and we have no immediate plans for next steps.

Craving time to myself, I march out of the house with no heed to the lectures that'll follow once it becomes apparent that I'm gone. I've no intention of leaving the property, but I need to catch my breath from all the lessons. Without thought for where I'm going, I find myself by the gargoyles.

This side of the house is in the sun and has no direct connection to the sunroom which, like the kitchen, is a gathering point. I pause comparing the gargoyle's positions. Today the gargoyle with spikes lining its jaw is in a sitting position and the one with the dagger-tipped mane is laying down with its paws outstretched.

As I move closer, I hear a soft rumble. The spiked

gargoyle is purring and there's a cloaked form scratching behind its ears. A prickle of fear and excitement races through me at the thought of catching somebody that might know some useful information. Before I can react, the faint crunch of gravel far up the driveway startles the crouched figure. The individual straightens and turns. My orb fades out in my palm when Brynlee scowls at me from under her cloak like a sullen twenty-year-old who is displeased that someone dared to interrupt their temporary escape from responsibility.

"What are you doing out here?" I bark.

"Kori, I could ask you the same thing."

I nod and stretch "Fair, but what are you doing?"

"Spending a few minutes with Galox and Daken, like I always do," she says. When I just stare blankly, she rocks on her heels. "This is Galox," Brynlee waves a hand at the spikey gargoyle. "And this is Daken," she indicates the stretched-out one.

"The stone gargoyles?" I surprise myself when the disbelief in my voice isn't as pronounced as it would've been days ago.

Brynlee doesn't see my internal grimace. She smirks. "Stone? You keep telling yourself that, Cousin." She brushes past me, talking over her shoulder as she goes, "Don't worry, I just fed them, so they should have a pleasant manner for a while."

She's in a mood so I don't bother questioning if she's teasing me. I reason that they wouldn't be here if they were a threat to people staying on the property. I stare at the gargoyles while listening to Brynlee's receding footfalls. When everything is silent, I breathe deep. *Safe as anywhere else, I guess.*

I plop down on the ground between Galox and Daken. When neither gargoyle moves nor makes a sound, I feel foolish that it was a thought that crossed my mind. The part of me that disowned my magical heritage wants to deny Fin's and my experience with the gargoyles ten days ago. I'm cursing under my breath that ten days have already passed when I hear someone crunching down the driveway in my direction. I'm relieved to see it's Fin.

"What are you doing out here?" I quiz her.

"Searching for you, of course!" She drops beside me. Immediately Fin scratches behind a round ear that ends in a pointy tip, on the gargoyle known as Daken.

"Um, what are you doing?" I ask.

Fin looks at me and she bursts out laughing.

"What?"

"Nothing, it's just that after everything that's happened, you're still fighting the fact that this shit is real. Not just real, but our reality!" She swings her hands dramatically and accidentally swats the gargoyle. A low, guttural sound erupts from him, making us both jump. "Shit. Sorry, Daken!" She starts a soothing stroke on its neck.

Reality. My eyebrows are resting up near my hairline as I review Daken's oversized visible fangs and the numerous spikes dotting the puffy part of his face where a lion's whiskers would be. "How do you know the gargoyle's name, Fin?"

Fin giggles. "I know Daken and Galox are a gargoyle

couple. They've been protectors of this property for hundreds of years!"

I blink at her, and she laughs harder. Before she can say what else she knows about Daken and Galox, Noah bellows for me from somewhere up the driveway. We go silent and stare at each other, waiting to see if he'll call again.

"Kori, where are you?" Noah's louder this time.

My eye twitches. Fin reaches out and places her finger over my involuntary eyelid spasm. Her voice comes out in a whisper. "Come on, maybe if I provide you with a breather from all this in-our-face magic, then you can come back feeling open and ready to accept."

She gets up and starts running toward the road. There's no thought required for me. I hop up and follow. We reach the tree line and Fin plunges right in, crashing through to the road on the other side. I'm surprised to see the Willys MB parked and waiting for us.

"Fin?" I race to jump in the front passenger's seat.

"I had Roger park it here. I need a sandwich from my favourite restaurant and you, my friend, as I already mentioned need a break. Sit back, relax, and get into a new head space." She mashes her foot down on the gas pedal and the Willys shoots forward, kicking up a wall of dust and gravel behind us.

"I think I'm going to try one of your Turkish coffees today, but tell me about them first," I yell over the wind ripping past our heads.

"Well, it has a high caffeine content, but they add extra sugar to cut the bold coffee flavour!"

"Sold," I say as we enter the outskirts of Lindsay.

"Good, but I'm picking the food for us. I've been wanting you to try the avocado and goat cheese sandwiches. They're one of my favourites." We stop for a red light. Fin must see me scrunch my face up because she laughs. "You'll love it with its mashed avocado and sprouts." She pulls the Willys into the alley and parks so close to the wall that I have to climb over the door to get out.

"No, you wait here!" she says, eyeing the alley. "Last time we went inside together, you were a shit magnet. Remember, Miss Hum-and-Poop?" She laughs as she struts to the door.

I lean against the Willys and watch the opening of the alley. I float my chakra stones on my palm, thankful for this moment to myself but before I can enjoy it too much, the door flies open and Fin comes running out at full speed. She's empty-handed, which makes me nervous about what's inside to set her on the run. My chakra stones drop into my hand, and I make a fist.

Fin charges toward me and grabs my wrist, yanking me down the alley behind her. She casts a glance over her shoulder, checking for someone or something, and tightens her grip on me.

"What is it, Fin?" I holler. I see nothing and turn my eyes forward to keep from tripping. Fin yanks us into an oversized rear entranceway to a closed store. She stuffs me in behind her before she peeks out.

"What is it, Fin? What's out there?"

She pulls her head in and turns to face me. A wave of alarm goes off in my brain. Her face is unreadable. I try to get some distance between us but the cold brick wall is flat against my back. When I can't access my magic, my alarm grows to full panic.

I study Fin's face. Her electric-green eyes aren't green, but a deep brown and her face has an intense sadness. Suspicious, I sniff the air. My nose fills with the bouquet of cardamon, cedar, and lavender with undertones of cinnamon. "Belamey Adelgrief?" I whisper.

Whoever it is takes a step closer and their lips pull into what's supposed to be a comforting smile. Another step, their body is up against mine and I've no doubt this is Belamey, as the heated energy I've come to associate with him radiates off his body. I'm surprised to find my panic level is almost gone.

My gut instinct that served to keep me safe as a police officer isn't screaming danger. This man's actions are controversial, but he isn't a threat to me. Something else is going on with him. I slit my eyes and scrutinize the face. Belamey's handsome features replace Fin's feminine ones as he lets the disguise drop.

"Hello, Kori. Forgive my precaution in blocking you from your magic, I didn't want you to attack me when you realized I wasn't Fin . . ."

I feel him release my magic, then he cocks his head and bends close. There's a moment when I think he's going to kiss me, but his head moves until his lips brush my ear. "It's getting harder to find time alone with you." He lingers with his head close to mine while the smell of him intoxicates me and garbles any comments.

My eyes close to savour his fragrance. I give my head a shake to clear the fog that his proximity creates in my brain, which works just enough for me to take control of my arms and shove him away. He laughs. It's a deep, playful sound that gives me shivers.

I push away the thoughts of his muscled body pinning me to the wall in an act of desire. My voice comes out strangled. "What are you doing?"

Belamey's eyes travel the full length of my body and I feel angry with myself for wondering if he likes what he sees. "You're flushed, Kori."

"How did you disguise yourself as Fin?" I ask, ignoring his comment on my heated state. I shelve my confusion about his effect on me. I'm trying to work through enough uncomfortable stuff, and since Alivia and Holden's safety is connected to me figuring out my magic, my unwarranted attraction to Belamey can wait. *Attraction? Really? What's the matter with me?*

"You're getting stronger. I'm surprised you haven't figured out the cloaking trick. It's just a variation from masking, but then again, why change any of this?" He traces his fingers down my sides, which sets my nerve endings tingling and my fingers ache to return the touch.

I push at him, but he's expecting it and he grabs my wrists and pins them in between us so we remain hidden in the doorway. "Always the smouldering Ember, but we don't have time to get dirty today, Kori," he teases with a twinkle in his eye that I haven't noticed there before. "Fin will return soon. I waited until she was in line to order before I came to see you. She was so intent on the menu that she wasn't paying attention to much else."

I observe the alleyway over his shoulder. "What do you want, Belamey? And how did you know I was here?"

He smiles at me and lifts one eyebrow. I swallow in response, but before he can play with me any further, Fin's voice rings out.

"See, we have so little time together." He raises his hand up between us and wiggles his fingers. There's a playful tickle on my scalp and clear sparkling particles pull from my hair onto Belamey's palm. "I placed these on you that day I was in your bedroom, it's the reason I was there. It's so I could find you if you needed help." He studies my face. "They're hunting, Kori. Until they have you, or the Ember stone, or both, they won't be satisfied."

I glance at him and at the alley. "Fin!"

Belamey tuts. "Be careful, Kori Ember. Not everything is as it seems." He takes my hand and dumps the particles into my palm. "That's all the sparkles I placed on you. Your choice if you want to keep them so I can't find you . . ." He looks over his shoulder. Fin's feet are pounding up the alley. "I came to tell you Holden and Alivia are safe for now. My safety requires you keep me being the one who shared this with you our secret." His eyes stare into mine and there's something there that surprises me.

"How do I believe—" Before I can finish my question, his lips brush over mine and fire shoots through me. My mouth parts and I lean into him.

Fin's voice calls my name. It echoes in the alley, and I'm left staring at a swirl of smoke where Belamey was a few seconds before. *What is this smoky magic he uses?*

I haven't seen anyone else . . . Alaric's memory! Nekane used it to escape after he thought he killed Alaric. My hand without the sparkles has a pressure in it and I realize Belamey slipped an item into it before he disappeared.

I let the particles fall to the ground, not sure if I can trust Belamey or my judgement where he's involved. I step into the alleyway so Fin knows where I am, planning to see what Belamey has given me. Fin slides to a stop with her throwing knives in hand. Her head swivels as she searches for a target. I stare at her. She examines me and the alley, not convinced to put her knives away. "What the fuck?" She hisses.

A chilly breeze gusts down the alley and Fin and I both turn in the direction that it's coming from. The breeze gusts with a faint smell of decay. Fin's arm cocks and throws as the first of the hollow men appear in front of us. Her knife stabs into him and he scatters into dust, which blows our way on the now-cold air.

"Run," Belamey's voice is urgent in my ear, but he's nowhere to be seen.

Without having to be told twice, I ram the unknown object into my pocket, grab Fin, and charge for the Willys. Fin has us peeling out of the alley backward at full speed as several hollow men glide toward us. Shrill banshee cries fills the air like they're sounding an initial battle cry.

"Hold on," she screams as she whips the steering wheel to the right and rockets us forward into traffic.

Fin speeds by cars and plows through a red light, trying to put distance between us and the alley. She doesn't decrease her speed at all and soon we're flying down country roads. I'm surprised when she zooms past the driveway and I panic, wondering if a second fake Fin has duped me. The smug smirk on her face reassures me that I haven't and I subside into my seat. She takes a right onto a grass cow path and lessens our tempo.

"Where are we going?" I ask now that she can hear me easier.

"To eat and have privacy while you explain what just happened?"

"Eat?"

She flicks her head. "It's on the floor in the back under that blanket. Hopefully the coffees are still upright given our fast getaway from the alley."

We motor into an old gravel pit. Fin drives to the far side and parks so we have a view of the road. She hops out without a word, reaches in, and grabs the food. "You get the coffees." She slides onto the hood of the Willys.

I grab the square coffee tray, marvelling that the coffees, set up diagonal to one another, kept the tray from tipping. I slide up beside her. Before Fin eats, she passes me a sandwich on toasted rye bread. I inspect it with curiosity. It's green inside, with avocado, sprouts, and thin slices of cucumber. I also see specks of white, which I assume is goat cheese, and there are vibrant orange pops. "You said nothing about tomatoes."

Fin just shrugs and keeps eating.

I bite down and stare off over the pit. I'm pleased with the creamy and cheesy taste of the sandwich, which also packs a nice crunch. The tension drains out of my body as I chew. Fin is sipping her coffee, watching me as I finish eating. She passes me my drink and I'm surprised to feel warmth coming off it.

"So, tell me about Belamey?"

I whip my head at her so fast that I almost knock myself off the car. She's laughing at me when I form the word. "How?"

"His smell was clinging to you in the alley, and you were grinning like an idiot!"

My fingers go to my lips before I think better of it.

"No!" With eyes as wide as mine, we assess each other.

"Wait, you could smell Belamey on me?" I ask with a bit of hope because I'm worried that my preoccupation with his smell is some kind of sign of my muddled desire.

"Of course, I can smell him! How do you think he makes himself smell so exquisite? That man's scent is delicious?" She licks her lips and her face takes on a dreamy state.

I sigh and try to relax. My mind is spinning about what I should reveal to Fin. She's watching me over the rim of her disposable cup. Fin is obviously not someone Belamey was trying to warn me about or he wouldn't have appeared when she and I were together. I feel on edge, but it isn't Fin making me feel that way. It's the overall unknown of our experience in the alley.

I'm staring at Fin but not seeing her. Refocusing on the gravel pit, I fill my mouth with coffee. The pit is a mix of plateaus and dips with reddish-brown sand and gray stones. Patches of green vegetation grow at random intervals on that hillside. I try to ground myself by imagining myself running barefoot and leaping off the side to feel that moment of euphoria as I free fall, plunging into the soft grainy sand with my feet gliding through the coolness of the granular powder.

Fin clears her throat. I push my eyes up to the blue sky. There's cloud cover in the distance moving our way. I take a sip of coffee and launch into a monologue about Belamey and I in the alley. When I finish talking, I lift my coffee, not caring that it's cold as it flows over my lips.

"He loves you," she announces.

The liquid passes over my lips with a shocked mouthful of air. Sputtering and choking, I slide off the hood, coughing, and bend over, sure that I'm going to die from my coffee inhalation, but Fin just sits on the Willys, reasoning out her theory. I miss most of it and there's some that I choose to ignore. When I get enough unrestricted air, I shoot daggers at her from my eyes.

She has the audacity to roll her eyes at me as she slides off the Willys. "Don't worry, your secret is safe with me, but when you see him naked, I want details!"

I throw my empty disposable cup at her.

"What?" She mocks innocence.

A crack of thunder sounds in the distance. The sky is now a nasty gray. If we stay, the storm will catch us. We hop in the Willys. The wind picks up. Drops of rain mist the air when we hit the main road. Thunder cracks and lightning bolts dance.

"Your mother will love the beautiful smouldering babies you and Belamey are going to make," Fin says as she turns us onto the driveway.

"The silence between us on the drive here was almost perfect, Fin!" I purse my lips.

Fin gives a whoop and she can't contain her smile. She stops teasing me though.

The rain is coming down in sheets, obscuring our vision, but I catch a slight view of the gargoyles. "Fin, something is off. Look at Daken and Galox." Both gargoyles are crouched down, their shoulders hunched, their heads low, and their eyes peer forward. "They're watching, almost stalking,"

Fin speeds right up to the deck and stops as close as she can. We can't see Galox and Daken or the front of the house from the deck, but their behaviour stays in my mind as we jump out and run up the stairs. As soon as we hit the deck, I can't feel the rain anymore, but the beat of it hammering on a dome overhead is loud in my ears. The Grogda siblings stop pacing and analyze Fin and I before they return to their steady back-and-forth patrol of the deck in cassowary form.

"Love your rain dome," Fin calls over her shoulder as we tumble into the sunroom, dripping wet and shivering.

The birds are milling about in their usual manner, giving no indication that anything is amiss. I consider if the weather could be what's effecting the gargoyles, but that doesn't make sense. They were hypervigilant, not behaving like the weather was causing discomfort. Fin is shaking the water off her ebony bobbed hairstyle like she's a dog. I gauge the sunroom, but the only strange thing is that Birdie isn't out here.

Fin reads my mind. "She isn't in here all the time, Kori."

"I can't believe I'm stuck on this, or even considering it at all, but the gargoyles are on edge, Fin."

She shrugs. "Maybe." She looks outside. "Maybe the storm has them on edge. Come on, let's go get our lecture for leaving the property." She saunters into the kitchen.

I survey the sky before I follow Fin. "Or maybe they see something we don't," I mumble without emotion.

Chapter 18

Everybody, except Hellzel and Dugal, is in the kitchen when Fin and I enter, but nobody is interested in our escapade. Roger's eyes lock on Fin, who beams a smile at him. I'm not as fortunate with welcoming greetings. Mom takes a second to cast me a death stare, but that's where it ends. She turns to the discussion unfolding.

A new person, a stranger to me, arrived while Fin and me were gone, and from the bits of conversation I'm catching, he had a hard time getting to us. Fin doesn't wait to see if anybody is going to change their minds about lecturing us and she tugs me straight through the kitchen. She stuffs me into the bathroom to shower and flings clothes in from the dresser while I'm enjoying the hot water stinging my skin.

"Don't turn it off, Kori," Fin says from inside the bathroom.

"Fin, get out!"

She laughs. "Hurry."

I peek around the shower curtain, and she tosses a towel at me, drops hers, and moves to get in the other end of the shower. I hop out and wrap in my towel.

"Oh, relax you prude," she sings. "We already established that your vagina isn't golden!" She pauses, waiting for me to respond and when I say nothing she continues, "Wait for me. I don't want to miss anything. Something must be going on. Did you see there was an unknown person at the table?"

"I agree something is going on," I say loud enough for Fin to hear over the running shower. "I'm less concerned with the stranger than the behaviour of the gargoyles," I remark under my breath.

I dress and perch on the bathroom counter, listening to Fin sing her rendition of a current popular radio song. While she finishes showering, I rest my head against the wall. She pauses mid-chorus and pops her head into view in a mess of lathered shampoo. "You mention in your steamy alley encounter that Belamey put something in your hand. Now is a good time to see what it is." She disappears behind the shower curtain and continues singing.

I stare at the spot where Fin's head was and shake my own before fishing in my wet clothes for the mysterious item from Belamey. My hand feels a ball shape and I pull it out. It's a crumpled up paper. I smooth it out and pause.

"Well?" Fin says, building the word right into the lyrics of the song.

"It's a paper folded into a mock envelope," I call over the shower water.

Her head pops out, but she doesn't stop singing.

"Alivia used to leave me notes tucked and creased this way all the time when we were young." My hands tremble as I grab the middle V-shaped section marked *pull* and I pull. The note gives way, and I fold it down and press it flat on the counter.

"The day they took him, Holden was drawing this picture. I watched him fold it in half twice and stuff it in his pocket. He wanted to finish it after dinner," I mumble.

Fin disappears behind the shower curtain. "Proof of life. Holden's drawing refolded by Alivia."

My eyes wander to the unfrosted window and then the sky, wondering what game Belamey is playing and why. My eyes land on the large white bird flying over the house. "Strange, there's an albatross circling the house."

Fin's head pokes around the curtain to view me and then the window. There are other birds swooping into the yard. Snarling silences Fin's singing and I almost fall off the counter. It isn't until this moment that I appreciate the sheer breadth of the lion gargoyles. I watch as one after the other they leap off the ground and pull birds, the albatross being one of them, out of the sky like they're just bothersome flies.

"You read Daken and Galox correctly, Kori," Fin says with a warm tone which she follows with a sharp intake of air. "Looks like we made a stupid mistake not mentioning it to anybody when we came in." Then she's on the move.

She wastes no time running naked down the hall, leaving a water trail behind her on her flight to the dresser. She's a fleshy blur when she hollers a warning on her way by the kitchen. I slide into the room, calling out my alert that we're under attack. The words are barely out of my mouth when a blast hits the house so hard I'm sure the walls will crumble.

"They've thrown a holding dome over us," Aunt Rune and Brynlee say in unison.

"What's a holding dome?" I look up at the ceiling.

"It keeps us all in the space it covers," Aunt Rune says. "There's no way through it. It doesn't penetrate into the ground, but there's no magic for tunnelling, so we're stuck for now."

"We can't get out unless we weaken it enough to shatter it, but that takes a certain skill." Brynlee's mischievous smile is so big it's comical on her face.

Fin slides into the kitchen, and everyone pauses. She's dressed like Lara Croft from the movie *Tomb Raider*, decorated with various sized knives instead of firearms. "What?" she asks the room. "These are my main knives," she points to the belt on her waist, "and these are spares." She swishes her hands downward at four belts of knives, two on each of her thighs.

"And those?" I point to the mini-knives belted to her left bicep.

Her eyes cut past me and before I can register what she's doing, a knife zings by my head and lands in the chest of a hollow man trying to breach the doorway between the sunroom and the kitchen. I swing my eyes to Fin, who shrugs.

Noah wastes no time in thundering directions. "We need to take this fight outside to keep the safe house from falling! Rune and Brynlee, work on collapsing the dome. Ague, do what you do. Fin, you know your role.

Everyone else, let's go to battle."

Even the stranger arms himself with magic and races from the room. I'll have to ask about him later. I move to follow everyone, but Noah blocks me. "Not you!"

I squint at him. "Like hell, not me!"

"You'll stay in here. Something has changed if they are attacking. Until now, we were certain they weren't aware of you and your connection to the Ember stone. Kieran knew, but he's dead. They're here for you and the Ember stone. It's the only thing that makes sense. One step outside, and you'll be gone. Do you not understand how much relies on you and that stone? If they get you and the Ember stone, then they'll use Alivia and Holden to force you to do anything they want with it.

"The Cleansing happens once the Ember stone is in the Cleansing room, which Nekane would never allow, but you can access its raw power anywhere once you know how and once you are strong enough. You exclusively!

"Ask yourself, Kori, what wouldn't you do to keep your sister and nephew safe? There isn't anything Nekane wouldn't do, Kori, if he had that kind of power, you and the Ember stone together, to control. Human subjugation would only be a start. So, you'll stay here! Stay with Fin. Her job is to keep you both safe. Fight from in here with that goal in mind!" He turns on his heel and races into the sunroom. I see Noah tackle someone using their combined momentum to pull them across the table in a flurry of feathers and birdseed.

My cop self is screaming at me. I'm trained to run

into danger, not hide or run from it. "You aren't a cop anymore, Kori, and these isn't normie problems." Fin, as always, accurately reads me, which is why she and I will make a great team inside the safe house.

A second knife flies past me and hits its mark. "Stop throwing those blazing things so close to my head!" I yell at Fin. I have orbs readied in both my hands, but I'm distracted by the feeling of burning on my skin where the Ember stone sits. *Why is it burning my skin? And why now?*

"Get behind me then, idiot." Fin smirks as she lets another knife fly.

"Auntie," Jayce's scared voice calls from the hall.

"Smoke and ashes." I dive behind Fin. I'm between her and Jayce and his eyes are teared. His body is shaking, and he's holding two dwarfed orbs that I've never seen before. They're glowing and pulsing in his palms so dramatically that I pause, concerned with what they do.

"Jayce? It's okay. You can let those orbs fade." I steady my voice.

"No, I keep Auntie Fin safe."

Fin is crouched low in the doorway, unaware of us. I move toward Jayce. "No, honey. That's not your job."

Jayce's shining eyes glance at me and then Fin. "Mommy said that I have a special magic for keeping people safe." His hands come into the air, and he claps them together. There's a blinding flash as the two orbs collide and merge into one. A streak of light follows when Jayce flings the orb at Fin. There's time for my eyes to go wide before the orb smashes into her unsuspecting body. Her body takes on a soft, glowing outline. I swallow and watch, waiting for something untold to happen. I don't have to wait.

Fin releases her throwing knife and attempts to dive behind the wall to avoid an oncoming attack, but she's too slow. A black orb with electricity pulsing through it hits her in the side and she slams into the wall. I know because of the wild pulsing inside this orb that it's a death orb that's hit Fin, but she's alive. She's crawling. I grab her arm and yank her away from the entry.

"Thank you," she whispers to Jayce, who beams at her, and she wipes the tears off his cheeks.

I creep toward the entry and push my head out close to the ground. The burning on my chest has increased threefold and I feel as if there's fire coursing through my veins. I'm fighting to control my movements.

There are cloaked forms working ferociously at a charm on the entranceway. A charm that wasn't there a few minutes ago when Fin's knives were working to keep the goons at bay. I catch sight of Birdie in the sunroom behind the cloaked forms, she must have warded the door just after Fin was hit. Birdie shifts into an owl, snatches one of the cloaked forms in her talons, and carries him from sight.

I glance at Fin and Jayce just as he launches one of his special orbs at me. It's like a large pinch where it contacts my body, and then a soft tickle runs over my skin. The intense heat where the Ember stone touches my flesh is shielded and I can feel the fire in my veins fade. I smile at him and re-focus on the entranceway.

Sucking a deep breath, I bowl a sound-wave orb

across the kitchen floor. I watch as the tiny, listless orb grows and picks up speed. It hits the feet of the cloaked form and blows him backward into the depths of the sunroom.

"That'll take him a minute to recuperate from." I pull my head into the hall.

Fin has repositioned herself at the far end of the hallway. She's throwing knives into the living room in the direction of the sunroom doorway. I swallow a lump in my throat. We've been so focused on the kitchen entrance we didn't check the entrance from the living room. Birdie's presence in the sunroom to ward the kitchen entrance makes sense if she'd been close by, dealing with the second doorway.

Jayce is propelling clear orbs the size of marbles out into the room faster than Fin is throwing knives. I do a double take when I see the case of small-scale throwing knives, but there's no time to wonder where they came from. The commotion at the kitchen entranceway re-alerts me to the cloaked forms, back with renewed vigour. They have an extra body working as a magical overwatch so they don't get surprised. I push out a deep breath, wracking my brain for a safe retreat point.

The charm hisses and steams. The invisible barrier is now visible as a pane of glass with cracked spider webbing branching out from their main point of attack. I recall Birdie hopping through her door charm the night the cassowaries arrived and I feel like we have seconds before they're through.

"Retreat!" I scream as I pound down the hall toward the stairs. Fin scoops Jayce up and hits the stairs with me on her heels. I'm almost knocked off my feet when the front door on the landing flies open. Brynlee runs in, banging the door behind her. Frustrated, I wonder why we can't ward access points so that they're unusable to everybody, but I also understand the danger with limiting entrance and exits in an emergency.

"Dome is almost down," she says, as if she expected me to be there. She knits a glimmering spiderweb, stretches it, and tosses it over the doorway. I watch as it grows to cover the full area of the door and attaches to the surrounding wall. It fades into a fraudulent spider's web coated with morning dew. "Kori, you do it to the top of the stairs. It'll offer a measure of protection to the stairs, enough to slow them down." She flicks her head at the steps that lead up. "Hurry!"

My web replica gives off a flickering light like a flame. Under different circumstances I would take a moment to be impressed with how easily I accomplished this on the first try, but this isn't the time. I toss it up the stairs, but I don't wait to see what happens. I thunder down the steps behind Brynlee. Fin holds Jayce in the basement, unsure which way to go.

"To the potion room," Brynlee yells as she turns to run in the opposite direction. A scream and poof of dust let us know that my charm works and in spite of our efforts, The Society of the Blood Wind is in the safe house.

"Come on." Fin races past me.

Brynlee has now disappeared down the hallway. *Where's she going?* "Blazing hell! Carter."

"There's no time. What'll they want with an unconscious normie anyway?" Fin yells. "Come on."

With a glance up the stairs, I start toward the end of the hall after Brynlee, but she's already running my way with Carter stumbling behind her. Dust in the wake of another scream has me turning on my heels and running in the potion room's direction. I screech to a halt inside the doorway with my hands in the air, hoping Fin realizes it's me before the knife leaves her hand. Brynlee and Carter race through the door and smack into me. Fin assesses and drops her throwing arm without letting a knife fly. Brynlee latches the door shut and laces one of her webs over it.

Carter is leaning over. His hands are clutching the sides of the table and his body is swaying. His eyes are opening and closing. The sleep charm must have been a potent one because he's struggling to shake off the effects.

"He's awake?" I blurt out.

"I woke him. We'll need his help," Brynlee says.

"What's he going to do, wag his penis at them?" Fin says with exasperation.

We can hear movement and voices in the hall. Fin pushes Jayce behind her and tells him to get under the table. He scrambles under and miniature clear orbs start rolling out. After Jayce's life-saving orb skills I'm curious to see what these ones can do and a bit anxious, too, but there's no time to have a safety conversation with him.

"We need muscle. My charm holds magic people and hollow men, but humans come right through." A dissatisfied sneer covers Brynlee's face. "I haven't mastered the other half of the charm, not with enough stability to use it when we're this close to the web."

The door handle turns, and a tall, muscular guy races into the room. His feet hit Jayce's orbs, and he goes skidding like a cartoon character with his arms pinwheeling. A simple but effective orb. Based on the threads attached to it, it'll time out and disappear in less than five minutes. A new round of mini orbs spills across the floor, but these are rainbow coloured.

A cloaked form tries to enter, but he bursts into dust when he hits the charm, and his momentum sends the particles flying into our faces. I miss seeing the next man enter the room, but I hear explosive sounds from ground level and a crash, followed by a clatter as his body clears potion bottles off the table. I make a mental note to learn how to make Jayce's rainbow exploding orbs.

Potion bottles in this room are bound to have anything in them. It's reasonable to assume some of them were empty, but not all. I glimpse broken glass, quarks, liquids, powders, and dried herbs littering the floor. The air takes on a malodour that can't be described; it's so rank that it'll overpower the hollow-men stench.

I'm hoping my olfactory system will climatize and not deaden. Since we aren't perishing, I assume that the contents aren't lethal or having any kind of dangerous reaction with each other.

Fin takes the next guy out with a well-aimed knife throw. Brynlee is throwing orb shields to block the attacks from two unfamiliar Spellbinders positioned on either side of the doorway. Their arms are all that come into view, releasing their cowardly attacks.

Recovered, the first man is closing in on Carter. He's revived enough that he's squared off with his attacker. I hear grunts as they land blows on one another.

I square off with a different man. He dives at me, and we go down. In a tangle of limbs, we grapple for a grip on each other's neck. We tussle on the floor until we hit the table leg hard with my opponent's posterior. The air rushes out of him into my face. His foul breath—a blend of onion, spices, and steak—makes my stomach lurch, but I take control of the moment and ram my knee into his crotch, forcing the last of the air out of his lungs. He curls up into the fetal position, groaning.

Hands grab my shoulders, digging painfully into my skin. I'm lifted off the ground and tossed like a ragdoll. I release a stunted electric orb as my back hits the wall, but I can't get my footing. I slide the short distance down the wall and my body hits the floor as I watch the orb sail toward my attacker, hitting him in the chest.

The initial hit causes a stumble, and the hood falls. I'm shocked to see the oversized muscle machine is a woman. Her body convulses with the voltage from the orb, but she just shakes it off and keeps herself moving my way.

I swallow and climb to my feet as she moves forward. I'm surprised when her body jerks backward. An arm seizes her neck in a chokehold and legs ensnare her waist; she keeps advancing. Carter is clinging to her. I can see his biceps straining against her tree-trunk neck.

"Move," he yells over her shoulder but I don't have time.

As the woman swings her fist, the masculine features of her face pinch tight in concentration. I duck. She swings over the place where my head was seconds before. Her body follows the force of her punch, exposing her side. I throw a fist-shaped power orb. It hits her under her ribcage but above her hipbone. I'm pleased to hear air forced out of her lungs, even if it's a small amount.

It hasn't impacted her and neither have Carter's attempts to slow her. I'm in her crosshairs. She's swaying her body side to side to dislodge Carter while moving in my direction. I have nowhere to go.

She stops and tips her head to the side, listening. All I hear is silence. The sound of fighting has stopped.

She grabs Carter's leg and rips him off of her, discarding him on the ground like a sack of potatoes. He scrambles to his feet as she points a menacing finger at me before she turns and runs, dragging the other functioning enemy behind her. Whatever she heard, it was her cue to leave.

We're all stunned by the abrupt retreat and stand staring at the door. I scan the area. Fin and Brynlee are on the other side of the room, exhausted but uninjured. Jayce is crawling out from under the table and Carter is peeling himself off the floor. There's a ridiculous amount of dust littering the room. I'm coated in the powdery grime.

"I do NOT wag my penis at people, Fin," Carter says.

"That's insulting."

Fin huffs and I can tell she's preparing a monologue about Carter and his penis. They're welcome to their verbal banter, but I've no desire to listen to it. I set my jaw and peek into the hallway. Satisfied that it's deserted, I step out and hurry for the stairs. I can hear familiar voices gathering in the kitchen.

Roger is the first person I see as I enter the room. He's uninjured, but he's covered in more hollow man dust than me. Heedless of the mess he's creating, he's vigorously brushing at himself.

"Beautiful," Noah teases as soon as he sees me. I slit my eyes at him. "What?" He raises his hands. "All I'm saying is that you look great wearing that ashy smoulder."

I turn my back on him. "Is everybody okay?"

The Grogda siblings, as people, enter the kitchen from the sunroom, supporting each other and dripping with blood. As I assess their state, I realize that I should refer to them as Hellzel and Dugal out of respect for their help and loyalty. Our relationship deserves a first-name comradeship.

Birdie comes in behind them with the stranger. "Living room," Birdie chirps to Dugal and Hellzel. *Seems Fin and I are the only people who don't know the new guy.* "Astrid and Rune are providing treatment in there," Birdie explains.

I look over my shoulder at Noah, hoping maybe he'll answer my question. He nods and moves up beside me, all joking gone. "We sustained several injuries, but our defenses held, and we had no fatalities."

I swallow and sigh in relief. "What was that?"

"A test of our defenses and response to their attack," Alaric says quietly.

"The whole thing took minutes," Noah says in an equally subdued tone.

A strong manure odour fills the kitchen and I take an involuntary step, trying to protect my senses as it chokes my nostrils and coats my taste buds. This miasma could be a weapon.

Everybody has a hand over their noses and mouths. An awkward bird enters the room with its orange mohawk jiggling with each step. It's a mash-up of other birds but with a blue face like a cassowary. The smell is getting stronger as it gets farther into the room. It stops walking and releases a gassy noise out of its stubby beak. The odour is so strong at this point it stings my eyes and I close them against the stench.

"What in the fiery blazes is that bird?" I sputter and spit the words out trying not to taste the air.

"It's a hoatzin, also known as a stink bird," Birdie says. "Pearle!" She shrieks. My eyes fly open in time to see the chicken-sized, stinky bird transform into Grama Pearle.

"Guess we know why she doesn't shift very often," Fin says from the hallway.

Grama Pearle aims a big smile at me. "Gotta love a good fart and a great belch."

My mouth drops open as my eyes go round. Fin's laugh is wholesome, demonstrating her enjoyment of Grama Pearle's antics. I feel Jayce race past my legs, calling for Great-Grama Pearle.

Noah is unphased by Grama Pearle's comment. "We need to recoup and prepare in case they attack again. Tightening our defenses is a must."

I run a hand over my face, trying to reset my features.

"Carter!" Mom's voice rings out in surprise. She doesn't keep the disgust from her tone.

She was never a fan of Carter, but his affair and our divorce put him at the top of her list of despised people. I hang my head in defeat, the last thing I want to do is explain to Mom that Carter is here because of a penis hex.

"Hi, Mom," Carter says as he moves past me. Oblivious to her aversion, he hugs her like nothing has changed.

Mom is stock still, but her eyes cut to me. "You have some explaining to do, young lady!"

Chapter 19

The rest of us use elbow grease to tidy up and reset the house charms and wards, while our injured rest to allow the mojo to heal them. Having taken the brunt of the initial attack, the Grogda siblings are in no shape to return to guarding the deck tonight.

We're trying to set a night watch schedule when the sunroom charm triggers a warning that someone has entered. This, by itself, isn't too destressing. We've added a new charm for additional protection. Now whoever gains entry will be wrapped both physically and magically.

The alarming part is not one of us has energy right now to deal with enemies who stumble into the trap. The arrival of someone to the sunroom reminds me that I still haven't found out who the stranger is. Obviously, he's a trusted ally but knowing a little more would be nice. First this surprise guest, then the stranger.

With a sigh, I follow Alaric and Noah to the sunroom. I can't see because the two of them move like a wall ahead of me. The rain has stopped, and it's a cloudless night. But the only light is from the sliver of moon shining through the windows, which does nothing to

The Ember Stone

help me see. I push between them to see a scruffy man with an amused face.

"Not the most welcoming greeting I've ever received," he says in a low rough voice, "but not the worst either."

His tall, open stance seems to take up a lot of space in the sunroom, and it's easy to see that he's not the least bit troubled by being vulnerable in his bindings. The man's pale blue, almost clear eyes focus on me when he reaches up in an elaborate stretch and enormous yawn. Startled, I whip my head at Alaric. He's the only one who could have released this man's magical bindings. Alaric's face is impassive as he watches the newcomer.

"Alaric, my man!" the unknown man says. "Got your message, but barely. Something, or someone, hell-bent on keeping your message from getting through attacked the poor bird. Good bird, though. Sorry for its loss."

Alaric moves to greet the man. I watch as they clasp each other from forearm to forearm with their hands at each other's elbows. They lean in for a hug with their arms braced between them and they thump each other on the back with their free hands. Alaric and this man must have an interesting history together, some kind of bond, for Alaric, always so impassive, to provide a heartfelt hello. When they finish their greeting, the man dips his head at Noah and then addresses Alaric.

"Take it I missed the fun," he says.

Alaric nods.

I clear my throat, hoping to get an introduction to this mystery man, but the three of them just look at me. I'm not sure if they're teasing or testing me, and I don't care. I push my shoulders back, raise my chin, and step closer with my hand extended. "Kori Ember, and you are?"

To my surprise, the man breaks into a throaty chuckle. When he's finished laughing, he grins at Alaric. "She's exactly as you described her!"

Exasperated, my foot taps the floor while I await a response. They're watching me. The man chuckles and grasps my hand in a strong, warm embrace. "Griffin."

I wait for more of an introduction but when it's clear that there's nothing forthcoming, I turn toward the kitchen. "You men and your one-word names," I huff as I walk away to the sound of Griffin's throaty laugh.

A few seconds later, Noah, Alaric, and Griffin enter the kitchen. Fin makes a soft moan that's ignored if anyone besides me heard it. "Where do these chiseled he-men come from?" Based on her low voice and pained tone, I know the question isn't meant for anybody but herself.

I scrunch my face up at her so it's clear that she knows I think she's an idiot and I turn to the men. My breath catches and I hope that nobody notices. In the full light of the kitchen, Griffin presents as a very attractive man about ten years my senior. I note the confident stance as he faces us, shoulders back, chest forward, feet spread with one hand loosely resting in his perfectly fitting jeans and the other arm hanging at his side. Fin notices my double take, and she leans in close to me. "Caught you," she whispers in my ear.

I glance over my shoulder at her so she can see me. Meanwhile, I missed Griffin being introduced to the stranger who I still have no names for and Noah has almost completed introductions to Grama Pearle, Birdie, my parents, Brynlee, and Aunt Rune. I'm mid-eye roll when he reaches Fin. She gives one of her sultry smiles. "Single," she says.

I rest my forehead on the palm of my hand. By the way Griffin chuckles in response, I know I'm not the sole person they briefed him about.

Alaric relaxes against the counter while Noah continues. "Griffin will take the night watch so we can rest. We'll reconvene in the morning for the 'now what?' conversation."

When nobody moves or says anything, Noah dismisses us in his most authoritative voice. I give him a curtsey and drag Fin out of the room before she can embarrass herself with any sexually suggestive offers. Formal introductions to the unknown man will have to wait a bit longer.

"What an excellent specimen," Birdie hoots.

Griffin has shifted. Fin peeks into the kitchen and gives a stifled shriek before disappearing behind the wall. I shrug at Birdie, Noah, Alaric, and Griffin the buzzard before leaving. Fin is in the hall, almost quivering with excitement.

"What?" I ask.

"Did you see the rugged and handsome bird that Griffin turns into?" she breathes.

"Were we seeing the same bird? Isn't Griffin a black-bearded vulture?"

"I could stroke the rusty orange feathers on his belly. Oh, or maybe the gray-black plumage on his back."

I don't try to keep my eyebrows from rising to the top of my forehead. "What's wrong with you?"

"Did you see the creamy colour of his head and the contrasting dark beard?" She continues.

"Are you kidding me right now?"

Fin looks at me, but she's seeing something else. "You know what?" She doesn't wait for an answer. "Often, when that kind of vulture mates, the female has multiple partners," she says, licking her lips. I hadn't been sure at first if she was joking around, but based on the dreamy look stuck on her face, she's attracted to Griffin, the man and the bird.

I grab her arm when I realize she's heading to the kitchen, and I drag her behind me. "Fin, where's Roger? Did you eat him whole because I haven't seen him in a few hours?"

"Hmm," she mutters absently.

"Roger? Do you remember him?" I ask, pushing her toward her bed.

She shucks her clothes while staring at the doorway. I wave my hand in front of her face, trying to get her to focus. She sighs and sees me for the first time since she got a glimpse of Griffin, in both his human and bird form. "Roger is one hundred and five in troll years and nineteen in human. The numbers don't work out for us; just over a decade younger than me is too much of an age difference. A decade older I could appreciate, but not younger.

"Even if our ages were closer, sex isn't his thing. Roger's, I mean. He doesn't want to have sex! I respect that, but you know how I feel about my own sex.

Anyway, I think he's giving me some space to calm my heated parts," she says, slipping into bed. "I think I found a new way to accomplish that," she mumbles before she starts to snore.

More like a new sex toy. Shaking my head, I climb into bed. I fall asleep, thinking about the strange reaction the Ember stone had when we were being attacked. I should ask Grama Pearle about it, but the thought of feeling naked and on display, which is how I feel every time my magical ignorance is spotlighted, doesn't have me racing to find her. Besides, it was just a heated feeling, I rationalize.

I wake to an empty room in the morning, and I know without question where Fin has disappeared. When I come into the kitchen, I'm surprised because I see almost everybody is present except Fin.

"Good," Noah says. "We're waiting for you, as well as Fin and Griffin." He reaches for the coffee pot and dumps a large amount into a mug for me.

I take the mug from him. "Where's Fin?"

She's setting the stage for her sexual advances, I think to myself.

"She volunteered to go wake Griffin up," Brynlee says dismissively. "Hellzel was feeling better and relieved Griffin from the deck a few hours ago so he could rest."

"You want to grab Fin so we can get started?" Noah asks, prepping another round of coffee grinds.

I set my coffee down and wander into the hall. I tap on the bedroom door, which isn't latched shut so I give no thought to intimate privacy, and I push it open. "Smoke and ashes," I exclaim with surprise as I get an eye full of a topless Fin astride Griffin.

Griffin bunches the blanket over the lower halves of themselves. I appreciate his modesty. Fin smiles and waves at me like she's on an amusement park ride at the local fair. My eye twitches. *You bested me on this one, Noah,* I think to myself. I wink at Fin. My words come out in a gush of air, "We're waiting in the kitchen for you guys." I clear out before I see more.

As I walk into the kitchen, Noah shoves his elbow in Alaric's side. Alaric is struggling to hold his impassivity. There's a twitch at the corner of his mouth. I'm aware of Carter mumbling jealous comments about sexy men and the glory of their erections, but my eyes are for Noah.

Noah is holding his laughter in as I stop and take a calm and deliberate sip of my coffee. I set it down, never taking my eyes off him. Then I charge across the kitchen fighting to keep my own smile off my face. "You knew, and you sent me on purpose!" My voice cracks with suppressed laughter.

He breaks away from the counter and races from the room. I glimpse shocked faces as I bolt after Noah with thoughts of payback.

Noah positions the sofa between us. He's laughing while his hands are up in surrender. I don't hesitate.

Using the sofa as a support, I vault over, banging into him with full force. Noah locks his arms around me and allows my momentum to take us down in a controlled fall. We wrestle for a few minutes before I feel a sharp tug on my left ear. Noah stops trying to pin me and is grimacing. His head is tilted in a way that suggests a hand is pulling on his ear too, but there's nobody there.

The pulling increases and we're pried apart and forced to climb to our feet to avoid our ears being pulled off. I'm on my tiptoes, craning my eyes for the source of this pain, when Mom steps into view with a grim face. As children, Noah and I had our ears pulled by her often for fighting, but my memory of it feels inhibited likely a product of my shunning magic. My cheeks burn when I realize that she's using magic to yank our ears today, like we're youth. *Using magic.*

"Just like you two are kids," she says, releasing our ears and smiling. "Well, children, we're waiting in the kitchen. It would appear Fin and Griffin have . . ." she pauses, thinking about her choice of words, but finds none and just walks away instead.

I catch Noah's eye and we burst out laughing. Once we've regained our composure, we head to the kitchen. I take note that Carter isn't present and assume that he's napping since the sleeping charm is still attached to him, just not as potent. The discussion started without Noah and me and in the few moments that we were gone, and it's already decided that we need to abandon this refuge.

"Where are we going to go?" I butt into the conversation.

Grama Pearle's hazel eyes hold me. I can see that she's struggling with an internal battle. It's Mom's voice that supplies my answer. "Home!" The room has gone silent while everybody thinks that answer through.

"You can't be serious!" I say.

"The Ember family home is the best place for us now that The Society of the Blood Wind knows where all of us are and we know what they want," Grama Pearle adds.

"After yesterday's attack, they know our strengths and weaknesses here," Noah adds, nodding his agreement with the plan. "They're getting desperate to get the Ember stone, and Kori too. So, home would give us the playing field advantage."

"Didn't The Society of the Blood Wind already attack Mom, Dad, and Grama Pearle at our home?" I ask as I recall the first day I went to the Ember house.

"No," Noah says. "The Society of the Blood Wind ransacked the Ember house, but your family was already at the wartime safe house. And they might have been in the Ember house off and on since then, but as you know from the day you and I were attacked there, the Ember house has secrets."

My eyes flit from one of them to the other. They're committed to the idea. "What else don't I know?"

"There's a lot about our home that you didn't allow yourself to learn, Kori," Mom says so softly that I'm speechless.

Noah cuts in. "We weren't sure who took Alivia or why. We had assumptions but nothing concrete. No point to take a stand if we don't know the who, what or why of the fighting. So, I moved your family as a precaution and to buy time to get some answers.

"When the wartime safe house was compromised regrouping here and deciding what next made more sense than trying to move them to the Ember house as well as you guys too. It seemed too risky to have so many moving parts happening at once. Besides, this is a safe house so it has its own secrets and defenses."

I joggle my head to clear it and remember that I haven't told anybody but Fin about the drawing from Belamey. Struggling for words, I fish the drawing out of my pocket and smooth it out on the table.

Noah recognizes it since he was there when Holden stuffed it, unfinished, into his pocket. Something scary flashes in his eyes. "Where did you get this?"

Ready to meet his challenge, I fire back two words. "Belamey Adelgrief."

The room erupts, everyone talking over each other. People stand up. Hands are waving, fingers are pointing, heads are shaking, and tension is building. Mom's magically amplified voice cuts through the noise, telling us all to zip our lips. Her eyes fix on me, and she gives a slight nod to show that the floor is mine. I swallow and detail the adventure Fin and I had in the alley by Just Flavours.

"The thing I don't understand is why does Belamey have Alivia and Holden?" Fin interrupts.

Everyone eyes her. She brings her hand up and waves a finger. I stay quiet.

"Unless he had them both all along?" Birdie offers.

"But why?" I try to work through the idea and my

bizarre encounters with him. "Fin was right. He's our inside man!" I blurt. "He has to be the secret that Mouz died trying to convey to us. He—"

"WAIT!" Fin hollers so loud that she startles herself. I suck in air and glare at her. She's shaking her head side to side, using her body as a shield to point at the unknown man in the room. "Before we say anything," she says in a regular tone of voice, "who's the newbie? I know he arrived before we got attacked, but Kori and I haven't formally been introduced to him." The room falls silent and I'm not sure if Fin's question has caused insult.

"I'm Talon," says the smallish man with big round eyes and a permanently surprised expression. There's something about him that seems familiar, but I can't put my finger on it. "Birdie's son," he finishes.

I feel my mouth drop open and I make a conscious effort to close it. Curious how this information will be received, Talon is bobbing and weaving his head. I sneak a peek at Birdie.

Although Fin and I were the only ones who didn't know Talon's name, it seems limited people knew of the relationship between Birdie and Talon. She's also alert to how we'll handle Talon's admission. She isn't in owl form, but all I can think as I watch her posture is that her feathers are ruffled.

Grama Pearle tuts and moves closer to Birdie, giving her hand a squeeze. The tension Birdie is holding drains away.

"Enough said," Fin says reaching to shake hands with Talon.

I'm not sure who's more surprised when Talon speaks, us or Talon. "The other birds didn't make it to their intended recipients. I'm sorry to tell you fifteen or more birds lay dead close by. It's a sign of the times that messengers need to be warded to travel. It seems unlikely that there'll be other help available to assist us." His round eyes lock on his mother. They lower their heads, and we take a minute of silence for the fallen birds.

Nobody feels like speaking, so we make our way to the deck in silence. I watch in wonder as people shift and take flight off the property.

"How can we leave with no plan and no outside protection?" I say to the receding birds.

Talon hops, reminding me that Birdie is his mother. "Watch," he chirps at me.

His soft-skinned hands are pushing and pulling a gummy twine of magic. I goggle at him when he bobs his head down and takes a bite of it and chews. After a few minutes, a bubble pushes out from between his lips and breaks away, growing bigger. The bubble moves into the sky, overtaking the birds and causing them to disappear.

I rub my eyes, blink, and turn to Talon, who is hopping on the spot while he pulls another round of magic gum between his hands. When Noah, Fin, Talon, and I are left on the deck, I scratch my head. "Now what? What about Noah and Fin? Wait, can you shift, Noah?" I ask.

Talon gives a hoot. "This will be fun." His hands are working hard at pulling the magic gum. He's handling double the amount and his slight frame is struggling. "Here," he sings, shoving his hands at me. "Help me pull this."

Before I give consent, my hands are immersed in the magic.

"Faster," Talon chirps.

I copy his movements, and the gluey threads adhere to my hands. Now that I'm holding and working the magic gum myself, I can see shimmering flecks and colours being kneaded into it. As I work it like an oversized marshmallow being agitated between my palms, it's heating up. It gets squishier and stretchier.

"Mouth and chew now," Talon cheeps, and I do it without thinking. I'm surprised that it's airless and flavourless in my mouth. I see a bubble form on Talon's lips, so I blow. Soon we both have very enormous bubbles growing from our puckered mouths.

Crunching gravel precedes the Willys MB with Roger at the wheel. The bubble detaches from my mouth on its own and I'm in awe as Talon manipulates the two bubbles into joining. Together, their size is large enough to envelop the Willys.

Fin and Noah are already in the vehicle. After I climb in, Talon cacoons us with the bubble. Talon's voice is muffled, but our vision doesn't change. "Drive safe. See you there."

I cast a worried look at Noah. "He's going to fly in his own bubble of cover. He'll be fine," Noah reassures me.

Roger spins the tires, and we tear off down the driveway.

Chapter 20

My eyes peruse the house, searching for green and coal-tinted magic twines left by The Society of the Blood Wind. But there's nothing visible.

"Talon swept it a few days ago to prepare for our return," Noah says offhandedly.

I frown at Noah. "But I thought the decision was just made for us to come here?"

"It was, but we were thinking about it and planning to discuss it then we got attacked."

Fin reaches over and gives Roger a big hug before she pokes her finger to pop the bubble. She hops out of the Willys and stretches herself skyward. "It feels good to be home," she says, sashaying toward the front door. I can't control my eye roll or head shake, but I plan to follow her just the same.

I exit the vehicle. "Aren't you coming in, Roger?"

Roger gives me a half-hearted grin. "No, Kori, not today, but our paths will cross soon. Protect that stone with your life." I barely step clear of the vehicle before he drives off.

Noah calls to me over his shoulder. "He's guarding the safe house with Daken and Galox."

I watch the direction the Willys disappeared in. Noah and Fin are out of sight as I trudge up to the door and stop in the entranceway. Everyone else has already continued into the depths of the house. I pull the old wood and glass front door closed and glance down the stairs to Grama Pearle's store.

There are no telltale signs of rubble from the spilled big basin of stones the day I first came home. Wondering about the state of the walls that the goons hammered, I consider the stairs and I'm about to go see when the sounds of talking and laughter reach my ears. I sigh, dismissing the option to hide myself away in the hideyhole.

Curiosity gets the best of me when the noises that I associate to Birdie's sunroom are present in this house. The sunroom birds were in the safe house when we left. I follow the chirps, tweets, and trills down the hall, expecting to find a temporary structure set-up outside on the deck, but as the exterior kitchen door comes into view, it's closed and therefore not where the source of the chirping is emanating from.

The birds are louder. An undersized, round bird with a yellow throat is hopping along the bar of the ceiling light between the bulbs. I blink at it, hoping it might disappear. It doesn't, so I ignore it and try to block out thoughts of feathers and feces on the countertops.

The louder commotion is in the library. The room is filled with birds of various sizes, colours, and species. Fin is the only human in sight and Noah the only Spellbinder. My left eye gives a slight twitch as I survey the room. "Fin?" I choke out over the chirps and feather ruffling.

She flicks her eyes at me, and then ignores me as she studies the birds. I suck air, cross my arms, and tap my foot as I watch feathers drift on the air currents and soil whatever surface is free from anisodactyl feet and bird seed. Fin wheels on me, exasperated. She strolls toward me, turns dramatically, and stands on the top of my feet with her heels, pinning me to the spot and bringing an end to my foot tapping. Before I shove her, she points at the birds and yells names.

"Talon," she hollers, pointing at an owl with a surprised facial expression. He transforms and Talon's equally astonished human face is staring at us. It wasn't the sunroom birds at all, these are the Spellbinders that flew here from the safe house.

She identifies a few more birds and explains that they're friends of Alaric's here to help us. Fin turns to the two owls. One is lanky with long ear tufts and the other is a large stocky owl with rounded ears. Fin points to each owl, naming Brynlee and Aunt Rune. That leaves a woodpecker, a compact blue bird with a black throat, a swan, a baby morning dove, a steely blue gray hawk with reddish bars on its underparts, and the bird that I saw in the kitchen.

The little dove shifts and Jayce is jumping up and down yelling, "Watch me, watch me!" He transforms into a dove and then into his boy body before he comes running at me like I'm the most important person in the world.

I smile despite everything and laugh as I scoop him up into my arms to enjoy the crushing hug that I know he has ready for me. Meanwhile, Fin points at the remaining birds who are waiting for her to guess who they are. One at a time faster than I can follow, she calls out their names. I think my maternal grandparents were the swan and the hawk. I don't know whether my dad or uncle was the blue bird or the woodpecker. Regardless, all of them are in front of us, smiling and nodding at Fin.

The one bird that I can associate with a person is Mom. She's in the kitchen behind me in human form. It's ironic: Mom is the undersized bird with the yellow throat that I was worried would poop on the counters. If I've ever seen her in bird form, I can't recall it.

I push my fingers into the skin beside my eye, which is now fully twitching, as Grama Pearle and Birdie shoot up alongside me, having shrunk themselves to monitor whatever kind of game it was that Fin was playing. Nobody seems interested in explaining what's going on. I keep the fingers of my one hand on the corner of my eye and shove Fin off my feet using my free hand. Alaric, who was sitting statue-like in a chair, reaches out and steadies Fin.

"Kori!" Grama Pearle admonishes.

Birdie hoots and walks away. I watch her and the others drift off into the house before I turn to Fin. She and Grama Pearle are busy discussing something unknown. I butt in, feeling left out and at a loss for what Fin was doing. "What was that?"

"Just practicing," Fin says.

"Here, Fin." Grama Pearle passes a medium-sized sketch book to Fin. "Educate yourself using this and I

know you'll be ready. It has a number of hostiles in it."
Grama Pearle pats me on the shoulder and withdraws
into the depths of the house.

I raise my eyebrows at Fin.

Fin gives me one of her best smiles and flourishes a
knife in the air between us. "I'm training, of course." I
blink at her and wait. She disappears her knife and
shakes her head. "I feel responsible to know everyone in
their bird form as well as I know them as humans. I
don't want to throw a knife at them in the last battle."

"The last battle!" I say with exasperation. "Smoke and
ashes, Fin, this isn't the final destruction of the world."
I shut my eyes tight and knead my fingers in circles at
the corner of my eyes as I suck in slow, inhales of air.
When I open my eyes, from my position in the library, I
see Fin walking through the kitchen. I close my eyes for
a few more seconds, taking deep breaths. When I cross
the kitchen to the dining room, Fin has a cup of coffee
in her hand and she's flipping through the sketchbook
Grama Pearle just gave her.

"You should have a coffee, Kori," she says as if
everything is proceeding as normal. "Your sister is an
amazing drawer."

"Is that Alivia's sketchbook?" I ask, smiling at the
memory of the soft smudges of lead that are always on
Alivia's drawing hand.

Fin slams the book shut and points to the
coffeemaker. "Coffee first. You and I both know where
you're concerned coffee keeps people alive."

I can't turn down the rich smell of fresh brew. I select
an oversized mug from the cupboard, fill it to the brim

with rich brown liquid, and take a relaxing sip with my back to Fin. I follow that with a deep breath of the warm steam rising off my cup, then move to the dining room and slide into a chair.

Fin is right. Alivia's drawings are breathtaking. Between the detail, the way she handles colour, and her use of light and shadow, the images come to life. Each page is a skillful composition of an enemy bird labelled in Alivia's neat printing, with the type of bird by common title and the name of the Spellbinder associated to it. "I can't believe these are actual birds," I say to Fin.

"Right? And who comes up with these names? Vampire finch, dracula parrot, Inca tern." She pauses, and a devilish grin crosses her features.

"What?"

She giggles. "Well, if Carter could shift, I bet his bird would be cock-of-the-rock!"

"Fin, he isn't here to hear you."

She shrugs, "It's how his and my relationship is built, Kori."

Kieran's and Kyson's bird drawings in the sketchbook bring our laughter to a halt. We skip past their images and stop on a Nicobar pigeon. Alivia has captured the image using dark green intermixed with gray and blue, bronzy-orange for the lengthy plumes trailing down from the neck, and metallic green for the rest of its plumage. Its sturdy legs and feet are dull red with yellow claws. It's such a strange bird that it has an annotation.

"Listen to this," Fin says, leaning in to read it.

"Known by the nickname Dodo. Legal name unknown. Dodo!" She says with a laugh. "I haven't heard of Dodo before now, no mention in conversation. Have you?"

"Nope. Seems a fitting name based off the bird," I say. I've found the bottom of my coffee cup so I excuse myself, planning to let Fin continue what she's dubbed studying.

"Wait," she calls, reaching under the sketchbook and pulling out a folded paper. "It's from Grama Pearle," she says, passing it to me.

I turn the paper over in my hands, inspecting each side. Visually, it's a normal sheet of paper, but I sense there's more to it.

"Well, open it," Fin says. "I'm curious what it is."

I unfold it and note that the title written in Grama Pearle's flowing hand is *Lesson Schedule*. Beneath the title she has penned the names of every Spellbinder in the house; each name corresponds with a time and lesson. I'm shocked how many of us there are. Before I formulate any other thoughts, Grama Pearle's voice literally comes out of the paper, not corresponding to any of the written words. "This is my lesson to you. Review these weaves and leave a note for me with Fin. I know you're going to burn your lessons to the ground today!" She makes a kissing sound, and the weaves snap out of focus.

"Brilliant!" Fin says, eyes on the pages of the sketchbook.

I glance at Fin, the sketchbook, and then at the coffee pot, questioning my decision to not have a second cup. I sigh at the list. There are sixteen people listed with half-hour intervals. If I don't get a hustle on, I'll be late for my first lesson. I sink my voice message into the paper, and pass it to Fin.

I wander off, looking at the catalogue of activities. They range from magic shields with Noah, charms with Aunt Rune, to mental magic with Ague. Some activities will hopefully only need to be restimulated skills, but others are new. I've no idea what some of the words mean but they boil down to magical focus, continuance, and stability. I stop and hold the wall, waiting for the wave of light-headedness to pass. This is no time to succumb to the feeling of being overwhelmed.

Somehow this program is supposed to help me accept my magic and break down the defences I used to distance myself from it after Jaxton's death. All things requiring mastery before I can move on to more complex magic. I need to do more than beginner's magic, and faltering beginner's magic at that, before it'll be safe to use the Ember stone.

Feeling mentally and physically exhausted from the day's lessons, I drift up the stairs from Grama Pearle's store. I'm pleasantly surprised when I move into the hall and an array of warm, mouth-watering aromas hits me. Lifting my chin, I draw in the rich smells of Grama Opal's cooking. I follow my nose, knowing that Grama

Opal has been very busy cooking with the gas stove and with magic; tonight, we're going to feast. The kitchen is a hive of activity, with people moving dishes of food, plates, glasses, and several other items required for an Ember family feast.

I stop at the entranceway to the kitchen, and he's there, standing behind me, leaving me both relieved and frustrated that the ward placed on the Ember house guards against motive. I don't need to turn to know that it's Belamey. His scent is filling my nostrils and the heat from his body is radiating through me, creating a sensation of longing in places I don't care to acknowledge that he's having this effect on.

Everyone has fallen silent, and each person wears their own varied manner of shock, except for Fin. Her face cracks into a broad grin. "Hello, dark and dreamy."

"What are you doing here?" Noah barks. His body is tensed in anticipation of Belamey's response. Fin's comment about Noah's unresolved feelings for me pops into my mind as I watch his reaction to Belamey.

I sweep the room with my eyes, noting no magic at the ready. People are shocked by Belamey's presence, but not threatened. They're confident in the wards ability to control antagonistic entry.

Ignoring Noah, Belamey snakes his arm around my waist. "Come with me, please," he says with his voice low. I nod once and he pulls me tight. I feel like a human shield that's excited about its proximity to death. Shutting my eyes, I steady myself and raise my palm to the room. Belamey's husky voice is close to my ear. "We need to speak," he says, barely loud enough for anyone else to hear. "Alone," he says louder as he reverses.

"Got it," Fin says. "We're going to speak alone," she tells everyone present as she struts toward Belamey and I, intent on following us.

I glance at Grama Pearle, standing close to Birdie. They're subtly bobbing their heads up and down in silent agreement to some opinion they share. Belamey doesn't stop reversing until we're outside. Fin walks facing us, grinning the entire time.

The Grogda siblings, in bird form, are patrolling past the front stairs as we come out. They assess us, but move on. Like everyone inside, except Noah, they don't judge Belamey as any kind of threat. Belamey releases me and I put space between us, questioning in my mind my reluctance to do so. Fin positions herself close to me.

The air has a chill to it, and I shiver without the warmth from Belamey's body. He notices and a questionable smirk pulls at the corners of his mouth. "You're welcome to cuddle in and I can prolong my vowels so we can enjoy the moment." His brown eyes move down my body, and I quiver, but this time it isn't from the cold.

I suck in the chilly air and cross my arms. Fin surveys me and then Belamey. "So, we're alone." Her tone suggests she isn't convinced and her eyes scan for threats that might be hiding. She's evidently decided that Belamey isn't a threat, believing her theory of his love for me.

There's a rustling in the trees behind Belamey and knives materialize in Fin's hands from nowhere. The neckless hawk speeds through the leaves in a blur of motion to perch on a branch close to us. "It's The Recruiter," she yells, jumping up and down and waving her arms. Her knives aren't in sight. "Rumour is he's rebuilding his team because of all the drama in your magical world. They need a group to try and maintain the balance," she yells at me over her shoulder. "Pick me, pick me," she hollers at this bird, who doesn't acknowledge her commotion. "I love adventure and I'm so good at teams."

"The who?" I blow out an exasperated breath. "Fin, tone it down!"

She's still waving at the bird like a maniac, but she's whispering as she beseeches him for a spot on his team.

Belamey ignores both Fin and the bird like neither pose a risk. *Does he know The Recruiter?* He's so close to me that I can feel the warmth from his body. He's a foot taller than me, and I tilt my head up to see his face. His tall stance doesn't change as he inclines his head down to lock eyes with me.

"Alivia and Holden are no longer safe. Their location has been compromised," his husky voice echoes in my ear as I try to process what he's saying.

I'm surprised by the gentleness of the finger he presses on my lips, but he's not looking at me. His predator-like body is tense and his eyes are scanning. Everything has gone silent.

"Don't move," he whispers. I arm myself with orbs and scan my eyes up over his shoulders.

"Fin!" Belamey calls out crushing me against him, and he swivels us with his finger still pushed to my lips. One of Fin's knives sails through the spot where

Belamey and I just were and clips the wing of a crow. The bird twirls in the air, squawking.

Belamey fixes on me with his intense sadness. "They've been watching me, spying to determine if I'm the leak." I understand the word "they" to mean his father, Nekane, and his grandfather, Dolion. For them to suspect him of being a traitor would be crushing if it weren't true, but here he is, betraying them. Something isn't adding up.

A second crow's wing is clipped by another of Fin's knives. "Get to my place. That's where Alivia and Holden are," his low voice comes out quiet. Without warning, he replaces the finger he has pressed against my mouth with his lips.

He draws away from me and I'm startled as he shifts. In a puff of dark gray feathers and wingbeats, he rises toward the heavens. I watch as he turns and dives. Talons like a grizzly bear's claws are attached to his legs, as thick as a child's wrist. Stretching out, he snatches the two injured crows from the ground.

With short broad wings, he takes flight almost straight up into the sky, unhindered by the extra weight. A series of loud caws echo in his wake as a third crow chases after him. A flurry of feathers in the tree branch tells us the hawk has taken its leave as well.

I throw a protective dome over Fin and me to make sure we aren't under attack. The Grogda siblings' big, feathery black bodies come sprinting from opposite corners of the house, drawn by the shrieks from the crows. I double my protection dome, thinking about a jump attack from those muscular legs if they don't recognize us. I swallow and we move close together as the cassowaries close the distance. Fin's arm comes up with a knife and my eyes go wider than I thought possible. "Don't worry. I'm just going to bean them with the handle end," she hisses.

She doesn't release the throw, though. Dugal and Hellzel both stop. Recognizing Fin and I, they bob their naked blue heads at us, causing the two red wattles on each of their necks to wobble. They turn and go in opposite directions back around the house. Satisfied that we aren't under accidental attack by the Grogda siblings or any enemies, I drop my protective domes.

"So, Belamey is a harpy eagle," Fin says with a grin. "Sexy! Same bird as Alaric, did you know? Interesting coincidence. Strong birds for strong men."

I choose to ignore her display of bird knowledge and address a different issue instead. "Why were you not throwing to kill?"

Fin stops. "Sorry," she says. "I keep thinking you've been learning the same things as me, but your training is very dissimilar. The crows were in the sketchbook, the back half, but you were already off doing your lessons by then." She hooks arms with me and aims us for the front door, where Noah is now surveying the skies.

"The crows were just kids! I can't remember their names, but I asked Grama Pearle about them because Alivia had drawn them all on one page of the sketchbook, but all the other birds had a page to themselves." She glances at me for a response, which I provide in the form of my eyebrows speeding toward my hairline. Her studying and knowing the birds takes on a new importance. "Enemy kids, yes, but still kids. I just wanted to knock them off their flight path so they wouldn't hurt you." She stops and turns me to face her. There's a look on her face I've never seen there before. "They're trained to kill," she says, and the revulsion in her voice echoes her guise.

I widen my eyes at her. "They weren't here for me," I mumble, trying to digest the bombshells of information and another layer to Belamey's sadness is revealed.

Fin gives me a tight hug. "Belamey will be fine. I bet he drops the kid crows somewhere safe and makes sure they lose his trail. Plus, if anything goes wrong, The Recruiter followed them. Come on." She angles us for the stairs.

"Wait," I say, stopping Fin and spinning her toward me this time. I glance at the treetops. "Why did you call that little hawk The Recruiter?"

"There's a book in the library about The Recruiter. The Recruiter rounds up the best of the best for a stealthy team that fights the good fight from the shadows. It was dormant for a long time. You'll have to read about it yourself, we don't have time for me to explain all of it to you. But with the things happening lately, some we've been made privy to and others we haven't, it was time for his team to be reborn." Her smile is pasted on her face and her head bobs in acknowledgement of her own words. "He's recruiting."

I can't help wondering when she reads all these books, but I decide now isn't the time to ask. "That's the bird that I keep seeing everywhere." I wait, as if the hawk might reappear.

"It must be trying to recruit me," Fin whispers. She takes a turn searching the treetops. "It makes the most sense, don't you think?"

I blink at her.

"Oh. Maybe it wants to recruit you, too."

"Kori? Fin? What are you two waiting for?" Noah calls from the deck, unaware of the visit from the crows.

I take a second to roll my eyes at Fin. She shrugs. "We'll see." She grabs my arm and leads us up the deck stairs, ending the possibility for any more of this conversation. Noah holds the door open, and we go inside.

The door has just closed when someone hammers on it. I crank it open, ready for just about anything except what's there. Carter grins at me. "I was napping when you guys left," he says. "Took me a while to walk to the main road and get a lift, but here we are. Me and Jackhammer," he says calmly, no doubt in his mind that leaving him behind was an oversight. To be honest, I can't say if it was or wasn't. Things were chaotic.

I gag in response to his referral to Jackhammer. Impervious, he brushes past me into the house, talking about his trip into town as two creatures, one human and one penis. I note that his symptoms from the spell are present, but that his eyes are a bit clearer. He twitched at his inclusion of Jackhammer in his sentence, visibly conscious and uncomfortable about saying it, but still compelled.

Fin is giggling and following him down the hall. Noah is muttering under his breath and trailing behind Fin. I turn to the door and look at the cloudless sky, which is fading from blue to gray.

I hear Fin saying that we need a plan. I sigh and push the door shut, taking a brief second to ensure the wards reset when I latch the door. I turn and hurry down the hallway. We've a few hours to get organized and extract Alivia and Holden from Belamey's place. There's no time to speculate about what Belamey's role is until after my sister and nephew are safe. My instincts indicate that Belamey is telling the truth.

Chapter 21

A group, five paces ahead of me, comprised of Noah, Grama Pearle, Birdie, Astrid, Alaric, Griffin, and Fin seat themselves at the dining room table. Fin is relaying Belamey's message. I cast a scowl at Fin, hoping she doesn't try to work her love theories into the narrative. She blows me a kiss and stays to the pertinent details. Sucking a deep breath of air, I turn away from Fin, and blow my breath out. Then I interject myself into the conversation. "I think we need to assume Belamey's place is being watched."

"That won't be a problem," Grama Pearle responds.

"Oh?" I say, massaging the corners of my eyes.

Noah slides a hot cup of coffee onto the table in front of me. "I don't like it, Pearle."

"You don't like what?" I ask, blowing on my steaming mug. "Thanks, by the way."

"I don't suppose you'll sit this one out?" I see defeat on Noah's face, so I gaze at Grama Pearle without answering him.

"Belamey lives in Mouz's old house," she says, like this should have meaning for me. I sip my coffee and wait for the explanation. "There's what I'm going to call a clandestine door into the house."

"Sure, if you're four inches tall!" Noah huffs and his defeat makes sense to me.

He lacks the magic required to shrink, a reminder that each Spellbinder's magical strengths and skills are different. One of us would have to shrink while holding on to him and then maintain physical contact with him to preserve his shrunken size. It would be too much of a safety risk if he got separated from us. I steal a peek at him over my coffee cup to see that he's almost visibly steaming because this plan can't include him.

"It's dangerous, Pearle," he continues, "whether I can go or not."

Grama Pearle tailors her stance so she can lay a wizened hand on his shoulder. I'm not sure if Noah is aware of what she's doing with that hand, but I can see meager lines of magic drifting from her fingers. I watch, noting the flow of soft greens and browns. It has a calming effect, like enjoying a soothing cup of tea. Even from this distance, I feel at ease and more stable.

"I know what you are doing, Pearle," Noah says, with the edge gone from his voice.

Grama Pearle smiles and pats his shoulder. "The plan now, please, Noah?"

Noah nods and sighs. "Okay, a team of four-inch-high people will enter the tunnel."

"Sorry, what tunnel?" I interrupt.

"It's an old plumbing drain in the basement. When the plumbing was replaced, it should've been removed, but it never happened. Its drain cap used to be left open. Mouz positioned the cap to appear sealed, but it wasn't.

He used it to come and go without detection," Grama Pearle explains.

"Like I was saying, a team will enter the house. They'll find Alivia and Holden and come out the same way." Noah's hands are laced behind his head and his tone is warm. Grama Pearle's calming magic perhaps is more like tea spiked with a generous dollop of liquor.

"Sounds easy enough," Fin says. "I mean, assuming there are no traps or magical wards, and assuming there are no hollow men, Warped, or otherwise unfriendly Spellbinders. Then you have to hope Alivia and Holden are there, and you can get to them, and get them to the basement. Oh, and what if the cap . . ."

"FIN!"

Fin stops talking. She raises her shoulders up and down in an act of indifference. "What? I'm just saying it might not be so easy."

My foot is tapping rapidly. "So, who's going with me?" I see Noah wince, but he says nothing to discourage me.

"Alaric, Griffin, and Astrid will go into the house with you for the extraction," Noah says. Each of them nods in agreement as he says their names. "I'll position at the exterior of the tube in case of trouble."

"I'm driving," Fin cuts in.

Noah keeps talking as if she hasn't spoken. "Rune will be outside the house somewhere. Her night vision as a barred owl is well suited to the watch the exterior and I think she left about half an hour ago to sit on the house, anyway. Everyone else will stay here. Get ready because we're leaving in a few minutes."

Nobody wastes any time and I'm surprised how

quickly we're parked a few houses down from Belamey's two-story, red brick home. Even with tinted windows in the vehicle Fin borrowed from her lot, I feel exposed. Noah creaks the door open for us and we climb out and drop to the ground one at a time as four-inch humans. It's a dark night and the streetlight happens to be out. *Imagine that*, I think as I look skyward, trying to spot Aunt Rune.

The entrance to the pipe is near the road among some bushes. The pipe is four inches, so we're going to be walking bent over or crouched. Alaric leads us in, followed by Astrid, and then me, with Griffin taking up the rear. We walk a distance into the tunnel in pitch blackness before we use light orbs because we don't want to draw any inquiry.

I cut off thought of sewer rats, snakes, and anything else that might hunt for a nice four-inch-tall evening meal. I use my shirt to block the rotten egg moldiness that hangs in the air, wishing I had asked a few questions about "the old plumbing drain," which is actually an old sewer line. It feels like an eternity before Alaric's light orb casts a soft glow in the tunnel.

I glance at the cylindrical walls, thinking we were better off in the dark. I tug my shirt higher on my nose and focus my line of vision on Astrid. It's a long walk for a four-inch person. Alaric stops and waits for us all to huddle in. He looks at each one of us to make sure we're ready before he pushes the ABS pipe cap. It doesn't move. Our whole plan is shot if that cap has been screwed on.

Griffin brushes past me and they give the cap a good

shove. It groans and there's a crunchy sound as the dried debris around the lip of the cap crumbles and the cap gives way. I cringe, expecting to hear an echoing bang when the cap hits the floor, but the sound is a muffled thud. Carpeted basement floor in a house this old seems unlikely.

Alaric and Griffin jump out of the hole, wasting no time unshrinking themselves. Astrid nods to me and I follow her out. The first thing I see when my feet hit the ground is dull red feet with yellow claws standing on a dirt floor. I would've missed seeing the bird standing there, silent and unmoving, if I had of sprouted up to regular size like everybody else did.

I lift my gaze, and my eyes go wide when I see the heavy-set pigeon from Alivia's drawing of Dodo. I can't tell if us materializing out of the pipe has stunned or scared the bird. I fling a dissipating dome over it to restrict its movement and muffle any sounds he might make once it shakes off its temporary inability to react. I shift into my full human height.

"Nice throw," Astrid says. "How long until he's free?"

I smile at the new trick I learned, basic with an intermediate twist. Dodo can't transform into human form until the dome dissolves, and he can't call for help or attack us with magic. He's controlled but not harmed. "An hour," I answer. "Why is this floor dirt?"

"The house is old, built in the early 1900s," Astrid says wistfully.

I put a foot on the narrow wooden stairs and test my weight, unsure if this staircase will hold. They don't look like they've had any maintenance since they were built.

The door at the top is aged wood with a substantial gap under it. I can see under the door that it's dark on the other side and with my hearing magically amplified, I can tell it's silent, too.

The stairs creak and quake under my weight. I push the door open faster than I would have liked, but the stairs are protesting loudly and trembling. I'm sure if I don't get off them, we'll go down together. Astrid pushes us into a galley kitchen. The dim light coming in the solo window gives an impression of a sleek, bachelor kitchen with black marble, brick, and wood. I smell notes of cardamon and cedar and wonder if Belamey is okay.

"Did the stairs fall?" I whisper to Astrid.

"Not yet, but the men won't be coming up because their weight will likely bring them down." She flicks her head at the kitchen's exit.

"Wait," I say. "Let me practice searching with my magic." I cast out feelers of magic to sniff through the house like a scout. It takes a few moments. Astrid is watching me for a response. "Just Alivia and Holden in the house. Top floor. Far corner."

Astrid nods. She points for me to go right and motions she'll go left. Cautiously, we enter the dining room. I make my way to what was once the servants' staircase and head up, knowing Astrid is moving through the living room. She'll take the main stairs up at the opposite end of the house.

Astrid's approach will bring her closer to Alivia and Holden's room. Our split approach, is an extra precaution to try to ensure at least one of us reaches Alivia and Holden. We've no idea what to expect and we have no idea if Alivia and Holden know they aren't safe.

These stairs are cramped and creaky and there are questionably twisted floorboards. The hallway upstairs is narrow and dark. The air is as chilly as if we were outside, which makes me think the windows are open. I make my way along the wall, not wanting to cast any light in case there are eyes watching from outside.

Without warning, Alivia is racing down the hallway toward me with Holden in her arms. At the same instant, an owl shrieks a caution. Astrid comes flying up the stairs as Alivia races past. Flapping of wings and bird calls break out as birds fly in the open bedroom windows.

Alivia thrusts Holden at me, her eyes full of terror. "Get him out now!"

I have time to register that Alivia is clean and rested. Then Holden's arms grip me and I can feel his body shaking. His face is in my neck, making wet tear stains on my skin. Alivia and I lock eyes. A dark figure emerges from the bedroom closest to us. Other figures are coming out of the shadows into the hallway behind her.

"GO!" Alivia yells. "I'll slow them down." She turns and rushes headfirst into the dark figures advancing on us. The last thing I see is Astrid's blue tail feathers sail out the open hall window. I turn and flee down the stairs with Holden in my arms, hopping over the twisted stairs to avoid tripping.

The kitchen remains empty as I race through. I hit the stairs and they hold until I reach the bottom before they collapse into a heap, throwing debris from the dirt floor into the air.

Coughing and spitting, I see Alaric near the entrance to the old plumbing drain, and he's monitoring the door to the kitchen. He's almost eager for someone to come through it. I also see Griffin is in the tunnel with his arms outstretched for me to pass Holden to him. Holden is squirming in my arms and saying words I can't hear. Alaric continues to watch the door.

"Shrink, Holden. We need to go," I say as he squirms out of my grasp.

Much to my surprise, he races across the room toward the dome holding Dodo. Holden uses magic to release the dome. He grabs the bird by its neck and starts dragging it, yelling, "Shrink, shrink, shrink."

I goggle as both Holden and the bird shrink. No time to argue or question it. Alaric grabs them and passes them to Griffin. *Friends?*

Feet walking on the floor above us echoes through the basement. Before I shrink, I push a projection of me into the dining room upstairs. I set my projection to run and hide in the living room, hoping that it'll provide enough distraction for us to escape down the plumbing tunnel before the projection fades.

I manipulate dirt and water elements from the plants in that room to spin on the air currents. Alaric lifts me into the tunnel. Sounds of confusion drift down as enemies thunder into the living room and an onslaught of earth and water hits them, my magic-made tornado.

"Nice," Alaric says. He throws an orb of some sort up at the upper door before jumping and shrinking. He lands in the plumbing drain with us, mercifully not misjudging his shrinking jump. I can hear Griffin's footfalls moving down our escape route. Alaric pushes me along at a brisk pace. A loud explosion solves the mystery of Alaric's orb. My ears ring and ache.

The explosion has disturbed the dusty basement floor. The blast wave has debris hurtling down the tunnel behind us, threatening to overtake us and choke off our ability to breathe. The impact on our bodies at this size in this closed in space will be devastating.

I push my body harder, but I can only go so fast when I can't stand up straight. I can see the tunnel's exit, but the blast catches us before we reach it. A strange sensation of floating takes over. My arms and legs spin and flail forward out of my control. I twist and tumble. Scattered pieces of dirt and waste batter me. *Ironic*, I think.

I surround us with a bubble, and push out at the air currents, trying to control the closest ones so we can surf the blast wave. I curse my shrunken size. My body is carried out the end of the tunnel with Alaric behind me, but I've gained enough control to ride the currents like a bubble caught in a storm.

The bubble bounces, but we remain safe inside. When it hits the grass a second time, I can't hold it any longer and it pops. We skid on our bottoms across the cold blades of grass, coming to a stop concealed from sight in the bushes.

My ears feel plugged, so I ram my fingers into them, wincing and shaking my head. Alaric's hands grasp my head, holding it in place. I watch his lips move even though I can't hear what he's saying and nod that I understand. He releases me and points. All I see in the indicated direction is a moonless night and an empty street. If Aunt Rune is still out there, she's nowhere in sight.

There's no time for questions.

Alaric masks himself and I know without being able to see him he's moving along his indicated route. I sigh and wish I hadn't because it creates a strange hissing pressure in my ears. After masking myself, I step out of our hiding spot. I cast my eyes to the sky. Shadows of birds exit and enter the upper windows of the house. *Alivia, where are you?*

I turn from the bearing Alaric wants me to walk and face the house. Looking up at the expanse of brick, I wonder how to get back inside and get her out. Cords of magic choke off mine, severing my masking and making me visible if anyone looks my way.

A cold fear washes over me. I'm visible. The Ember stone on my chest comes alive with warmth. Without realizing what I'm doing, I reach for the heat the Ember stone is producing instead of pushing it away. The magic trapping me explodes and I pivot to fight, but it's Alaric behind me. I catch the surprise on his face but it disappears to his normal indifference. I do a double-take when he nods his approval.

The sensation from the Ember stone fades. We aren't masked, but Alaric seems unconcerned. He's thrown a dome over us that resembles the bushes, vines and leaves of different sizes and hues of green.

Alaric's lips are moving, and I strain to make out his words. "They probably moved Alivia," I manage to read his lips. I'm thankful for once that he isn't a long-winded man.

He turns and starts moving in the direction that he originally wanted us to go, masking himself. I look at the house one more time and swallow. Our one chance to rescue her and we failed. Now we don't know where they've taken her, and even if she's still inside, we've lost the element of surprise and it would be an all-out fight to get her out.

"Holden," I whisper. I mask myself and run in the direction that Alaric was moving. The street is empty and I can't see any sign of Alaric, but I keep running.

I barely sense the slight contracting pressure that I race through, but it's enough of a warning. Skidding and swinging my arms, I work to stop myself before I bounce off the big tire that has materialized in my path. I come to rest with my four-inch body pressed against the tire. I let out a sigh, recognizing the vehicle as the one we arrived in.

Wisps of a creative weave hang in the air. Griffin placed a dome, one that allows things to move in and out of it without disturbing its protection, over the vehicle to hide it until all of us returned. I'm looking up at Noah. He's gesturing and his mouth is moving, but I can't hear. I stare at him, my ears still suffering the after effects of the blast wave.

Alaric's regular-sized hand drops in front of my eyes, and he snaps his fingers at me. I blink and let myself bloom up to my regular five-foot-three height. Noah stuffs me in the open back door and hops in the front, pulling Holden onto his lap. Holden's arms pin the pigeon. I cock my head sideways, watching the docile bird, wondering why it isn't struggling.

Fin rockets away from the curb. I faintly hear what I think are the words, "Will the dome move with us and keep our location hidden?" I assume that I'm correct because Griffin's head is bobbing up and down.

"Astrid?" I say, watching the surrounding faces. Noah puts his finger to his lips and shakes his head from side to side. "What?" I say, leaning forward to watch his mouth, straining to hear.

He has his neck craned sideways so I can see his face. "Stop yelling!" are the first words that I understand from reading his lips, coupled with hints of syllables I hear. "Redirected them," Noah says, before turning frontward in his seat and ending any hope of me knowing what he's saying.

Griffin taps me on the shoulder. I sit back and turn to stare at his lips. His smile curves from the corner of his mouth up his cheeks to twinkle mischievously in his almost clear eyes. Then he brings his hands into my line of sight and he's rubbing his palms together rapidly. I can see magic building and I'm reminded of normie children building static through the friction of their hands.

He stops and moves them toward either side of my head. I survey his face as he claps his hands down over my ears. His smile fades into impartiality, which with him is a gentle grin. I see the scruffy handsome features that attract Fin.

I feel a warm tickling pressure in my eardrums. The pressure becomes a mild tug and soon a whistle fills my ears. It's like my ears are sealed and pressure is trying to escape and creates the high-pitched hiss in the process.

Griffin's grip on the sides of my head tightens, and I wonder if he's going to crush my head like a grape. Instead, there's a subtle pop in both my ears. He releases my head and searches my face with his eyebrows raised. I blink and realize that I can hear the hum of the tires moving over the pavement. I can hear breathing from the people in the vehicle and I can hear Fin humming along with the radio.

"It's best to stay quiet for a while, Kori. Overly loud noises or just listening to a conversation could cause permanent damage," Griffin says with his face turned to the window.

Nobody in the vehicle is talkative. I nod and slouch watching Holden stroke the plumes trailing down the strange bird's neck.

The bird isn't trying to escape. Holden's eyes are closed, and his movements become less pronounced. In just a few moments, it appears the boy and bird will be asleep. They're friends then, but who is Dodo and what's his story? Time to figure that out when they wake. I note the comfort between them and wonder about the development of their relationship over the last few days, and then I wonder about Belamey.

Noah is watching out the window and talking in hushed tones to Fin. I can't hear what he's saying, but she's nodding and glancing out her window too. Leaning over, all I see is a dark, empty sky. I tip my head against the headrest and close my eyes to the emotions that threaten to overtake me. *Sleep*, I whisper to myself, and

I allow my body to stop fighting.

Chapter 22

I hear hushed voices. I stretch my body, noting the frame of my bed beneath me. My bed. I'm in the Ember house! How did I not wake up before now? I shoot straight up with my eyes wide, too wide, because the glare of the morning sun is an additional surprise. I blink rapidly to gain focus. My sun-struck eyes and startled brain swear there were three boys in my room; Jayce, Holden, and a teenager I've never seen before.

My eyes adjust and I choose to ignore the fact that I was in the vehicle last night fully clothed and I'm now wearing my tank top and undies. I've no memory of it. Instead, I search for the boys.

Jayce's head is turning from me to Holden. Holden has wide eyes and a gap in his pouty lips. Dodo, the stocky bird, is peeking his head around Holden, blinking black-brown eyes at me, and cocking its head in jerky motions. Granted I have no basis of comparison for the pigeon's behaviour, but he seems skittish. If my sleep groggy brain is correct about a teenager standing where the bird now stands, then that supports my reading of his nervous energy.

"Boys," I say, adding a smile. "Boys, where is the boy

you were just talking to?"

"No boy," Jayce says.

"No boy," Holden repeats, bumping into Dodo.

"Holden, Auntie saw another boy."

"No boy," Holden repeats with tears threatening.

"No boy," I say to him, shaking my head to emphasize that I heard him. No point to scare them more then they already are. I slip off the bed onto my knees. "It's okay, you aren't in trouble. Auntie just wants to know who you were talking to."

Holden considers for a minute. Dodo makes a coo sound. "Run!" Jayce hollers, racing from the room. Holden flees on unsteady legs, with Dodo wasting no time following.

I scrub my hands over my face. *That could've gone better.* I'm thankful when I see fresh clothes folded on the chair.

Noah hands me a fresh cup of coffee when I stroll into the kitchen. I draw in a deep breath of it and sigh. "Thank you."

He's smirking. I decide to ignore the smirk because I'm not ready to find out how I got into bed last night. The house is quiet. "Did the boys and Dodo run through here?" I ask. The words are no sooner out of my mouth when a commotion starts in the hall.

"No, Uncle Carter! NO!" Jayce and Holden are yelling in unison. Both boy's voices are marked by tremors, they're fearful of something but I know that it can't be Carter. He dotes on them and they adore him.

I cringe at the use of the title uncle and glance at Noah. Before Noah can comment, Carter comes into the kitchen, acting out a role in the theatre of the absurd, with Jayce attached to his left leg and Holden attached to his right. Carter's face and neck are flushed and his expression is pinched.

Jayce is on his tummy, dragging behind Carter with his tiny arms holding tight to Carter's ankle. Holden is affixed on top of Carter's other foot with his arms and legs clinging to Carter and he's trying to bite Carter's leg through his pants. Carter is jiggling that leg to keep Holden's teeth from digging in. In addition, Carter's hand is latched onto the upper arm of a familiar teenage boy with dark eyes and stringy shoulder-length hair.

"You were in my room this morning," I blurt out, happy that my grip on sanity hasn't gotten as thin as I feared.

Fin, who has a clear view from her chair in the dining room, claps her hands, delighted with the entertainment. Griffin makes a non-committal noise in his throat.

The boy's eyes are wild, almost feral. He shifts in Carter's hand and leaves Carter holding the leg of the nicobar pigeon. Surprised, Carter hollers and opens his hand as if the bird is on fire.

Dodo drops to the ground and doesn't move for a second, stunned. I feel a bit stunned myself because Carter's reaction is a sure sign that he saw the transformation, and saw it for what it was: magic. *Burning brimstone, why now? This is bad.* A myriad of scenarios roll through my mind, but I clamp my thoughts off. Dodo and the boys are foremost right now.

Holden and Jayce leap toward Dodo the bird, and

Dodo shifts into a teenage boy. With a speed and strength that I don't think any of us were expecting, Dodo scoops up Jayce and Holden, one under each of his arms, and he runs full speed, head down, at the kitchen door that leads into an open backyard.

Noah moves to stop him, but the teenager flings a glittery surface the size of a manhole a few steps to the left of Noah. It's suspended in the air and Dodo amends his course, jumping through it with Jayce and Holden.

The shimmer on the surface of the manhole obscures the location on the other side. The three of them disappear. It happens so quickly that I see part of the weave. It's a soft, wavering string of moonlight intertwined with what my mind classifies as star dust. If I could see a full set of threads for it, I think I could duplicate it.

Carter is making strange noises and wringing his hands. Noah is standing in front of the kitchen door with his mouth hanging open.

Fin jumps to her feet. "Cool!" The word hangs from her lips.

Then a noise comes from the backyard.

"Yes, short-range conveyance. Children love it because the location is unforeseeable, game-like. You might end up where you want or you might not. Point is that it's unlikely they'll get off the yard using manholes, but they can evade us quickly enough." Griffin straightens from his lean on the counter, and he throws a similar shimmering manhole into the air, winks at Fin, grabs my arm, and tugs me through with him before I can question the hole's reliability.

There's a brief catch in my breath as I cross through the shimmering surface. It feels like I have dropped over the first hill of a roller coaster when really I'm stepping, horizontal, from one side of the hole to the other. Then I'm in the backyard with a teenager who is pleading with Holden to leave with him while assuring Holden that Jayce can go too. Griffin's shimmering manhole blinks out.

"Hey," I yell, whipping a magic cord around Dodo to bind his magic. *No time to question how I figured that out,* I tell myself. Griffin tosses a dome over us to conceal us from any watching eyes. He waits while I deal with the situation, his stance relaxed with his arms crossed.

"No, Auntie," Holden yells, running at me and hammering on my leg with a fat fist and big tears.

Jayce is trying with his limited knowledge of magic to remove my wrap from this teenaged boy who has become a friend. Jayce's unsuccessful efforts are tiring him. I reach down and scoop Holden up.

"Shh, I won't hurt your friend," I say loud enough for everyone to hear. "I just don't want him to run off with anybody. It's preferable that he doesn't run off at all."

Negotiation wasn't my strong suit as a cop, but when I catch the boy's eye and there's terror there, I try to give him a reassuring smile. I whisper in Holden's ear and put him down. Holden is quick to follow my instruction. He scampers to the boy and takes hold of his hand. The boy relaxes a bit, which is the effect I wanted.

"Jayce?" Jayce stops his magical efforts. "I'll free him in just one second. I promise." I watch while Jayce reaches for the boy's other hand. "Okay, young man," I address the teenager, firmly. "I'm going to release my hold on your magic, but on the condition that you join us inside for some breakfast and a chat."

Jayce and Holden, both bouncing on their feet, are smiling up at Dodo. The teenager swallows and nods without looking up. I can't see his face, but his head is moving left and right as he glances at Jayce and Holden.

"Nope. Young man, you need to look at me and answer." I've set the magic in place between Dodo and I that will bind him to his words so that I don't have to worry if he's telling me one thing while planning another. It's not visible or detectable but it'll hold him like an invisible cord to the commitment he makes. *Thank you for that lesson, Ague. And thank you to myself for being one in a million Spellbinders who can learn the technique.*

Ill at ease, the boy lifts his head and, more apprehensive, his eyes rise to meet mine. "Yes, ma'am," he whispers.

"Good, let's go inside." I combine what I saw of Dodo's and Griffin's weaves, and create a glimmering manhole to hopefully take us into the kitchen.

Griffin saunters through first while I shoo my hands at the three boys so they'll follow him. I step through behind them, confident thanks to Ague's binding magic that Dodo is true to his word.

Even when I'm expecting it, it feels like I'm dropping over the steep slope. It's quick, though and, within seconds, I'm in the kitchen with a clear view of the dining room. Fin is putting juice, pastries, and a fresh coffee pot on the table. Jayce and Holden abandon the teenager to scramble up on chairs. The teenager casts his eyes at me, and I raise my eyebrow and smile as I move to sit at the table.

"Come on," Fin says, patting a seat with a glowing smile.

The teenager swallows again. He creeps to the table, eyeing the spread of treats. His tongue darts across his lips and he tears his eyes from the food, unsure.

"Help yourself." Fin is smiling. The teenager assesses her for a second but says nothing. "I'm Fin," she says.

The teenager is salivating at the pastries. "I know."

"Who are you?" Fin asks, letting no surprise register in her voice. She's relaxed in her chair with her head tilted to the side as she feigns mild curiosity.

The teenager looks at Holden. Holden is pulling pieces of his pastry apart and making a sticky mess of himself. Sensing the teenager's eyes, Holden smiles up at him. The grains of sugar that fall off the corners of Holden's lips distract him from the teenager.

"I'm Dodo," the teenager says, reaching for the coffee pot. Nobody at the table says anything. I don't know what's more surprising. That this young man, who is maybe sixteen, drinks coffee, or that he calls himself Dodo.

I watch as he pours a large cup and hunches over it. Fin and I glance at each other, and she reclines her chair. "Sugar?" she asks Dodo.

He finishes a soft blow on the liquid and takes a sip. "No, thank you. I drink it black, like Belamey." His chin comes up and his voice doesn't waiver. It's the first time I've seen him act as anything other then self-conscious, scared, and unsure.

I raise my eyebrows and lounge back. "So, Dodo, why do my nephews believe you are their best friend."

"Friends," Holden mimics, casting crumbs of pastry over the table in front of him.

Dodo squirms, crosses and uncrosses his arms, and if he could sink into the seat and disappear from sight I'm sure he would.

"Okay, well, maybe tell me why you were lurking in Belamey's basement?" I ask.

Dodo clutches his coffee cup like he needs protection and the mug will provide it. He redirects his gaze to watch Holden. His voice is quiet when he speaks. "Belamey asked me to keep him safe." Dodo gestures at Holden. He's louder with his next sentence, he's trying to be firm but there's a shake to it. "Belamey told me to keep Holden safe, just like Belamey protected me."

"Who did he keep you safe from, Dodo?" I ask keeping my voice low, but he doesn't answer. "Who did Belamey tell you to keep Holden safe from?" Dodo raises his eyes and I'm saddened by their haunted aspect. "Okay, what can you tell me, then?"

"Belamey said that I can trust you," Dodo answers so quietly that I almost don't hear him. He lowers his eyes to his coffee mug. "Kori?" He says, shocking me because he knows my name too. "Are you going to save us from the evil that is growing stronger in the Spellbinders?"

I blink at Dodo, unsure of how to answer. My hand moves to the Ember stone. *The Cleansing.* Dodo brings his coffee cup to his lips but pauses, "Kori, is Belamey going to die?" Dodo's eyes stray up to meet mine for a split second and the concern in them is heartbreaking.

Grama Pearle enters the room, and I'm thankful for the diversion. Dodo transforms into a bird, dropping his coffee mug onto the table but not before Grama Pearle sees him as human. I block out the image of Dodo the bird perched in a chair. When I open my eyes, I focus on Grama Pearle.

"That's new," she says, flicking her hand at Dodo.

I nod in agreement. "He's a skittish little thing, boy and bird."

"What do we know about him?" Grama Pearle asks. I take it to mean she's talking about the teenager. I don't answer, though, because Birdie has entered the dining room. She's staring at Dodo the bird with a look that suggests the children leave the area.

"Jayce and Holden," I say to the boys. "Can you take Dodo and show him the room where you have your toys, please?"

Both boys make faces of happiness before they grab Dodo and scurry away.

I gaze at Birdie. She's fixated on the spot where Dodo the bird was just sitting. "Birdie, do you know that bird?"

She blinks at me from behind her big round glasses like a spell has been broken.

"The boy and the bird go by the name, Dodo," I say to Grama Pearle, thinking that perhaps I misread Birdie's response.

"Maybe five or six years ago," Birdie says, "Nekane was after a boy. The boy wasn't well known, but it wasn't a secret in the Spellbinder community that his parents, who lived as normies, weren't nice to him because of his magical abilities. One day, his parents put him out on the streets and left him to fend for himself. He was too young, ten or eleven. Nekane wanted to take him in and make him a Society of the Blood Wind henchman."

"Typical Nekane, thinking to make himself a recruit or weapon, as if people are dispensable items," Grama Pearle interrupts. "I remember hearing whispers, but that boy wasn't the last of the miscreants, runaways, or otherwise impressionable individuals that Nekane began grooming."

"He never groomed that boy, Pearle." Birdie purses her lips at her for interrupting. "Nekane never found the boy. In fact, nobody reportedly found the boy. Some people questioned that he existed. After a while, people stopped talking about it and Nekane found other Spellbinders to recruit."

"And you think Dodo is that boy?" Fin jumps in.

"He fits the age the boy would be now. The bird type fits, too," Birdie chirps. "I had a bit of extra interest vested in this case because he was slotted to live at the safe house with me as an apprentice. A way to give him a home, a purpose, and a future."

"But why would he be at Belamey's house? And why would he be so loyal to Belamey, unless . . ." my voice trails off as I put the pieces together with the new information that we're learning about Belamey. "Clandestine, he took the boy in to keep Nekane from using and corrupting him!"

I do the math in my head, guessing Belamey to be

about thirty-four would've made him twenty-seven or twenty-eight when he took Dodo in. We know that Dodo can shrink, so coming and going via the sewer pipe makes sense. Given how skittish Dodo is, it wouldn't surprise me if he never left Belamey's house.

"Sure," Fin says. "But let's talk about Dodo's parents. How'd they have a child with magical abilities? One of them was a Spellbinder, right?" she asks.

I shrug, not one hundred percent sure of the answer.

"Yes, Fin one of his parents was a Spellbinder that's the only way he would have magical abilities. Spellbinder and normie intimate relationships happen and magic is the dominant gene. Some couples never have children, and in relationships where they do, the normie is usually like yourself and open to magic. There have been families where the normie parent stayed conditioned to not see and their family functioned, but the normie parent often has stories about strange things happening.

"In Dodo's case, one parent was hiding their magic. But why hide it? That's something that I don't have an answer to, especially when hiding it comes between yourself and your own child," Birdie chirps. "Maybe the parent had repressed magic so thoroughly that they didn't remember it as being part of themselves. Both parents could see Dodo's magic because it's where their dislike of him came from, so their conditioning was faulty on some level. They died in a car collision about a year after they put Dodo out of the house, so whatever their motives, they died with them."

We sit, thinking about that. "Poor Dodo," Fin

mumbles. "Why would a Spellbinder want to be with someone they have to hide their true self from?" she asks. Then she claps a hand over her mouth and flicks her eyes at me.

"Point taken, Fin." I huff and clench my jaw. I force my next words over my lips. "I wasn't hiding my true self from Carter so much as I was hiding it from my self." I fight the nausea that the omission causes and I hurry to change the topic. "Well, Jayce and Holden have taken to Dodo. I get the impression Dodo and Holden spent time together at Belamey's place," I say. "Speaking of Belamey's place, what happened to you and Noah while we were inside his house, Fin?"

"Not much because we were under Griffin's dome the whole time. We could see and hear, but we were invisible to everyone else." She shrugs. "Orders were provided to me. No matter what, I was to remain the getaway driver, but I was hoping for an opportunity to use my mad throwing skills."

I give her a hand flap. "What about Aunt Rune or Astrid? What happened to them, did you see? Are they here?"

"Astrid flew off in the opposite direction from us, drawing a bunch of birds after her. She's used to flying at night. I expect she'll be here soon. She would want to make sure nobody followed her," Noah says, very sure of his answer.

"And Aunt Rune?" I ask, deciding to let his sureness of Astrid be.

On cue, Aunt Rune sweeps into the room. "I'll answer that, Noah."

Noah gives a bowing wave out in front of himself turning the floor over to Aunt Rune. She gives him a glare and a cackle before she turns to me. "A mixed flock of birds was coming from the west, and I identified some of them as henchmen for The Society of the Blood Wind. So, I sent up a warning shriek. That, of course, drew them to me and allowed you to escape.

"When I took to the skies to draw them away, I saw another group coming in. I shook a bit of my sleeping charm off my tail feathers at the group behind me. A few birds dropped from the sky in a deep sleep. I drew a few others away and led them through other sleeping charms, booby traps, I had set up when I first went to Belamey's house." She laughs, a harsh and raucous noise, before she continues.

"I looped past the house after, and the birds knocked out by my charm were still sleeping. I did see Alivia being taken out to a dark SUV and Nekane was one of the five Spellbinders escorting her out, so he must have arrived after I drew the birds away. I wasn't able to attack five of them on my own. I took a disjointed flight home in case there was anybody watching."

I blink at her, unsure what to say or do.

"Apple?" Fin asks. I don't know where the apple came from, so now I'm blinking at Fin.

Aunt Rune cackles and plucks it from Fin's outstretched hand. "I've a plan for this one," she says as she leaves the room.

"That's not creepy at all," Fin mumbles. "Wait, there's a potion room here? I don't remember ever being in a potion room." Fin shoves her chair out and darts after

Aunt Rune.

I prop my head on my fist and close my eyes, so my rapid blinking doesn't give me a seizure. This has been my stress tick for longer than I can remember, this and the twitching eye muscle.

"Let's figure out what this last fiasco taught us about The Society of the Blood Wind," Noah says.

I creak an eye open. Even with his back to me, I can hear the coffee brewing, so I decide to close my eyes and wait.

"You fill me in later, dear," Grama Pearle says. "Birdie and I are going to speak with Dodo." They head down the hall, chattering.

I don't open my eyes until Noah waves the hot cup of coffee under my nose. Inhaling deeply, I accept his offering. I'm startled because while my eyes have been closed, Alaric and Griffin have joined us.

Fin comes hurrying into the dining room. "Aunt Rune threatened to use the sleeping charm on me if I didn't leave," Fin huffs. "Oh, I meant to tell you, Kori. After you went through the manhole, Carter was falling asleep on his feet in the hallway. I've settled him on the sofa." She plops herself down in a chair.

I feel the edge of my eye tingle, so I take a big gulp of my burning hot coffee to curb a full-blown eye twitch. When I've recovered from the burning sensation, I take a smaller sip. "Okay, Noah. You asked what we learned?"

"We learned that the Tall Drink of Water, or as you like to call him, Belamey, is fighting for the good guys," Fin says proudly. We stare at her. "What? His intel was good, and he was keeping Alivia and Holden safe, not to mention that he has been keeping Dodo safe for years." She smirks. "Where do you think he is? The Society of the Blood Wind must be hunting him now. Should we be worried about his safety? What am I saying? He's able to take care of himself if all of this is any indication."

"We learned The Society of the Blood Wind has an unknown number of supporters ready to do its bidding." I pull my eyes off Fin.

"Yeap, and that Belamey's place isn't safe. They moved Alivia, and she's now in the hands of the enemy," Noah adds.

"Did we identify any of the birds or the Spellbinders that they shifted into? Or do you think Grama Pearle or Birdie could, if any of us could provide a description?" I ask. Trying not to dwell on Noah's information about Alivia, I move my fingers to the corner of my left eye and start a slow circling while I clutch my coffee cup in my other hand.

"I didn't," Fin says. "But I'm going through Alivia's sketchbook again. So far, Dodo is the only bird I recognized from those pages. Nekane, Dolion, Aza, and Kyson were not part of the flock of evil that descended on Belamey's house. As for describing, I don't think I could do it without mixing details up."

"Same," I agree after I sift through the jumble of birds and Spellbinders in the hallway when Alivia passed Holden to me. It's a blur.

"Birdie and I've been talking with Dodo," Grama Pearle announces as she reenters the room with Ague on her heels. "He's a very interesting young man."

"Did you learn something from him, Grama Pearle?"

"Hopefully you didn't learn anything by using Ague's special interrogation skills," Fin interrupts. Ague's melting red lipstick lips stretch into an elaborate grin, but she says nothing, content to let us come to our own assumptions. Fin makes a choking noise and I'm sure she's dreaming up a million horrible tortures and assigning them to Ague's questioning techniques. I shoot a *grow up idiot* glance at her to cut off any more of her absurd comments and noises before turning to Grama Pearle.

"Grama Pearle?"

"Dodo believes Nekane wants Alivia because of her talents for healing and her awareness charms. She's one of the most gifted Spellbinders of our time in regards to healing," Grama Pearle says.

Catching sight of my face, she adds, "Make no mistake, Kori, he wants you and the Ember stone, too." She sighs. "The Society of the Blood Wind has always had the balance of power tipped against them, even though they continue trying to reorientate it. If they get possession of the Ember stone, the balance of power will change. The Cleansing forces a personal rumination of sorts, one that allows each of us to scrutinize our own motives and character and then come out the other side of the process with a positive outlook and an internal balance that's revitalized." As she talks, her voice grows quiet until her words just fade out.

"Am I correct about Belamey's allegiance, Grama Pearle?" Fin asks, cutting her eyes to me and narrowing them.

"Belamey Adelgrief fights with us." Grama Pearle eyes Ague.

"HA!" Fin says as she dances out of the room.

I pull a full breath and clamp down my irritation at Fin's noise of triumph. "How can we be sure?"

"I just am. But to satisfy anyone who doesn't believe, let's remember, Ague is very good at discerning if someone is being honest or telling lies. Her chance will come to use that skill with Belamey," Grama Pearle says.

I peer at Ague and swallow, thinking about Dodo and what he might have experienced. Ague's grin is tight, but she manages a theatrical laugh that screams of villainous intentions.

"You're a psychological nightmare, Ague Draven." Grama Pearle's laugh is equally nefarious.

I feel my eyes pop. It's a visible reaction because both Grama Pearle and Ague's laughter change to one of genuine pleasure. I huff at them and stomp my foot, making them laugh harder. The group discussion is over.

Chapter 23

I'm trying to shake off Ague and Grama Pearle's laughter as I round the corner into the living room. I'm hoping to find the room empty so I can be alone to watch the skies for Astrid and float my chakra stones to calm myself. Stopping in my tracks, I cock my head to the side to explore my options. After all our years of friendship, Fin's ability to surprise me with her antics should be ineffective, yet she regularly pulls it off. I can't help my curiosity. "Fin," I whisper, in case she's asleep.

"Yes?" She doesn't open her eyes or raise her head off the book she's using as a pillow.

"It's just, well, what in the fiery blazes are you doing?"

"Practicing osmosis," she says matter-of-factly as if I should have reasoned that out. "You know? The unconscious process of taking in information, ideas, and knowledge."

"Right," I shake my head. In silence I move to the window and lift my eyes to the fall skies, noting the haze has passed. The blue sky is clear and almost cloudless.

Fin's voice startles me out of my trance. "I used to study for our exams this way in high school," she says. "Bet you didn't know that."

I turn from the window. I can't tell if she's joking or if she believes herself. She's lying on the book, but she's watching me. I give her a polite smile and an eyebrow raise.

She sits. "Don't be so doubtful. Don't you remember how good my marks were?"

"You're brilliant and quick-witted as well as a tiny bit dramatic and eccentric."

She's gawking at me and formulating her rebuttal.

I sigh, glance out the window, and move to a chair. "Okay, so what are you using your osmosis talent on today?"

Pleased that I've accepted her so-called talent, Fin smiles and lifts Alivia's sketchbook. "I know almost all of them now!"

I nod and hold my polite smile in place as I try to control how wide my eyes want to go. "Hey, where's Carter? Wasn't he sleeping on the sofa?"

"He was. With this less potent sleep charm, he's awake off and on for sometimes an hour plus. Brynlee and the boys took him outside to get some fresh air. She and I agreed to keep track of him, make sure he's fed, watered, and gets bathroom breaks. I put an air mattress on the floor in the boys' room for him and another for Dodo. He agreed to help Carter in the night, if needed."

"Thank you, Fin."

"Birds," Fin says, and I think she's referring to the sketchbook. "Astrid and . . ." she pauses and leaps off the sofa, grabbing me by the arm and dragging me behind her.

Through the window, I see Astrid's blue bird being trailed by a bird with short, broad wings. *Alaric as a harpy eagle.* As Fin tugs me through the room, I wonder when Alaric left the house and how he found Astrid to accompany him.

Fin cranks me close to her and drapes her arm over my shoulder. She's bouncing on her toes.

"I think that your osmosis trick did something questionable to your brain, Fin," I tease. "System overload." I bounce on my toes.

She smirks.

There are feet coming up the front stairs now. I try to turn and head down the hall to put on a pot of coffee, but Fin's arm tightens and slips up toward my neck until she has me in a loose headlock. "What are you doing, nutball?"

"This will be fun, Kori," she says in a know-it-all tone that makes no sense to me.

Astrid strolls through the door. She pauses, amused with me struggling in Fin's headlock. I flash a tight-lipped smile. "Excuse me a second." I stomp my heel down hard enough on Fin's toes that she loosens her grip, then I yank her arm down from my neck and move my body to her side. Giving Fin an *I hate you* glare, I turn to Astrid. "Glad you're here. Where's Alaric?"

Concern marks Astrid's face. "He's not here?"

"He was right behind you as you were flying in." The doorway is open and Fin is bouncing on her toes.

"Oh," says Astrid, her voice increasing in pitch, as she understands something I don't. "Alaric isn't with me." She moves into the house and the doorway remains empty. I gaze to her then to the door as a shadow darkens it. I feel my eyes bulge and my mouth drop open as Belamey steps in the front door and closes it behind him.

"Kori," he says by way of greeting.

Fin gives an excited giggle, clapping her hands in satisfaction. She gives me a raised eyebrow to say *See?* Grabbing my arm, she drags me stumbling backwards down the hall. "We'll check the coffee situation," she yells to Astrid and Belamey over her shoulder.

"I, I . . ." my brain is trying to make sense of what is happening. I can't get my sentences to formulate fast enough to keep up. Fin releases me in the middle of the kitchen. Besides us, this room and the dining room are empty. I stare at Astrid and Belamey, who followed us. I'm happy I have the presence of mind to close my mouth and put my eyes back in their sockets, but I'm confused.

Fin dumps the bit of coffee left in the pot down the sink and is busy prepping to brew more. "Is that what took you so long, Astrid? You had to find Belamey?"

"It's time that all our players are on the same page," Astrid responds.

I'm recuperated enough now that I jump into the conversation. "Astrid, I don't understand what you're trying to tell us or how you knew where to find Belamey!" I can feel my defenses stirring, and I remember Belamey warning me that some things aren't what they seem.

Astrid casts a look in Belamey's direction. "Let's just say for now that Belamey and I share a mutual friend."

Belamey nods in agreement.

Fin spins and I can see the wheels turning in her mind about this mysterious mutual friend. "Fin," I say before she spouts out theories. "Can you please find Grama Pearle, Noah, and whatever other adults you think need to hear what Astrid and Belamey have to say. Then bring them to the dining room."

She gives me a pouty lip for impeding her questions about the mutual friend, then she hurries from the room.

"Belamey!" two voices yell from the hall and thundering feet follow. Jayce, Holden, and Dodo race toward Belamey. Dodo slides to a halt, letting Holden race by him. Jayce stops by the entrance to the hallway.

I'm beyond shocked when Holden flings himself at Belamey's legs, hugging them for all he's worth. I'm more surprised when Belamey chuckles deeply and scoops Holden up. Calm, Dodo crosses the kitchen. He waits while Belamey puts Holden on the floor.

"Dude!" Dodo says, putting out his fist.

Belamey's smile is bemused. "Dude!" They fist bump and make an exploding hand gesture. "They treating you well?" Belamey asks like he isn't the person out of place in this scenario.

Dodo just nods.

"Excellent." Belamey's eyes catch sight of Jayce, still at the mouth of the hallway, watching the exchange with fidgeting feet. "You must be the big brother I've heard so much about," Belamey says to him. Belamey thrusts his hand forward. "I'm Belamey Adelgrief."

Jayce's face emits a huge smile. He rushes forward

to shake hands with Belamey. "I'm Jayce Ember. It's a pleasure to meet you, Mr. Adelgrief." Jayce is doing his best imitation of a grown up.

Belamey ruffles Jayce's hair. "You can call me Belamey, young man."

I blow out an exasperated sigh, wondering about the absence of rational behaviour in my life. Part of me wants Belamey to be the enemy, so I can gloss over the unexpected feelings he stirs in me. But here he is, winning over the heart of my nephew, no signs of sinister motives. I cast my eyes to Astrid, but she's just smiling at the interchange. Footsteps and voices in the hallway draw our attention.

"Dodo, can you please take the boys to play with their toys? This conversation won't be child-friendly," Astrid says.

Dodo glances at Belamey, who nods his agreement. Dodo rounds Jayce and Holden up and they leave the room as Fin leads Grama Pearle, Birdie, Noah, and Alaric in. Noah appears displeased.

"Coffee is ready. Let's take this meeting in the dining room," Fin directs. She prances across the kitchen and places the full coffee pot onto a tray she has prepared with mugs, sugar, and milk. She doesn't wait for agreement as she sashays from the room.

"Come, come," Grama Pearle says, following Fin.

Alaric and Astrid hang back to lean against the wall like a lethal overwatch, but I'm not one hundred percent sure who they're worried about. Birdie perches on the edge of her chair with her big eyes locked on Belamey. Fin has chosen a chair so close to Belamey that her knees are touching his while she studies him in a different way than Birdie. She's like a child that's infatuated with a previously taboo toy; the hot evil enemy is now friend. That and she's a flirt. Grama Pearle is the only one of us who's untroubled by Belamey's presence except, of course, Belamey, who is nonchalant.

Before we can say anything, Ague appears at Belamey's side. She blinks into sight beside him, having entered the room masked from sight. He couldn't have known she was there, but self-assured, he doesn't flinch. "Belamey Adelgrief," she purrs his name like he's a long-desired specimen.

Belamey shocks me again. He stands, reaching out his hand to Ague without question. *Is he volunteering to be read?* He must know Ague's innate ability to read the people she touches as well as control them if she chooses.

"Doctor Ague Draven," he says with awe. "I'm pleased to make your acquaintance."

When Ague grasps his hand, he pulls her in for a welcoming embrace. When he releases her, Ague has a smeared grin that spreads from ear to ear. She inclines her head and gives Grama Pearle a very clear nod. Ague moves to the side to listen.

"Now that Ague's test is done," Noah speaks up, with a blatant glare at Belamey. Fin's opinion about Noah and Belamey's feeling for me make my mouth go dry. *Is that what Noah is so upset about?* It's clear Noah would've been happier if Belamey failed Ague's test. "Astrid, do you care to clue us in?"

Astrid doesn't move from her place against the wall. "Sure, Noah," she says with remarkable patience. "As soon as I saw our extraction of both Alivia and Holden wouldn't be successful, I knew we would need different help." She gives a shrug and flicks her eyes at Belamey.

"That's where I come in." Belamey relaxes in his chair with a cup of coffee.

"Get on with it, Adelgrief," Noah barks.

Belamey takes a sip of his coffee and places it down on the table. "Noah, I consider us to be on a first name basis, so please, call me Belamey," he says with a firm, but friendly manner.

I stomp my foot when I see Noah is gearing up for another comment. "Move on," I say to everybody, but I fix Noah with a steely stare. Noah glares at me before returning his scowl at Belamey. Noah's aversion to Belamey doesn't seem to be an issue anybody wants to get tangled in.

Belamey leads the conversation. "The first thing is that once Nekane got his hands on Alivia, he stashed her somewhere and he alone knows where. He isn't sure who to trust, so he won't risk anyone knowing where Alivia is. He's counting on her to be his ticket to either the Ember stone, or Kori, or both. So, I've set a meeting with Aza Tier.

"My plan is to feed her some information about a meeting between myself and Kori. As long as Ague shares with me how to get Aza to act in our favour, the control trick, then it *should* work. The goal is to draw The Society of the Blood Wind to one specific place." Belamey pauses and scans the room to see if we're following the plan. I scan the room too and note assorted confusion on almost everyone's face.

"Ah," Belamey says. "You didn't think I knew about Ague's ploy with Aza? Astrid told me. As she mentioned to Kori and Fin when we arrived, Astrid and I have a friend in common. Anyway, returning her as a spy was good work."

He throws his hands up, palms forward. "Relax, your secret is safe. Good choice of a puppet, by the way, because Aza has a bit of a desire to be in my presence." He shoots a pointed look at Fin's knees, which are brushing up against his. "I used her desire to get her to agree to meet me away from the eyes of The Society of the Blood Wind."

Unabashed, Fin locks eyes with Belamey. "That's very astute, Belamey," she says, rolling his name over her tongue.

"Oh, smoke and ashes, Fin. Give it a break," I say.

"Don't be jealous, Kori. You know how I feel about you," Belamey says. I watch him with astonished eyes as he slants his body and whispers like we're the only two people in the room. "I'm patient, and I know your feelings will catch up."

The whole room falls silent, and Belamey and I stare at each other. I can't look at anybody, I feel flustered and breathless. My mouth has gone dry and I'm unsure how to respond. Noah stands abruptly and marches away.

"Told you so," Fin says to me, like we're in a grade-school argument, her eyes tracking Noah's retreat.

I'm about to flip her the finger when Grama Pearle

speaks up. "Well, that's all very interesting, but let's discuss this meeting with Aza."

"Right." Belamey clears his throat and moves his eyes reluctantly from me to Grama Pearle. "The meeting is today, in a few hours. Astrid and I thought it best to not delay. There's too much at stake."

"I'll go with Belamey as his unseen back up," Astrid interjects.

Belamey nods. "Pearle, I'm going to tell Aza the meeting is set for the Cleansing chamber. Is your tunnel from the store to the chamber passable?"

"It is." There's no surprise in Grama Pearle's voice when Belamey mentions a hidden tunnel from her store to the Cleansing room.

I glance at Astrid wondering how much she told Belamey and if she has other allies she hasn't told us about. I'm also curious about her and Belamey's relationship.

"I'll tell Aza that Kori and I are meeting there in two days' time, in the evening." Belamey continues.

"Wait, why?" Fin asks. "Why do we want Nekane to come to us and this Cleansing chamber?"

Grama Pearle answers. "We don't know where he has Alivia, Fin. If Nekane dies trying to resist the Cleansing, and there were Spellbinders who died doing just that, then Alivia's location will die with him.

"The Cleansing can't wait. Things have gotten too out of hand and the balance of power is very close to tipping in The Society of the Blood Wind's favour. The longer we wait, the greater the risk that the Ember stone, or Kori, will wind up in their hands. Plus, the closer you are to

The Cleanser, the more powerful the effect." Grama Pearle explains. She nods at Belamey to continue.

"I'll then set another meeting with Aza for the same day to make sure that she has leaked the information to Nekane, or someone close to him." Belamey casts his eyes to me and to Grama Pearle. His voice comes out low and questioning. "Is she ready for this?"

I know he means me, but I'm unsure what he means by *this*. I'm too wrapped up in the explosion of information since Belamey and Astrid arrived to get upset about him questioning me being ready for anything.

"She has to be." Grama Pearle turns to me with sad but serious eyes.

Perceptible only to me, the Ember stone on my chest flares once in a wave of hot and cold, as if it's marking the end of our meeting. Everyone is moving with a purpose. Belamey is following Astrid. They move like a team that has worked together before. Birdie is hopping after them, chirping about gathering the troops and telling them the plan.

"Alaric," Grama Pearle says before he can disappear.

He says nothing but nods and flicks his head in a *follow me* motion.

"Come on, girls," Grama Pearle says to Fin and me as she accompanies Alaric down the hall.

The house is alive with everyone's energy and ambition. The four of us head straight down to the store in silence, but feel charged as well. The store is tidy, with everything in its proper place. I disengage from the group and hurry into the storage room to see the damage they did to the walls with the sledgehammer. Nothing is badly damaged, only slightly chipped. Debris from the assault has been cleaned up, and the passage is hidden. I wonder if there are other secret doors in this space and where they might lead.

There's the sound of a shelf being moved. Inquisitive, I hurry to the main room. Alaric has pulled the wooden bookshelf out from the wall, the same bookshelf where I found the Ember stone holder. It's swivelled out to the left on unseen door hinges, revealing an expanse of brick wall and a bunch of dust and cobwebs. *Why is the shelf hinged to the wall?* I can't see what Alaric's hands are doing, but nothing exciting is happening.

"Hasn't been opened in years, Alaric." Grama Pearle moves to place her hands on the wall. A flare of brilliant yellow sweeps out from under her hands and cascades across the surface of the wall like a hungry flame. The webs and dust disintegrate under its power. The wall itself groans a low long creak in response.

I blink when Alaric heaves and the wall gives way, moving right with a grinding action of stone grating against stone. The tunnel beyond is pitch black and noiseless once the echoing of stone contacting stone dies away. I swallow, remembering the narrow passage behind the hidden door in the storage room. I've no desire to enter a confined space.

Alaric tosses a light orb into the tunnel. Relief washes over me when I see a regular-sized passage, more like a rock hallway. Alaric steps aside and looks down at Grama Pearle. She smiles and pats his arm. "I can take it from here, Alaric. Thank you. The hard part was opening it after it's been sealed for so long."

Alaric nods and strolls toward the basement stairs. I know Fin has hurried off into the store. "Just a minute, Grama Pearle. Don't leave without me." Her feet are thundering back, and she stops next to me. Candle in hand, her eyes flare wide with excitement. "Ready?" She sparks a lighter and her candle comes to life.

I stifle my comment about getting a flashlight. There won't be one in the basement, and I'd be shocked to find one anywhere in the house. Grama Pearle loves candles; even when I was a kid and the power went out, she wouldn't use a flashlight.

Grama Pearle smiles. "Excellent, Fin. Can you please light a few of the torches that you find along the wall so that our walk won't be in darkness? Just a few, please."

Fin skips ahead to light the first torch. They're staggered on opposite sides of the wall at five feet intervals. Grama Pearle winks. "Come on, Kori. It's best you see where we'll be meeting at least once before the Cleansing, so you know what to expect. Your focus and acceptance, at least in regards to magic, do better once your mind has had time to process it. Since you can't practice the Cleansing, we can at least prepare you by showing you the space." She turns and enters the tunnel.

I follow her and Fin, trying to figure out what Grama Pearle is talking about. I give up on my effort to decode Grama Pearle's statements. The dim light from the torches casts a soft glow on the walls. There are strange drawings of symbols, images, words, and pictures. I slow to look at them. None of the markings are familiar and they make no sense to me.

"Another time, Kori." Grama Pearle calls over her shoulder. I cast my glance in her direction, but she's not facing me. She's following Fin. "You can investigate it all on a different day. We don't have time today. This is a long walk."

I look at the walls one more time before hurrying to catch up to Grama Pearle and Fin. Fin is rambling on and Grama Pearle is adding the occasional word or sentence to the conversation. I trail behind them in silence, watching the strange wall designs.

"This one, Fin." Grama Pearle indicates a particular torch. "And, please, pass it to me when it's lit."

Fin holds her candle up to the torch and, as it sputters and puffs into life, an open doorway to a large room is revealed. She lifts the torch down, lights it, and passes it to Grama Pearle. Fin blows out the stub of her candle, and keeps it pinched between her fingers. Grama Pearle enters the room with Fin on her heels. I'm the last to enter.

The Ember stone screams as I cross the threshold. The sound is deafening, and its burst of power is so unexpected that my body doubles over and I drop to my knees. I grab my ears with my hands to protect them.

Waves of intense heat and cold burn on my chest where the Ember stone sits. My skin tingles as sparks of fire flash on my flesh. The power coming off the Ember stone is overwhelming. I'm unprepared and struggle to defend myself, warring for control.

Terrified, I scream with the Ember stone.

I throw my arms straight up into the air, desperate

to purge myself. A surge of violent blue flames shoots up my body and off my arms. I'm conscious of the flame as it hits the stone ceiling and ripples across it with a dull orange glow, a fire wave searching for a surface to crash against. Then I crumple to the ground as darkness washes over me.

Chapter 24

My brain notices my body in a laggy, lazy way, like a patient coming out of anesthesia. I'm struggling to recognize my location and remember what happened, but I can't. Nor can I shake the fog in my brain. Fight as I might to get to the surface of my consciousness, I don't make it and the blackness engulfs me.

I'm not sure how much time has passed before my eyes creak open and I groan. I feel sick and chilly.

"She's awake," I hear Fin say.

The shuffling of feet precedes the faces of Grama Pearle and Fin popping into my line of sight. "Good," Grama Pearle says and hurries away.

"Fin?" I mumble.

"Shh, we've been keeping you hidden. You're lucky that didn't kill you. We're all lucky. That thing is super powerful," she says, flicking her hand at the Ember stone. Fin's head tips to the side, listening.

The room is dimly lit. I'm in the storage room of Grama Pearle's store laying on a cot. I explore my chest with my hand; my flesh isn't burnt or tender. The Ember stone is there, but it's quiet and without a temperature. I touch my ears and decide that they're intact, too. "Fin, what in the blazing hell is going on?"

Fin scoots onto the cot to sit with me. "You don't remember your blood-curdling scream, fire throwing, or collapse into unconsciousness?"

Eyes shut, I push my hands against my ears. The memory of the Ember stone screaming is strong, and I recall vivid shades of blue. I open my eyes. Fin is watching me. I blink at her and shake my head.

"Grama Pearle says it was the Ember stone that knocked you out. She was shaken up. She didn't know the room and the stone were connected, but she thinks that the connection is what caused you to pass out. We've been hiding you and what happened for hours, hoping you would regain consciousness before anybody asked questions.

"She told me that Spellbinder children start learning to control their magic as soon as they display signs, which varies from child to child, but typically age five." Fin scrunches her face at me and there's tension in her voice. "You trained from four until ten, when Jaxton died. For twenty years you've been without training. You're learning basic childhood magic."

I ignore the parts of her speech about learning magic. I'm well aware of the choices I made and the reasons. "Why hide me?"

Fin looks at me like I have rocks in my head. "Kori, I'm not fooled about why you're here or why you are trying to pick up where you left off twenty years ago. I know you recognize that humans can't save Alivia, but Spellbinders can. Pretending to be a Spellbinder for a limited time frame isn't enough. Kori, if you can't control the Ember stone, we don't want anybody to know that. Grama Pearle says that hope is going to be a critical part of what comes next. We don't want to cause any panic."

I mull that over but discard it because I'm not sure what I'm doing. I just know I want to get Alivia home. Which I suppose is Fin's point. I need to be either all in or out. I appreciate Fin's opinion. She has a way of seeing things that I sometimes don't catch right away. "Did you see inside the cave?"

Fin's eyes sparkle. "Just quick because you went down like a sack of potatoes," she says with teasing disapproval. "It's all stone. It's been renovated, creating a bar area and stools carved out of rock. They carved fancy stone holders into the wall to hold the torches. There are multiple entrances that appear to be tunnels like the one we accessed, and they all have torches secured to the entranceways. I didn't explore or ask Grama Pearle about them yet. I imagine all the entrances are concealed.

"If a normie pulled that shelf back in the store, they'd never know the wall opens to a tunnel. As for Spellbinders' knowledge of the entrances, I'll have to put that on my list of questions to ask Grama Pearle as well as whether the door can be opened from the inside." She rubs her hands together, happy with the list she's formulating. "Anyway, there is one tunnel on the far side of the room with no torch, which seems strange . . ."

"What?"

"It's just that I can't imagine hanging out in there, given the story about the room's creation."

"Creation?"

"Grama Pearle said the room has a power of its own and that the power comes from deep in the earth. Some ancient entity burrowed up from the center of the world into that room and made a deal that resulted in the Ember stone and Cleansing in the Cleansing room and the whole ritual for keeping balance tipped in favour of goodness. The entity fled after, never to be see—"

Grama Pearle's return stops Fin's talking. She crosses the room to my cot and hands me a glass. I sit up, noting the weakness in my body like general fatigue making my movements and cognitive function weary and laboured. "It's fluorescent slime in a cup. What am I supposed to do with it?"

"Drink it. We need to get upstairs for dinner. We've already been gone too long." Grama Pearle is watching me, and her hand is clenching the cremation necklace with Grandpa Ian's ashes.

Without warning, Fin pinches my nose and pushes the glass to my lips. I shake off her hand and glare at her. Undisturbed, she just shrugs.

"You better head upstairs, Fin, dear." Grama Pearle flicks her free hand at me to hurry me up.

Fin mimes that she's holding and drinking a cup. She smirks and leaves.

My chin trembles as I lift the glass. The liquid is thicker than I expected, and it doesn't pour as much as it glides in a gradual blob into my open mouth. I try to block words like ooze and seepage from my mind as the green goop spreads onto my tongue. I fight my gag reflex and swallow the swampy goo. I flick my tongue in and out of my mouth, frog-like, trying to dislodge the memory of its taste and consistency.

"I'm sorry, Kori." Grama Pearle says, and I think she means for the foul thing she just pressured me into ingesting.

"It's okay, Grama Pearle. I've tasted worse."

She gets closer. Her hands pull down my eyelids to see the pink of my eye. She turns my head to see inside my ears, then face forward. "Say 'ahhh' and stick out your tongue," she orders.

I shake her hands off my head. "Why? What did you feed me?" I'm licking at my hand to get the coating off my tongue.

With amazing speed, Grama Pearle's hand flashes out and grabs my tongue. In response, my eyes go wide, and I make strange noises of protest, but I can't pull my tongue from her grip. "Shh," she says, examining my tongue. She releases it and pats my shoulder. "Feeling better yet?"

I take a minute to assess my body and realize that the weakness is gone. I feel energized and ready to move. Surprise must register on my face because Grama Pearle gives a bark of laughter. "It might taste bad, but it sure works. A couple of the ingredients aren't the easiest to get so it isn't a drink I make often." She pauses. "I said I was sorry a few minutes ago because I didn't know the Ember stone's connection to the Cleansing room would activate it, Kori."

"Connection? Is that the deal Fin started to tell me about?"

"Probably. The entity emerged at a time when

humanity had fallen so far, we lived in darkness. It appeared with two stones that bound it to the light. It wanted free and it offered a key to save us from darkness in exchange for two lives and a family bound to their sacrifice. If an explanation was offered about how the stone works, it wasn't passed on in the histories. We know that the two halves of the stone need to be together to balance each other, so there must be something to that, which causes it to spread outward once it's activated in the Cleansing room."

The Ember stone feels heavy around my neck. "Grama Pearle, the two lives are they . . ." My head lowers to my chest.

"The stones sucked in the lives, took on the form that hangs from your neck, and the entity bound them to the Ember family."

"Which is why it's an Ember that's The Cleanser."

Grama Pearle nods. "Time for us to go upstairs," she says, walking off. "Come on," she calls from somewhere in her store. I can hear her feet moving up the stairs.

My hand moves to the Ember stone. I sigh and follow Grama Pearle. I notice the door to the tunnel is closed, but someone left the shelf ajar. Grama Pearle is nowhere in sight as I inspect the wall. *How did I get to the store?* I'm puzzling about it.

"Kori," Fin calls from the top of the stairs.

"Fin, wait." I hurry up the stairs. She waits for me and I lean close to whisper. "How did you and Grama Pearle move me from the cave into the store?"

Fin aims a smile down the hall. Satisfied that nobody is going to hear, she whispers, "Floated you with magic," and she walks away.

I swipe a hand over my face. But I pause mid-swipe as it occurs to me that I missed making my argument about going with Belamey and Astrid to meet Aza. I stomp my foot before following Fin to the kitchen.

"Where is everybody?" I ask Brynlee as she tries to herd Jayce and Holden past me and out of the kitchen with Dodo trailing them.

"Carter is sleeping in Jayce and Holden's bedroom. Grama Pearle, Fin, and Birdie are in the dining room, waiting for Astrid and Belamey to return. Everyone else is off carrying out missions of preparation like we were told you've been doing all afternoon," she says.

I purse my lips at Brynlee, readying a reply, but Jayce and Holden snatch her hands and pull her down the hall. I watch their retreat before I speed into the dining room. Fin pats the chair, and I sit down. Grama Pearle and Birdie are busy chewing and staring at their food. Without skipping a beat, Fin pushes a plate in front of me. My plate has golden toast on it; maybe it's a grilled-cheese sandwich. My tummy gives a gurgle and I sigh. I haven't eaten since breakfast so I scoop up the warm bread and chomp down.

My grilled cheese crunches. *Grill cheese shouldn't crunch.* I'm thinking of spitting it out when the sharp cheddar hits my taste buds, making them twinge. I can't help it. I chew. The flavour in my mouth explodes with cheese, smoked bacon, and what my taste buds identify as sour apple. I tip my sandwich sideways to investigate. The thin slices of apple peek out from under the melted cheese, which is topped with the crispy bacon. I glance at Fin.

She nods at me. "You bet I made that. You love it, don't you?"

In response, I take a big bite. Then I take another bite, enjoying Fin's state of happiness with her creation, but I choke when Belamey enters the room alone. My brain hasn't harmonized with the notion of Belamey being one of us enough to see him not only here but wandering around without being monitored. Fin pounds me on the back unnecessarily while everyone else ignores us. "Where is Astrid?" I say between coughs.

"Here," she says, coming into the dining room.

Belamey strolls over, scoops the other half of my sandwich off my plate, and sits down beside Fin. "You make this?" he asks her.

Smitten, she just nods at him. Her hand is still on my back, but it's just sitting there like she forgot its existence. I shake it off and shoot a glare at her, before directing it at Belamey. I recognize that my irritation is a result of my dissatisfaction with my ability to adjust and accept. It's one of the things I admire about Fin. *Cut yourself some slack. You're trying to come to terms with a lot of stuff right now.* Neither of them takes any notice of me as they discuss the various items that they each enjoy cooking into their grilled-cheese sandwiches.

I give up on them and turn to Astrid. She's already deep in conversation with Grama Pearle and Birdie. All I catch is that the meeting went well. Watching me, the three of them lean in close, whispering. I see the cords of magic go up and I lean in my chair to wait. I won't hear their conversation now. Fin and Belamey have moved on to the best method of cooking a grilled cheese. I roll my eyes and close them.

"Belamey," Grama Pearle's says. I open my eyes to see Grama Pearle give Belamey a *come here* finger wave, which he responds to without question. I gape at them as they replace the sound block after including Belamey in their discussion. Gawking at them, I see nodding, some smiles, a bit of chuckling, and then they come to a decision. So, they needed privacy, which suggests that someone was being given an opportunity to say no to something without all of us knowing what it is. The sound block drops.

Fin squirms in her seat. "This is going to be good!"

Astrid claps a hand on Belamey's shoulder, nods to Grama Pearle, and takes her leave from Birdie. She's gone from the room and still, nobody is speaking.

"I can't take it," Fin blurts out. "Tell me what's happening."

Everyone, including me, looks at Fin, who shows the faintest hint of colour in her cheeks, which I know is a sign of excitement and not embarrassment. "What? I need to know."

Birdie gives a hoot but says nothing. Grama Pearle fixes me with a *hang in there* stare and clears her throat. "Belamey," she says.

"I've been told that you need assistance with the Ember stone," he says in his husky voice. His eyes burn into me.

"What!" Exasperation is my foremost emotion. "What makes you an authority on the Ember stone?"

Belamey's eyes assess me in a way that makes me feel exposed. He yawns like he's bored with everything. "Pearle, I need to sleep first."

She nods at him in response, even though his focus is on me.

"Okay, tomorrow then." He turns and takes leisurely strides from the room.

"Where's he going?" Fin asks watching the spot where Belamey was like he might come into sight.

"His room," Birdie says, causing me to choke on a mouthful of air.

"His what?" I sputter.

Birdie gives another hoot and leaves. I raise my eyebrows at Grama Pearle.

"Okay, do you want to know which room is his?" she asks, trying not to let the smile that's pulling at the corners of her mouth slide into place.

"Yes, she does. What a great idea, Grama Pearle," Fin says.

Resting my eyes, I place my elbows on the table, and use my palms to support my head while I rub my temples. "Can you at least shed some light on why Belamey needs to help me with anything, let alone the Ember stone?"

"Good question," Fin says. I feel her hand on my back as she makes small circles. I suck in a deep breath. "Good, Kori. Just breathe."

"Smoke and ashes, Fin." I sit up and throw my shoulders back to dislodge her hand.

"Just trying to help," Fin says with a pout.

I purse my lips. Her sulk changes to a smile that

stretches into a big grin with a giggle. Grama Pearle is trying to sort through what she thinks I need to know versus what I don't. I lounge, cross my arms, and wait the few minutes it takes her to figure it out.

"Particular duties are often assigned to each person in a group or organization. The Society of the Blood Wind is the same," she says, casting a glance toward the kitchen. "Belamey's job was to become a subject matter resource on the Ember stone and its history."

Fin's head is bobbing up and down and she's smiling. "He's a subject matter expert for the Ember stone. Makes sense."

"No, it makes little sense," I argue.

"Well, we haven't been sure if Belamey was going to be the biggest hurdle or our best ally." Grama Pearle's hazel eyes focus on me as she leans in over the table.

My blood boils. "You knew about Belamey's allegiance?"

"No, not exactly." She cuts her eyes to the kitchen and to me. "It's more like we were estimating the likelihood. We tried to encourage him to join our side whenever the opportunity presented."

"Like Mouz," Fin says, her head bobbing in acknowledgement.

I cast my eyes to Fin and then to Grama Pearle. Then I narrow my eyes at Grama Pearle and lean in, but I direct my statement to Fin. "This time, I'm sure there's something Grama Pearle isn't telling us."

It's Grama Pearle who nods in acknowledgement. Fin scootches her chair in closer and arches her body over the table. Grama Pearle and I stare at each other, each of us trying to wear the other down. I'm aware that Fin is moving her head between us so she can see who breaks first. Grama Pearle flicks her fingers and tendrils of magic float up and create a soundproof dome with the three of us inside. Satisfied, I break my stare and sit with my arms crossed. Fin relaxes too.

"Belamey's mother—" Grama Pearle begins.

"Holy shit nuggets," Fin blurts out. "You knew Belamey's mother? Does Belamey know?"

I place my hand on Fin's shoulder. She pauses in her string of questions and I give her a very subtle head shake.

"Rye Adelgrief, or Juniper, as Birdie, Mouz, and I knew her. She married into the Adelgrief family," Grama Pearle begins again.

"Her name was Rye Juniper?" Fin interrupts.

"Fin!" I stomp my foot for punctuation. Both of Fin's hands fly up and cover her mouth. "I aught to glue your hands to your mouth with a bit of magic to keep you quiet," I say.

"Yes, Fin, Belamey's mother's name was Rye Juniper." Grama Pearle pauses, watching Fin.

Fin tips her hands so that her mouth is uncovered. "Is she missing then, or dead?" she says in a rush. Fin whips her head to me with big round eyes like she can't believe she asked a question, and she slaps her hands over her mouth. I tap my fingers on the table and wish that I had a coffee.

"I'm not sure if Rye is missing or dead but, for now, that's one mystery best left unsolved." Grama Pearle peeks toward the kitchen before she resumes talking.

"Rye was deep undercover with The Society of the Blood Wind. She had used Nekane's affections for her to get inside the group. She thought he would tire of her and move to a new girlfriend, but he didn't. At that point, she was too far in to stop playing the part, for reasons personal to her." Grama glances at Fin, expecting another interruption.

Fin's hands drop to her lap. "Was she faking her love for Nekane?"

"At first, but as is the way with many things, time can change them. After Belamey was born, everything was different for Rye. She had to make impossible choices that I imagine caused her internal struggles every day." Grama Pearle's smile is sad. "The story spread by the Adelgrief family is that Rye fled, but there was no trace of her and no sign that she tried to leave with Belamey. We've been hoping that the part of Rye that directed her moral compass in the laws of magic and the rights of humans would pass to Belamey, through genetics and teaching."

"But you weren't sure until now," Fin finishes. "Wow!"

"We don't know what Belamey knows or accepts as truth," Grama Pearle says as an afterthought. "Making direct contact with him would've put him in danger with The Society of the Blood Wind. Plus, Birdie and I gave Rye our word that we would wait for Belamey to come to us, if he ever did. "I think it best we don't explore the matter until after we get Alivia home safe." The side of Grama Pearle's mouth turns down, showing a depth of sadness she's trying to hide from us, and perhaps from herself.

"So many secrets," I say.

Grama Pearle closes her eyes and gives a tiny nod. "There's so much you never accepted. You didn't want to be part of the magical world we live in, Kori, and no matter what we did or didn't share, it wouldn't have changed that for you," she says. "Knowing your choice, it was safer for you to not know these things. That way they couldn't be used against you."

We sit silently, each of us lost in our own thoughts. "If any of us had known you were going to be responsible for the Ember stone, we might have made different choices, but what is done is done. I'm sorry, Kori." Grama Pearle releases the sound dome. "Tomorrow, you learn whatever Belamey can teach you about the Ember stone."

"Grama Pearle, why does Belamey know so much and our family doesn't?"

"The written history books containing information about the Ember stone were stolen. Memory Keeper history of the Ember stone was eventually committed to paper and Memory Keepers stopped passing those memories on until it was only the books that knew the details. Not a wise decision, but . . . When they were stolen, the knowledge was, too." She searches my face for understanding.

I tip my head, "Another mystery until now?"

"Sadly, it was. Until Belamey told us." She raises a hand. "We can only deal with one issue at a time; the history books will be dealt with after Alivia is rescued and the Cleansing is complete."

She gets up and walks from the room.

Fin and I sit looking at each other. "I'm coming to learn, too," Fin says. "I like Belamey, but we should tread lightly until we can be sure of his love for you." Her hands fly up in front of her like she's surrendering to the tongue lashing she knows is coming from me, so I just roll my eyes.

Fin and I make our way through the sleeping house to our room. I let her take the bed and I flop onto the air mattress clothed and close my eyes.

Chapter 25

I come into the kitchen to find Fin smirking over her coffee cup at Belamey. "Belamey's favourite restaurant is Just Flavours," she says to me without so much as a good morning or any other form of greeting.

"What else compares?" Belamey takes a big bite of the experimental breakfast sandwich the two of them were working on.

I hit Belamey and Fin with my best neutral cop semblance. Fin crosses the kitchen and passes me a coffee mug. Her focus is Belamey, and I'm not sure how she doesn't fall on her face before she reaches me.

"Who knew he was cool and normal?" she whispers with her focus on him. "When you two hook up, I'll have a new best boy friend!" I barely keep the mug she's passing me from dropping to the floor. She lets go without checking to see if I have a hold of it before she walks away, positioning herself closer to Belamey so she can return to the conversation I interrupted.

"I think you already do," I mutter. My cheeks colour when I register that her relationship comment about Belamey and me wasn't what I reacted to.

I drop my eyes to my cup. It has a bit of coffee near

the bottom of the mug. It's been doused with milk, making it a creamy brown. There's no steam rising from the mug. Suspicious about this cup and the coffee being second hand, I turn it in my hands so I can inspect the rim. I find lip impressions. I massage my forehead with one hand while I discard it in the sink using my other.

"What, no coffee this morning?" Belamey asks between bites. His tone suggests he knew Fin was handing me a used mug, even if she didn't. It's hard to tell because he is eating, but I think there's a smile playing at the corners of his lips. He's amused by Fin's enthusiasm to make him her friend.

I sigh and pour myself a coffee in a clean mug. When I turn, Fin is giving me her *what's up* face. "I prefer to drink a full, hot cup of coffee and not the dredge from someone else's discarded mug." I blow on the top of my coffee and inhale the delicious steam.

Fin stares at me, confused.

"Picky," Belamey says emotionlessly, yet I detect amusement.

Belamey and Fin look at me. Fin's expression is one of confusion and Belamey's is merriment. I don't bother trying to fight my eye roll, but I put a bit of effort into its speed and size. I let my eyes sag left and start making their way up in my eye sockets. When I finish my drama, Belamey and Fin are still staring at me, so I give a *cheers* gesture with my coffee cup and bring it to my lips. When I lower it, I'm pleased to see they've stopped staring and resumed their conversation about food.

I lean against the counter and close my eyes while I finish my coffee. "Well, the chef lesson was great, guys, but the clock on Alivia's safety is counting down, so if we could move on to lesson number two, that would be great." I infuse my voice with determination so that my other emotions—worry, fear, and discomfort, to name a few—don't shine through.

Belamey crosses the room in two strides and stops facing me. His brown eyes look down at me. His gaze slides off my eyes and moves toward my chest. I track my eyes down in time to see his strong fingers brush the skin of my chest as he plucks the Ember stone away from my flesh.

"Is it talking to you, Kori?" he asks. "Maybe a sensation or a sound?"

I swallow and try to calm the flutter in my stomach that his touch creates. He raises his eyebrows at me and waits. After a few minutes, he nods. He lowers the Ember stone to my chest and whispers in my ear. I'm so distracted by the heat from his hand and the soft stroke of his fingers tracing the Ember stone where it lies on my skin that I hear nothing he says. He draws his hand away.

I swallow and watch him. But I've no idea what he said and I'm fighting the urge to stomp my foot at myself when Fin hooks arms with me. She steers me down the hall. I can hear that Belamey is following us, and I realize Fin heard what he said. I don't ask her because I don't want to draw attention to the fact that I was distracted by my attraction to Belamey, so I trust Fin heard him. She's leading us to the tunnel heading to the Cleansing room.

I'm surprised that the stone door is open. Belamey

steps up beside Fin and me. He glances first at me and then at Fin before he looks down the dark tunnel. In a very cliché action, he snaps his fingers, and we watch as the torch closest to us lights up in a brilliant flash of fire. Each torch, all the way down the hall, ignites, one after another in a domino effect.

"Nice," Fin says, clapping her hands. I give an eye roll that neither Fin nor Belamey sees because they're peering down the tunnel. Belamey gives a smirk and turns to me.

"Our goal, Kori," Belamey says, "is to help you control external stimuli and connect with the Ember stone when it needs you and you need it and to help you stay connected. It's the best we can hope for with the time we have left." He gives a decisive nod. "If you had formal training, we wouldn't need to worry about your control of outer distractions. If we had more time, our approach to everything would be relaxed and less distressing."

I blink at him.

"Let's do this," Fin says from behind Belamey.

"You aren't going to like this." Without warning, Belamey wraps me with magic like a lasso, and starts pulling me into the tunnel. His actions cause a wave of panic to flood through me.

"I can feel your fear," he says to me in his low, rough voice.

My eyes go wide, and I stop pulling against the bonds. It surprises me when I feel Belamey's desire burning through the magic tying us together. I can sense it faintly, but it's there nonetheless. Just before he releases the bond, I feel that he's pleased with the lesson.

"Okay?" I ask him not one-hundred percent sure what I'm learning from this. I'm trying not to let thoughts of his desire complicate my thinking.

He pulls the corner of his mouth up at me. "The lesson is two-fold. First, that's always there, those ties to the Spellbinder, that sense of their feelings and emotions. It can sometimes provide clues to motives and reactions. Awareness of the tie is less obvious, but for a Spellbinder as powerful as you, it should never be a question. Second, when you quieted your inner turmoil, you became aware of important things you were missing. Be in the moment."

"Is it just the emotions of Spellbinders that Kori can read?" Fin blurts out.

Belamey turns to Fin and to me. "Probably not, eh, Kori?"

I swallow and give Fin a slight nod to let her know I'm attuned to her. I pause and move closer to her, leaning in to whisper, "Horny."

Fin licks her lips and glances at Belamey as if to emphasis her horniness. "Always," she giggles. "I'm hoping for five or ten minutes with Griffin tonight." She winks.

"Now, can you sense anything else?" Belamey asks.

I scrunch my brow. Without warning, Fin flies up into the air and drops toward the cement floor. Belamey catches her with his magic before she hits the ground, but in those few seconds, I feel Belamey's amusement and Fin's shock and excitement. I also feel something that I wasn't expecting. The Ember stone is primed to respond.

I note the alternating waves of heat and cold, one way the stone speaks to me. This message means that it's ready to answer me. Belamey reads my awareness of the Ember stone through my facial expression, and nods his approval. Fin is on her feet, adjusting her wardrobe with a tug here and some smoothing there. She casts a glance at Belamey and then at me.

"Did it work?" she asks Belamey with a big grin. "Can you hear the Ember stone, Kori?"

I feel my eyes go wide.

"You didn't think we spent all morning talking about food, did you?" Belamey's husky voice cuts in. "There were other ways to test this, but this was fun for Fin and I, and with all our limitations, it made the most sense. Work with what we have."

I slide my eyes to him and shrug. The Ember stone has quieted and returned to a neutral temperature.

"Think of the Ember stone as a power source that you can connect to and use to increase your own power. But you lack the focus; external distractions both inside and outside of yourself are a problem. The Ember stone functions somewhat differently inside versus outside the Cleansing room. So, outside the room, you can increase your magical powers, any of them, but inside the Cleansing room, the Ember stone has one focus and that's the Cleansing. Only magic within you that's central to the Cleansing will be intensified."

I narrow my eyes, preparing to blast him about minding his own business when it comes to me, my ability to focus, and my magic, but he grabs my hand

and starts running into the tunnel. I stumble until my feet figure out what's required. The Ember stone flares when my body jerks forward, but it stabilizes because there's no threat.

We keep running down the hall with no sign that we'll stop. I'm aware that Fin is running down the hall behind us. I also know that her anxiety is growing, but I don't know why.

"Belamey, stop!" she yells from behind us. "Belamey!"

Belamey ignores her and keeps running, dragging me with him.

"Kori," Fin yells and I can hear the panic in her voice. This isn't an orchestrated lesson. "Stop, you're almost—"

Fin doesn't finish her sentence and there's sudden silence in the hallway. The Ember stone is pulsing temperatures. I look back, hoping that I won't trip. Fin is stuck in the hall. I can see her and the surrounding hallway. I also see that she's banging her hand like a crazed mime hitting a wall. Her mouth is moving, but I can't hear her. I can feel her anxiety move toward fear.

Belamey is emotionless. Given the circumstances, my brain expects to feel cold-bloodedness from him, but there's nothing. He has blocked Fin from following us, using some kind of invisible wall that is soundproof as well. It's part of his plan, but I've no idea why. Is he trying to illicit some kind of response from me and the Ember stone again?

My foot catches the floor and I whip my head forward, trying to maintain my balance and momentum. The Ember stone's pulsing is increasing in intensity and it's getting louder. I use my body to speak to it and its energy responds to me.

"Belamey," I yell. "Let go of me."

Belamey keeps running. He doesn't loosen his grip, and he doesn't acknowledge that he heard me. I notice the Ember stone doing what can be described as speaking, with hot and cold pulses and humming. It knows where we are, and it senses the Cleansing room. It's readying to Cleanse.

Its power is increasing. I'm struggling to maintain control. Belamey has slowed his pace, but he keeps moving us. He's aware of the struggle between the Ember stone and me.

We're almost at the entrance to the room. The Ember stone is starting a low keening that I believe will mount into a scream if I can't get control. This is how it started the last time, except this time I'm aware now of myself and the Ember stone as an extension of me.

The ice pulse of it shoots through my veins, crystalizing my blood, while waves of heat spark on my skin. I'm sure it's a matter of time before I burst into flames. There's a scream echoing in my brain as the Ember stone and I engage in a tug-of-war contest for control.

My knees buckle and some distant part of my brain signals there should be pain, but my body isn't registering it. My vision blurs. My body arches backwards and my head tilts up as the Ember stone and I scream as one. Sight, feeling, sound, and consciousness die away for me in that one gut-wrenching sound.

I wake on the cot in the back room of Grama Pearle's store. The room is dark, but I hear voices talking in the other room. I have to focus to make sense of the words. The first voice is Belamey's. "She won't be ready, Pearle." His voice is deep with concern.

Grama Pearle's question is a mumble.

Belamey answers. "The Cleansing room and the Ember stone are both an ancient energy, harnessed from the centre of the earth. Think of the room as an electrical receptacle and think of the stone as a power cord infused with its own power. As the two get closer together, the power arcs. When the stone is in the room, 'plugged in,' the power builds and needs a conductor. That's where The Cleanser, Kori, comes in. A conductor doesn't fight its role. Imagine a lightning rod that repelled the lightning instead of diverting it. Devastating. Kori can do this but she isn't letting herself."

I can't hear Grama Pearle's response.

"She's the strongest Spellbinder I've seen or read about in the histories, but she's also grossly negligent of her powers. And she fights them at every turn. I don't believe that she's consciously aware she's fighting them because she has trained herself to fight them for so long," Belamey says. "This is dangerous. And I haven't read anything in the histories to suggest anything like this has ever happened before."

Grama Pearle's voice is quiet, but I make out her words this time. "She has to succeed, Belamey." Even in her hushed tone, the strain in her voice is evident. "The Society of the Blood Wind and all they stand for will prevail and they'll ensure there is never another Cleansing."

I push myself into a sitting position, and a wave of dizziness hits me. I slam my eyes shut and hold onto the cot. The ringing in my ears makes me miss a chunk of the conversation.

When I can hear, Belamey is talking. "I swear it will be done, Pearle, even if it costs my life to save her and our people." His footfalls go up the stairs. I've no idea what he just committed to. I roll my eyes at myself for missing part of the discussion and wish I hadn't because another wave of dizziness washes over me.

"Kori," Grama Pearle says.

I slit my eyes open, trying to avoid any action that might make me dizzy. Grama Pearle is holding a glass out. I accept it but push it at her when I see the familiar fluorescent liquid.

"Drink it," she says in her no-nonsense voice.

I sigh and bring the cup closer to my body. I stare down into it, then I upend the sludge into my mouth.

"Do you know what happened?" she asks me while I choke down the drink.

I nod and shrug in response. She waits, saying nothing. I flick my tongue in and out of my mouth a few times and breathe deep. "The Ember stone and the

Cleansing room."

Grama Pearle purses her lips.

"What?"

"Not quite, Kori," she says. "It's you and the Ember stone fighting for control, when you each need to give over to the other and act together."

She watches me. I watch her.

Pointing at me with her index finger, her tone is sharp. "Nobody can force you to do this, and we can't show you anything more then we already have." She shakes her head at me, turns on her heels, and walks away, mumbling. "So much depends on a woman who continuously refuses to accept . . ." I don't hear Grama Pearle's mumbling because she turns into the main part of the store and goes upstairs.

I sit alone in the quiet and I lift my hand to the Ember stone. I'm not sure if I'm expecting it to say "hello" in greeting, but I feel disheartened by its silence. With a sigh, I lower it to my chest and make my way to the entrance of the tunnel, pleased that Grama Pearle's drink has stopped my dizziness.

As I stare into the tunnel, I hear Belamey's voice up stairs talking to Astrid. *The meeting.* I turn and bolt, racing up the stairs two at a time. I slide on my feet at the top of the stairs, skidding to a stop at the main entrance to the house. Belamey and Astrid watch me.

"Feeling better, I see," Belamey says.

"Hello, Kori," Astrid says pleasantly. If she knows what happened, she isn't giving any sign.

"Hello, Astrid," I say before turning to Belamey. "I'm coming with you. I want to be at your meeting with Aza.

Hidden, of course," I say to make sure that my intent is clear. I'm driven by a need to feel useful, I can do stakeouts, handle informants, gather investigative information, provide backup . . . And I can do it with ease and comfort, not like the magic.

"Okay," he says, stepping up to me so the fronts of our bodies are touching as he reaches behind me for the doorknob. He slides his body across mine and toward the now open door. "Come on." He shifts into a harpy eagle and flies out.

Astrid smiles at me and whips a cord of magic at the door. She transforms into her blue bird form and soars after Belamey. She grips the cord of magic in her claw, and it trails behind her.

Unsure of what happened, I swallow. I had expected an argument. I check for witnesses, but I see nobody, so I shift and zoom out the door after Belamey and Astrid. Astrid's cord of magic goes taut and dissipates as it pulls the front door shut.

Chapter 26

I'm surprised when I realize our flight path is taking us to the old drive-in theatre. We shift into human form at the concession stand. I feel exposed with the two open fields on either side of us and only the big outdoor movie screen for cover. I'm more shocked when Belamey unlocks the door and waves us in. *Why does he have keys?* As I walk by, I give him wide-eyes.

Belamey shrugs. "I'm thinking of this purchase as a business investment."

I turn, my mouth gaping open. "You bought the drive-in?"

"Yeah, it's been part of the town since the mid-1950s. I couldn't see letting it go under. So, I bought it. I want to preserve it, its history, and its place as part of the town." He shrugs.

A car speeding over the gravel road in front of the drive-in reminds us why we're at the theatre. We stop talking and hurry inside. It's dark and redolent of stale popcorn and spilt pop. It takes a while for my eyes to adjust, but when I can see, Astrid is nowhere in sight. "Where's Astrid?" I hiss at Belamey.

He points upwards, and I cast my eyes in that

direction. The concession stand has no ceiling. It's open space up to the A-frame roof with a few rafters and two oversized ceiling fans. There are two octagon-shaped windows on either side of the building. I see the silhouette of a person perched on a rear rafter. The window is too high from the beam for her to see out it in bird form. I nod. "Okay, where do I go?"

Belamey is close enough to me that when he flicks his eyebrows at Astrid, I'm able to see the movement in the darkness. "Right," I say.

Before we can do or say anything further, Astrid's voice interrupts us. "She's coming. Belamey, she isn't alone!"

Belamey shifts, flies up toward the window, and transforms into his human self. I follow and transform into human form on the beam behind him, leaning in close to see out.

Aza's wingspan is huge, and I'm amazed watching this big bird soar on the air currents without flapping its wings. The black and white plumage of her wings is eye-catching and the feathers on her wing tips remind me of outstretched fingers. That's where her beauty ends though because her featherless head is ugly and vulture-like. Once I've had my fill of Aza as an Andean condor, I search the skies for whatever else Astrid saw.

I see a familiar red-tailed hawk. *Kyson Adelgrief.* I swallow, trying to work through the implications. "She isn't flying like she's scared for her life."

"I don't think she knows he's there. He's far enough back, and Aza is trusted by The Society of the Blood Wind so she's not spied on. She wouldn't be looking for a follower." Astrid whispers. "She's under Ague's control, so she wouldn't have told anybody."

"But Kyson wouldn't tail her if there wasn't someone to be killed," I say.

Astrid is reticent, but I see the shadow of her head nodding. Aza has landed on her strong bird legs. Kyson comes in to land a short distance behind her. Red tailed hawks are formidable hunters, as is Kyson. She won't know he's there until it's too late.

Aza transforms. Her time released from our captivity has done nothing to tame her feral state. She's standing there, and it's apparent that she doesn't know Kyson is behind her.

"He's going to kill her," I exclaim. Kyson's arm snakes around Aza's neck and he grabs her head with his opposite arm, breaking her neck in one fluid motion. Before her slender body hits the ground, he shifts into bird form and soars off in the direction they just came from.

I'm speeding toward Aza's lifeless body in my hummingbird form before I give it thought. I glance at the sky, but Kyson is nowhere in sight. I can hear Belamey and Astrid following me. My thoughts are of Alivia when I place my hands on Aza's forehead. No decision is required. There's no line I won't cross to rescue Alivia, just as there was no line Jaxton wouldn't have crossed to protect me.

Trying not to think about the warmth coming off her skin, I use my pointer fingers to slide her eyelids up. I don't look at her eyes as I glide my thumbs gently but quickly onto the iris and cornea part of her eyeball. Her eyes seem to be the same temperature as my fingertips and it's the moistness alerting me that I have my thumbs on her eyes. Astrid and Belamey shift into human form, frozen to the spot watching me.

I'm expecting images to present themselves to me like when I viewed Alaric's memories, but that isn't what happens. Looking through a dying person's eyes isn't the same as collecting memories, and any Spellbinder can do this unlike being a Memory Keeper.

The name, looking through a dying person's eyes, suggest a visual connection but that's not the case at all. The connection I make is a physical one with Aza's eyes and then I probe with feelers of magic that are triggered by the connection and I assume by her death. A shiver runs down my spine as Aza's voice speaks in my head.

It's soft at first, like a distant whisper that's a struggle to understand, but her volume and pace increase, like she's eager to confess while she still has a voice. I want to speak to her and ask her questions about the things she's telling me, so many sad things. Her voice fades. Then she goes silent.

I remain where I am, fighting my emotions. *I'm sorry*, I say in my mind. And I think I hear her say that she's sorry, too.

Belamey's hand is on my shoulder, and I can hear him and Astrid calling to me. My hands don't want to release Aza. I feel weak and heavy. Astrid's voice is there, but it's far away. "You know she has to let go, Belamey. Get her to let go before Kori's life drains down into Aza's and we'll lose them both."

I'm distantly aware of a pulsing heat and coolness on my chest. A husky voice reverberates in my consciousness. Belamey's voice? Waves of hot and cold flow through and over me from the Ember stone. The voice is calling my name. A high-pitched cry of pain grows louder in my ears and it's turning my tired heaviness to active energy.

Fear grows, and it's jumbled with anger. There's a violent skirmish between my consciousness and the pull of death. I understand the high-pitch cry as the Ember stone calling to me and I embrace the waves of hot and cold to support the strength I need. I use it to separate from Aza's body and as I break away, both physically and spiritually, a wave of nausea overwhelms me. Turning to the side, I vomit.

The Ember stone goes quiet. *Did the Ember stone and I just connect? If so, how?* I wipe my mouth on my hand and turn to face Belamey and Astrid. I see sadness in Astrid's eyes but there's understanding as well. She gives a teeny head nod.

Belamey is watching me, and I can't tell what thoughts are moving behind his eyes. "We need to go," is all he says as he scans the sky.

Something inside me feels different. No part of me cares what anyone thinks of my actions, and I'm prepared to deal with the consequences as long as I get Alivia home. *Is this acceptance of my magical abilities on some level?*

"We can't leave her here." I push myself up off the ground.

Neither Belamey nor Astrid object. They just nod in

unison. Astrid's hands move in a weave I'm unfamiliar with, but I don't have the desire to acknowledge or learn it. She places the fabricated netting under Aza, causing her body to become weightless.

Astrid tosses magic mesh on Aza to make her disappear. Before Astrid shifts, she creates a cord so she can transport Aza's body for burial. Astrid flies off with Aza in tow and she doesn't give a backward glance.

I turn to Belamey. "I—" but he shakes his head.

"Not here," he says, "In case Kyson returns." He transforms and takes to the sky. I scowl at the ground where Aza's body lay moments before, and then I glower in the direction Kyson flew. I sigh and shift, flying off after Belamey.

The flight home is a blur. I'm thankful to follow Belamey's flight path. The three grayish bands that mark his tail feathers are my focal point while I fly. Belamey lands on the roof of the Ember house and transforms into human form when I land close to him. I shift too and adjust myself to keep my balance.

We aren't seen or heard because Belamey has thrown a dome over us. I'm happy perched up here where I don't have to answer questions about the meeting. I feel a numbness I don't want to explain to myself or anybody else, but I think of Alaric and his loss as well as him looking through Kieran's eyes. Those two things are as connected for him, like Alivia's safety and my looking through Aza's eyes are.

Belamey is staring off into the distance and not speaking. I gaze in the same direction, and I'm awed by the view. The sun is sinking behind a distant row of houses and the glow is an orangey-red colour. Blowing out a breath, I suck in a gulp of chilly air, hoping it might wash away my numbness.

"I don't think that Alivia's safety has been compromised," Belamey says, and I can feel his stare.

"What do you mean?" I ask, glancing at him.

"Kyson killed Aza instantly and left. If there was suspicion that she was meeting someone, especially one of us, he would've waited because we would've been his target. Aza wouldn't have been the initial target. But that's not what happened. Aza *was* the target."

"She told them you and I were meeting in the Cleansing chamber later today. They killed Aza to make sure she couldn't change her mind and tell us that she blabbed our meeting plans," I say with a certainty provided to me by Aza's last words.

He nods. "Makes sense. They killed her to silence her, which also means they don't know she was setting them up. I don't think they know she was meeting me today. Kyson was likely waiting for her to go somewhere alone so he could eliminate her." Belamey is quiet for a few minutes. "I had a plan to pull her out and get her somewhere safe. I know there's always a risk when a person spies, but most of them get a choice to spy or not. This feels . . ."

He doesn't finish, and he doesn't need to. I'm wrestling with the same discomfort. I think about it and sigh. "It makes sense with what Aza shared with me." I swallow. "She said Nekane is coming to the Cleansing room, and he's bringing his very best, plus anyone else he can." I stare at the sinking sun.

"Kori," Belamey says. Closing my eyes, I wait for whatever he's going to say. "I know you're struggling to regain some sense of feeling," he continues in the same low tone.

I tip my head to one side, assessing him, then I gaze over the rooftops.

His voice is quieter than I'm used to, and it cracks with emotion. "I've done what you did." He pauses, considering. "For me, it wasn't out of love or concern for another's safety. They forced me to do it as an initiate."

My head snaps in his direction and my eyes feel a sting of cold air where they've widened in surprise.

"You've heard of the initiations then?" He asks.

"I was told that it wasn't a practice anymore," I say.

"That's what most people believe. Things that happen within The Society of the Blood wind and with its members stay within the infrastructure." He gives a snort of displeasure. "It has to stay. It's one thing for people to assume something is going on, but in the absence of physical evidence, what can be done?

"What's important is you can regain that sense of feeling. You did what you did out of necessity. And no, that doesn't make it right, but you aren't The Society of the Blood Wind. But sometimes we must operate or even live in the grey areas." There's a grim twist to Belamey's mouth. "Sometimes, in order to protect the people we care about, we have to do things that border on immoral or are plain evil."

I stare at Belamey, blinking, not sure what to say. He winks at me and careens backward. I watch wide-eyed as he does a series of somersaults and pitches over the side of the roof. In seconds, a harpy eagle soars up before diving toward the front door. When I can't see him anymore, I bring my eyes up and scan the treetops. When I see the hawk on the tree branches, I am not surprised. Sighing, I turn away. I'm too distracted to care about it.

I sit on the roof until the sun is gone from the sky and a chill has set into my body. My thoughts cycle through the events that transpired since I found out Alivia was taken. I'm not the same person I was when this started, but I'm not sure what that means.

I recognize that magic is a part of me, and I'm trying to accept it. I contemplate what Belamey said. Depending on the outcome of tomorrow, there's the possibility none of this will matter.

Chapter 27

While I've been outside, Belamey has summoned everyone to the dining room. I'm not sure what he's shared, but they know some details of the meeting including that I looked through Aza's eyes because the room falls silent when I enter.

"Tell us what you know from Aza, Kori." Grama Pearle says without pause.

I nod before making eye contact. "Nekane is planning to lead the mission into the tunnels. He believes it'll be an ambush to capture me and the Ember stone. If that fails, he'll kill me to avoid the Cleansing happening. He isn't aware of the Ember stone's connection to the Cleansing room."

My last comment generates some confused expressions, and I remember that only Belamey, Fin, Grama Pearle, and I have knowledge of that. I hurry on, hoping to avoid any questions about it. "Alivia will be with him. Her healing abilities have made her a new favourite plaything for Nekane."

Noah stands. "Alivia's ability to bring people back from the brink of death is a skill unheard of in Spellbinders for centuries now. It's a promising tool for someone like Nekane, who practices extreme methods of torture. How many times can a person resist telling their secrets when they are brought to and from the edge of death over and over? Looking through the eyes is limited to that small window of time, but the limits on how many times a person can nearly die are unknown." He leans on the wall and crosses his arms. His comment triggers vivid pictures in my mind from Aza's commentary, and I squeeze my eyes shut against them. *So much pain.*

"Kori, do you know when he's coming?" Grama Pearle asks.

I open my eyes and nod. "Yes. He plans for The Society of the Blood Wind to enter from all the tunnels that they can access, but he wants to wait until he's sure we're inside the cave. So, he plans to let the meeting start before he enters the tunnels. He also plans to station people outside the house so they can breach here at some point." I cross my arms and raise my voice a bit. "There's always that possibility that Nekane fed Aza a false plan, given his trust issues, but when weighed against his arrogance, he didn't know she was meeting us and he knew he was going to have her killed, so why not tell her the truth and let it die with her?"

Several heads are nodding as if Nekane's plan doesn't surprise them. It's the obvious course of action. And they agree with my evaluation of his distrust versus his arrogance.

We suspected this would be Nekane's response to Belamey and I meeting. So, we planned for it already, and we'd been waiting for verification which we got from Aza. Noah nods at Alaric. "Well, let's get down to the details."

Alaric pulls himself off the wall and leaves without a word. Griffin follows him. Birdie and Talon disappear after speaking with Grama Pearle, and a number of other people leave. Mom grasps my shoulder on her way past.

"Good," Noah says when the room clears.

Grama Pearle, Belamey, Noah, and Fin are left in the dining room with me. I raise my eyebrows at Noah. He shrugs.

"Thank you, Noah." Grama Pearle smiles. "We," she says, looking at everybody except me, "are the ones that need to get Kori into the Cleansing room and keep her safe while she's there."

She makes it sound like it's going to be the easiest job. I slide into a chair, trying to hide the shakiness in my limbs, and I'm grateful that they can't see my racing pulse, the tightness in my chest and lungs, or the fear that's causing these responses.

"Okay," Fin says, "but how do we get her into the room? She loses consciousness just getting close to it."

I can't help giving Fin a squinty glare, but I keep my words to myself. She has stated the truth.

Fin positions her mouth so her lips brush my ear. "Nobody is judging you, but you. We maybe don't agree with your decision to shun your magical heritage, but we all know life happens. We make choices and then we have to show up every day and live with them. And here you are, Kori. You showed up. Be proud of that."

With Fin's perceptiveness, I wonder how much she has packed into that statement. I sit and listen, content not to talk for now.

"I've a plan for that, Fin." Grama Pearle cuts her eyes to me. "But we won't discuss it just yet, I prefer to share the details when it's time to execute it." I catch a flicker of Grama Pearle's eyes in Belamey's direction, and I see him give a subtle bob of his head. Grama Pearle's furtiveness makes me think I'm not going to like the plan.

Noah clears his throat, and the conversation moves off in a different direction.

The smell of fresh coffee is strong in the kitchen. Dawn breaks after a sleepless night filled with planning and various forms of preparation. I'm thankful for all the preliminaries because it keeps my mind busy, and keeps everybody else occupied with preparations, too.

So far, I needed to share the bare minimum of what I learned from Aza and no explanations for my action, meaning I've not experienced criticism or judgement for it. For me, reliving looking through her eyes is woeful because I know now that she was so much more then what she presented on the exterior.

She was so eager to have her voice heard before she died. There was such depth of emotion hiding in her.

She wanted to save me and our people but a life living with The Society of the Blood Wind crushed her confidence and left her feeling powerless. After the next steps of this fight are over, I'll make sure to share the truth about her.

The dawn has brought dark, angry rain clouds. I wonder if it's an omen, but I shake the thought off. Rain cleanses and it'll be good weather for catching a much-needed nap. With the meeting set for evening, we plan to be through the tunnel and positioned inside the cave and Cleansing room by late afternoon.

I wake to the sounds of commotion and race toward it, fearful that the attack has started before I hear giggling intermixed with statements of encouragement. I skid to a halt in the kitchen when I catch sight of Fin chasing after Dodo. He wastes no time throwing one of his glimmering manholes into the air and racing through it, to appear in a different part of the kitchen. The manhole blinks out before Fin can access it. It's tag, refashioned to practice the skill of crafting and using manholes.

Fin changes direction but loses Dodo as he jumps through one of his manholes. A smaller shimmering manhole appears, and Jayce comes racing out, pats Fin on her bottom, and jumps into a manhole that he has ready. Fin spins to grab him and it's Holden's turn to pop out of a shimmering manhole and swat at Fin before diving through another.

It's clear by how much time passing between the boys' disappearing and reappearing that the manholes are taking them to random spots in the house before they return to the kitchen. I can't help but smile, watching this game. Fin and the boys are enjoying themselves, and for a few minutes I forget about what's coming.

"I think they're ready," Noah says, strolling up behind me. He stops to watch the fun.

"Ready for what?" When he says nothing, I turn. He's staring at me. I shake my head at him. "What?"

He sighs and rubs the back of his neck. "Well, even though Griffin, Alaric, and a few of their reinforcements will be in the house, we can't leave Dodo and the boys with no way to keep themselves safe," he says, stretching his hands in a wide wave to indicate the space. I catch the notes of frustration in his voice.

I wince and gaze at the game in the kitchen. The momentary joy I felt at watching them seconds ago fades in a heavy sadness. *So much depending on . . . me.* "Right, Noah," I say in a flat voice.

The game ends, and Fin bends over, huffing a bit from the exertion. She's wearing a big smile when all the boys give her a hug.

Everything moves posthaste after that, and I'm standing in front of the tunnel that'll lead us to the Cleansing room. It's just the five of us, myself and the four people set as my guard. Alaric, Griffin, and four more of their crew are remaining at the Ember house to keep The Society of the Blood Wind from breaching there.

The fact Alaric is staying is surprising. Given his aspiration to extract vengeance on Nekane, I would've thought he'd want to be in the best position to access him. Regardless, everyone else started into the tunnel in groups over the course of the last few hours. Now, it's our turn.

"Okay, Kori, now you get to know the plan," Grama Pearle says, moving in close so I can see her steely stare. "I waited to tell you because I know you aren't going to like it."

Shocking. Something else that I'm not going to like. *I can't wait to hear what it is*, I think sarcastically.

I notice right away that Grama Pearle is wearing more than just one cremation necklace for protection. I recognize Grandpa Ian's ashes in the onyx urn. It calls to mind the ghostly form of his snowy white owl protecting us from The Society of the Blood Wind.

I assume the two white and silver urns are Great-Grandmother Effie and Great-Grandfather Luther, but I don't know their birds. Before I can ask Grama Pearle questions about the urns, she narrows her eyes. "Remove the necklace. Belamey will carry the Ember stone until we get you and it to the platform inside the Cleansing room."

My eyes are almost popping out of their sockets. Before I voice my objections, Belamey is behind me, undoing the clasp.

As the clasp on the necklace releases, I grab the

Ember stone and yank it forward. Spinning, I put distance between me, Belamey, and our group. I face them once I'm in the tunnel. I can feel the Ember stone responding to me. It's pulsing hot and cold in my hand. "Smoke and ashes, Grama Pearle, that's the plan?" My voice quivers with the anger that I'm struggling to control.

Belamey hasn't moved. He's just watching me in amusement. I flick my eyes to Noah, anticipating his support. He looks like he's sucking on a lemon and piercing his foot with a nail. I can't believe his response, and my eyes flair wider when Noah crosses his arms, untalkative. I disregard him and gape at Fin.

"No support here, Kori. You know how I feel about riding dark stallions." She shakes her head like she's trying to clear it. "I mean, you know how I feel about dark stallions riding in, all sexy and strong, to save the day." She glances at Belamey and sighs.

I roll my eyes. Grama Pearle is giving me her best stern expression, the one that she used to give me when I was a child. It used to terrify me, but I'm not a child anymore. I hold my ground and stare at her.

Neither of us are talking. Seconds tick by in silence. I'm considering turning and running to the Cleansing room, but I know that Grama Pearle is correct in getting someone else to carry the Ember stone temporarily. I also know that Belamey, as the least likely option, is the best choice. His magic gives him a strength and protection that Fin and Noah don't have. Grama Pearle will already be a target for The Society of the Blood Wind, so she can't carry the Ember stone.

I sigh, resigned, and hold the Ember stone out for Belamey. I look away with my hand outstretched. Belamey's two strong, warm hands cup mine and he moves his body so that he's in my line of sight. "I'm hurt that you hesitate to trust me," he whispers so that only I can hear.

I focus on Belamey. He's motionless while I search his face and eyes. He's still cupping my hand, which is clenching the Ember stone. I'm surprised to find that I do trust him. I wiggle my fingers and release the Ember stone into his palm. He nods at me but says nothing. It's Grama Pearle that speaks. "There's one more thing, Kori."

I swallow and glare at her.

"*You* can't perform the Cleansing alone," she says. "Not with your history of resistance and lack of training."

I bite back the sarcastic *thanks* comment. "Obviously," I say instead and wonder if I'm missing something.

"Your magic is strong, Kori, but you're untrained," she continues. "So, you need to let Belamey join his magic to yours when he passes you the Ember stone. It's a direct joining and not like the feedback you're able to pick up from other Spellbinders using magic against you."

She holds up her hand to keep me from talking. "Belamey knows the most about the Ember stone, so it has to be him, and he'll help you do what needs to be done." She sounds confident, but I see a flicker of doubt on her features.

I don't like it. I dislike anyone thinking I can't succeed, almost as much as I dislike not succeeding. Grama Pearle knows that about me, and she's never in my life doubted me, so this could've been a calculated guise. Either way, the effect is the same. It strengthens my resolve to succeed.

"We need to hurry," Noah says, slipping past Grama Pearle and I. He drags his hand across my shoulder blades to encourage me to walk forward. I shake him off and move along the tunnel close to Grama Pearle.

"What does that mean, join his magic?" I ask.

"Sounds sexual," Fin says from close behind us. Grama Pearle and I both ignore her.

Because we can't use any light, moving through the tunnel is laborious, and it's hard to judge where we are. "Its time to stop talking," Noah hisses.

Grama Pearle flicks her hand at Noah dismissively, even though he misses the gesture because he's the leader. "I wouldn't call it invasive. It's more intimate," she whispers. "His magic will enter you, then it'll seek your magic."

She pauses, gauging her time-constrained explanation. "Think of it as two threads twining to make a length of rope. And," she says as an afterthought, "you'll need to grant Belamey permission to complete this coupling."

"Wow! Coupling, that's such a great word." Fin breathes.

"Shhh," Noah hisses.

We walk in silence until we enter the cave. I can make out the shape of the bar and stools Fin described to me.

Behind us, sounds of feet running in the tunnel echo into the cave like the beating of a drum. The feet are getting closer. "Guys," Carter's voice hollers.

He must've woken up and wondered where we were. Given that I've no idea what Griffin, Alaric and crew, and Dodo, and the boys are doing at the house, Carter may or may not have spoken to them before he wandered into Grama Pearle's store. Given that we left the entrance to the tunnel open for ease of access, he obviously decided to explore. The sleep charm must be wearing off. He seems to be asleep less and less.

"Somebody shut him up and send him away," Noah whispers.

We pause as Fin slips into the tunnel. A slight commotion follows Fin's disappearance and then it goes quiet. Seconds tick by before Fin appears at the cave's mouth with Carter. They're shooting glares at each other.

"Carter, get out of here," I hiss, exasperated.

Noah places a hand on my shoulder. "He's here now, Kori. There's not much to be done about—"

"I'm here too," a nasally voice interrupts.

The voice has a familiarity with it that makes my skin prickle. A massive woman comes charging out of the darkness with lustrous hair tied in a low ponytail. There's no mistaking that manly face and tree-like neck. This is the woman Carter and I fought in the basement of the safe house.

"You!" Carter charges forward to meet the hulking woman head on. "I wasn't quite myself when we fought the last time she-man, but this time—" There's a jarring sound as their bodies slam into one another blocking out anything else he says.

My mind races to our encounter with her in the basement of the safe house. She didn't use magical assaults on us. She used very low-grade shields, a lesser version of what Noah can do, to protect against magic attacks. I decide that she's muscle for The Society of the Blood Wind and with Carter's police training, he can take care of himself. That's all the time that I can spare to worry about him.

"See, everyone has a purpose," Fin calls out. I'm not sure to whom she's addressing this comment, and I don't get a chance to ask. Noah and Belamey grab my upper arms on each side of my body to ensure I don't involve myself in Carter's fight.

"Time to go." Noah says as he and Belamey manoeuvre me forward. "We don't have time to spare for Carter right now."

Sounds of fighting fill the darkness. Occasional flashes of magic light up the space, revealing moving shadows of havoc.

"Where is it, Pearle?" Belamey calls out.

"Should be straight ahead about ten more feet," she calls. "I'll stay at the opening of this second tunnel to buy you guys some extra time. I've a few magic tricks up my sleeve." I hear her voice one more time over the sounds of fighting, "Believe, Kori, in magic and in yourself."

"Duck," Noah says, pushing my head into the second tunnel. This must be the tunnel that enthralled Fin, the one with no torch, marking it as a less-used space.

My brain fills with questions about the tunnel's and cave's purpose in between Cleansings. Were they used for meetings or travelling between points? I let my thoughts continue to wander as a distraction about what's to come. I'm forced to walk crouched because the ceiling is so low.

This second tunnel is so dark I can't see shapes or outlines. There's no way for me to be sure Belamey and Fin are preceding or that Noah is trailing.

Puffs of air move strands of my hair. I can hear the soft paper swoosh of wings moving in the space above my head. *Bats!* That explains the musty, acrid smell. I regulate my breathing and try to relax.

Our group has stopped walking in what I assume is the next section of the cave. The ceiling is a lot higher here. I'm standing straight and straining my eyes in the darkness, but it's too dark to make out the details of this space.

Belamey moves in front of me. I know it's him by his smell and I can feel the heat from his body. Voiceless, he grabs my hand and directs me through the dark cave and up a couple of stairs.

He bends toward me until his husky voice is speaking low in my ear. "We're on the platform now, Kori. It's time for me to join my magic to yours before I return the Ember stone to you. I can't use the Ember stone. Only you can do that. But by joining our magics together, my magical strength can fuel yours. Do I have your permission?"

I'm barely able to nod my head without bouncing it off his body. Satisfied that my nod indicates my trust and cooperation, he straightens himself and I feel like a schoolgirl waiting for a first kiss. To ease my discomfort, I close my eyes and let my arms hang loose at my sides.

I feel a warmth enter my body. There's just a bit of it at first, like Belamey is testing me. There isn't anything unpleasant, like I feared there would be. Just as I'm relaxing to the idea of Belamey's magic joining to mine, he gives his magic a forceful push, and the warmth radiates into me like a wave of unexpected heat.

My eyes fly open in shock, fixing on Belamey. I know the heat of his magic isn't just magic. It's a part of him. It's an intimate awareness as his magic swirls and blends with mine.

I feel overwhelmed and strangely excited. Belamey smirks, and he moves so the front of our bodies touch. "It's my first time, too, but I've studied for years, curious about it," he says, his voice warm with pleasure.

I feel flushed and hot in unexpected ways from our magics joining. My breathing has increased with my heart rate. Belamey's smirk holds as he locks eyes with me. "Imagine what else I can do," he breathes.

I swallow, letting my thoughts wander a bit before my eyes snap wide in realization. "You sense me the same as I sense you!"

His eyebrows pull up the tiniest amount, but he says nothing. I was so absorbed with the strange inner feeling of Belamey's magic that I missed his hands securing the necklace around my neck. His hand touches the skin of my chest, cradling the Ember stone, but I can feel the strength of the Ember stone calling to me now that it's this close to me.

"Ready?" he asks me. His brown eyes probe mine, suggesting I don't need to answer.

Hesitantly, he pulls his hand away, allowing the Ember stone to fall against my flesh. In seconds, there's ice moving through my veins and fire sparking to life on my skin. My eyes glow and I can see everything in the darkness.

My fight or flight response activates, ingrained from a life of conditioning and a career marked by danger. Belamey has dropped to his knees as he struggles with the weight of the power surging between me and the Ember stone. I know it's my inability to give over control, to work with the Ember stone, that's drawing his strength the most. I also understand that his magical strength keeps me conscious.

Now, I'm a fiery beacon on this platform. My amber eyes take in the battle and carnage in this section of the cave. My need to save them would cripple me if it weren't for the fight I'm locked in with the Ember stone.

I fight against it, exerting my force on it unsuccessfully over and over while at the same time yelling at myself internally not to be scared and that the Ember stone isn't trying to hurt me. We're partners with a common goal. The threat isn't to my personal survival. The threat is to the survival of all the people I care about. The threat is to humans and Spellbinders alike.

Belamey's hands drop to the ground. The weight of the struggle is crushing him. His body sways on hands and knees.

I don't see any magical threads, but Nekane appears on the platform with Belamey and I. His brown eyes leer at me from the shadows of his face. I see whispers of Belamey in the dark handsomeness that Nekane's known for. Locked as Belamey and I are with the Ember stone, we're powerless to defend ourselves from him.

Where are Fin and Noah?

One side of Nekane's mouth pulls up while the other remains in place and he runs an aged hand through hair that is more salt than pepper. He hides his age well, with his straight back and well-kept body, but he can't hide his evilness. The self-satisfied quirk of his mouth, the glare in his eyes, and his lack of emotion mark him for the cold-hearted man he is. He kicks Belamey in the stomach.

I hear the air explode out of Belamey as his body lifts off the floor from the force of the impact. Belamey's hands give way, and his arms drop to support him on his elbows. "Useless waste, just like your mother," Nekane spits at Belamey.

Belamey's lack of response to Nekane coupled with no attempt to protect himself is all Nekane needs. He disregards his son, realizing that Belamey is bound to me by his magic and that his fate will mirror mine.

In his hand, Nekane fashions a glacial blue lightning bolt. Panic washes through me. He faces me like we're the only people in the cave. "Don't worry, Kori, your struggle will be over soon. No more Cleansing. My family's work, my work, will be rewarded today. On this day, the Ember family will die, with you leading the way."

He's weaving the lightning bolt while he talks, confident that nothing can stop him from driving it through me. So, he doesn't see the harpy eagle descend on him.

Alaric's eagle is modified from the original species by its size and strength. Talons larger than a grizzly bear's claws mutilate the skin of Nekane's face. The combination of surprise and pain stops him, and the partial lightning bolt drops from his hand, vanishing.

As Nekane's hands grip his torn face, Alaric, as a harpy eagle, grabs onto Nekane's forearms and yanks him off the platform. Nekane lashes out blindly with his magic. The eagle gives a sharp scream and Nekane falls to the floor, landing on his posterior, stunned.

I see it all, but I'm locked in my own struggle, powerless to help. *No, not powerless. Embrace it,* my inner voice whispers. I imagine Jaxton beside me, lionhearted, encouraging me to stop flailing and accept who I am and accept the Ember stone as my ally.

The eagle dives at Nekane with outstretched feet. The talons are skin deep in the flesh of Nekane's chest before he has recovered from his fall. If there wasn't so much noise, I'm sure the crack of ribs breaking as talons latch onto the ribcage would echo throughout the cave. Some ribs must've detached completely, but enough ribs are intact for Alaric's large wings to pull him and Nekane's lifeless form skyward.

There's an opening in the cave's roof that I hadn't noticed before because it's obscured by overgrowth. Alaric blasts it away with magic as he soars through, taking Nekane's limp form with him, trailing blood like red rain. Dim light enters the cave from the hole in the ceiling. I'm astonished by the size of this space.

The Ember stone's scream is low in my ears. It's a sound that I wasn't aware of a few minutes ago. There's a lessening in Belamey's magic. The strain of joining his magic with mine while the Ember stone and I remain locked in battle is killing him.

I'm aware if I can't do this, everyone is going to die. *This is the reality that I'm meant to live.* I push out a surge of anger that flares the fire on my skin. I can feel Belamey's strain through our joined magic.

"Kori!" Fin's voice calls out over the mayhem.

My eyes feel like balls of fire in their sockets as I search for her in the chaotic cave. When I lock my gaze on her, she lets a knife fly. It flies in slow motion. I see Fin's adaptability, her trust in me, her belief in me. I understand that she accepts her fate, as Jaxton accepted his. It's my turn to bear mine, all of it and not just pieces.

As the blade comes toward my head, I don't move or flinch. The knife's trajectory is so close to me that the air currents from its flight path pull at the flames coating me. I don't see her second knife throw. The suddenness of it flying past the opposite side of my head causes me to blink.

My eyes lock shut. *Let yourself see*, I scream at myself.

In a flash of fire and smoke, the good and bad defining moments of my life rise from my subconscious and merge into balance. As I acknowledge them, I feel something inside of me drop into place and I see me and all of my imperfections as perfectly me.

I'm a Spellbinder, a powerful one. With this new

understanding, I reach for the Ember stone. This time, when it reaches back, I don't fight it and the connection comes easy, innate.

With my acceptance, the ice in my veins liquifies and the fire on my skin flares. If the connection to Belamey remains, I don't feel it because it no longer feeds me. I've now surpassed the stage of being a fiery beacon.

The power of the Ember stone coursing through me elevates me off the platform. I hover, visibly burning with a strange blue icy flame. I keep my eyes open. My vision tightens into a narrow tunnel and then explodes out.

I can see everything magical and every Spellbinder in the cave or elsewhere in the world. It's like my third eye has opened. I can feel waves of heat and cold radiating out of me, searching to touch each Spellbinder. There are millions of us.

When I focus, I can see those waves as sparks of fire and ice sent out to create balance in each Spellbinder. The fighting in the cave has stopped. Those who haven't fled in fear now stare in awe.

As the balancing sparks of fire and ice touch them, some of them slide to the floor in a temporary sleep. Others turn their eyes inward, trance-like, for introspection. Regardless of how they respond, the sparks work the same: a forced self-analysis of one's own motives and character. When they wake from sleep or trance, it'll be with a clean slate, a positive outlook, and the ability to reinvent who they want to be.

The sparks have touched each Spellbinder worldwide, restoring proper balance, and I can feel the power of the Ember stone recede. I sensed sparks for Alivia and Belamey, both alive, but the Cleansing was happening too swiftly to identify each Spellbinder. How I managed to pick them out is beyond me, perhaps because they were the top of my thoughts.

I sink to my feet on the platform. Exhaustion washes over me as the Ember stone's connection severs. My legs buckle and powerful hands grasp me and lower me to the ground. "Makes sense that it's you," I mumble to Noah.

He smiles at me and waves to someone I can't see. "Does it make sense that it's me, too," Fin asks, popping her head into my line of sight. I hear the pride and love in her voice, no teasing. Noah slips sideways into a sleep, somehow having managed to resist long enough to ensure my safety.

I manage a nod at my best friend before my eyes close and I welcome my own slumber.

Chapter 28

I wake on the living room sofa to the sounds of muffled conversation and laughter. Warm streams of sunlight come in the window and create a laziness I haven't felt in a while. The environment feels different. It's happy and safe. I feel different too, more connected to life than I have before.

The Ember stone. My hand flies to my chest. The Ember stone slipped behind my body as I slept, but it's secured to my neck. My connection to the Ember stone feels different, not so much a connection as a residue left behind after an intense bond. Before I can give this any thought, I'm startled by Grama Pearle.

I hadn't heard her feet as she entered the room. Her steps are awkward, and I realize there's a bandage on her foot. Not a life-threatening injury, but one serious enough that curative healing was needed. I see mojo working on the area.

"You noticed that quickly," she says to me, inclining her head at the Ember stone I'm cradling over my chest.

I understand she isn't talking about her bandaged foot. "Grama Pearle, I can't hear the Ember stone." It's unclear to both of us if I'm asking a question or making a statement.

Grama Pearle moves over to the sofa. I sit up so she can fit beside me. "It won't speak for generations now, Kori, because its job is done, but parts of its power will remain with you, perhaps forever, even after the Ember stone is separated from you."

"Why wouldn't the Ember stone be with me?" I feel silly asking because I realized this on some level right from the beginning. It had been under guard before, so why wouldn't it return?

Grama Pearle's eyes stray to the corner of the room. Roger is standing in the shadows. My mind makes the connections. "Roger's taking it home to the rock trolls, isn't he?" I clutch the Ember stone, but the familiar pulse of heat and cold isn't there. I swallow. "It'll be guarded by the rock trolls until the next Cleansing."

Roger is watching my hand with the Ember stone. I nod. There will always be a Spellbinder like Nekane who wants to stop the Cleansing for their own purposes. The Ember stone is a power that is safest locked away and under guard until the next thousand-year cycle.

"I need to go, Pearle," Roger interrupts.

Grama Pearle nods to Roger. "It's time to take it off, Kori."

Roger steps closer. I stall with a question. "Was any of Birdie's story about Roger true?"

Grama Pearle chokes on her words. "Yes, Roger was with Birdie for the reasons she shared." She pauses, taking a deep breath, like what she's saying is painful. I gawk at her. The corners of her mouth tug like she's trying to give me a reassuring smile before she continues. "But Roger was also there knowing that when he returned home, whether to stay or be released from the tribe, he would take the Ember stone with him."

I fiddle with the clasp, to buy time to decide how I feel about what's happening. I'm conflicted with relief that the Ember stone and the Cleansing aren't my responsibility any longer, while I'm also sad to part with the Ember stone because it represents for me my own accomplishments, acceptance, and growth.

Grama Pearle, sensing my hesitancy, continues with her explanation. "The rock trolls have an ability to remain impartial to the all the drama and politics that go on with the human and Spellbinder worlds. It's what makes them so good at their role, guarding and following the rules set out to keep items like these safe and available for use when the time occurs. The Ember stone will be safe with Roger and the rock trolls. And it was decided that Roger will stay with his tribe."

The necklace releases and it settles into my hand. I stare down, trying to reconcile everything this stone has been responsible for. As I swallow, I see Roger's gray-skinned hand moving toward mine. I fight the urge to snap my hand shut as he plucks the Ember stone up. Then I can't look away from my empty palm even when Grama Pearle stands to give Roger her goodbyes. When the front door closes, I'm still staring at my hand. I notice that there's a feeling of weight lifted from me, but the strange connections I felt when I first woke up are present.

In silence, I revisit the Cleansing. "Alivia?" As I ask, I

realize this is one thing that's different for me. I can sense people. This new ability is a leftover power from the Ember stone's magic during the Cleansing. I sense Alivia, but I'm not sure if sensing her is enough to know she's okay or where she is.

"She's fine, Kori. She's in the dining room with Holden, Jayce, and a few others." Grama Pearle says with a smile. "Jaxton would be so proud of you."

Her comments are received by me as more of a caress than a punch. *I'm proud of myself too.* I search Grama Pearle's face. "Are you okay?"

"I'm okay, Kori. So many of us are okay because of you," Grama Pearle says, but the smile on her lips doesn't touch her eyes.

"Grama Pearle?"

She nods and reaches over to take hold of my hand. I swallow and wait for whatever is coming. "Not everyone that went into the tunnels came out," she says.

Eyes closed, I filter these new connections, scanning first for those closest to Grama Pearle. Aunt Rune and Brynlee are tired, but otherwise okay. I rush to check Mom and Dad, and they're also fine. My eyes fly open. *Birdie!* "Oh, Grama Pearle, I'm so sorry." I don't need or want details of her death. Knowing she's gone is painful enough.

"My bestie, Birdie," Grama Pearle says, and I can hear the tears in her voice. Tears well in my eyes. We hold each other. I'm not sure which of us is supporting the other as we cry. Eventually, I dry my eyes and pull away from Grama Pearle.

"Talon?" I ask.

Grama Pearle produces a Kleenex from the sleeve of her shirt. The noise she makes as she blows her nose is loud and resonant. She sounds like a Canada goose. "Besides his intense sadness over his mother's death, he's otherwise well. He left this morning to go to the safe house. It'll be his responsibility now. The purpose of the safe house will be a bit different, not covert, although what happens inside will be secret, and new wards and charms will be required. Regardless, it'll still need an attendant." A smile plays on the corners of her mouth as she thinks about Talon taking over Birdie's responsibilities.

I hear the door in the kitchen open and close, but it isn't clear if someone has come in or gone out. Tired, I sigh. "I need a coffee, Grama Pearle, and I need to see Alivia."

Grama Pearle nods and we help each other up. My body is stiff and weak. We're almost in the hallway when Holden and Jayce come flying in in full pursuit of Dodo in bird form. Holden and Jayce are laughing and squealing with pleasure while Dodo is making a noise that sounds like "doo-doo." The three of them dodge our legs and disappear into the house.

Alivia and Noah are talking in the dining room. I'm pleased by the smell of fresh-brewed coffee. I stop Grama Pearle before they can see us, worried about everyone's exact location. "Where's the family?"

"Rune took her family home right away so she could make her potions and charms to fix them up. Your other grandparents went home to sleep and will return for dinner. Your parents are sleeping upstairs," she explains. "Everyone had an active role in the battle, but you can ask each of them about that later."

Before I can ask after anyone else, Alivia runs into the room. She launches all 105 pounds of herself at me but we manage not to go down in a heap of arms and legs. The hints of lavender in her wavy ash-brown hair are a familiar Alivia fragrance. It relaxes me because she's here and safe and because lavender is infused with calming properties.

We lock our arms around each other and I'm not sure which one of us is squeezing harder, but I know that we're both wheezing. I tap her back, our cue to each other that we're tapping out of our hug status. We break away laughing, tears in our eyes.

"You should know, Nekane was with me in my kitchen. I had closed my eyes, questioning my confidence, when there was a soft sound behind me, and the scent in the air changed." Alivia inhales deeply through her nose. "I smelt muted notes of something earthy, sweet, and spicy. It was Belamey. Only scant hints of the scent were reaching my nose because the fragrance was being wafted, likely to prevent Belamey from being detected. I saw Nekane release his magic in my direction, but the pain never came. My body bent in half as I was yanked backwards in a vacuum-like effect that created neither sound nor feeling. Everything went black."

"Belamey." I whisper.

"He's fine. Him and Fin went to Just Flavours." Alivia's smile is soft as she hooks arms with Grama Pearle and, using her other hand to grab mine, she leads Grama Pearle and I both into the dining room. Noah is by himself, and he just finished pouring me an oversized mug of coffee. He's pretty battered, but in good spirits.

He sets my coffee cup down to give me a one-armed hug. I hug him, trying not to crush his slinged arm. I slide into my chair and take a sip of my coffee. "Where's Alaric?" I ask. I can feel Alaric with my new sense, but he's very different. He's faint and distant.

When no one answers, I look from face to face. Noah gives a subtle headshake, and his voice is soft. "Gone."

I shut my eyes, remembering the blood on his feathers after Nekane's counterattack on him. I remember the powerful wings of Alaric's bird lifting Nekane's lifeless body out of the cave to dispose of as he saw fit, an unknown to us. *Gone somewhere to never be seen or gone as in dead?* I wonder, but I don't clarify the thought knowing that he wouldn't have shared his intentions. Alaric had no plan to come out the other side of this battle the same man that went in. He completed his mission. Either way, he's resting.

The room is quiet as we sit thinking our individual thoughts. None of us is sure what to say. The heaviness deepens. The exterior door off the kitchen opens.

Hearing Fin's voice rambling on about food and flavours brings a smile to my face. The sight of Belamey makes my insides quiver because I've no idea how to respond to him or what to feel. Anxious, I cross my arms. Each of them is carrying a ridiculous number of food bags.

Fin sees me and drops her Just Flavours bags on the

table and launches herself at me, crushing me in a big hug. "Girl, you are straight fire, badass, the bomb, the—"

"Fin?" I interrupt.

Fin stops and raises her eyebrows. She places her hands on her hips and waits.

"Did you get coffee?"

"Turkish, baby, but they're in the car." She turns toward the bags. "Can you get them, please?" Her face is a mask of strange excitement.

I blink at her, trying to read her bizarre look. I'm also trying to do my best to ignore Belamey so I don't have to look at myself or our relationship when Fin links her arm through mine and drags me from the dining room, mumbling about getting plates from the kitchen. She releases me once we're out of earshot. "Belamey checked on you while you were sleeping. It was so romantic," she says. Her dreaminess vanishes. "You need to go get the coffees now, please," she urges.

"I'll go with her, Fin," says Belamey's husky voice close behind me.

My skin prickles and my mouth goes dry. Fin's eyes flash in excitement. She's bouncing on her toes as she turns and starts gathering plates. Belamey and I are almost out the door when Fin calls, "Don't forget the coffees."

I stop and scrunch my face up, planning to give Fin the third degree about her perplexing behaviour, but Belamey hooks my waist and leads me down into the backyard.

I freeze in the yard when I see the sharp-shinned

hawk that's been shadowing me on and off since I was a police officer. My assumption was that he was monitoring the Ember stone and that whole situation, but seeing him here now doesn't fit with that speculation.

It dives off the branches of the closest tree and aims its flight path straight at us. I've pressed myself backwards, unsure of what to expect. Belamey is like a wall behind me and I'm conscious that I'm pressed up against him and that he isn't moving, nor is he the least bit concerned by the hawk.

The hawk shifts within a few feet of us and I'm not surprised to see a familiar thick-necked man who I arrested several times for causing a disturbance. I roll my eyes at the realization he is, in fact, sometimes a bird. He's not crazy. I wonder if he staged those arrests to test me or make contact in a way that wasn't suspicious to his role as The Recruiter.

"What is this?" I ask without directing the question at either Belamey or the man.

The man studies me with dark-brown, speckled black eyes. "Do you know who I am, Kori?"

I take a minute to assess him. He's nodding at me encouragingly.

"The Recruiter," I say.

"This is an official job offer, Kori," the man says by way of acknowledging my answer.

I reposition so I can see Belamey and The Recruiter. Belamey gives me a shoulder shrug. "I'm going to get the coffees," he says and wanders off.

My attention is on The Recruiter. I'm trying to control

the size of my eyes, which want to pop out of my face. Close-lipped, I watch him.

"I'm sure you figured out both Belamey and Astrid work with me," he says. "Kori, I've been waiting a long time for you to be ready. We need a Spellbinder like you on our team."

"I don't understand," is all I can manage and for once I'm not talking about the Spellbinder part.

"Well, we don't have time to get into specifics now. However, the snippets you've been told about me, and my team's work, is accurate. You can speak with Belamey or your friend, Fin, to learn more. Fin has a flare for life that we need on our team, normie or not, and she was quick to accept my offer."

"Fin?" My voice is raised in pitch. I'm so surprised that I forget to close my mouth.

The Recruiter smiles and winks. "I'll take that as a 'yes,' Kori. Welcome to the team. I'll be in touch." Saying nothing more, he shifts and disappears into the sky.

Belamey returns with two trays of coffee and a medium-sized paper bag clutched in his teeth. Dazed, I take one of the trays from him and head toward the kitchen door. I hear Belamey remove the bag from his teeth into his free hand. I hold the door open for him. His brown eyes lock with mine as he walks through the doorway.

"Welcome to the team," he says in a low tone as he continues past me.

I look at the sky before dropping my eyes down. I'm not sure what makes me think of Nekane, but I do. Closing the door, I call to Belamey. Nekane's death can't be easy for him, a complicated grief. He turns. "I'm sorry for your loss, Belamey," I say. "Will you grieve for him?"

Belamey considers his answer. "I grieved for my parents a long time ago," he says with that intense sadness clinging to him. He scratches his jaw, turns, and walks into the dining room. I follow.

Fin takes the tray out of my hands and replaces it with a single cup of coffee. "Welcome to the team," she whispers with a big smile before she steers me to the table.

Before she moves away, I whisper, "Where is Griffin?"

"Mission, he's one of us," she winks. "He said he'll call me as soon as he can. Now, here's what you need to know," she says, waving her hand over the spread of food. I know she's trying to give us all a semblance of normal, sharing with the people she cares about some of the things she loves.

With the introduction of food, the tension in the room drains. It offers a focus for our actions and conversation. Fin points to a rustic-looking, whole grain sandwich with sliced pear and kale. I can also see thinly sliced chicken and melted Brie on this sandwich. "Fig-glazed chicken with Brie," she says. "That one is an apple, turkey, and Brussels sprout sandwich. I know it sounds strange, but they make the apples and Brussels sprouts into a slaw." She kisses her fingertips and pushes them out into the air.

"That's my kind of sandwich," Grama Pearle says, reaching to grab one. "Thank you, Fin. This is just what we all need."

"I'm dying to try this one." Fin smiles at the sandwich

she just picked up. "It's chicken, arugula, mango, jalapeño, and feta cheese." She chomps down without introducing the other items on the table.

The food Fin didn't identify includes strawberry oatmeal bars with a vanilla glaze, chocolate-covered strawberries, and mini apple fritters. I'm surprised to see both Noah and Belamey bonding over fig-glazed chicken and Brie.

I select a waffle sandwich, but find that it isn't made with waffles. It's multigrain bread pressed on the waffle iron. I inspect it before taking a bite. I see deli turkey, thin apple slices, Colby cheese, and bacon. The flavours dancing across my taste buds after my first bite tell me that there's Dijon mustard and mayonnaise on this sandwich, too. I hadn't realized how hungry I was and I'm busy devouring my sandwich when Carter walks into the dining room.

The amiable conversation falls silent. Carter is staring down at the front of his thin sutra yoga pants. Everyone is looking at Carter's pants as well. There's nothing left to the imagination.

"Will he remember all this?" I ask Grama Pearle.

"No, Ague is good at what she does. As soon as he leaves our house, his memory of all the magic will start to fade. When he crosses the threshold into his own place, he'll believe he's arriving home from a hospital stay after an incident at work left him honourably discharged. We made sure that his reality will line up in the human world. Pension and all the rest of it."

"Do we know what really happened to Carter? There's still mystery surrounding what happened to him that night and why—"

Before Grama Pearle can answer, Carter lifts his head from his unmistakeable erection. His eyes are wide, and his cheeks redden. His mien makes it clear that the spell has worn off. He clears his throat, "If you'll excuse me." He turns and hurries from the room with what had been until recently his typical pronounced sense of dignity.

I'm not surprised that it's Fin who breaks the stunned silence. "Wonder if he has a reunion planned," she says with a mischievous grin. "Consulting Dr. Jackoff. If I was a betting woman, I would say he's going to paddle the pink canoe, spank the monkey, box with the one-eyed champ, cuff the carrot, shuck the corn, wrestle the—"

"FIN!" We say in unison before we all burst out laughing and I'm thankful to feel new beginnings.

If you loved *The Ember Stone*, be sure not to miss the next adventure from *The Ember Files*. Here is a special preview.

Book 2 of The Ember Files

"Where do you find such friends, Belamey the Eminent?" Bradig asks. From the top of my vision, I see Belamey shrug and Bradig nod. I drop my head back down before Bradig returns his attention to me. "Raise your eyes human and address me, if you will," Bradig commands.

I make a fast eye roll before lifting my head. I'm surprised by the squinty, thin, angled eyes that are assessing me. They're luminescent-orange set above chubby cheeks, a mouth, and a nose that are accentuated like the muzzle of a cat. I blink and nod my head, briefly considering Bradig's aged faced before I give a response. "Lord Bradig, I too am honoured to be in your supreme company."

Bradig's hiccups seem to have stopped for the moment while he continues to assess me. "This one is unworthy. I have decided it to be true." Bradig declares to the room. He waves for Belamey to move closer. Bradig pulls a very sharp-looking axe from his belt. "We must kill her."

For information on Shari's next book, please visit her website at http://sharimarshall.ca.

Book Club Reading Guide

1. What do you think of the book's title? How does it relate to the book's contents? What other titles might you choose?
2. If you could hear this same story from another person's point of view, who would you choose?
3. How was your experience of the book? Were you engaged immediately, or did it take you a while to get into it? Did reading the book impact your mood? If yes, how so?
4. How did your opinion of the book change as you read?
5. If someone asked you to summarize this book in ten words or less, what would you say?
6. What was your favourite quote or passage?
7. Did the world the author created feel realistic to you, or was it lacking in certain details?
8. Is the ending satisfying? If so, why? If not, why not and how would you change it?

CPSIA information can be obtained
at www.ICGtesting.com
Printed in the USA
JSHW012158070623
42889JS00011B/428